W9-AXK-169

GAMES DIVAS PLAY

OTHER TITLES BY
ANGELA BURT-MURRAY

The Angry Black Woman's Guide to Life,
coauthored by Denene Millner and Mitzi Miller

The Vow,
coauthored by Denene Millner and Mitzi Miller

GAMES DIVAS PLAY

Angela Burt-Murray

Published by

†THOMAS & MERCER

This is a work of fiction. Names, characters, organizations, places, events, and incidents are either products of the author's imagination or are used fictitiously.

Text copyright © 2014 Angela Burt-Murray
All rights reserved.

No part of this book may be reproduced, or stored in a retrieval system, or transmitted in any form or by any means, electronic, mechanical, photocopying, recording, or otherwise, without express written permission of the publisher.

Published by Thomas & Mercer, Seattle

www.apub.com

Amazon, the Amazon logo, and Thomas & Mercer are trademarks of Amazon.com, Inc., or its affiliates.

ISBN-13: 9781477820162
ISBN-10: 1477820167

Cover design by Paul Barrett

Library of Congress Control Number: 2013920602

Printed in the United States of America

DEDICATION

To my husband, Leonard, for always being my biggest cheerleader.
To my sons, Solomon and Ellison, for being the sunshine in my life.
To my parents, Diana and Howard, for unconditional love.
To BCFL for friendship, laughter, and cupcakes!

PROLOGUE

It would be easy to get the key to the hotel's penthouse suite. We had stayed at the Four Seasons several times, so no one would dare turn me away. And, of course, his sorry ass had been too lazy to find a different location to be with that bitch.

"Hello," chirped Christian, the hotel's concierge, as I approached the large walnut desk. "How may I help you?"

I forced a smile, shrugged my shoulders, and said, "Silly me, I forgot my key." I adjusted the large tinted Chanel sunglasses that covered my puffy red eyes.

"Of course, I'm more than happy to make you another key," Christian said as he slid the card key into the machine and then came around the desk to present it to me. "We had some of your favorite champagne delivered about an hour ago, so enjoy!"

I thanked him softly through clenched teeth, then turned away.

Key in hand, I walked across the busy Manhattan lobby, my black patent leather Christian Louboutin pumps clicking along the hotel's marble floor. The weight of the gun in the pocket of my navy silk Burberry trench coat tapped lightly against my thigh as I walked to the private elevator. The gun gave me the confidence to do what I needed to do.

After all, promises were made.

Slipping the card key into the security slot in the elevator, I pushed the button for the penthouse suite and leaned back against the mahogany-paneled wall. It was unfortunate that it had come to this, but he had given me no choice.

The elevator glided silently up to the fifty-second floor to the $35,000-a-night suite. The elevator doors opened directly into the luxurious penthouse, and I smiled tearfully at the memory of the many nights we had shared here. And now this was where our relationship would end.

The forty-three-hundred-square-foot suite was so large that I knew they would never hear my arrival. I walked through the spacious living room and faced the panoramic view of the sun setting over New York City. A large bouquet of fragrant orchids sat in the center of the art deco glass coffee table. Pieces of clothing were strewn carelessly about the living room, and a pair of Nike sneakers had been kicked off under the coffee table. Two empty champagne flutes sat next to the flowers along with a half-empty bottle of Veuve Clicquot. I picked up the crystal flute and stared at the wine-colored lipstick print along the rim. I tossed the flute next to a lacy black La Perla bra, which lay on the buttery linen couch. *Bitch.*

I walked down the hall toward the master bedroom, my heels sinking into the thick dove-gray carpeting, which muffled my steps. One of the large onyx double doors to the bedroom was slightly open, and as I got closer, I could hear their moans. I slowly pushed the door open so that I could slip into the darkened room. The heavy gold damask curtains were closed, and the flame from a jasmine candle flickered on the nightstand next to the bed, casting dancing shadows on the creamy wall. I clutched the gun in my pocket, and saw the couple right where I expected.

They were so caught up in their lovemaking, neither of them noticed they were no longer alone. I could see the outline of his long, lean frame, the silky white sheets tangled like vines around his muscled legs. She sat atop my man, thrusting her hips into him. His large hands, the ones I used to love, cupped and massaged her breasts as he pushed back up into her. She threw back her head and raked her long nails along his broad chest and moaned deeply.

"Oh, baby," she said in a husky voice as she now started to move faster.

His hands slid down her toned back and squeezed her round bottom as he pulled her into him.

"Oh yes, baby," she purred, leaning down to slip her tongue into his waiting mouth. My eyes narrowed as I watched them kiss each other passionately. I moved deeper into the room's shadows and closer to the bed.

Suddenly he wrapped his arm around his lover and flipped her onto her back so that now he was on top. Now I knew I had the perfect shot.

Promises were made.

As my mind flashed back to memories of our relationship, tears began to stream down my cheeks behind my sunglasses. Slipping the gun out of my pocket, I stood at the foot of the bed and raised it level with his broad muscled back.

And then I pulled the trigger.

After all, promises were made.

CHAPTER 1

Nia

The woman was dead.

Her limp naked form lay in the twisted heap of trash next to an overflowing garbage bin in a dark alley. Her battered face was partially obscured by a long curtain of dirty blond hair matted with blood. Two plainclothes cops warily surveyed the body, looking for clues.

"Damn shame," muttered the police officer as he waved his flashlight around the crime scene. A scrawny gray cat stepped out of the shadows and tentatively sniffed the corpse before rubbing its body up against its dead mistress.

The dead woman suddenly sat up, sneezed, and pushed the cat away.

"Cut," yelled the director, Rich Benson, as he jumped out of his chair and threw his script down on the sidewalk. A bell rang, and the bright lights came up, illuminating the dark downtown Los Angeles street. "What the hell are you doing, Dead Woman Number One? You're supposed to be dead, for Christ's sake!"

"I know, but I'm allergic to the frickin' cat," the dead woman whined with a thick New York accent as the wardrobe assistant threw her a robe to wrap around her shivering body.

The frustrated director kicked a garbage bin. "This scene isn't working for me," he said to one of the writers as he raked his hand through dark brown hair that was a little too long for his age. "And tell casting we need a hotter dead woman who isn't allergic to fucking cats!"

This scene wasn't working for me, either, but since I was the senior entertainment editor for *Hollywood Scoop!* magazine, it was my job to write about this shitty cable drama, *Vice 911*. The show was about a precinct of New York City cops, who, in between hopping in and out of bed with one another, managed to solve a case or two. And tonight I had to craft a riveting cover story on Gabriella Rodriguez, the busty new starlet on the show that Deadline.com called "*Baywatch* meets *Law & Order*." Clearly, this assignment was totally worth the $186,000 I owed in Harvard student loans.

Everyone on the set was cold, pissy, and tired. It was two thirty in the morning, and they had been shooting the scene where Gabriella's character, Officer Jessie Cortez, the hot new Latina rookie who just transferred into the seventy-eighth precinct, and Captain O'Leary, the rogue alcoholic veteran who ran the dysfunctional police unit, acted on the sexual tension that had been brewing between them over the past couple of episodes. The two horny coworkers had pulled into the dark alley to get it on, when the car's headlights picked up the outline of the body.

Sex would have to wait.

But not for too long, of course. Rich insisted that every episode contain some sort of climax. Literally.

"Ritchie, I'm not happy with my scene," Gabriella purred as she tottered in platform boots over to the director. She twisted one of the long black tendrils framing her toasted-brown face and caressed Rich's arm through his leather jacket. As a former telenovela star, Gabriella tended to overdramatize every scene with her wide brown eyes, pouty red lips, heaving bosom, and heavily accented dialogue.

Her signature tight black blouse skimmed faded low-rise jeans that looked like they were painted on her body. Her lush red lips were, of course, pouting. In yesterday morning's *Hollywood Scoop!* story meeting, the beauty director told me that Gabriella had just signed a cosmetics contract to be the spokesmodel for a new shade of red lipstick named after the show. Unfortunately, the makeup endorsement was not enough of a scoop for my boss, Kris Kensington, so I needed to find a story angle fast to keep her off my ass. Stuffing the last bite of a stale walnut brownie into my mouth, I scribbled down some more notes about the last scene and started to make my way over to Gabriella to finish our interview so that I could go the hell home.

But before I could catch her attention, Rich put his arm around Gabriella's waist and walked her away from the garbage bin. They began to talk in hushed tones. I paced back and forth, waiting for them to finish so that I could follow up on Gabriella's last comment that she thought her character could be a female role model. Given that the show's only female viewers belonged to the Female Police Officers Union that was trying to get the show canceled due to its "misogynistic portrayals of women serving in the line of duty," who was this chica kidding?

Out of the corner of my eye, I saw Gabriella whisper something in Rich's ear before her tongue snaked out and flicked his ear. Rich popped her on her ass and followed his star into her trailer. Clearly, the rumors whispered on the set and around town that they were sleeping together were true.

Maybe there was a story here for me after all.

—

Did she just fire me?

Oh shit. Did this crazy heffa just fire me? My head was spinning as I tried to get my brain to focus. I saw my boss's thin coral lips moving, but I was hearing no sound. She tapped one of her black patent leather Tory Burch flats on the glass coffee table strewn with *Hollywood Scoop!* magazine layouts and cover mock-ups of Gabriella Rodriguez kneeling in the sand on the beach in a bright red ball gown.

Could Kris have possibly come up with a less original cover-shoot concept? Demi Moore, Jennifer Aniston, Uma Thurman, ring a bell?

I wanted to rip into her about her tired *Vanity Fair* rip-off, but this probably wasn't the time.

Mario, the manorexic weasel from human resources, sat next to her on the cream sofa in her office, absentmindedly picking at an old acne scar on his pockmarked cheek.

Focus, Nia.

"Look, Nia," Kris snapped impatiently, "like I said, I'm sorry, but we have to let you go."

"But why?" I said as I tried to regain my composure. I felt hot, and my hands were suddenly clammy like they used to get in seventh grade. "I routinely scoop the other celebrity magazines and even the blogs with my A-list sources, so what could you possibly be firing me for?"

"In the online teaser you posted on the website yesterday for your Gabriella Rodriguez cover story, you wrote that Gabriella and Rich Benson are having an affair. And that sloppy reporting has resulted in me having to spend my morning on the phone with Rich's extremely irate publicist and our own legal team, as well as trying to kill Keith Kelly's *New York Post* column on your whole screwup. Rich's lawyer says they are going to sue if we don't run a retraction. And the network is threatening to restrict our future access to *Vice* and all their other shows and talent."

"Retraction?" I exclaimed. My mind quickly raced through the online teaser piece I wrote for the cover story that would hit the stands Friday as I tried to figure out what I could have written that would cause me to be fired. "For what?"

"For saying Gabriella and Rich are having an affair," Kris said with an exasperated sigh. "This is a major embarrassment for both the studio and Rich. And Rich's wife is already threatening divorce."

"Well, maybe Rich shouldn't be fucking Gabriella Rodriguez, then," I snapped. "Look, Kris, I saw them with my own two eyes making out on the set—I walked in on them in her trailer—and I merely wrote down what I saw. And when I asked Gabriella about it after Rich left, she gushed about how they were made for each other. She clearly wanted me to write about their relationship."

"It doesn't matter, Nia," Kris snapped back. She took a large manila envelope from Mario's outstretched hand and slid it across the coffee table to me. "This has come down from corporate, and their decision is final, so we have to let you go. I think you'll find our severance package very generous. Today is your last day."

As the only black editor at *Hollywood Scoop!*, I've paid my dues over the last five years. I'm used to getting my fair share of shit from this insecure woman and having to fight not only to get my stories the coverage they deserve but to get the magazine and website to give any coverage to black Hollywood. But I've never in my entire eight-year career as a journalist not been backed up by my boss when I wrote the truth. It's just not done. But Kris and I never really got along because I'm not good at hiding how I feel about people I think are stupid. As my assistant, MJ, had warned me numerous times, my facial expression tended to say it all. But I've never seen Kris sacrifice one of her reporters when threatened by lawyers. After all, this is celebrity journalism we're talking about; threats of lawsuits are par for the course.

"But I followed the editorial guidelines regarding legally sensitive stories and sent the piece to you prior to posting and asked for your comments," I said as I suddenly realized what Kris was trying to do. "You never got back to me."

It wasn't unusual for Kris not to respond to flagged copy since she spent most of her time schmoozing publicists, lunching with her celeb friends, and party hopping as the face of the magazine. So in order to meet their daily deadlines, most of the reporters had gotten used to moving forward if they had the story cold, had all the proper backup, and hadn't heard back from Kris within two hours of sending her a story. And usually she responded only if there was a problem. But it was clear this time that lazy-ass Kris hadn't read my post, and now that corporate was up in arms, she was throwing me under the bus for not doing her own damn job.

"Nia, don't try to blame me for your sloppy reporting," Kris said in a bristling tone as she flicked an invisible piece of lint off her black pants. "It's quite unfortunate. But you really should have proper sign-off before posting such a sensitive piece. The simple fact of the matter is that you went off on your own, without the proper approvals, and now you have to pay the consequences."

"Nia, I'm happy to walk you through the terms of the severance agreement back in my office if you like," Mario said, jumping into the conversation. Kris was clearly finished with this matter and finished with me.

"You don't have to walk me through shit trying to get me to act like we all don't know what's really going on here, Mario." Fighting back hot tears of frustration, I grabbed the envelope from the table and left Kris's office.

Walking past the rows of cubicles in the *Hollywood Scoop!* newsroom for the last time, I fought to keep my tears of humiliation in check and regain my composure. I buttoned the jacket of the olive-colored suit that my mom had ordered on Home Shopping Network for me last month. I had worn it because I had assumed I'd be doing TV interviews today for my big exclusive story. When I put it on this morning, I knew MJ would hate the suit, but my mom would love to see her baby wearing it on national TV. How was I going to tell my mom I got fired after all she had sacrificed to get me out of the South Side of Chicago?

Whispered conversations among clusters of my former colleagues ceased as I made my way down the long corridor to my office. People wouldn't even look me in the eye. Clearly, the word that I had been canned was already out. I squared my shoulders and stared straight ahead.

A movie scene suddenly flashed through my mind from Spike Lee's *Jungle Fever* where Wesley Snipes's character was forced out of the architectural firm he helped build. As he was storming out of the office, he pointed out and ripped down the model buildings hung up around the office that he created. I wanted to do the same as I passed the framed cover blowups on the wall. George Clooney's humanitarian trip to Darfur? My exclusive. Julia Robert's long-awaited *Pretty Woman* sequel? Absafuckinglutely mine. Jennifer Lopez's implosion? All mine. Of course, none of the stories I wrote on black Hollywood made the walls. No Tyler Perry. No Wayans Brothers. No Steve Harvey. And not even the black Oscar-winning elite like Denzel Washington or Halle Berry was good enough for Kris's precious wall of fame. As she would always say in our editorial meetings, "It's not me. I'd love to put more black stars on the covers of *Hollywood Scoop!*, but black talent just doesn't sell magazines."

I managed to suppress the overwhelming urge to jump up on the nearest desk and point out my obvious and meaningful contributions to this bullshit publication and the injustice of it all.

As I neared my office at the end of the hallway, I saw MJ standing outside his cubicle. He was dressed in his favorite black skinny jeans, hot pink V-neck shirt, and fitted black blazer with the sleeves pushed up to his bony elbows. A large man in gray slacks and a blue blazer watched him put items into a box. Another similarly dressed man was stationed outside my office door. It then dawned on me that I was now to suffer further humiliation by being thrown out of the building by a wannabe cop.

"Miss Bullock, I'm here to allow you to collect your things from your desk and then escort you out of the building," said the security guard who was normally stationed in the lobby. I always told MJ that he reminded me of Stanley from *The Office*.

"What's going on, MJ?" I asked, ignoring him and turning my attention to my assistant.

"Girl, I guess we both been fired," said MJ, chewing loudly on his favorite watermelon-flavored Bubble Yum as he tossed the contents of his desk into a large cardboard box. "While you were in with Kris, I got called to HR, and they dropped the bomb."

I felt my blood pressure rising. My face was suddenly hot again. It was one thing for Kris to fire me to cover her own laziness, but messing with MJ was quite another.

MJ was the best assistant I'd ever had, and we had been a team for the past five years. A former cosmetology school dropout who had been working at the Platinum Scissors salon in Inglewood, he won me over after a brief conversation at the shampoo bowl. When I complained to him that I was having difficulty getting a quote from Angelina Jolie for a story I was doing on the rise in female action heroes, he whipped out his cell phone and called a friend who does her daughter Zahara's hair. "You know they had to come to the hood to show them how to do that child's head," he had quipped while waiting for a callback from his homegirl.

Within ten minutes I was on the phone with Angelina and had my quotes. As fate would have it, I had just been promoted to senior editor and was in need of an assistant. I was sick of the résumés of children of studio execs being passed to me, so I hired Marquis Vaughn Jackson on the spot after a twenty-minute conversation when I realized he was connected more than I was in the Hollywood underground world of stylists, makeup artists, and assistants. He got up to speed quickly and made frenemies in a backstabbing *Hollywood Scoop!* office that at first didn't know what to make of the five-foot-ten black man with a spiky Mohawk and a rainbow assortment of skinny jeans (before they were all the rage). Loyal and plugged into all things pop culture, MJ had proven himself indispensable to me over the years. And with the requisite gay man's taste for fashion *and* drama, he also felt it was his duty to dress me for high-profile interviews and award shows and to counsel me on my rocky relationship with my live-in boyfriend, Eric. His only fault? A borderline stalkerish obsession with Beyoncé. But he was so good at his job that all could be forgiven, even the daily Queen Bey who-what-where-when news alerts he felt compelled to share with me and anyone walking past his Beyoncé-plastered cubicle and on his popular personal blog Beyoncelicious247. And since he was the only other black employee at the *Hollywood Scoop!* Plantation, as we jokingly referred to our day jobs, I knew boyfriend always had my back.

I was just sorry that today I didn't have his.

"Ms. Bullock, we were told to escort you and Mr. Jackson from the building. Please step into your office and quickly collect your things. You have ten minutes," the guard said curtly as he stepped aside and gestured with his fat arm into the office.

"Ten minutes? I can't even load my contacts and files from my computer in that time," I replied. And goodness knows MJ couldn't take down all his beloved Beyoncé memorabilia and deflate the life-size blow-up doll of the singer that I got him for his last birthday in that little bit of time, either.

"Ms. Bullock, I must inform you that your contacts, company files, and computer are all property of Hollywood Scoop Media, so you are only allowed to take the items that are clearly visible on top of your desk, personal items in your desk drawers, but absolutely nothing off your computer's hard drive."

This joker must be crazy. I had spent years busting my butt to build a database of the most coveted e-mail addresses, cell phone numbers, birthdays, rehab hideouts, doctors, lawyers, bail bondsmen, and personal notes that crisscrossed all levels of Hollywood's who's who labyrinth. It was my lifeline. Without it, I couldn't do anything as a journalist, and it would be next to impossible to re-create. MJ's Spidey senses must have started tingling, because he seemed to know exactly what his girl needed at that moment: a diversion.

"First of all, mall cop . . . ," MJ said loudly, staring down the offending guard while grabbing his best friend, Bey. He knocked his box of belongings on the ground in the process, causing them to spill out all over the floor of his cubicle. "Who in the Blue Ivy hell are you calling Mr. Jackson? Mr. Jackson is my daddy, and as far as I can tell, he ain't the one getting fired!"

Now, if there is one thing straight men don't know how to deal with, it's an angry gay man clutching a blow-up Beyoncé doll. And these two were completely flummoxed. As MJ launched into a full-on tirade about his rights being trampled on and how he was going to launch a complaint with the National Association of Black Journalists and the EEOFG—the fake Equal Employment Office for Fabulous Gays that he threatened to call on me at least twice a week for some perceived slight—the two guards tried to placate him and help him pack up his things, so I slipped into my office and closed the door. Sitting down at my computer, I quickly plugged a flash drive into my Mac and began dragging files over to the drive icon.

"Come on . . . ," I said to the computer, tapping my foot nervously. I then accessed MJ's computer through the network and began copying his files as well.

"Don't you touch Beyoncé! Don't nobody know where your hands have been, mall cop," I could hear MJ screech haughtily. I laughed and shook my head as I imagined the guards trying to help MJ pack but not realizing they were taking their own lives into their hands by manhandling Sasha Fierce.

As the final files loaded onto the flash drive, I rummaged through my desk, throwing folders into the box. Then I grabbed my journalism awards from the top shelf of my bookcase and added them to the box, covering the folders. I heard one of the guards turn the knob to the door of my office, so I turned and quickly snatched the flash drive out of the computer and slipped it into my front pocket.

"Are you ready, Ms. Bullock?" Stan asked, exasperation in his baritone voice.

"Absolutely," I said, grabbing the box of *my* belongings and marching past him with my head held high. "Let's go, MJ."

"Right behind you, boss," MJ said as he slipped on his tinted Gucci shades, tucked Sasha Fierce under his arm, and grabbed his box while humming Beyoncé's "Irreplaceable."

—

Assuming that HR tool, Mario, would forget to cancel my corporate American Express card for at least another day or so, I agreed to spring for "we've just been fired" drinks. MJ and I were going to meet at Coltrane's after we dropped off our stuff.

Truth be told, I also wanted to go home, see my boyfriend, Eric, and cry to him about the injustice of it all. Maybe I could convince him to go with us for drinks as well.

Eric, a struggling website developer, worked out of our cramped West Hollywood apartment. We were introduced by a mutual friend at an old-school skating party, and I fell hard for the six-foot web geek with ebony skin, a blinding white smile, and a wicked sense of humor. Eric and I had been together for nearly two years—with no ring in sight as my mother was fond of reminding me every chance she got. He claimed he wanted to get his business on solid footing before we got married, but I was starting to think there was more to it. And recently things had gotten so strained between us as we each worked around the clock to build our respective careers that we had little time for quality interaction, let alone sex. We seemed to fight more often than have meaningful exchanges. He had also been staying out later than usual with his friends, or seemed to always be going off to some tech conference to "network."

Slipping my key into the lock of our third-floor apartment, I walked in and dropped my sad little box with what was left of my journalism career and the black Marc Jacobs purse I splurged on last week to celebrate my twenty-ninth birthday on the worn leather sofa. Biting my lip, I wondered if I could take the purse that I had maxed out my credit card for back to Neiman Marcus. Money was going to be tight until I found a new gig, and I knew Eric couldn't cover all the bills. The coffee table overflowed with copies of *Hollywood Scoop!* and other magazines and an ashtray full of Eric's cigarette ashes. I dumped out the contents of my box and then swept the pile of magazines into it, dumped the ashes on top, and placed it by the front door for Eric to take out with the trash.

As I made my way to the back of the apartment, I heard a high-pitched giggle coming from our tiny second bedroom that Eric adopted as his home office. He must be Skyping with a client, I thought, so I walked softly along the worn hardwood floors to the door and pushed it open. I could see the back of his head as he sat in front of his three-screen monitor setup. The middle screen was partially obscured, but as I came closer, I could make out the image of two naked women sitting on a bed.

"Oh, daddy, is that how you like it?" cooed a buxom woman with long blond curls as she got into a kneeling position and rubbed a large black dildo between her breasts and then pushed it up to her pouty red lips. The other woman, an equally large-breasted brunette with a short pixie cut and heavy black eye makeup, positioned herself behind the blonde, massaging her breasts and then moving her hands down the woman's body.

"Yeah, baby," Eric moaned. "That's it. Do it for big daddy." Suddenly I noticed Eric's arm moving up and down in his lap and heard a squishy noise as he leaned toward the large computer screens. He twisted his body and used his free hand to push a button on his keyboard, and the other two monitors came alive with the images of the naked women as the sound of their moans echoed around the small room. He then quickly dipped his hand into my Crème de la Mer moisturizing cream, which sat on his cluttered desk next to the keyboard. The brunette roughly turned the blonde's face toward hers, jammed her tongue down her throat, and kissed her roughly as her hand dove between the woman's thighs. Eric groaned deeply, and his body began to jerk.

"What the fuck . . . !" I yelled as I came up beside Eric and saw his erection covered in my $300 face cream. Startled, Eric swung around in the direction of my voice so quickly that he knocked the jar of the luxurious Parisian cream onto the hardwood floor, cracking the jar. I pushed him hard in the chest away from the computer, and the wheels of the chair jerked out from under him as he fell back onto the floor. Startled by the noise, Eric's playmates on-screen looked up into their webcam.

"Are you OK, honey?" asked the pouty blonde. "We can't see you anymore. Did you climax?"

I picked up the cracked jar of my favorite face cream and threw it at Eric's chest as he tried to stuff himself back into his jeans. He then got up on his knees and quickly punched a few keys on the keyboard, causing the three screens to go black.

"Is this what you do all day while I'm at work?" I screamed. "What the hell is this? You're jacking off to Internet porn with my face cream? Do you know how much this stuff costs?" In that moment I wasn't sure if I was more offended by his cyber cheating or his jerking off with my favorite beauty treat.

"Nia, it's not what you think. They are clients!" Eric stood up in front of me, wiping his greasy hands on his pants.

"A client? Muthafucka, how stupid do you think I am?" This broke-ass Negro had the nerve to think I was going to believe these cybersluts were clients?

"No, really!" he said, rummaging through a stack of papers on the side of his desk. "Look, here's the name of their company: DoMeBaby .next." He shoved an invoice at me. I scanned the heading and saw there was indeed a company called DoMeBaby.next that had engaged Eric to develop a virtual sex site.

"Uh . . . OK, but what's that got to do with you jerking off with my three-hundred-dollar face cream? What are you doing? Test-driving the site?"

Eric fell back on the futon shoved up against the wall and dropped his head into his hands.

"Look, I'm not proud that you found me this way. And of course I wasn't testing the site. Damn, a brother was horny as hell because it ain't like you're giving it up these days." Was he actually trying to blame this pathetic shit on me? I thought we were just going through a rough patch and this relationship had to be going somewhere after

I had invested nearly two years, my credit score, and my heart. But maybe those weren't enough.

"So let me get this straight: I come home to find you jerking off to porn like some perv in the middle of the afternoon, and somehow this is my fault?"

"It's not like it's real sex! I didn't even touch them," he whined.

"You know what, Eric? I'm done. Get your shit, and get the hell out of my apartment." I started throwing his stuff into an empty milk crate he had used to store hard drives.

"I really can't believe you, Nia," Eric snorted. "I love you, but you take things way too far. We've been together for two years, and you're throwing me out over this?"

"Did I stutter, Negro? Get your shit and get the fuck out!" He got up from the couch and began to walk out of the room.

I followed him and said, "You know what? I can't even stand to look at you, so I'm leaving, and you better be gone when I get back."

Eric tried to grab my arm as I rushed past him, but I twisted out of his reach. I grabbed my purse off the couch and left the room, slamming the door for the second time today.

—

"Don't stop drinking now, bitch!" MJ said to me as he gestured to the bartender at Coltrane's to pour two of America's latest unemployed workers another round of Hennessy. I'd lost count of the number of rounds after I shared my tale of finding Eric with his pants down, especially after MJ started laughing at my plight.

"I can't believe you laughed at me. You know I love Eric!" I threw back another glass of the cool dark liquid.

"Girl, please. That wannabe Mark Fuckerberg wasn't never about shit and didn't deserve you. And deep down you know you were bored with his computer-programming ass, anyway. Look at you! You're gorgeous and could do so much better!"

I looked into the mirror behind the bar at my reflection. While I appreciated MJ's sideways compliment, I definitely wasn't feeling gorgeous today. I was five foot eight with deep honey brown skin, high cheekbones, and almond-shaped dark brown eyes. My perfect rows of white teeth were thanks to the best cosmetic dentist in Hollywood (he hooked me up after I made a call to get his daughter an internship at Paramount). I also had curves Eric joked would make Jessica Rabbit jealous. My short black Halle Berry haircut set me apart in the land of pageant hair weaves, and Eric always said he loved the way I wore it with confidence.

"I mean, damn, could you possibly be with someone any more boring than Eric?"

"Shut up, MJ. You just never liked him because of that time he tried to fix you up with his accountant." I snickered at the blind date Eric had tried to arrange between MJ and the straightest gay guy I had ever seen.

"You're damn right I'm mad about that shit," MJ said, snorting and standing up to give a showgirl-worthy twirl in front of his bar stool. "Look at me, girl. I'm far too fabulous to evah, evvvvvah date an accountant. What the hell was Eric thinking? I mean, I hate when you people try to set us up because you think, 'I know two black guys who are gay, so I should hook them up.' No!"

"'You people'? What do you mean? It could have worked if you weren't so damn bitchy." The evening had gone horribly wrong. MJ could barely hide his disdain for the accountant who clearly fell in love with MJ on sight.

"When I say 'you people,' I mean my straight friends. First of all, I'm gay with a capital *G*, capital *A*, capital *Y*, and all of the glitter, leather, and lace-covered fabulousness that entails. The accountant, on the other hand, was a 'homosexual.'" MJ always uses air quotes around "homosexual" to describe uptight men he feels are only gay in the dark and nowhere near as fabulous as he is.

"OK, well, you could have exercised some home training and at least stayed for the rest of dinner."

"Why? There was no need to waste my precious time when there are plenty of fine and fabulous men out there dying for some MJ in their lives."

"You are crazy as hell," I said, shaking my head at the memory of the failed setup.

"And that's why you love me, sister." MJ leaned over and kissed me on the cheek as he slid back onto the bar stool. "So what us gon' do now that we ain't got no jobs? You know I ride or die for you, girl, but MJ isn't going back to the shampoo bowl."

I couldn't even think about that right now, but I knew we had to find something fast before Kris and Hollywood Scoop Media blacklisted me throughout the entire industry. I toyed with the idea of a wrongful termination suit and called an employment lawyer friend who told me I definitely had a case. But I knew even if I won the case, after months of litigation and a six-figure legal bill, no one would ever hire me again and my career would officially be over for real.

Even though I couldn't process the idea of finding a new job, I knew I'd need to get my act together quickly, because with Eric moving out, I needed a new gig ASAP to keep a roof over my damn head.

"Bartender, keep 'em coming." I raised my glass, waiting for a refill.

—

The persistent and annoying vibration of my cell phone was what finally woke me up. I rolled over in the queen-size bed Eric and I used to share, still dressed in the suit I had worn yesterday—the shittiest day of my life.

MJ and I had drowned our collective sorrows in endless rounds of Hennessy and mojitos and bad karaoke at Coltrane's. I had managed to stumble home at some ungodly hour and had fallen straight into bed. I now tried to raise my throbbing head up from the pillow, but it was too heavy. I blindly felt around with my hand to grab the phone off the dusty nightstand. I could only manage to open one eye to squint at the flashing number on my phone. I saw a New York area code, but I didn't recognize the rest of the numbers, so I let the call go to voice mail. The caller didn't leave a message, choosing instead to call back less than a minute later. I answered, figuring whoever it was wouldn't do anything but keep calling until I did.

"Hello?" I mumbled hoarsely. The scratchy sound of my own voice made my head throb even harder. *No more mojitos. Damn you, MJ.*

"Hey, girl. Wake up. It's Vanessa," said a much-too-cheery voice on the other end of the line.

"Hey, V.," I said. My voice cracked as I registered that the happy tone from another planet was that of Vanessa King, all-around home-girl and my former college roommate. We both earned our stripes growing up in rough neighborhoods, me on Chicago's South Side and Vanessa in Compton, and we became fast friends the moment we stepped on Harvard's campus freshman year with the same inner-city chips on our shoulders.

I sat up in bed, raking my hand through my short matted hair, mad at myself that I hadn't tied it up with the scarf last night. As the memories of yesterday's firing and last night's breakup rushed into my consciousness, I fell back into the pile of pillows on my bed, groaning. "Oh, my head."

"Damn, girl. Aren't you too old for hangovers?" Vanessa chuckled. "Wake up, heffa. I need to talk to you."

"Girl, if only you knew. I just had the day from hell." I slowly recounted the past twenty-four hours to Vanessa. As I repeated the details of the single worst day ever, I tried to quiet the rising nausea in my stomach with a swig of the Pepto-Bismol I kept in the nightstand drawer. I placed the bottle back in the drawer stuffed with travel brochures, home decorating magazines, and real estate listings. This drawer might as well be called the drawer of lost dreams. I'd always loved to travel, and I collected travel brochures about all the places I dreamed of going with Eric. The magazines were dog-eared with furnishings and paint colors for the dream home Eric and I said we were going to buy for our family one day. Buying a home for my family would also be a part of a dream I'd had since I was a child who grew up bouncing from apartment to apartment when my mom couldn't pay the rent. I had always wanted to be the first in my family to own a home. But what family? What home? I'd been busy giving my life to *Hollywood Scoop!* for the last five years, and now that Kris has tossed me out on my ass, I had nothing to show for it. No family, no man, no memories.

As I heard my seven-year-old godson, Damon, laughing in the background, my stomach clenched. Would I ever have children of my own? Or had that possibility died along with my journalism career and my relationship with Eric?

"I'm so sorry," Vanessa said. "Why didn't you call me?"

"I should have. That certainly would have been better than going out with MJ's crazy ass. MJ, who made me have another drink every time I mentioned Eric's name because he said he was officially black history. You know he never liked us together."

"MJ's possessive ass never likes you with anyone," she snorted, laughing. "He's like a jealous boyfriend who doesn't want anyone else to have you. Except no sex."

"Stop playing. You know there's no one for MJ but Ms. Beyoncé. I do believe that boy would go straight for her."

"I know that's right." Vanessa giggled. "So what are you going to do about a new gig? You should come out here to New York and find something new."

Vanessa had been saying this to me for weeks, ever since she and her husband, NBA All-Star Marcus King, was traded to the New York Gladiators. I've sat through enough teary phone calls over the years to know that Vanessa was looking at this trade as a fresh start for her husband's career and their struggling marriage. She told me that having me there would give her some support and a real friend in a city full of fakes.

"I may just have to, girl. Knowing Kris, I'm sure I'm blacklisted at all the LA media companies." I had worked really hard to get to this point in my career, and the thought of starting over brought tears to my puffy eyes. I let a few fall onto the pillow, sniffing hard to stop my running nose.

"Ah, hell. I know you're not crying over that witch! We are better than that. No one gets the best of us!"

"I know but damn. Did she really have to fire me?" I whined into the phone, giving into my pain of losing both my job and Eric in the same day. I wasn't sure which hurt more.

"OK, look, I think I can get you a job interview within the week if you'd seriously consider moving to New York."

"Really?" I didn't dare get my hopes up.

"Yeah, a soror of mine, DeAnna George, is the president of the publishing unit of PrimeTime Media Group, and over dinner last week, she was telling me about all the drama she was going through to find a new editor for one of their properties, *DivaDish* magazine and the website."

"I'll take it!" I said quickly into the phone. Suddenly the thought of a new job and a new life three thousand miles away from *Hollywood Scoop!* and Eric sounded like a lifeline I couldn't afford to pass up.

"Well, slow down, sister. It's not my job to offer, but you know I'll put in the serious good word and lean on her to make it happen. She's always trying to get Marcus and me to give one of her publications an interview, so I'm sure she'll be salivating if she thinks I owe her something." Vanessa laughed.

"For real, V., you know I've always wanted to run my own show, and no one is better connected than me. That brand is hot and has a lot of potential."

"Consider it done. I'll call her as soon as we get off the phone."

I smiled and thanked my best friend for always having my back. We caught up on how the move was going, her search for a new home, and getting Damon settled into a new school.

"So why are you calling me from a new phone number?" I asked.

"Kareem got me yet another cell phone," Vanessa said, sighing into the phone.

"Kareem is still on the payroll? I thought you were going to get Marcus to fire him and get a new agent? I know that's your man cousin and all, but he has no business managing Marcus's career. He's so shady."

"Girl, don't I wish. You know I want that bastard out of our lives, but he's fam, and if I learned nothing from Marcus during our marriage, don't nothing come between him and his boy." Basketball players were notorious for carrying childhood friends and family members on the payroll, but Marcus had upgraded his cousin to agent/manager, giving him a damn near twenty-four-hour presence in Vanessa and Marcus's marriage. A former basketball star himself, he had grown up with Marcus. The two of them actually looked more like brothers than cousins with the same six-foot-five frame, ebony skin tone, and lean, muscled athletic build.

"OK, forget Kareem. This is like your third new phone number in the last six months. What's Kareem up to now?"

"Kareem says it's a new security thing with us moving to New York. I'll explain when you get here. Look, I've got to bounce and take Damon to his doctor's appointment. I'll call you as soon as I speak with DeAnna. Hopefully you guys can get on the phone together today."

"I really appreciate this, V. Honestly, you have no idea."

"No doubt, girl. We always have each other's backs. You just hurry up and get your butt to New York."

She laughed, and then her voice turned serious. "After all, I need my best friend in the same city if I'm going to survive the concrete jungle."

CHAPTER 2

Vanessa

"M arcus!"

"*Marcus!*"

"Mrs. King!"

"*Marcus and Mrs. King! Over here, please!*"

The flashing cameras and the bright lights from all the TV crews were blinding. I tried to put my head down and into Marcus's back while he clutched my hand as we made our way through the screaming crowd.

I couldn't remember the last time he held my hand.

I could smell the hypnotic scent of his Prada cologne through the dark gray wool of his double-breasted Zegna suit, which was complemented by a crisp white-and-black pinstripe shirt with French cuffs, gleaming onyx cuff links, and an ebony silk tie. My man looked like $150 million and worth every penny the New York Gladiators were paying him.

And I was holding my own today if I did say so myself.

At twenty-eight, and after giving birth to our son, Damon, I could still turn a brother's head with my lush curves, tiny waist, and full breasts that stood at attention. My milk-chocolate skin gleamed with Donna Karan body-sparkle lotion. A bright red silk Roland Mouret off-the-shoulder knit dress hugged my Coke-bottle curves that would make Pam Grier look anorexic in comparison. I paired the dress with black patent leather Jimmy Choo platform stilettos. Walter, my hairstylist, had slicked back my thick jet-black shoulder-length hair into a chic high ponytail with a pompadour that elongated my features. My favorite makeup artist, Kiki, who had come to our apartment at what seemed like the crack of dawn, had done her magic, too. I inherited my mother's flawless deep mocha skin, so Kiki opted for Bobbi Brown's ultrasheer foundation and highlighted my high, sharp cheekbones with a shimmery bronzer. My eyes, large dark brown pools flecked with hints of gold in the light, were accented with smoky shades of honey gold and warm brown. Kiki added a few silky lashes in the corners for pop and arched my thick black eyebrows to perfection. For my lips, she finished with a matte crimson shade from Dior that was a bit brighter than I'd normally choose, but today was a very special occasion.

We were aiming for the stage in the front of the Madison Square Garden pressroom where Gladiator owner Davis Jennings, Coach Brad Townsend, and Kareem stood applauding at the front of the room. As we tried to weave our way through the throng of screaming reporters, I smoothed down the front of my dress and silently prayed that my hair would stay in place with the rising heat in the tiny room. I have hair like Oprah; it's superthick and seems to grow overnight. Everyone thinks it's a weave, and sometimes it has a mind of its own, so hopefully Walter had used enough pomade to keep my edges in place. The last thing I needed was photos of raggedy flyaways in the front of my hairline to pop up on those nasty gossip blogs.

The Madison Square Garden pressroom was packed, as well it should be.

After all, the King had finally come to New York.

Marcus's trade to the struggling New York franchise had been speculated about for months. He was billed as the silver bullet that would bring a championship to the Big Apple, and the entire city—from the mayor, to the tourism board, and fans posting videos on YouTube—had been pushing for him to come. And I was, too. It was time for a fresh start, not only for Marcus's career but also for our marriage. It was time to leave the scandal behind us.

Marcus and I had been so happy in the beginning of our marriage. We met our junior year at Inglewood High School. He was the star basketball player and had all the girls chasing after him, but I played it cool. After all, I was fine as hell and had all the boys sniffing around me, so there was no need to chase. Once I decided to give him the time of day, there were immediate sparks. He was fine and he knew it. I was cute and I knew it. But the first night we met, we talked forever, and it was as if everyone at the school faded away. He was tall with smooth dark skin, cheekbones that could cut glass, full juicy lips, sexy hooded ebony eyes framed by impossibly long lashes, and a smooth, confident walk that looked like a panther's. He approached me in the school hallway and without comment walked me away from the guy who had been trying to spit some tired game. I was hooked and he knew it.

I had always been focused on my classes and getting out of Inglewood as quickly as possible, but I hadn't counted on falling in love with Marcus. We tried to see each other as often as we could, but with his rigorous practice schedule and my mom keeping me on lock with my studies, it was tough. His cousin and best friend, Kareem, was also on the team. Handsome basketball stars who looked as if they could have been brothers, the two of them ran our school. I could tell Kareem didn't like that Marcus and I had started dating. I was standing in the way of him and his boy and the harem of girls that seemed to trail them in the hallways Monday through Friday. Kareem ate up the attention, but Marcus soon had eyes only for me. Kareem couldn't understand why he settled for one girl. I'm sure he had hoped after graduation things would cool off when we all headed off to college, but they didn't.

After we graduated, Marcus and Kareem went to UCLA, and I flew east to Harvard with dreams of becoming a child psychologist. A long-distance relationship was tough, but Marcus and I made it work. One night when Marcus and I returned to his dorm after I had managed to scrounge up enough money to fly home to LA to celebrate his birthday, Kareem had left a little present of his own: a buxom blond stripper wearing nothing but Marcus's game jersey in his bed. Marcus tried to get me to laugh off what he said was Kareem's little prank as he pushed the pouting girl out of his room, but from that moment on, Kareem was officially on my shit list. So when Marcus came out of UCLA as a first-round draft pick for the Phoenix Lasers and named Kareem as his new agent, I wasn't happy that he was going to continue to be a part of our lives. A car accident had ended Kareem's college ball career a few months earlier, and Marcus was determined that he and his cousin would live their NBA dream together, so I kept my mouth shut.

Marcus felt like he owed Kareem since he wasn't able to get to the pros like he did.

I always suspected that Kareem was shady, but every time I tried to talk to Marcus about my concerns, he shut me down. He just couldn't or wouldn't see that Kareem didn't have our best interests at heart, and I knew someone else could have done a better job managing him. I wouldn't have been surprised if he had been stealing money from us, but there was no way to tell, because Kareem had a tight grip on our finances. Even during our quarterly financial review with Kareem, I was never quite sure how much Marcus had made and how much was going out. Marcus only halfway paid attention, so he was not even concerned that something could be wrong.

We were excited that he had finally achieved his dream of playing in the NBA. We knew we wanted to get married eventually, but right before the draft our senior year, I found out I was pregnant and Marcus was adamant that we get married right away. We didn't want our child to grow up without a father in his life, so we went down to the justice of the peace that summer and got married right after he signed his contract with the Lasers. We moved to Phoenix, and our little prince, Damon Marcus King, was born six months later. Our little family was complete. And I prayed we would always be that happy.

As soon as we moved to Phoenix, the other NBA wives tried to school me in the treacherous realities of being married to a professional athlete. And while I listened patiently, I believed that Marcus loved me too much to succumb to the groupies who would be lying in wait in every city to which they traveled. I learned the way the game was played. These tricks, white, black, Latina, Asian, Martian, whatever, were relentless in their pursuit of our men. And thanks to sites like Balleralert, those hookers could track their movements, share their hookup tips, and post their freaky sexcapades with players. Not to mention the whores that would flash their bare vayjayjays from the stands as players ran up and down the basketball court, and the bitches that would bribe a hotel housekeeper to let them into a player's room and would lie naked across his bed, willing to do whatever he wanted after a game on the road. I heard so many unbelievable groupie-gone-wild stories from the other NBA wives that my guard was up even though I thought that wouldn't ever be something we would have to deal with. I trusted Marcus, and I knew he loved me.

For the first four years of our marriage, we were blissfully happy. I stayed home and raised Damon, putting aside my career dreams and telling myself my priority should be my family. I traveled with Marcus as much as I could, but three years ago I started to notice a change in Marcus as his star really began to rise and the pressure on his career increased along with the temptations. It seemed like everyone wanted a piece of my husband. Whether it was the media dissecting and critiquing every step he made on the court on *SportsCenter*, the coaching staff pushing him and his teammates to bring home a championship, or other players in the league trying to make a name for themselves by talking trash to or about him on court and in their own interviews, the pressure was intense. The worst for me was the chatter on the blogs. Instead of covering Hollywood's leading men, they soon wanted to cover nothing but basketball players, their million-dollar contracts, lavish lifestyles, and sexcapades. The attention was relentless as the sites posted every picture they could get and featured straight-up lies speculating about players' relationships, marriages, and sexuality. It was a dirty business. I tried to stop reading them, but of course whenever friends and family members saw something about Marcus, they always forwarded the links to me.

As the years went on, I tried to hold things down at home. But during the season, it seemed like he was barely home, and when he was, he was distant and short with me. I wanted to have another baby, but Marcus kept saying it wasn't the right time. It seemed like what media thought of him meant more to him than what I or his son did. Sometimes when Marcus was on the road, I tried to call him in the middle of the night to make sure everything was OK. When I couldn't reach him, I'd reach out to Kareem, who was always traveling with his one and only client, and then I'd get a call back from Marcus with some excuse about missing my call while in the shower. I didn't want to believe what my instincts were trying to tell me, but when photos of Marcus and beautiful women at nightclubs began popping up on the gossip blogs, I knew I could no longer ignore what I felt. When I questioned what was going on, he denied he was having affairs. But when my husband stopped trying to have sex with me, especially after he'd been on the road, I knew he had to be getting it from somewhere.

I thought about hiring a private detective, but I was afraid the tabloids would find out, so I knew I had to figure it out on my own. My first stop was Marcus's cell phone, which wasn't easy to get because he kept it attached to his body like an extra kidney. He jumped whenever it buzzed with an incoming text message or ran across the room to retrieve it whenever it rang. He even took it into the bathroom with him when he showered, claiming he was expecting an important call from the coach or Kareem. So one night while he was sleeping, I went looking for his phone.

He had long since stopped charging it on the nightstand next to our bed, so the first place I looked was on top of the island dresser in his huge walk-in closet, but I didn't see it. I didn't think he would take a chance of it being too far away, so I took my own phone out of the pocket of my robe and dialed his number. When the call connected, I heard a faint buzzing sounding in the closet. I couldn't figure out where it was coming from before his voice mail picked up, so I hung up and called again as I walked around the closet, pushing back the hundreds of shirts, jackets, and suits hanging along the walls. The buzzing was getting louder, so I knew I was close. As I made my way to the very back of his walk-in closet, the noise seemed to come from the ground. Pushing my way through a wall of heavy suits and pushing aside rows of pristine size-sixteen sneakers, I found the phone stuffed into the toe of one of his Nikes. The cord to the charger snaked out of the side of the phone and plugged into an outlet on the bottom of the wall. He must have just had that installed, as I didn't remember there being outlets in the back of the closet.

Shaking and fearful of what I might find, I began my search. His phone was locked, so I tried a bunch of codes: his birthday, Damon's birthday, my birthday, and our wedding anniversary. On the last try before the phone locked, I input his team number twice: 2323—after all, life had been all about him for quite some time. The phone unlocked.

I scrolled through his text messages and saw that most of his correspondence with his teammates, Kareem, and family members was fine. A number I didn't recognize appeared in his phone log and text screen, but the messages were deleted. With no way to retrieve the deleted messages, I decided I had no choice but to call the number. I pushed the button to dial the unfamiliar number and held my breath as I put the phone to my ear. It rang twice, and then a woman's husky voice answered. The voice was low and sexy, and I doubted it was because she had been sleeping; this was probably how she sounded every time my husband called her.

"Hey, baby. Did you wake up in the middle of the night thinking about me?"

I could barely catch my breath as I clutched the phone to my ear.

"Baby, are you there?" she asked. "Marcus, you woke me up, so I hope you're going to at least give me some hot phone sex to hold me over until Miami."

I clutched my stomach, which was suddenly tied in knots. Hot tears streamed down my face. Marcus was scheduled to leave for a game against Miami the next day.

"Bitch, who is this?" I screamed into the phone. "Who are you? Are you fucking my husband?"

The woman laughed and then hung up the phone. Blind with rage, I punched desperately at the buttons and redialed the number. This time her voice mail picked up, and I continued to scream into the receiver.

"You fucking bitch! You stay away from my family!" My screams must have awakened Marcus, because just as I was redialing the number, he ran into the closet and grabbed the phone from me. The panic on his face let me know immediately that he knew he was caught.

The next six months of our marriage were a nightmare. We went to counseling, and we talked to our pastor. Marcus swore he would stop seeing other women, and I spiraled downward into a deep depression. From the outside, we looked like the happy NBA couple. I continued my duties as president of the National Basketball Association wives organization, and Marcus continued to play the best season of his career. The only people I confided in were Nia and another NBA wife I had grown close to, Jacqueline Herman. I could tell Nia wanted me to leave Marcus, because she said just that at the end of all our calls, but Jacqueline encouraged me to stay. Married for ten years to Michael Herman, Marcus's closest teammate, Jacqueline was far more pragmatic. She shared her own stories of betrayal and how she and Michael somehow made it work. One such story left me breathless. A famous Hollywood actress that I loved in all her romantic comedies had showed up at their kids' holiday program demanding that Michael come out and leave his family and be with her. Humiliated in front of the other parents, Jacqueline had demanded Michael have the woman removed from their school by the police and that he take out a restraining order. Jacqueline was uncertain at that point if they could ever work things out, but somehow she said they did.

That's when I learned about the Road Code that some of the basketball wives and their husbands adopt. This rule essentially meant that what happened on the road stayed on the road, and that part of their lives never entered into the family home. No phone calls, text messages, accidental pregnancies, no STDs, no gossip on the blogs, and absolutely no falling in love. When the players were home with their families, they devoted their attention to their wives and kids. Some wives, she told me, had even gone as far as to create legal agreements that triggered steep financial penalties if the Road Code was broken. I told Jacqueline I didn't think I could live like that and knowingly share my man with other women.

"First of all, you're not sharing your man," Jacqueline told me. "You're protecting your family. If you wanted a faithful husband, you should have married Joe Postal Worker instead of a fine-ass basketball player worth millions of dollars. That man's walking around with a target on his back, and these scandalous chicks, who are throwing panties at him left and right, will stop at nothing to get him. And because he's a man who thinks with the wrong head, sometimes he's going to slip up. It's just sex with them, and it doesn't have to mean anything more. Your husband loves you, but at the end of the day, he's a man—and being a man who's a professional athlete takes it to a whole new level."

I didn't know if I could accept the Code and that Kareem could be the one facilitating these hookups as they traveled around the country. Marcus and I continued to go to counseling and meet with our pastor to discuss our problems. We took a vacation to Fiji, and things seemed to get better. I saw that Marcus was really trying and he was sorry he had hurt me. But last year I started to get that nagging feeling again that something was going on. The blogs were littered with pics of him at nightclubs while on the road, and there were always groups of women hanging in the background. He always reassured me that nothing was going on and that the women were just hoping to catch the eye of one of the single players.

Yeah, right. How dumb do I look? I wanted to say to him.

I managed to sneak a look at his cell phone again but didn't see anything out of the ordinary. I told Jacqueline about my suspicions. That's when she told me that Marcus likely had a second phone.

"After they get caught the first time, that's what they do," she said, chuckling. "They'll get a second phone and only take it out when they are outside the home or completely away from you. He might keep it in his car, in a bag, or even have a friend or his agent carry it. If you happen to come around when he has it on him, he'll pass it off to one of his boys or Kareem. Part of the Road Code is that you never have to see the calls or text messages. He'll never put it in your face, so maybe he's living by the Code and you don't even know it."

I thought about confronting Marcus but couldn't bring myself to hear the truth. I buried my anger and focused on my charity work with the Wives Association and raising our son while Marcus burned up the courts and took his team to the play-offs. New endorsement offers came in, and his star was burning brighter than ever. A nasty divorce could possibly put that all in jeopardy. And as Jacqueline pointed out, half that money was mine, so I needed to protect it in case at some point I decided to leave.

Then the dead cheerleader turned up in the desert, and everything changed.

One girl in particular had begun to show up in the background of the photos of Marcus on the road. Her name was Kalinda Walters, and she was one of the new Phoenix Lasers dancers. And while the team organization had very strict rules about players and dancers interacting (mostly driven by jealous wives trying to protect their territory and frustrated coaches trying to keep their players focused on the court), this twenty-something firecracker seemed to play by her own rules.

Marcus assured me nothing was going on with the nubile dark-haired beauty with the green eyes and DD breasts, but I felt like something wasn't right.

One of the reports contained gruesome details about the dancer's murder and the state her body was in when she was discovered: her cinnamon-brown skin had been carved up with jagged knife wounds, indicating that she had been tortured before a single gunshot to the head had ended her life, her long black hair was matted with dried blood, huge black flies swarmed the body, and maggots had started to harvest their eggs in the open wounds.

The Phoenix media jumped all over the murder of the sexy young dancer. Although there wasn't any hard evidence, they really worked themselves into a frenzy when they found out that detectives had questioned several of the Laser players, including Marcus, after finding their numbers in her cell phone logs.

Marcus denied any involvement with the girl, but the whispers persisted and swirled for months, both in the papers and online about a possible affair with Kalinda. Marcus assured me that nothing had happened between them.

The case went unsolved for several months with the police at a dead end. That's when the trade talks began. Marcus's free-agency contract was up, and everyone knew New York wanted him badly, but the team owner, Davis Jennings, was an ultraconservative business tycoon who abhorred scandal. Kareem and Marcus's publicist, Desiree Deevers, worked overtime squashing anything linking the dead dancer to their multimillion-dollar client. Nothing could be allowed to kill this deal. Marcus had always talked about playing for New York and wanted to get this deal done quickly. There was no more talk of the cheerleader. But in checking Marcus's history on his laptop, I saw that several times over the past few days he had logged onto GoldenGoddess, the personal website of a popular Los Angeles groupie Jacqueline had told me to watch out for.

We both couldn't wait to get to New York.

But for very different reasons.

No more cheerleader.

And no more threats.

—

The press conference finally ended. After answering questions for more than an hour, Marcus was exhausted but kept his smile bright as we left the stifling room of reporters. He confidently answered all of ESPN's questions about how he planned to lead the team to a championship, artfully spoke to *Sports Illustrated* about how excited he was to work with Coach Townsend and the current team roster, and he deftly avoided any questions from Deadspin about the "drama" he was leaving behind in Arizona. I saw Desiree in the corner jotting down the names of reporters bold enough to try to bring their questions around to that dead whore, and I knew she would have them banned from any future interviews with Marcus and the franchise.

Marcus and I were escorted out by a security team through the bowels of Madison Square Garden to the loading dock where we slipped into the back of the waiting limousine.

"Congratulations, my darling," I said as I relaxed my jaw, which ached from having a fake smile plastered on my face for the past hour, and sank into the soft buttery black leather seats. I turned to Marcus to kiss him on his cheek as the car pulled out from the underground garage and began to make its way through the heavy city traffic. "You've always wanted to play in New York, and now it's official."

"Thank you, baby," Marcus said, taking my hand and absentmindedly kissing it as he looked out the car window. "We've got a lot to do to get settled. You ready to look for a house?"

"Not really, but we have to get settled and get Damon in school."

"Yeah, little man's got to get into school, and we don't want to live in the apartment forever. At least we're out of the hotel, though."

When we first got to New York, we stayed at the Four Seasons hotel for several weeks, but as part of Marcus's deal with the Gladiators, we were offered a penthouse loft in Tribeca to live in until we found a home. It was beautiful space fully furnished, and I, too, was glad to be out of the Four Seasons—but it wasn't home.

"I'm going to start looking next week," I said, taking in the scene outside the tinted windows as a bike messenger whizzed by, nearly clipping the limousine driver's side mirror. Marcus picked up the interior phone to speak to the driver, Alex, and told him to drop him at the Four Seasons and then to take me home.

"Aren't we both going back to the apartment?" I asked. I had hoped the three of us would spend the day together, exploring the neighborhood and perhaps taking Damon to the Natural History Museum to see the dinosaurs.

"Uh, sorry, babe. Kareem set up this meeting with these guys from China who want to discuss some business opportunities for my brand overseas," he answered quickly. "They are going back tomorrow, so we have to meet today."

"Oh, OK. I guess we'll see you later, then."

"Yeah, hopefully not too late. These cats might want to have dinner though, so I'll let you know."

As the car pulled up at the door of the hotel, I grabbed Marcus's arm before he could step out of the car.

"Try not to be too late, honey. We want to see you, too." I looked into his dark eyes as if they could show me if he was telling me the truth. But I could no longer read his eyes.

"I'll try, baby," he said as he leaned in and kissed me quickly on the cheek before stepping out of the car. I saw Kareem grinning, at the curb, as he walked over to clap his boy on the back.

"Hey, V.," he said as he leaned down to speak to me. "Don't worry, I'll have your boy home soon. Unless he wants to go out and celebrate that big fat Gladiators contract I got for him!"

Marcus and Kareem dapped each other up with broad smiles across all of their features.

"I know that's right, man. You did the damn thing on that big fat contract," Marcus said to Kareem. "We did it, baby. We in New York!"

Before I could tell Marcus again that Damon and I really wanted him to come home early tonight so that we could celebrate as a family, he and Kareem turned away to walk into the hotel. As I pushed the button to raise the car window, I saw Kareem slip something in

Marcus's hand as they walked through the door of the hotel. A phone. My stomach sank.

Suddenly I got that all-too-familiar feeling in my stomach as Alex began to steer the car downtown. It was a pain that seemed to indicate that our fresh start might be turning into the same old thing, and I wasn't willing to let that happen. Pulling out my cell phone from my cherry-red Dior handbag, I dialed the only number that could help get my marriage back on the right track.

CHAPTER 3

Laila

D *amn, I'm a sexy bitch.*

Naked except for a thin lacy wisp of a black Agent Provocateur thong covering my freshly waxed kitty, a matching demi-cut bra, and six-inch fire-red studded Christian Louboutin suede platform pumps, I finished rubbing in the Carol's Daughter Sparkling Body Butter on my toffee-brown body before I prepared to position my glistening self for my camera phone. Slipping one of the satin bra straps off my shoulder, I pinched my dark cocoa nipples so that they stood at attention through the delicate French lace as if they were waiting for his hungry lips. I ran my hands through my dark brown curls, causing the long layers to frame my face with the amber and blond highlights my hairdresser put in this morning. I let the left side of my hair fall sexily over one of my hazel-green eyes.

Wearing the New York Gladiator colors of black and red, I was officially ready for my close-up. I grabbed my phone from the bathroom counter, placed one hand on my hip, and with my pinky finger, pulled up the side of my thong and positioned the camera to shoot. After reviewing the shot, I clicked forward, found Marcus's number, and typed: *Your "Welcome to New York" Present* and pressed "Send."

Marcus King will be mine. And judging from the immediate response to my text, it was going to happen sooner than I planned.

MK: *Damnnnn, baby. U got me horny as hell lookin at ur sexy assssss!!*

Laila: *Well, why don't U come get some of this brown suga. Lap dance? Shower sex? However U want it!*

MK: *R U in NYC???*

Laila: *Yesssss*

MK: *U got my soldier hard as a brick! Meet me at Four Seasons at 6:30. Ask for my man Christian at the desk and he'll hook U up.*

Laila: *See U soon*

MK: *And make sure U wear that sexy shit U got on now*

———

It was only 4:00, so I had time to take care of a little business before I got pleasured. I pulled up the number of Miki Woods, the fast-talking, Emmy-award-winning Glam Network executive in charge of programming who'd been stalking me about doing a reality show. Over the last few weeks, she had been putting on the hard sell to get me to at least consider shooting a pilot. Her concept was kind of hot. It would be the first-ever interactive web-based real-time reality show called *Whatever Laila Wants . . .* with the tagline "She's Every Man's Fantasy and Every Wife's Nightmare." It would follow my life as I build my "modeling career," party in New York City, and look for Mr. Right. Viewers would get to interact during the show through the show's website. Miki was blowing up my phone, salivating over the opportunity to be the first to capture my rumored relationship with New York Gladiator Marcus King. Showing Miki our X-rated text message exchanges over the past few weeks had only whet her appetite even more, and it was getting my offer price close to seven figures.

"Hey, Miki, it's Laila," I said when her assistant, Tyra, patched my call through to her boss.

"Hi, Laila!" Miki gushed into the phone. "How are you? Did you see the press conference today?"

This chick ain't even slick, but I decided to play with her. Maybe I could even turn this seven-figure deal into eight.

"Press conference? What press conference?" I asked coyly.

"Marcus King's first press conference as a New York Gladiator. Every local news channel carried it live. This is big news, Laila."

"Oh yeah. He told me he was doing something like that today."

"Now, Laila, let's cut to the chase. You know Glam Network wants to do this show with you. And I promise you *Whatever Laila Wants* is going to be huge! We'll put our entire marketing muscle behind it to ensure it's a ratings smash, and with Marcus moving to New York, the interest in the two of you is only going to get more intense."

"I agree, Miki. But opening up my life to your cameras is a big step. I don't generally like to . . . well . . . kiss and tell."

"I know, but we'd really be breaking new ground in the reality TV space with this concept."

"I don't know, Miki. You're really asking a lot . . ." I let my voice trail off and heard her breathing quicken, but I could tell she needed a little push to raise her offer.

"Check your e-mail, Miki. I sent you a little present."

"Oh my God" she exclaimed into the phone after she opened the e-mail containing my most recent text exchange with Marcus along with my photo. "Is this from Marcus King? Are you really about to go meet him? Can I send a camera crew to meet you?"

"Are you crazy? Of course you can't send a camera crew. First of all, we don't have a deal, and second of all, you can't scare Marcus away before I get him. So back the hell up." This nut was about to mess up everything before things really got official.

"OK, I understand, but this is too hot! Laila, I'm willing to raise our offer to one million dollars for the first season and will include a guaranteed second-season option for two million dollars if the show hits predetermined ratings targets. I know a hit when I see one."

Deciding to do my own million-dollar reality show for Glam Network was a no-brainer. But I knew as soon as I signed those papers and word got out that I was doing a reality show, my married man and New York Gladiator's new franchise player could get skittish. Admittedly, the gossip blogs were already speculating about our relationship, thanks to some well-placed tips, but an actual show could have Marcus trying to get as far away from me as possible—no matter how good my kitty kat was. So in order to have my cake and eat it, too, I'm going to have to be patient, and so are Miki and Glam Network. It will be worth it in the long run for all of us.

"Look, Miki. I love that you believe in me and believe in this show. I really do. I promise you I'll seriously think about it, talk to my agent, and get back to you."

"OK, I know you have to get going to the Four Seasons," she joked. "Are you sure we can't send a crew over?"

"Talk to you later, Miki." It was showtime.

—

I know I'm going to get what I want. After all, I always do. Everything and everyone I've ever wanted in my twenty-three years on earth I've gotten. I've been blessed with model looks and a curvaceous body made for sin, and it hadn't been difficult for me to learn to work my charms. My mother had groomed me from day one for the good life. And while Daddy did his best to provide for his two angels, I knew that if I really wanted the life I deserved, I was going to have to get it on my own.

Dropping out of college after two years at Howard University, I had moved to LA with my best friend, Darryl Simmons, so I could pursue modeling and he could start his party-promoting career. I never ran with chicks—too much drama and jealousy. I always got along better with guys. Most of them wanted to get me into bed, of course, and Darryl was no exception in the beginning. But once I put them in the friend box, they were only too happy to hang around, hoping I'd change my mind and give them a little taste.

Once we got to LA, Darryl and I were like kids in a candy store. We got a cheap but decent apartment, hung out all night at the clubs, and slept most of the day. Darryl hooked up with some Mexican cocaine dealers he met at one of our favorite nightclubs and started his own little side hustle with them. While drugs were never my thing, I didn't complain because Darryl's dealing paid for the roof over our heads, put food in the cabinets, and kept me from having to get the typical actor's job of waitressing at some shit diner.

At first I really did try to make an honest go of it and made the requisite rounds of the agents and casting directors, but I found the price for signing was usually a taste of my golden kitty kat. Unwilling to get on the casting couch to audition for a tiny part in a local car insurance commercial, I quickly surmised there had to be a better way to become a star.

Because we went out every night, Darryl and I started to make connections. My looks got us in the door, and Darryl's cocaine introduced us to a whole new crowd of Hollywood actors, video directors, and athletes. I branded myself the Golden Goddess and started to get requests for video appearances and men's magazine photo shoots. I shot a few videos for hot rappers and R&B stars. After one video where my entire scene took place in a glass shower, the calls for more videos and dates with rappers started coming in. Everyone seemed to want to work with Laila. But hooking up with rappers who just wanted to pass me around to their crew wasn't what I wanted. Most of their money wasn't real, anyway. Everything on the set, including their platinum jewelry, six-figure cars, and clothes, was rented for the shoot. Plus, dating a rapper didn't have a lot of cachet and wouldn't put me on a red carpet, in magazines, or on TV. But professional athletes were a different story. They had real paper and an affinity for beautiful women like me.

Ever the budding entrepreneur, Darryl figured we needed to start self-promoting my "talents," so he started my GoldenGoddess website, which showcased all my photo shoots, magazine covers, video clips, and my personal blog where I talked about the party life and answered reader questions. While I knew it wasn't anything more than a site for pervs to jack off to my glossy images, we started to get a lot of traffic. The hot urban websites started featuring me, and people in the industry took notice. And then I met Marcus King and everything changed.

Darryl and I had gone to the NBA All-Star game in Las Vegas after getting hooked up with tickets from one of his clients, Kareem Davis. I'd never been to All-Star before, but from what I'd heard, it was a who's who of pro athletes and the women trying to land them. What I hadn't counted on was the level of groupie talent, models, and actresses in attendance. Everywhere you looked, there were model chicks looking like they stepped right off the cover of *Vogue* in the lobby of all the hotels as well as tramps in barely there G-strings and pasties popping it and dropping it like they stepped off the cover of *Smooth* magazine. And all these chicks were serious about their game. Staying four to six deep in a room, they were decked out in their most scandalous gear and highest stilettos. But never the one to be intimidated by another beautiful chick, I knew I could more than hold my own.

Our first event was the hottest ticket: the opening weekend black-jack party at the Mandalay Bay Hotel and Casino. When we were welcomed into the VIP area, I immediately turned my attention to the evening's hottest attraction. Standing in a corner of the room surrounded by a group of other boldfaced-named players, Marcus King stood out. He was simply delicious. Wearing a crisp white shirt that showed off his dark ebony skin, he scanned the room, and our eyes connected. I held his gaze, smiled, and raised my champagne glass to him. He raised his own glass and smiled, his sexy lips revealing perfect white teeth. He then turned to a man standing next to him. I assumed the man was his brother because they looked so much alike and had the same gait and mannerisms. The man nodded his head to something Marcus said. I knew I had been given the approval. A shiver went through my body in anticipation of what was to come. The man turned out to be Kareem. He asked me for my number and told me to expect an important call later in the evening.

Now, because I was a mistress of seduction and master of the game, the one thing I knew about rich black athletes was that groupie ass was a dime a dozen, and if you gave in too quickly, you'd be nothing more than memory and story to share in the locker room. If you wanted to be more than a one-night jump-off, you had to hook them. So I played the game. When Marcus sent me a text, we had a playful and sexy exchange, but I didn't meet him at his hotel at 2:00 a.m. as he requested. Darryl warned me that I was taking quite a chance because Marcus could have just moved on to the next chick, but I knew if I was going to be more than just a blow job, I had to play my cards right. So I didn't sleep with him that weekend but kept in contact via text and invited him to check out my website and look me up when he was in town the following month to play the Los Angeles Vikings.

He called as soon as he landed, and we made plans for a discreet outing—dinner and dessert in his hotel suite coordinated by Kareem. As one of the league's most visible franchise players and a married man, Marcus could ill afford to have a messy affair splashed all over TMZ. The sex had been as electric as I had fantasized. To keep his attentions and affections, I'd have to keep the intrigue going, so I made sure that every time we saw each other, I surprised him and left him wanting more of the Goddess.

What married women don't understand is that when it comes to sex, you can't just give it to your man whenever he wants it. You have to be excited, enthusiastic, and adventurous. And when you're dealing with someone like Marcus King, a multimillion-dollar pro-athlete who can jump into bed with a new movie star or model every single day of the week, you really have to step up your game. So whether it was handcuffs, blindfolds, blow jobs on the private jet, or bringing a little blond friend along for the party, I did it all, and Marcus never knew what to expect. And that's what kept him coming back for more . . . and kept his wife's bed cold as ice.

And while I thought we'd have fun for a couple of months and I'd get some wonderful presents and maybe even that fly new Mercedes I had my eye on, what I hadn't expected was the deeper connection that developed between us. Marcus was funny, sensitive, charming as hell, and the king of the league. He listened to me talk and wanted to hear my opinion. We began seeing each other as often as we could. Kareem would fly me into the cities Marcus was playing, and he whisked me out right after the next game. And after each meeting, it became harder and harder for us to part. I could tell he was getting in deep with me, and I was quickly doing the same.

I never worried about his wife, and he never mentioned her. And like most NBA wives, the woman soon to be known as the ex-Mrs. King hadn't really maintained her looks. She was cute enough, but she always had a tired expression on her face. The First Lady of the NBA, as she was known, stood no chance against me and my plans for her soon-to-be ex-husband. Sometimes she did intrude on our evenings together like when his main cell phone would ring while we were in bed and he'd have to answer. He would apologize and take the call in the bathroom. He had recently got a separate cell phone for me because he said wifey was always checking his phone for text messages and e-mails from other women. I never understood why women didn't know that there was no more of a turnoff than a crazy jealous woman. But she wasn't my problem, and soon enough she wouldn't be Marcus's, either.

CHAPTER 4

Nia

*B*reaking news alert: Marcus King spotted at NYC hotel with video vixen!!??

"Dammit, Marcus," I groaned as I read the e-mail from Che Williams, intrepid *DivaDish* senior entertainment editor, and tossed my iPhone onto my cluttered desk before staring out the window of my corner office in Midtown Manhattan.

"Ooh, girl," said MJ as he walked into my office, his iPhone in one hand and another large brown box from my mom with more clothes from the HSN that she bought for my new job. He dropped the box on the coffee table in the seating area of my office, slid the frosted glass door closed behind him, and flopped his slim frame in one of the smoky Lucite chairs facing my desk. "Did you see Che's e-mail?"

"Of course I did," I snapped as I sat down in the black leather chair behind my desk and raked my fingers through my new short, spiky do. When the *DivaDish* reporters had breaking news that needed an immediate response, I instructed them to copy MJ on the communication so that he could find me quickly for approval.

"Whatcha gonna do, EIC?" he drawled. "You know this is a big story, and our readers are obsessed with Marcus King since he got traded to New York. Whenever the writers post anything about him on the site, it gets tons of page views and comments. I bet you that tramp-ass Laila James is the one that leaked the story. Golden Goddess, my ass."

Suddenly both of our iPhones buzzed with another incoming message from Che.

Got video!!!

I clicked on Che's message, and the short video clip opened on my screen.

Shit . . .

Marcus King was hard to miss. And with a $150 million contract with the New York Gladiators, he had a target on his back for every reporter and every wannabe paparazzi with a cell phone camera. The clip was grainy and unsteady, but I could hear Che's persistent voice yelling in the background, "Marcus King, over here!"

When he saw Che's camera aimed at his grill, he threw up his hand to block his face as he walked out of a Manhattan hotel lobby holding a woman's hand. The woman, dressed in a short, tight turquoise Hervé Léger dress, quickly pulled the dark glasses off the top of her long dark hair, slipped them on, and then dropped his hand. But it was too late. The video ended as Marcus rushed by Che and jumped into a waiting car. The woman immediately turned and ran back into the hotel.

It was definitely Marcus in the video. And it was definitely Laila James, the Golden Goddess, with him.

"Damn . . . How dumb do you have to be to try to leave a hotel with your ho in the middle of Manhattan in broad daylight?" MJ asked as he shook his head.

I knew Che was waiting for my response before she posted her latest scoop to the *DivaDish* website. It was sure to get a lot of traffic and put our fledgling site on the map.

But I wasn't sure what to do with this juicy exclusive because, after all, it would kill my girl Vanessa, and she was the one who helped me get this new job.

—

Vanessa had hooked up an e-mail introduction to her soror DeAnna George, the president of PrimeTime Media's publishing unit, just as she had promised. Desperate for a new job and anxious to get the hell out of Los Angeles and as far away from Eric as possible, I quickly drafted a twenty-page proposal for DeAnna, outlining my vision for the magazine and website. Shortly after receiving my proposal, DeAnna, who, as fate would have it, was in LA to meet with advertising clients, arranged to meet for lunch at her suite in the Beverly Hills Hotel.

It was apparent immediately that DeAnna George was wicked smart, had an edgy sense of humor, and played to win. One of the only female presidents at PrimeTime Media Group, a New York–based conglomerate of publishing, social media, and TV networks, she hadn't gotten to the top by playing nicely with others and sharing her toys. Average height and well toned, she had a light brown complexion and a razor-sharp, chin-length jet-black bob with a widow's peak. I took her age to be a well-preserved fiftyish. A Google search had yielded several business accolades and a few nasty stories about her underhanded office politics and quick temper, so I'd need to push for an ironclad contract to protect myself if she offered me the job. I walked her through my proposal, laying out my vision for the weekly magazine and daily website, which seemed to impress her.

"I want the *DivaDish* brand to be the must-read for women of color both in print and online, and I think you're just the woman to take the brand to the number one position," she said with a hard glint in her dark eyes as she slid a black folder across the table to me. When I opened the folder, I was happy to see an employment contract. The salary, while in the mid six figures, was a little lower than I would have liked for this type of position, but when I tried to address that, she quickly shut me down.

"Let me be clear, Nia. All PrimeTime Media contracts are nonnegotiable," DeAnna said. "Our human resources department has done all the necessary research on the marketplace, competition, and, more importantly, they have done the research on you. So, since you were fired from your last position and Kris Kensington seems to be doing her best to sully what's left of your reputation, this offer seems more than fair."

Ouch, girlfriend did not play. I had to swallow my ego and my first impulse to shove the contract back across the table and tell DeAnna where to stick it, but unfortunately she was right. Just within the last week I had started to realize how limited my options really were. My calls and e-mails to contacts at outlets that had previously expressed interest in my work went unreturned and unanswered. The word was out. My career was officially DOA in LA thanks to Kris, and her version of my firing was sure to get to the East Coast media outlets within the week as well. But while I digested that this could be the only job offer I received and that eking out a living as a freelance writer wouldn't cut it, I knew there was one thing that DeAnna had to agree to or I could never take the job.

"OK, I can accept the salary, but one point that's nonnegotiable for me is that I must be allowed to bring my assistant, Marquis Jackson, with me." I sat back in my chair and stared back at DeAnna. I was ready to walk away over this point, and she knew it.

"Fine. I'll have legal adjust the contract to include your assistant, Marquis, and send the revised agreement to your home this evening to sign."

I accepted the terms of her offer, and within forty-eight hours, human resources had arranged for my apartment and MJ's to be packed up and the contents shipped to New York.

When we arrived at the *DivaDish* offices, MJ jumped on decorating the office. He'd done a great job. There were a plush cream-colored sofa, two black linen and chrome chairs, and a glass coffee table with chrome furnishings. A fifty-four-inch HD flat screen was mounted on the wall along with a series of black-and-white photographs of celebrities behind the sofa and a large zebra-skin rug on the floor.

I got busy meeting the new team, whose members seemed bright, competitive, and passionate about the brand and the growing audience.

They were all young, hungry, and ready to put *DivaDish* on the map, but the senior editor, Che Williams, had really distinguished herself as a dogged reporter with a knack for landing juicy scoops, great underground contacts, and a hip writing style that readers really liked. There was only one bad apple in the bunch: a self-important fashion reporter named Basil Greene whom DeAnna had personally hired. Lazy, loud, and with an affinity for long lunches and cocktails, he quickly got on both MJ's and my bad side.

Up by six o'clock and in the office by seven thirty each morning, I spent the first half hour of my day scouring competing websites. I then checked the chatter on our Facebook page and Twitter account, posted some questions to spur discussion, and then responded to e-mail. At eight thirty, I met with the editorial team to talk about the day's assignments, brainstorm new articles, and review the hottest celebrity photos from the photo agencies to make our selects for the day. We'd then review any overnight star sightings, breakups, or makeups, and our marketing and social media teams would review traffic patterns and develop new content opportunities and campaigns.

Being editor in chief for *DivaDish* was fun and fast-paced. I reported on the celebrities that *I* cared about, like Gabrielle Union and her hot romance with Dwyane Wade; the opening of Steve Harvey's new movie; Usher's baby mama drama; Beyoncé and Jay Z's daughter, Blue Ivy; Kim Kardashian and Kanye's latest antics; and Zoe Saldana's blockbuster. I no longer had to pretend to be just as obsessed as my former *Hollywood Scoop!* colleagues with the likes of just-plain-old-boring Jennifer Aniston.

The first two weeks DeAnna left me alone to get acclimated and gel with the team. But by week three, she included me in her weekly update meetings during which she reviewed the business, newsstand sales, and traffic goals in painstaking detail with all her editors. All the editors made sure to overprepare for the weekly torture sessions because DeAnna was exacting and icy, and she never missed anything.

I always walked out of those meetings thankful I had a contract in case she ever decided to bounce me out the door over some bullshit.

The best part of my new job was finally running my own show and no longer having to answer to people like Kris Kensington. I assigned the stories. I set the pace. I decided whom we covered and to whom we gave a pass.

And now that meant I had to decide whether to cover my best friend's husband's affair.

—

I decided to put Che off for a little while longer and told MJ to let her know that I had received her e-mails and to hold on posting the story while I attended my weekly meeting with DeAnna. I opened my office closet door and looked into the full-length mirror on the other side of the door to check my look before going into battle.

Before we came to work at *DivaDish*, MJ had insisted that I needed a wardrobe upgrade. And he knew my mom would be sending boxes of "business separates" from the Home Shopping Network that he would have to donate to Goodwill, so he called his friend Harper Stevens, a personal shopper at Bergdorf Goodman, and arranged for a complete makeover. Standing naked and vulnerable in the bright, unforgiving light of a Bergdorf dressing room, I knew I was in good hands with Harper. She was fly in a boho chic kind of way, assessed my body and taste in minutes, and returned with an armload of skirts, blouses, dresses (I couldn't even remember the last time I'd worn one), and jeans, declaring my new look would be urban elegance with edge. I didn't even know what the hell that meant, but MJ snapped his fingers in appreciation, so I knew there was no going back.

The hardest part of the makeover? Aside from blowing my entire *Hollywood Scoop!* severance package, spreading the balance of that afternoon's purchases across three credit cards, and spending more on clothes in one afternoon than I had spent in total over the last five years, it was getting used to the heels. Now, don't get a sister wrong. I *l-o-v-e* a fabulous shoe. But prior to moving to New York, I saved my shoes for industry events and nights out when Eric managed to plan something for us that didn't involve a movie ticket or restaurant with a paper napkin dispenser on the table, but MJ and Harper assured me that being taken seriously in Manhattan was all about having a mean shoe game. This explained the acquisition of seven pairs of flatform pumps, calfskin booties, peep-toe stilettos, and one sick-ass pair of over-the-knee black leather boots that I had no idea where on earth I would actually wear. There wasn't a flat in sight.

And today's outfit had been one of my favorites. It was a little dressy for a regular day, but I was having drinks with Vanessa after work. The navy Zac Posen high-waisted skirt with an oversize brushed silver zipper running down the front hugged my full hips and skipped across the top of my knees, making my five-foot-eight frame look long and lean. The matching navy-and-black silk T-shirt with a netting of flowers on the shoulder made it hip for the office. Black suede pumps and an armful of black crystal bangles completed my look. Urban elegance indeed.

I spiked up my short cut and smoothed down the sides around my ears. I could feel it was almost time for a touch-up again. The jet-black color that my new stylist had recommended really worked with my deep brown skin tone. I hurriedly put on some clear MAC Lipglass before closing the closet door.

I grabbed a file with the site traffic data and new marketing plans, and walked down the hallway to DeAnna's office on the other side of the floor. The last editor to arrive was considered late by DeAnna.

The entire floor was bustling with activity. There were three other new digital properties inhabiting the floor with *DivaDish*. The northwest corner housed *TheSportsBeatz*, run by gruff former TV reporter Rodney Reynolds; this section of the floor sometimes sounded like an actual locker room with a bull pen of loud wannabe jocks tossing story ideas and often footballs around all day. The other property,

GospelWired, was headed by Michelle Miles, a holy rolling, sanctified sister who was always trying to bless me, share some scripture, or throw some holy water on me. I cut a quick left down the hall to DeAnna's office to miss Michelle. The last thing I needed was Michelle getting that holy water in my hair today, because then she'd be meeting her Maker a lot sooner than she intended.

Rodney and Michelle were barely civil when I came on board three months ago, so it was clear to me immediately that they considered me competition for resources and DeAnna's approval. I knew they would be no help in helping me get the lay of the land. Now, a knife in the back? They'd be more than happy to oblige. It was every publication and website for themselves, which was fine with me. As my mom always told me, keep your friends close and your enemies closer.

I stopped at the cubicle in front of DeAnna's glass office door. Her assistant, Joan, looked up at me from her computer screen over the tops of her glasses.

"DeAnna will be just a few minutes," she said in her usual clipped tone.

"Thank you," I said, and then took a seat in one of the upholstered chairs outside Joan's cubicle. Sitting there always made me feel like I was waiting to see the principal.

Michelle scurried down the long hallway, engrossed in reading her BlackBerry.

Out of the corner of my eye, I saw DeAnna's office door open and heard a familiar and grating guffaw. It was Basil, my wandering fashion editor.

He backed out of DeAnna's office and closed the door, never seeing me sitting outside Joan's cubicle.

What is my fashion editor doing talking to my boss?

"DeAnna's ready for you now," Joan said, interrupting my train of thought. She took off her headset and came around to lead us into DeAnna's office as if we couldn't find it for ourselves.

As Michelle and I followed her into DeAnna's office, I saw Rodney already seated on the sofa, and my antennae automatically shot up.

Why are my fashion editor and Rodney meeting with my boss?

I dashed off a quick text to MJ.

Saw Basil and Rodney meeting with D . . . What's up?

He responded quickly.

On it . . . Stand by.

I slipped my iPhone back into the pocket of my skirt, confident I'd have an answer on what sneaky little Basil was up to by the time I got out of this meeting.

With panoramic views of Manhattan's Central Park, DeAnna's office made a statement. Swiveling around in her large black leather chair from behind a desk that looked like command central from the space shuttle, DeAnna picked up her large black leather portfolio and pen and then made her way over to where we were seated.

Her bob slicked back off her face and tucked behind her ears, DeAnna wore a crisp white blouse with a large puffy bow knotted to the side of her neck, a snakeskin black knee-length skirt, and bright cranberry platform booties. She took her customary seat in the large leather and chrome chair with her back to the window. Bryan Phillips, the unit's finance director, slipped in quietly, carrying a sheaf of spreadsheets, and grabbed the other chair. Rodney and Michelle sat together on the sofa and put their papers and folders between them, clearly indicating that I wasn't welcome to join them.

What's going on with these two today?

Looking around awkwardly with nowhere to sit as if trapped in a bad game of musical chairs, I turned to ask Joan if she could bring in another chair, but she'd already slipped back out the door.

"Just take a seat on the ottoman, Nia, so we can get started," DeAnna said dismissively.

I removed some large coffee-table books and a tray and set them on the floor before taking my seat facing both DeAnna and Bryan, with my back to Rodney and Michelle. I sat tentatively on the edge of the ottoman, balancing my folder on my lap as Bryan opened the meeting with his weekly financial report.

His flat monotone voice droned on as he moved through the traffic, revenue, and expense figures for each of the sites. For *DivaDish* and *GospelWired*, Bryan's news was good. Traffic was up, revenue was climbing, and expenses were holding flat. But I heard Rodney shifting uncomfortably in his seat and shuffling some papers when Bryan got to his numbers, which were down across the board.

"What's going on with *TheSportsBeatz*, Rodney?" DeAnna said, turning an icy glance in the editor's direction.

"Well, as you know, DeAnna, there's always a lull in our audience traffic right before the NBA season starts. But this weekend the new season starts, and we will have some really good stuff to post," he said.

"In fact," he continued, sounding more excited than he should, given the numbers Bryan just shared, "we have story and video on Marcus King that's sure to create a lot of heat for the site."

Oh shit . . .

"What's the story?" asked Michelle. I tried to turn around on the ottoman as best I could in my tight skirt to look at Rodney. I wanted to be looking him dead in his eyes when he said he stole my story.

"As you know, we've just gotten video of Marcus King leaving a Midtown hotel with vixen Laila James." Rodney sat back against the sofa, keeping his gaze locked on DeAnna and refusing to look at me burning a hole in the side of his head as I started to speak up.

"But wait a minute, that's my . . ."

DeAnna cut me off, raising a manicured finger to let me know silence was expected.

"That's great, Rodney," she said. "Why don't you head back to your office and get that up right away?"

"But DeAnna . . . ," I started again, blood rushing to my cheeks. I felt hot all over. I clutched my pen and tried to restrain myself from jabbing Rodney's story-stealing neck with my pen.

"Just a minute, Nia," DeAnna said again with a wave of a glossy nail before she turned and told Bryan and Michelle that they could leave as well.

Rodney quickly gathered his things and left the office to go post my story on his struggling website before I could say anything, and Michelle slinked out the door behind him.

DeAnna turned her attention to me after the door closed behind them. Her gaze was cool and distant.

"I think I know what you were going to say, Nia."

"You do?" I was confused. How could she know what I was going to say?

"Yes, Nia," she said cryptically. "You were going to say that Rodney stole your story, right?"

"Uh, yes, actually I was," I said, looking at her quizzically. "How did you know?"

"How I know isn't relevant, Nia. What *is* relevant is that you had a story on superstar Marcus King that would have been a big traffic driver for your site, and you hesitated to put it up because you were worried about your friend Vanessa. The only thing that's relevant in this conversation is why you hesitated."

Yes, Vanessa was my friend, but she was also DeAnna's soror, which I thought meant something, but I guess I was mistaken. This woman was take-no-prisoners for real. Sorority bonds be damned.

"Wait a minute," I said. "Yes, one of my reporters got a clip of Marcus King in a compromising position, and I was taking a moment to decide how we should proceed. That was my video."

"Well, in the hour it took you to decide how to proceed, a *DivaDish* competitor could have jumped on the story and taken the lead," DeAnna said as she got up from her chair and walked over to her desk, sat down, and began scanning her e-mail in-box, indicating that she was wrapping up our meeting.

"And actually that video is the property of PrimeTime Media. It's not yours. So one of your internal competitors did what you were too afraid to do, and now they have the lead."

My phone began to buzz repeatedly in my pocket, and I knew it was MJ texting me with the news I now already knew. I'd later learn from MJ that Basil had overheard Che talking about the Marcus King exclusive in the office and had gone into the site's story queue, seen the story waiting for my approval, and then forwarded a copy of the clip to DeAnna to curry favor.

But how had Rodney gotten in the loop? There was no reason to think that Basil would go directly to Rodney, because then that Judas wouldn't have been able to score points with DeAnna. No, this snake had gone directly to her, and then she had been the one to pull in Rodney.

"I wasn't aware I was competing internally," I said as I gathered my papers and put them back into my folder. "But, believe me, DeAnna, I'm very clear now." I wanted to add "bitch" on the end, but that probably wouldn't have gone over too well.

"The web moves fast, and it won't wait for you to figure out your personal loyalties, Nia," DeAnna said over her shoulder as I started to walk out of her office. "And neither will I. Close the door behind you, please."

—

I sank back into the warm leather seats of the town car, thankful that my new job came with the perk of a car service but not thankful for much else after that afternoon's ambush in DeAnna's office.

What the hell was that?

I'd never worked at a place where titles within a company would steal one another's stories. And explaining to Che what had happened to her big exclusive had not been easy. Getting a story like the Marcus King video, however much I might loathe the idea of outing my best friend's husband, would have been huge for her career. I did manage to appeal to what was left of Rodney's journalistic ethics and get him to put her byline on the story and video on *TheSportsBeatz* site. And just as DeAnna had predicted, the story had taken off like wildfire that afternoon. Sites all over the web were linking and outright grabbing the video. The PR team had agreed to push Che to do the TV and radio interview requests that came pouring in. They were no dummies. Putting a young, pretty editor on the screen versus the curmudgeonly vet Rodney was a no-brainer.

As I was leaving the office, I saw Che getting her makeup done for an interview with *Access Hollywood*. Getting the byline and doing the on-air interviews seemed to have smoothed things over with her and shut down her initial threats to quit.

But I was more worried about Vanessa.

While she tended not to troll the Internet to read gossip blogs, she was still sure to have heard the news or seen the video. This was big news not only with urban sites, but the mainstream media had jumped on the story as well. I was actually surprised that Vanessa still wanted to get together, but perhaps she needed to talk.

I wasn't sure if I was going to tell her that my reporter had gotten the video. What could I say to her? And what was I going to say about the ongoing coverage that was bound to jump into high gear now that Marcus had essentially been confirmed as having an affair with the Golden Goddess?

CHAPTER 5

Vanessa

The dark Mercedes sedan headed downtown in the congested evening traffic, cutting seamlessly back and forth between a sea of honking taxis and cars. I stared out of the dark tinted windows into the crisp October evening. It was Friday night in Manhattan, and everyone seemed to be heading somewhere.

For a moment I was thankful that Marcus was leaving tonight for a game in Chicago, but then the familiar knot hit my stomach as I tortured myself with thoughts of Laila joining him in the Windy City. He tried to call me several times after the video hit the Internet, but I sent his calls to voice mail. I wasn't prepared to hear any more sorry lies about how it wasn't what I thought. I didn't think I could even look at him right now without clawing out his eyes.

I glanced down at my silver snakeskin Philip Stein watch to check the time. The larger face on the watch was on New York time and read six forty-five. I was supposed to meet Nia for drinks at seven o'clock. The second smaller face was set three hours behind on Pacific time, reminding me of home.

The black car pulled up in front of the Gansevoort Hotel. I gathered my black Gucci Python shoulder bag and tossed my BlackBerry inside. Alex opened the door and helped me out of the car. As I stepped out into the chilly fall evening, I braced myself for the conversation I was about to have with my best friend.

I know I have to tell her everything.

Walking into the dimly lit bar, I scanned the beautiful room. The dark walnut walls, soft light accenting the black lacquer tables with mirrored tops, and a whimsical mix of bright red velvet and leopard print chairs gave the intimate lounge a funky twist. Heavy gold damask curtains framed windows that looked out into the city streets. I immediately spotted Nia seated at a table in a dark alcove. As usual, my girl was intensely scrolling through messages on her iPhone while she absentmindedly stirred her dark amber cocktail.

I was glad to see she already knew that light and fruity girl drinks weren't on the menu tonight. Hard liquor only, thank you.

"Hey, girl," I said as I approached the table and leaned down to give her a kiss on the cheek.

"Hey, mama," she said warmly as she closed her e-mail and laid her phone on the table. Her eyes looked tired like mine.

"Sorry, I'm late," I said as I sat down in the leopard-upholstered chair across from her. "Traffic was murder." The waitress came over to ask Nia if she could refresh her drink and take my order.

"Yes, I'll have another, and she'll have the same," Nia said as she picked up her drink and threw back the rest of the remaining contents.

"Damn, slow down," I said with a chuckle. "Let me at least catch up."

"You're going to have to drink really fast to catch up with me."

"That's never been a problem for me, and you know I will still drink your little lightweight butt under the table." There had been many a night in Cambridge when we drank late into the night.

"Your hair looks cute," I told her as I admired the new shorter haircut that skimmed perfectly arched eyebrows and framed her big almond-shaped eyes.

"Thanks. Your man Walter really hooked a sister up at the salon. And Armond tamed a sister's crazy unibrow."

"I'm glad you liked Walter, and it's about time someone tackled your Groucho Marx brows. And since you got that Lasik surgery and got rid of those funky glasses, people can actually see your beautiful face."

"I know, right? The laser eye surgery was the bomb, and MJ was adamant that needed to be a part of my Manhattan makeover." She chuckled.

"Well, it all works, especially the hair. Walter's been after me to do something with this boring mess on top of my head, but I don't know what to do with it. Short hair is just so much work." I ran my fingers through my thick shoulder-length hair and tucked the long layered sides behind my ears. It wasn't like a new haircut would have kept my husband from cheating.

"You should totally try something new," Nia said. There was an awkward silence. I could tell that she wasn't sure if she should bring up the video or wait for me to do it. I didn't make her wait long.

"So, you saw the video . . . ," I said.

"Uh . . . Yes, I saw it."

"Can you believe it?" A single tear slipped out of the corner of my eye and slid down my cheek as I exhaled sharply. She reached across the table and took my hand.

The waitress returned with our drinks and placed them on the table. When she started to ask if we'd like any appetizers, I waved her away.

"How did you find out?" Nia asked.

"Well, this time I didn't have to go searching online to find it. He got Kareem and Desiree to do it."

"Hold up. Kareem called you about the video?" she asked, clearly incredulous that Marcus would try to get his agent to break the news of his infidelity to his wife.

"Oh yeah. They called, like they always do when there's some news about to break with Marcus. Now, my dumb behind thought they were calling to talk about some news related to the trade to New York. But nope, not this time. They told me that a story was breaking online, that it wasn't true, and they were doing everything they could to squash it."

"So how did you see the video?" she asked, then sipped her drink.

"I asked them what the story was, and they told me it was some video that someone took on their cell phone of Marcus leaving a business meeting, and that there was some woman in the background that the media was trying to link to him. So naturally, when I got off the phone, I searched online for the clip."

"Did you see it?"

"Yes," I choked out. "I must have watched it ten or twenty times, trying to talk myself into believing that he wasn't leaving that hotel with that skank trick Laila James."

I took another swallow of my drink. The warm liquid slid down my throat but didn't numb the pain in my chest like I wanted.

"I can't even believe this shit. We just got to New York, and he's already messing around after he promised me this trade would be a fresh start for our family."

"I'm so sorry, V." Nia handed me a tissue from her purse to wipe the tears that were now falling down my cheeks. "So do you need me to come over and help you pack tonight?"

"Pack?"

"Yeah, pack. Aren't you leaving his ass this time?"

"It's not that simple, Nia. We have a child."

"Yes, I know you have a child. Damon's my godson. But V., he's been cheating on you for years. How long are you going to take this mess from him?"

"You don't understand, Nia. You've never been married. It's much more complicated than you know."

"Complicated? How complicated can it be? I stood by your side while you both took those vows to love, honor, cherish, and be faithful. Or was it just you who promised to do all that?"

"Damn, Nia. I don't need your sarcastic bullshit right now. I'm dealing with a lot of stuff that you don't even understand."

"I saw the video, too, Vanessa. Despite what shady Kareem says, there's no way he wasn't leaving that hotel with that woman."

"You think I don't know that, Nia?" I hissed across the table at her. "You think I don't know for one hundred percent certain that he's fucking Laila? Of course I do. But it's not that easy to pack your stuff, take your son, and walk out the door."

"Why not? You've got money, you've got credit cards, and you've got friends. And all you need now is a pit bull divorce lawyer to start working on taking half that bastard's money."

"No, what I really need right now is a friend who'll listen to me." I slumped back into my seat, absentmindedly twisting the large yellow diamond on my ring finger. I took another large swallow from my half-empty glass. I needed to be numb.

"I'm listening, but you're not making any sense right now," Nia said, leaning across the table, her voice low and deep. "Look, I've never tried to tell you how to live your life. I've always been there when you've called me at two o'clock in the morning, sobbing on the phone, devastated because of Marcus's cheating. I've listened to you cry, and it broke my heart. I've listened to you after you went to therapy sessions, and bit my tongue. I've listened when you told me he said it's going to be different this time, desperately hoping like you that he had changed. But maybe, just maybe, it's not ever going to be different, Vanessa. Maybe, just maybe, this person that you married is who he is, and nothing you do and nothing he says is ever going to change that."

Nia had tears in her eyes, too. I knew she meant well and that she only wanted to do what she thought was best for little Damon and me. But she didn't know the whole story.

I wiped my tears again with the soggy tissue and then reached into my handbag for an envelope.

"This is why I can't leave right now," I told her as I slid a plain manila envelope with my husband's name typed neatly across the front across the table to her. No postage, no return address. "This came addressed to Marcus at the apartment yesterday."

Nia picked up the envelope and looked at me quizzically.

"Just open it," I told her. An icy cold chill went through my body when I heard her gasp.

"Oh my God, Vanessa," Nia said as she gripped the papers in disbelief. She began to go through them one by one.

The first page was a crude collage made up of tattered pieces of images of Marcus that looked like they were scratched and stabbed. The words *It's Your Turn to Die* were handwritten on the bottom of the page in a heavy black marker.

Nia turned to the second page, which had glued to it a grainy newspaper photo of Marcus holding Damon's hand as he walked down the street from our apartment. The photo had been splashed across the cover of the *Daily News* paper when we first got to New York two months ago with the headline "The King and Little Prince Come to New York." This photo, like the first, had the same manic slash marks cutting at the faces of my husband and the message, *You Will Pay for What You Did*.

The third photo I received this afternoon. The image showed me leaving a Manhattan boutique with an armful of shopping bags last week. Violent slashes marked my image as well, but this time the sender took the time to dig the razor deep into my eyes so all that was left were empty black holes. On the bottom of the page, written in the same heavy black marker, were the words *You Will All Die*.

Nia's eyes were wide, and all the warmth had drained from her face.

"Vanessa, when did you get these?" she asked, her brow suddenly furrowed and her eyes narrowed. She spread the papers out across the table, looking back and forth between them.

"These particular letters started coming after we came to New York," I answered. "The one of Marcus and Damon came last week. The third image, of me shopping, came today. In addition to this, we've also received threats on our cell phones and in e-mails."

"Have you gone to the police?" she asked.

"We can't."

"Why not? Someone is threatening your family," Nia said as she shook the papers at me, her voice rising in the trendy bar.

"Marcus says this type of stuff goes with the territory of being a professional athlete. Miss a key shot at buzzer, everyone hates you, and you get a barrage of hate mail. And, don't get me wrong: over the years, Marcus has received his fair share of angry letters from obsessed fans, religious fanatics, and racists. And since they call me First Lady of the NBA, occasionally there have been letters about me, but they tended to criticize what I wore or my hairstyle. This is very different. These letters are targeting our entire family. His mail usually goes directly to his fan club, which is managed by Kareem and Desiree, but these letters are coming directly to our home."

"Wait a minute," Nia said as she interrupted me. "You said these particular letters have come to the apartment now. Are you saying you were getting these kinds of letters sent to your home in Phoenix, too?"

I nodded my head slowly.

"And there's more," I said. I suddenly felt grateful to be able to talk to someone about this nightmare I'd been living for so long. I pulled three other large envelopes from my bag and gave them to her.

"This is all of them." These envelopes were heavier, containing printouts of all the text messages and e-mails we'd received.

"Oh my God, Vanessa. There have to be at least twenty here." The pile of grotesque images and hateful words covered the small table as she shuffled through the evil messages.

"Twenty-two," I answered.

"So, why exactly haven't you gone to the police again?" Nia asked, holding up some of the papers as if they were evidence of a crime.

"Because Kareem said we couldn't," I replied.

I told my best friend that when we first started receiving the letters six months ago, they always seemed to arrive when Marcus was on the road for an away game, and I showed them to him immediately when he returned.

At first we both chalked it up to some random weirdo who had somehow managed to get our home address. After all, in the age of Google, you can basically find anyone these days. But then the e-mails and text messages started coming, and I begged Marcus to go to the police. He talked it over with Kareem and Desiree who said if they went to the police, it would kill the trade with New York. They explained that questions were still swirling on the gossip blogs trying to link Marcus to the dead dancer, so this crazy stalker stuff would definitely spook the ultraconservative Gladiators organization.

Marcus would be labeled high risk, and no matter how stringently their lawyers drafted the morals clause, they wouldn't be able to fix the damage. This was a risk the Gladiators wouldn't be willing to take, especially given that their last big franchise player, Clint Beck, had been convicted of killing his wife after finding out she'd had an affair with a player on another team just three short years ago.

Marcus had long dreamed of playing professional basketball in a New York Gladiators uniform, and so he and Kareem begged me not to go to the police. Dutiful wifey that I was, I knew I couldn't stand in my husband's way. Kareem beefed up their personal security with two full-time bodyguards named Tyson and Bruce, and had CIA-level security installed throughout the house. We also kept a gun locked in a safe in our closet. I even took a series of shooting lessons at a local gun range, becoming a fairly decent shot. And once the trade went through, Marcus and Kareem assured me that the stalker was likely some crazed local and that we would all be safe in a new city.

But Nia wasn't having any of it.

"What do you mean Kareem said you couldn't?" Nia raised her voice again, causing people to look our way.

"Sssshhh! Can you keep your voice down?" I hissed. "I don't need this getting out."

"Maybe that's exactly what you need: for this to get out so the police can protect you and your family, Vanessa! I know he's family, but how much longer are you going to let that man run your life?"

I shuddered as I remembered the terror I felt nearly six months ago as soon as I opened the first envelope, which contained a slashed-up photo of Marcus picking up Damon from school.

And now this monster had tracked our family to New York.

CHAPTER 6

Laila

We are in love.

There's no other way to put it. And nothing, or no one, is going to stand in our way.

I cradled Marcus's head on my chest as he slept and kissed the top of his head. He stirred in his sleep, nuzzling my breast as he pulled my naked body closer to his. The early-morning sunlight began to peak through the heavy curtains and cast steaks of light across the sheets. Our limbs were intertwined. We couldn't get close enough to each other. This was heaven. I felt something stirring below his waist hitting the curve of my thigh. Round three would begin soon. He loved a taste of his brown sugar in the morning.

I know I don't have much time.

Careful so as not to wake him, I slowly stretched my right arm across the bed to the nightstand and felt around for my phone. My fingers danced on the marble top. After pushing two condom wrappers onto the floor, I found the phone behind them. Marcus shifted and pushed himself deeper into my leg. I knew he'd be awake soon and hungry for more of me.

Cell phone in hand, I quickly opened the camera application and pushed the button to turn the lens around toward us. I made sure to frame the shot to get his face and then adjusted the sheet to cover just the tops of my dark brown nipples. I looked down lovingly at my man and snapped the photo.

I'd love to take video of what I knew was about to happen next, but that would have to wait for another time.

—

After the video of us leaving the hotel hit the Internet, as I expected, Marcus had started to pull away from me. He texted me that we needed to cool things off until the noise around the video quieted down. He had a few shopping bags from Chanel sent over to my apartment, which let me know I was still on his mind. I told him I understood and would be patient.

I knew Vanessa was giving him hell, so the best strategy for me was to be understanding and loving versus the bitchy hysterical nag he was likely enduring at home.

Married women don't understand that while a major part of what makes a man cheat is of course the sexual desire they feel for women like me, the part that makes a man go deeper and lose all sense of rational behavior and fall in love is the way I make him feel. If I'm a sanctuary in life's storm—meaning a nagging wife—he would always come running back to me. So it was a few weeks before we saw each other again, but I was determined to make sure it was well worth his wait.

So when Kareem arranged to fly me to Chicago, I was ready with a plan. And since I knew Marcus would be feeling a little nervous about his wife sweating him about the video, and might be taking some heat from the conservative Gladiators organization, I knew I'd need to really pull out something special to keep him hooked.

—

The New York Gladiators beat the Chicago Blaze handily 106–89 that evening, so Marcus was in an especially good mood when he unlocked the door to our hotel suite. When he stepped in, I could tell he was pleased with what he saw.

Freshly showered after the game, he smelled like soap and the Dolce & Gabbana cologne I loved. His deep ebony complexion was freshly scrubbed, and the sexy stubble along his cheeks framing his bright white smile made him irresistible. He was dressed in black wool pants and a crisp gray shirt that peeked out from the collar of a thick black cashmere sweater that zipped up the front. The sleeves were pushed up and exposed his powerful forearms and his custom platinum and diamond-encrusted watch. Damn, he looked good.

But I knew I looked even better.

I greeted my man, dressed in a crimson plunging silk corset that laced up the back and matching sheer panties with a black garter belt, stockings, and eight-inch crystal-encrusted Christian Louboutin Daffodil platform pumps. My hair cascaded in long, glossy honey-blond curls swooped to one side and laid in a pool at the top of my breast. I looked into his dark eyes, which were hooded by long lashes, and kissed him deeply, sucking on his beautiful chocolate lower lip.

"Oh, you taste so good," I purred as I pulled the zipper down on his sweater and slid the soft fabric off his broad shoulders onto the floor. I wrapped my arms around him tightly and leaned my body into his. He picked me up with one arm and started to untie the silky straps along the back of my corset with the other.

"Not yet, baby," I teased playfully. "Come on in and see how much I've missed you." I gave him a glass of his favorite scotch, which was sitting on the table in the foyer.

The lights were dim, and there were scented votive candles around the sunken living room that overlooked the twinkling lights of the city and Lake Michigan. I led him over to a chair in the center of the room and told him to take a seat. He finished his drink while I picked up a rectangular velvet box off the coffee table. I walked back over to him and asked him to open it.

"What do you plan to do with those?" Marcus asked in a husky voice as he took out a pair of silver diamond-studded handcuffs, which sparkled against the black satin lining of the box. I laughed softly, took the handcuffs from his hand, and slipped them onto his wrists while I leaned in to kiss and softly lick his ear.

"Are you ready for the show?" I asked as I nibbled on his ear and moved down his neck.

"Oh, I think I'm ready," he said, looking down at the rising fabric of his wool slacks.

"Well, then let's get this party started," I said as I stepped away from Marcus and walked slowly over to the French doors leading to the bedroom so that he could appreciate the view. I pushed open the doors, and standing there waiting was the evening's entertainment.

"Marcus, I want you to meet Crystal," I said, looking over my shoulder at him.

Crystal, a brunette beauty with warm olive skin, full red lips, and piercing green eyes, wore a tight black leather corset, matching thong, and thigh-high black leather platform boots. Her straight jet-black hair hung down her back, the ends grazing the top of her thong. She was gorgeous if I did say so myself. Clearly not as fabulous as me, but she would do. I turned to look at Marcus and could tell he appreciated my selection.

I picked up the leather leash dangling from the diamond choker around Crystal's neck and led her into the living room. I turned on some music, and Raheem DeVaughn began to croon.

"Crystal wants to dance for you," I said as we made our way to him. "Is that all right, baby?"

"Hell, yeah. That sounds good to me," he said as he looked at both of us and licked his lips. "But it would be even better if I didn't have these handcuffs on."

"That's all part of the fun," I said, laughing huskily as I unclipped Crystal's leather leash and went to stand behind Marcus. My arms snaked around to the front of his body so that I could unbutton his shirt while Crystal began to move seductively in the candlelight. Dark shadows from her undulating body danced off the walls as she began her performance.

"Do you like that?" I asked Marcus as I bit his ear gently. Crystal bent over and began to flash her round bottom in his face.

"Oh, don't you want some of that?" I asked as I raked my nails along his broad chest and began to work my way down to his belt buckle. "Look at that juicy bounce."

Crystal wound her body slowly like a snake and whipped her long black hair back and forth across Marcus's chest. Standing in front of him, she put her hands on his knees and leaned in. I felt her warm breath on the left side of his neck. She played with his other ear as I kept whispering dirty little nothings to him. Her breasts were pressed against his chin. She reached around and unsnapped her corset, freeing her full breasts and displaying her erect dark nipples. She squeezed them and popped one of the long brown nipples in his mouth.

"Suck on it, baby," I encouraged. Marcus moaned. I could feel him straining against the handcuffs. I knew he wanted his hands free to really enjoy himself.

As Marcus continued to lick hungrily at Crystal's glistening breasts, she sat in his lap and began to grind her hips into him. She arched her head and back, thrusting into him, and the long strands of her hair grazed the carpeted floor. I pushed Marcus's open shirt off his muscled shoulders and massaged and squeezed his arms.

"Ride it," I commanded Crystal. "Does that feel good, Marcus?"

"Oh, yeah, but it would feel better if it was you," he moaned.

"Oh, it will be, baby. Believe me, I'm going to enjoy you all night. But let's have some more fun with Crystal for now."

I gave Crystal a look so that she realized I wasn't so caught up in her show not to remember that I told her she better not make my man orgasm. That was my job. And I could tell Marcus was just about ready for me. She got my message and began to wind up her performance with the big finish.

As she danced in front of him, I came from behind him and sat in his lap facing Crystal. His bulge had stretched out long and strong and strained against his pants.

Crystal leaned into me, and just as we had planned, she began to kiss me along my neck and reached out to untie the laces of my corset as I pushed my bottom back into Marcus. When the corset was completely undone, I raised my arms for Crystal to lift it up over my head. Marcus's breath began to quicken, and his wet tongue danced across my bare back. He was thrusting, pushing up into me from the chair as best he could with his arms restrained.

Crystal came back over and straddled us both. She wrapped her arms around Marcus's shoulders to steady herself as she began to grind her hips into mine, pushing me back into Marcus's lap. I threw my head onto Marcus's shoulder and closed my eyes as he began to kiss the other side of my neck. The pleasure intensified, our three bodies locked into one rhythm as we rocked back and forth in the chair.

Wet and more than ready to pleasure my man, I decided it was time to wrap up Crystal's performance. As I opened my eyes to give Crystal the signal, I saw her tongue snaking along the side of Marcus's cheek, heading toward his mouth.

Oh, hell no. I was very clear. Everybody knows in a successful threesome, you don't let the other girl kiss or actually screw your man. Crystal was the appetizer, and I was the main course. That's why you can't trust strippers around your man.

Stabilizing myself against Marcus's thighs, I suddenly pushed my body up, causing Crystal to tumble hard to the floor onto her back.

"Damn, what the hell . . . ?" Crystal said, pushing her hair out of her eyes as she stood up, rubbing her bruised bottom.

"Sorry, boo. I think we're finished with this evening's performance."

I could hear Marcus chuckle behind me. He knew why I'd done it, and that was fine with him because he was just as ready to get to the main event.

I scooped up Crystal's leather corset and leash from the floor, grabbed her trench coat from the hall closet, and then led her to the door. I handed her an envelope with her fee and shoved her whining ass out the door.

"Now where were we?" I said to Marcus when I returned to the room with a small silver key in my hand. I stood in front of him in my red panties, garter, and heels, stroking the key down my bare breasts. "You got something for me?"

"You know I do, and I'm going to show you as soon as you take these damn cuffs off. Stop playing, girl."

I walked behind him, dropped down on my knees, and unlocked the cuffs. Marcus stood up and began massaging his wrists.

"Maybe you want to put these on me now," I said playfully as I twirled the cuffs around my gold-flecked French-tipped finger.

"You damn right." And before I could get away, he snatched the cuffs from me, grabbed my hands, and locked them around my tiny wrists.

"So what are you going to do with me since I've been so bad?" I teased, pushing out my pouty lips.

Marcus's eyes were dark with desire. He quickly scooped me up in his massive arms and carried me into the bedroom. Any thoughts I had about a slow, romantic lovemaking reunion were quickly dashed as he bent me over the front of the bed. I heard his zipper come down. He ripped off the delicate red lace panties, and then he was thrusting inside me, causing me to gasp with pleasure. He pushed my shoulders down hard into the bed as he kicked my legs apart with his feet to gain deeper access. I pushed back up into his body as best I could with my arms constrained by the handcuffs.

He grabbed a handful of my hair and pulled my head up. He leaned into my body and began to whisper roughly in my ear.

"You like that?" he asked as he pushed hard inside my velvety warmth. I could barely catch my breath, so I just moaned in affirmation as I pressed my knees against the foot of the bed to raise myself up to heighten the pleasure.

"Oh damn. You're trying to make me explode, raising that pretty golden ass up in the air for me."

Suddenly Marcus was outside me. He pulled me up from the bed and pushed me down onto my knees in front of him.

I took him into my mouth and deep-throated him hungrily as he pushed his hips into my face while he palmed the back of my head.

"Yes, baby. That's it. Take it all." Marcus moaned, closed his eyes, and threw back his head. I felt him begin to thicken and pulsate. I quickened the pace and then switched up, licking along the large vein and swirling my tongue around the silky tip. I felt his legs shake.

Gotcha . . .

"Give it to me, baby. You know what I want," I said as I looked into his eyes, which were dark pools drunk with passion.

I licked my lips.

Ready.

Waiting.

Marcus groaned deeply as he pushed back into my warm, wet mouth, hitting the back of my throat with long deep strokes.

It didn't take long.

Spent and with me wrapped in his arms, he said it. The magic words.

"I love you, Laila." He mumbled sleepily as he cupped my face with his hands and kissed me gently on the lips after our second round of making love.

—

Now, I'm not stupid. I know you can't always believe a man who says he loves you right after you finish sexing him like crazy. And I know that ball players are sleeping with girls in every city behind their wives' backs. But it was the way Marcus said it to me that let me know he really meant it.

My plan was working.

But it never hurts to have a little insurance to move things along. I hit "Send" on the photo and softly placed my phone back on the nightstand, then turned around to wake up my man.

CHAPTER 7

Nia

After my meeting with Vanessa last week, I knew I had no choice but to contact my ex, Terrence. Since Vanessa wouldn't let me go to the police, Terrence was the only one who could help us. And we hadn't seen each other in five years, so that shouldn't make it awkward or anything.

Yeah, right . . .

Damn, the things I do for my girl.

I walked into the trendy SoHo French bistro and scanned the room. There he was, seated in a corner banquette. Before I could stop it, my mind began replaying the tumultuous relationship with him like a projector running in my head.

—

We met when I started as a cub reporter at the *New York Tribune* my first year out of Harvard. He was a rising star in the NYPD's notoriously tough narcotics division. Jake Irby, one of the crime reporters at the paper, always got a bunch of reporters together for drinks on Friday nights after work, and one night he took us to a dive bar in Hell's Kitchen where a lot of cops hung out. We were enjoying drinks and a couple games of pool when a long shadow was cast across our table. I looked up from my shot to see Jake talking to the finest man I had seen since moving to New York six months ago.

I estimated he was about six foot two, and he had the lean, muscled build of an ex-athlete. His smooth deep-mocha skin was clean-shaven except for a goatee that framed full, juicy lips. And as he talked and laughed with Jake, I could see Crest Whitestrips–perfect teeth. But his eyes, deep brown with sleepy lids and thick lashes, were what got me.

He was wearing dark jeans and dark brown Timberland boots. The sleeves of his navy-blue V-neck sweater were pushed up, revealing a tattoo on his forearm, but I couldn't make out what it was. His police shield hung from a silver chain around his neck.

Distracted, I missed my next shot, which was unusual for me because I had hustled other Harvard students to get most of my spending money in college. Eight ball was the easiest money I ever made.

"Ouch, Nia. Is this my lucky night? Am I finally going to beat you?" Jake asked as he turned back to me and took another swallow of beer. I could tell he was excited by the prospect of finally whooping me.

"I'm just trying to make our games competitive for once, Jake," I joked as I picked up my own beer off the high top table next and swallowed. I tried to play off the bad shot. I hadn't done something like that since I was eleven and my uncle Joe taught me how to play after school at his bar when I was supposed to be doing my homework. I'd been playing pool with the hardest of cats for over ten years, and I hustled throughout college, armed with all the tricks and angles.

"Has this beautiful young lady beaten you before, Jake?" Jake's friend asked as he looked at me and then chuckled. His eyes twinkled.

I had regretted not going home after work and changing. I smoothed down the sides of my medium-length layered bob and tucked my hair behind my ears. I had tossed on a pair of my favorite jeans, a black turtleneck, my old faithful Nine West boots, and my red leather blazer. Why did today have to be the day when everything decent I owned was at the cleaner's?

"She's gotten lucky a few times, Terrence," Jake said, trying to play off all the many cans of whoop ass I had opened on him for the last several weeks. I appreciated his bravado. "But it looks like I'm going to be the one getting lucky tonight." Jake broke the stack and watched as the balls scattered across the worn table. The ten ball went in the side pocket on the break.

"Cool. At least you got one ball in the pocket tonight," I said, laughing.

"Tonight's my night, Nia. I can feel it. Terrence, she's been beating me up a little bit, but tonight she's going down."

"Yeah, in your dreams, Jake," I shot back. OK, so now I knew his friend's name was Terrence. Jake surveyed the table, looking for the easiest next shot and not realizing that he needed to think three shots down the line to even have a chance of beating me.

Rookie mistake.

Jake hit the cue ball too hard, missing his planned shot.

"OK, well, I've got next," Jake's friend said as he laughed at his poor friend. He then placed his beer on top of a crisp fifty-dollar bill.

"Are you sure you want to lose all your money so early in the evening?" I asked, walking around the table to size up my strategy to run the rest of the table.

"I don't plan on losing," he said confidently. His voice was a deep honey-coated baritone.

"No one ever does, and then they play me," I said.

Jake missed his next shot as usual. My turn.

"Seven ball, corner pocket." I chalked my stick and set my position for my next shot.

"Three ball, in the side pocket."

The next five balls fell just as easily. In order to sink the eight ball and win the game, I had to squeeze by Jake's friend. And when I did, I swore I felt an electric current jump between us. I noticed he smelled like a fresh shower and soap. Nice. I hated pretty boys who wore cologne like chicks.

I bent over the table and lined up my stick. I could see out of the corner of my eye that old boy was sizing something up as well. I was glad I had at least worn my sexy low-rise jeans. I decided to give Jake's friend a real show and a last chance to pick up his money if he asked me nicely.

"Eight ball, corner pocket."

"I hate to say this, Nia, but it's impossible for you to put that ball in the corner pocket," Jake said, surveying the table. He was sure that he was going to get another turn at the table to try to redeem himself.

"Again, eight ball, corner pocket," I said, not lifting my head from the table. I drew back my stick and hit the cue ball hard. It shot across the table, then ricocheted around. Slowing down, the ball then gently tapped the eight ball into the corner pocket.

My work here was done.

The bar erupted in hoots at my victory. Jake hung his head and laughed.

"Damn, I thought I actually had a shot tonight." Jake handed me twenty bucks and headed over to his friend. "Be very careful, Terrence. Nia's a real shark." He clapped his friend on the shoulder and then headed over to the bar to get another beer to soothe his wounded ego.

"Is that true, Nia?" Terrence asked as he leaned against the table with a pool cue between his legs. He said my name slowly like he was trying it out for the first time, and I liked the way it sounded on his lips. "Are you a real shark?"

"Well, Terrence. It is Terrence, right?" I said, playing with him. "Since you've never seen me play before and I just waxed the table with your boy, I'll let you take your money back now if you're scared." I leaned against the table with one hand on my hip and the other holding out his fifty-dollar bill.

He laughed and took the bill from my outstretched hand, then placed it back on the edge of the table.

"Oh, now we're going to play for sure. But let's make it interesting." He looked up at the ceiling as if trying to think of an interesting wager; then he turned back to me.

"Fifty bucks if you win; your phone number if I win," he said with a smile, the light from the bar dancing in his eyes.

Oh shit. This brother is not slick. I know he's not trying to spit game at me. He is fine, though. And I haven't had anything close to a date or sex since I got to New York. This could get interesting. It could be nice to have a new friend with benefits.

"You're on. And I'll even let you break to give you a fighting chance." I walked around the table and got all the balls from the pockets as I sang Jay Z's song "I'm a Hustla, Baby" and then racked them up with ease.

"Well, I like your confidence. But it's going to be sad to see that pretty face crumble when I beat you like you stole something."

"Yeah, right," I said. "Let's go, Officer." It was on.

As the last ball sank into the hole, I turned to look at Terrence with a sly grin on my face, half expecting to see him scowling because he got spanked. Beating him down was probably going to end our little flirt fest since I knew most brothers couldn't handle getting beat by a woman.

"Well, at least you made it competitive," I said as I came around to the side of the table where he stood holding his fifty dollars out to me. I was surprised to see he had a slight smile on his face.

"Well, at least you have to give me a chance to win my money back. Double or nothing?" He winked at me as he began to collect the balls from the pockets, assuming I'd accept his challenge. I was disappointed he hadn't put my phone number back into the wager, but I tried not to let him see that.

"Sure, I could always use some spa money," I said cockily. I took off my jacket and laid it on the bar stool that also held my purse. "Loser breaks."

"With pleasure," he said with a focused glint in his dark eyes.

I never even made it back to the table. Terrence ran that table like a pro.

Jake busted out in laughter and slapped Terrence's palm.

Damn, I had been hustled by a hustler. I was slipping.

Terrence walked over to me, smiling with his palm outstretched. I'm supercompetitive, so it took everything I had not to ask for another round. I reached for my purse and pulled out my wallet. Of course, as usual I had little money on me because I never bother to bring money to a pool hall since I know I'm going to win.

I hadn't counted on getting hustled.

I looked up sheepishly at him and held out his fifty, Jake's twenty, a crumpled ten, and two fives dug out from the bottom of my bag.

"I can run to the ATM and get the rest," I said, my cheeks hot and red.

"That's OK," he said as he pushed the money away. "All I really want is your number, and we'll call it even." He smiled wide, his perfect white teeth shining.

Hell, yeah, you can have my number.

Long after Jake and the rest of the crew from the paper left, Terrence and I closed down the bar that night, drinking, talking, and playing more pool. At one point when I was down in another round, he cautioned me about a shot I was about to take.

"Look, I know you think you're hot shit and all because you beat me, but I've been playing pool for over ten years, which I learned from true hustlers on Chi's South Side. I know this is the shot to take."

"OK, OK, no need to jump down a brother's throat. But let me show you this right quick." He came up behind and lightly leaned on my back, placing his hands on top of mine on the pool cue. His breath felt warm on my ear as he talked about the shot I should take instead. As he talked, I could barely concentrate on what he was saying. I could feel his long leg muscles as they pressed into the back of my legs.

"So try that shot instead and see how it works," I heard him say as he stepped back. Shit, I'd been so caught up in him leaning up against me, I had missed everything he said. It had been a while since I'd had some physical contact. Time to play it off.

"I like my shot better," I said, and quickly took the shot, missing.

"Told you so," he said as he chuckled softly before he stepped up to take his shot and finish the table.

He beat me again. I was hooked.

That night, as we sipped our drinks and nibbled on hot wings at the bar, I learned about his childhood. He had grown up in Harlem with a single mom after his dad, who was also a cop, had been shot in the line of duty when Terrence was in the fourth grade. After watching his mother struggle to make ends meet, Terrence was driven to succeed so that he could help take care of his family. He attended the best New York City private schools through the A Better Chance program and went on to attend Columbia. He and Jake were roommates in college and had a long friendship. After graduation, he went into the police academy and for the last two years, he'd been assigned to the city's dangerous narcotics and gang task force while attending law school at night at New York University. His plan was to get his juris doctorate and join the DA's office as a prosecutor and then ultimately get into politics as a senator.

I'd never met a man who was so driven and knew exactly what he wanted to do with his life. Terrence was serious about his future.

I told him about growing up in Chicago and how, like him, I had a take-no-mess mom who fought to get me into the best city schools, which earned me a scholarship to Harvard. I told him I loved being a reporter, and while I was covering entertainment at the moment for the paper, ultimately I wanted to start a political magazine.

All of it sounded kind of flaky when I said it out loud in the face of a guy who just told me he tracks down violent gang members during the day and goes to law school at night.

"That's cool, Nia. I look forward to reading your stuff." No one I ever dated had said they looked forward to reading my stuff before. Most guys I had dated up to that point just wanted to talk about themselves, boast about their own jobs, and pretend to be interested in my life.

When the bartender flicked the lights off and on and pointed at the clock on the wall, I was startled to see it was two in the morning.

"Wow, where did the time go?" I asked as I slid off the bar stool to put on my blazer and pick up my purse.

"Time goes by quickly when you're having fun," Terrence said as he smiled and slipped on a well-worn brown leather jacket.

"Or maybe time goes by quickly when you're getting hustled," I said, heading for the door.

"Hustled? I'm a New York City police officer and future DA. Now does that sound like the type of cat that would hustle somebody?"

Laughing, we stepped out in the crisp Manhattan night. The cool air felt good after being in the stuffy bar so long. I stepped to the curb and put my arm up to hail a cab. Luckily, it was so late that there were plenty to choose from. A speeding taxi swerved over across the street, cutting off several other cars, and stopped in front of me.

"So, Nia, I never got your number," Terrence said as he opened the taxi's door for me so that I could slip into the backseat.

"Yeah, I know," I said, looking at him as I shut the door and then tapped the driver's plastic partition, telling him to pull off.

I turned around in the cab to look at him laughing as he stood in the middle of the street.

The next day, he called my cell phone while I was sitting at my desk. My pulse quickened when I heard his voice on the other end of the line. I was glad to hear from him but tried to keep my voice level because I didn't want to seem too eager.

"How'd you get this number?" I asked, pretending to be pissed even though I was grinning like a Cheshire cat when I heard his voice.

"I'm a cop—I can find anyone I want in this city," he said. "Nah, I'm just playing. Jake dimed you out."

"Jake, huh . . . I'll have to talk to him about giving my number to just anybody."

"Well, I'm not just anybody, and it's the least he could do for his old roommate," he said, laughing. I loved his laugh.

That night we met for dinner, and shortly after that we were pretty much inseparable. We got to know each other over long conversations into the night while dining at cheap hole-in-the-wall restaurants that only Terrence seemed to know about. We talked passionately about our favorite books, politics, and pop culture. We had heated discussions about the city's crime, the gentrification of Terrence's old neighborhood that could soon force his mother to sell their family brownstone, and New York's growing drug gang population.

But the best part of our relationship was the lovemaking. Terrence explored every single inch of my body with his hands and tongue. He had a precision I had never before experienced. He left me quivering and begging. And while I'd had my fair share of partners, nothing came close to the intense physical connection that we created with our bodies. I craved that man. I couldn't get enough of his chiseled brown body and the way he whispered my name when we made love.

In a word, I was sprung.

It was almost perfect. His job was the most difficult part of the relationship for me. I tried not to let him see how afraid I was, but whenever the news reported that an officer had been shot, I worried that it was Terrence.

And if it wasn't Terrence this time, I was certain it could be him the next.

My concern for his safety and what I felt was his cavalier attitude about his well-being were the source of the only arguments we ever had. I pushed him to speed up his plans to leave the force and join the DA's office while he finished his last year of law school, but Terrence said there was still more work for him to do. I tried to understand, but the fear wouldn't go away.

Spring came. We had been dating for nearly six months and were practically living together. We kept toiletries and several changes of clothing at each other's apartments, and at the end of our evenings together, we would decide where to sleep based on whose apartment was closer.

As summer approached, things were heating up with Terrence's investigation into the Mexican drug gangs. While he never specifically discussed the details of the case they were building, as a reporter I was good at piecing together information from the bits of his cell phone conversations I would overhear when he thought I was sleeping and from pumping Jake on the crime desk. As the temperature rose, so did the gang violence. There were many nights when Terrence was roused from our bed to go out to a new crime scene. I found myself unable to sleep until he returned.

At the end of the summer, I got a job offer in Los Angeles from *Hollywood Scoop!* We had just seen *Two Trains Running*, the August Wilson play, and I had planned to tell him about the offer and ask him to join me. We had returned to Terrence's apartment in Harlem when he got an urgent call on his cell phone. I began to change my clothes and could tell from his clipped tone that something major was going down. When he got off the phone, he came into the bedroom and quickly stripped off his slacks and shirt to change into dark jeans, a black T-shirt, and boots. He pulled out something from the back of the closet I hadn't seen before: a bulletproof vest.

"What's going on, Terrence?" I asked, my voice trembling as I watched him slip the protective vest over his head and attach the Velcro straps around his body.

"You know I can't talk to you about this, Nia," he said tightly as he sat down on the bed and pulled out a long metal box from underneath it. He unlocked it, and inside was a menacing-looking cache of guns of varying sizes. He quickly selected two, checked to confirm they were loaded, and slipped one into the waistband of the back of his jeans and the other smaller gun into an ankle holster.

"Terrence, baby, what's going on?" I asked as I came and sat down on the bed next to him and put my arms tightly around his waist.

"Nia, don't do this now. I have to go."

His eyes had changed from the bright, laughing eyes that always sparkled at me. They had a thunderous darkness and intensity I'd never seen before.

He grabbed a black nylon NYPD jacket from the closet and threw it over the vest. Then he grabbed his police shield off the dresser and put it around his neck. I followed him as he walked to the door, begging him not to go. There was a feeling in the pit of my stomach that told me something bad was going to happen.

Tires screeched to a halt outside. I walked over to the window and leaned out to see two unmarked police cars parked in front of the building, their engines running. They were here for Terrence.

"But I need to talk to you about something—"

As he reached the front door, he turned back to look at me as I came up behind him. He took my face between his large hands and saw the fear in my eyes. He leaned down to kiss me softly on the lips.

"Nia, I love you. I'm going to be fine."

That was the first time he said he loved me. My heart jumped, and tears began to slide down my face. I wanted to tell him I loved him, too, but before I could say anything, he walked out the door.

The next phone call I received was from his mother, Brenda Joyce, telling me that Terrence had been shot and was in surgery at Lenox Hill Hospital.

—

The rail-thin restaurant hostess, dressed in the ubiquitous tight black sheath, weaved her way through the room of lacquered tables, leading me to Terrence. Since I had last seen him in that hospital bed five years ago, I had changed quite a bit. My body was a little curvier and my hair much shorter. I could see as we approached the banquette that he looked the same, if not better, as he stood to greet me.

I was glad I had stopped by my apartment to change my clothes and freshen up my makeup before coming to dinner. I had hopped in a quick shower and then slipped into black Yigal Azrouël leggings, a black silk DKNY T-shirt top, and a black leather Prada blazer with three-quarter sleeves I pushed up at the elbow. Six-inch Alexander McQueen black woven platform sandals with burnished gold studs, a couple of gold round and square bangles, and a black lizard envelope clutch completed the look. Luckily, the weekly manicure MJ insisted I have was still passable. My favorite OPI purple wine color still looked glossy and fresh.

Terrence's uniform of jeans, boots, and jackets that he had worn when we dated had been replaced by a well-cut wool Italian suit, crisp white shirt with French cuffs, and black tie. I'd never seen him in a tie before. His hair was still closely cropped, but there were a few flecks of gray coming in that made him look even more handsome. His mocha skin was as flawless as ever, and his dark brown eyes still sparkled brightly when he smiled at me.

"Hello, Nia," Terrence said, his deep voice husky in my ear as he reached in to kiss me on the cheek. He ignored the awkward hand I stuck out as if former lovers seeing each other for the first time in five years would shake hands. I inhaled his scent. The clean soap smell was now layered with a hint of cologne. He always used to tell me he hated cologne, so what had changed? A new girlfriend's gift perhaps?

I scolded myself.

Damn, Nia, did you think that he wouldn't have a girlfriend or, hell, even a wife by now?

A man this fine—straight, educated, and employed—wasn't going to stay single forever. I snuck a glance down at his ring finger as I slid into the plush leather banquette and saw that it was bare. I cautioned myself that a naked ring finger didn't mean there wasn't a serious girlfriend.

"How are you, Terrence?" I asked, wondering why my heart was suddenly beating so quickly.

"I'm good. It's nice to see you," he said, settling back into his side of the banquette. The light from the small votive candle in the center of the table danced around. I was happy the waiter immediately came over to our table, giving me a chance to compose myself. I wasn't sure why I was suddenly so nervous.

"Good evening. My name is Blaine, and I'll be your server this evening. Can I interest the lovely couple in a bottle of wine this evening?" the waiter asked.

"Oh, we're not a couple," I jumped in to correct Blaine. "We were once. But not anymore."

"No, Blaine, we're not a couple, but it seems like she could definitely use some wine," Terrence said, chuckling.

"Oh, my apologies, Mr. Graham." A slight flush crept up Blaine's face. "Well, perhaps I can interest you and *your guest* in a bottle of merlot?"

"That sounds perfect. Sound good to you, Nia?" Terrence asked as he handed the wine list back to the flustered waiter.

"Sounds good to me as well," I said, shifting uncomfortably in my seat.

"Wonderful. I'll go get your bottle of wine, and you can have some time to look over your menus."

I glanced down at my menu, grateful for the momentary distraction.

"So, how are you?" asked Terrence, as he leaned toward me. I wished he would stay on his side of the banquette.

"I'm fine. Excited to be back in New York," I replied. "How have you been?"

"Good. I'm happy in the DA's office."

"The DA's office? You're not on the force anymore?"

"No, I left the force after I finished law school. I've been a special prosecutor in the district attorney's office for the last three years."

He told me that after his five years on the police force in the narcotics unit and three years in the DA's office, he was continuing his work in narcotics by working on the prosecutor's special drug task force to help state and federal agents to build cases against large international drug cartels.

"I've been working on some important cases that require me to pretty much split my time between New York and Washington, and I also spent some time in Colombia and Bolivia last month."

"Terrence, you did it. Just like you said you would. That's wonderful. Your mom must be so proud of you." I felt a flood of relief that he was no longer working as a cop. He was safe now.

"Yeah, you know my mom is just happy I'm no longer chasing down bad guys and in the line of fire anymore. But I try to tell Brenda Joyce that working in the DA's office has its own line of fire."

An awkward pause fell between us as I flashed back to our last encounter when he was lying in the hospital bed after being shot in the line of duty. His words had brought up an unpleasant memory for me. We sat across the table from each other, the silence weighing heavily between us.

"So, what are you doing in town?" Terrence asked to quickly change the subject.

"I got a new job. I'm the editor of a new magazine and website, *DivaDish.*"

"Congratulations, Nia. That's great news. Maybe we should have had Blaine bring us some champagne to toast instead of wine. When do you start?"

"Start?" I asked, unsure of what he meant. "I've been in the job almost three months now."

"You mean you've been back in my city for three months, and you didn't even call me?" he asked, sounding wounded.

"I did call you," I said defensively. "Last week, I called you to ask you to dinner to discuss something." Did he expect that I would call him when I got to town and we'd hook up like old times? Too much had been said and too much time had gone by. And I probably wouldn't have called him last week if I didn't need his help for Vanessa.

Our waiter, Blaine, returned to the table with the bottle of wine. He uncorked the bottle and presented the cork to Terrence who sniffed it and then held out his wineglass to sample the vintage merlot. Satisfied with the sample, he asked Blaine to fill our glasses. Not eager to return to his line of questioning, I jumped in and let the waiter know we were ready to order. I ordered the grilled salmon with asparagus, and Terrence said he'd have the lamb chops and spinach.

"Very good, Mr. Graham," Blaine said as he finished taking our orders before leaving the table.

I took a sip of the fragrant wine to calm my nerves. Why did I suddenly feel like I needed to be on the defensive?

"So, OK, you couldn't call a brother and let him know you were back in town," he said tightly, resuming the tense conversation. "What did you want to discuss?"

I decided to cut to the chase.

"Look, all bullshit from the past aside, Terrence, I called you because I need your help." I reached into my large clutch and pulled out the envelope Vanessa had given me with the threatening letters, e-mails, and text messages. I spread out everything across the table. I had placed each of the letters in an individual plastic sleeve in case there was any sort of forensic evidence that could be obtained from them. Although, given all the hands that had held the letters and the amount of time that had gone by, I doubted there would be anything traceable.

"What the hell . . . ?" Terrence began to pick up the pages one by one and examine them, turning them over in his large hands. "What is this stuff?"

I quickly ran down the story Vanessa had shared with me last week and told him the rumors about Marcus and the dead dancer in case that had any relation to the letters.

Terrence had met Vanessa once when she had come to visit me while we were dating. They had hit it off just like I had hoped they would, and that was why I knew I could trust him with her secret.

When Blaine returned to the table with some warm bread, I leaned over the photos to shield them from his eyes. When he left, Terrence began to look carefully at the letters again.

"She needs to go to the police," he said, thumbing through the ghastly threats.

"I know. I told her that, but she says they can't do it. Marcus recently signed his new contract with the Gladiators, and he and his management team told her they can't afford for this to get out. Initially they didn't want to jeopardize the trade to New York, and now that it's complete, they don't want to rock the boat."

"What kind of man puts money in front of his family's safety?" Terrence asked with his jaw tightening. "Just a cursory glance at these letters tells me that whoever is sending these letters is sick, and the fact that he or she managed to have them delivered directly to their homes in both Phoenix and now New York means whoever it is is serious. Dead serious, Nia."

"Look, I'm not trying to judge their marriage or judge how that man chooses to take care of his family," I said, my tone bristling, even though I felt the same way about Marcus not focusing on the safety of his family instead of his multimillion-dollar contract. "But I want to help out my best friend who is scared to death and feels like she has nowhere to turn." I released a heavy sigh, unclenched my hands, which had been balled up in my lap, and reached for my wineglass.

Terrence reached across the table and took my hand. I felt my heart jump as his large warm hand enveloped mine.

"I'm sorry, Nia. I don't mean to upset you, but Vanessa needs to understand the seriousness of this situation. These letters aren't just the musings of some random fan trying to get his favorite player's attention."

"I know, Terrence. She refuses to go to the police, so I came to you. But if you can't help us, then I'm sorry I bothered you." I began to gather up the letters and stacked them together again so that I could put them back into the envelope.

"I guess nothing's changed. It's always your way or no way, right?" he said as he sighed and shook his head. He took the envelope from me. "The first thing I want to do is have all the letters analyzed for

DNA as well as the handwriting. I've got to go up to DC tomorrow, and I've got a buddy at Quantico who will take a look at this stuff and keep it on the low. Once he reviews the material, we should have some sort of profile of this person, and then we can see where we want to go from there."

"Thank you, Terrence!" Before I could stop myself, I leaned in to hug him. His arm slipped around my body, and he hugged me back. Our embrace was familiar and warm, as though no time had passed between us at all.

But clearly things had changed.

"There you are, Terrence," a female voice called out.

Terrence suddenly pulled away from me and turned toward a woman quickly making her way over to our table. Terrence stood up and embraced a tall woman who looked like she just stepped off an international runway. She had glowing cinnamon-brown skin and sleek dark brown hair in soft-layered waves that caressed her bare shoulders. It was hard to tell if her best feature was the large golden-brown cat eyes framed by impossibly long dark lashes or her high cheekbones that could cut glass. Her tight black strapless dress hugged her curves, and it was clear she had just come from some sort of formal event.

I wanted to say, "Harpo, who dis woman?" but unlike Squeak in *The Color Purple* when she questioned her man, Harpo, Terrence was not my man. My stomach dropped.

"Hello, Vivica," Terrence said as he smiled. He greeted her with a deep kiss and put an arm around her small waist. "I thought you weren't going to be free until after the auction."

"I know, but I missed you, darling, so I snuck out of Russell Simmons's event early. I remembered you said you were meeting someone for dinner here, so I popped over," the woman said as she kissed him with full pouty red lips and wrapped her long, toned arms around him.

Someone? He told her he was meeting *someone?* That was who I was now, *someone . . .*

"Yes, I'm meeting my friend Nia Bullock for dinner," Terrence said as he turned to introduce me. I wasn't sure what to make of the "friend" label, but I tried to smile even though my face felt like it had hit the table and cracked.

"Oh, right—Nia!" the woman said brightly as she looked down at me from her Amazonian-model-height advantage.

"Hello, Nia." She extended a long elegant arm across the table to shake my hand. "I've heard so much about you." I managed to bite back the urge to say I hadn't heard a damn thing about her.

After she shook my hand, she leaned back into Terrence with her head on his shoulder, one arm around his waist while her left hand caressed the silk pocket square in his suit jacket.

That's when I saw the ring.

"Hello, Vivica, is it?" I said as I tried not to stare at the beautiful princess-cut diamond in the platinum setting on her ring finger. Suddenly I knew where I'd seen her before. She was actually a model. But not just any model. She did major advertising campaigns and had just appeared on the cover of *Elle* magazine's fall fashion issue.

"I hadn't gotten a chance to tell you yet, Nia," Terrence began. I already knew what he was going to say. I tried to shut the words out before I could hear them, but it was too late. "Meet my fiancée, Vivica DeWalders. We're getting married this summer."

Even though I had known what he was going to say, I felt like the air had been knocked out of me. Suddenly my face felt warm and a drop of sweat trickled down my back. I felt foolish.

"Congratulations, Terrence," I managed to squeeze out. "I guess we'll need Blaine to get that champagne after all."

CHAPTER 8

Vanessa

I wanted revenge.

I wanted a divorce.

With Marcus on the road, I was able to be alone with my thoughts, but I still wasn't ready to see him when he returned, so I told him to stay at the Four Seasons. That was two weeks ago.

What the hell was I going to do with my life?

I should have known better. I should have left Marcus when I first found out he was cheating back in Phoenix. Why had I believed that he had changed? Why had I believed that he loved me?

Most mornings I felt like a heavy fog was weighing me down. I was having trouble getting out of bed to walk the two blocks to drop off Damon at his new school. But today I forced myself to jump in the shower and put on a navy-blue Juicy sweat suit, because after I dropped off Damon at school, I had an appointment with the real estate agent the Gladiators' concierge had found for us. Dawn, who had already taken me out to see homes in Westchester and Connecticut, was meeting me in Alpine, New Jersey, at nine thirty. The swanky enclave with multimillion-dollar mansions just outside of New York was home to celebrities like Chris Rock, Mary J. Blige, and Eddie Murphy, but I really wasn't in the mood to look for a new house. I thought about canceling the appointment. After all, would I even need a new home for the three of us?

As I glanced down at my iPhone, I could see there were missed calls from Marcus, Kareem, and Nia from when I was in the shower. I wasn't in the mood to talk to any of them right now, but I planned to at least call Nia back when I got in the car to head to my appointment in New Jersey. We hadn't spoken at length since I told her about the stalker, but I knew she was working on something to help us.

As I went to put the phone back down on the nightstand, it buzzed again, and Kareem's name flashed across the screen.

"What the hell do you want?" I said into the phone.

"Look, V., I know you're upset, but you have to listen to me," Kareem hissed into the phone. We had both long stopped pretending to be cordial with each other, especially when Marcus wasn't around. Family or not, we couldn't stand each other. And while I always felt like Kareem wanted me out of Marcus's life from day one, he needed me to stay put so that I didn't cause problems with the Gladiators' owner. Still, that didn't stop him from being nasty to me. Ever since he had found out several years ago that I'd been trying to pressure Marcus to fire him and get another manager, the gloves had come off.

"Really, Kareem. What is it you want to say to me this time? Are you going to run down your usual routine about how I shouldn't believe what I'm seeing? Are you calling to tell me that my husband isn't sleeping with Laila?" I could hear my voice getting more shrill as I shot the questions out to Kareem and waited for his pathetic answer.

"Look, you're a grown woman, Vanessa. Shit, you know the deal better than anyone. You ain't no rookie in this here game anymore. You believe what you want about your husband, but you better not even think about walking out. You have to stay for the family." I could tell from his tone, he was taking great pleasure at my pain.

This was one of those moments I wished there was a way to slam down a cell phone in Kareem's ear as I disconnected the call. He had to go. I would never have a chance at saving my marriage with Kareem in the picture.

Shaking my head, I put three bobby pins between my teeth and twisted my thick hair up into a casual bun. I flipped the light switch on the wall as I walked into Damon's bedroom, which was decorated with a race-car theme and a life-size cutout poster on the wall of his hero dunking a basketball.

The morning sunlight streamed into the room through sheer curtains. I slipped into Damon's race-car bed beneath the window and wrapped my arms around his warm body.

"Good morning, sunshine," I whispered softly in his ear, trying to forget my heated conversation with Kareem as my son began to stir. I stroked his head and inhaled the scent of Carol's Daughter Vanilla Hair Honey in his short crop of tight curls.

"Morning, Mommy," Damon said as he yawned sleepily, displaying a missing front tooth. He turned over to face me, his eyes still closed and his yellow SpongeBob pajamas twisted around his body. At seven years old, Damon took after his father in height and with his deep brown chocolate skin. He was already tall for his age and towered over most of his second-grade classmates by several inches. His eyes were also like his father's—warm dark pools framed by long black lashes any woman would pay for. He got the deep dimples in his cheeks from me. I kissed his little brown nose as he wrapped his arms and legs around me tightly for what we called our octopus hug.

"Is Daddy home?" Damon asked as he untangled himself, sat up in the bed, and immediately looked at the poster of his father stretching toward an invisible basketball rim on his wall. Damon always woke up every morning looking for his best friend.

Marcus used to be my best friend, too.

"No, sweetheart. Remember, I reminded you last night that Daddy said he wouldn't be home until Saturday because he has games out of town this week? He'll be home tomorrow." Marcus and I were coordinating via text and Nicole, the indispensable nanny and cook the Gladiators' concierge found for us, to make sure he saw his son who didn't realize that his mom and dad were having problems. But I wasn't sure how much longer we could keep up the charade.

I pushed myself up and off the bed and walked over to his dresser to get his clothes for school. I selected some underwear, a bright red long-sleeve T-shirt with a growling T. rex on the front, socks, and a pair of jeans, and then laid them out on the bed.

"So I'm still the man of the house, then?" Damon asked as he took off his pajamas, dropped them in the middle of the floor, and stepped into his underwear. Before going out of town, Marcus always told Damon that it was their job as men to watch over Mommy and help her with anything she needs.

"Yeah, I guess so, *little* man of the house," I answered as I chuckled softly and picked up the pile of discarded pajamas to toss them into the wicker hamper in the corner of the room. "Well, little man of the house, let's go get some breakfast."

"Waffles and applesauce, Mommy!" Damon shouted as he quickly put on the rest of his clothes and went to get a pair of sneakers from his closet.

"Go to the bathroom and brush your teeth, wash your face, and put on lotion while I check on breakfast. And don't forget to get rid of the ash monster, little boy."

"OK, Mommy." Damon turned, put his arms out like Superman, and dashed down the hallway to his bathroom.

—

Nicole was already in the kitchen preparing breakfast when I walked in. The kitchen, which smelled of fresh waffles and smoky bacon, was a modern stainless steel and granite masterpiece that looked out into a large sunken great room with a recessed movie-theater-size plasma TV, gas fireplace, beige suede couches, and a bank of floor-to-ceiling windows that covered two walls and overlooked the Manhattan skyline.

"Good morning, Mrs. King," Nicole said brightly in her lilting Trinidadian accent as she poured sweet-potato batter into the Krups waffle maker. Damon had been on a major waffle kick for two weeks straight after he came back from a sleepover at his best friend Jacob's house. Jacob's mom, Mika, a former investment banker turned celebrity chef, lived two floors below us with her partner, Delilah. She shared her recipe for sweet-potato waffles with me after Damon came home begging for them. Drizzled with warm Vermont maple syrup and roasted pecans, they were pretty delicious, I had to admit, but unlike Damon, I didn't want to eat them every day.

On the granite island in the center of the kitchen sat a bowl of fresh fruit and a spinach and tomato omelet on a warming plate for me along with a small dish of homemade applesauce with cinnamon and crispy applewood-smoked bacon for Damon.

"Good morning, Nicole. Breakfast smells wonderful." I grabbed a piece of the warm bacon off the countertop and then headed down the hallway to the front door of the penthouse to collect the morning newspapers. I swore we must be some of the only people in New York who still got a pile of newspapers in the morning instead of just reading the news online.

I popped the last piece of crispy bacon into my mouth and then flipped through the heavy stack of papers in my arms as I made my way back to the kitchen. I put the newspapers aside on the large island and reached for the *New York Daily* to put at Damon's seat; I knew the first thing he would to want to see was how the Gladiators did in last night's game and see if there were any pictures of his dad. I didn't particularly care for that paper, a tabloid whose journalistic focus tended to be on gruesome crime dramas playing out in the five boroughs, political sex scandals, and sensational stories about rats overrunning the city, but Marcus said the paper had the best sports reporters in the city. They certainly seemed to love him now that he was a Gladiator, and he got a lot of back covers.

I hadn't watched the game last night because I couldn't stand the thought of seeing Marcus's face, so I had no idea if the Gladiators had won. While in a taxi yesterday, I heard ESPN's Stephen A. Smith on the radio lambasting the Gladiators over three losses in a row after what had seemed to be a hot winning streak. As I grabbed the paper, I noticed that Marcus was on both the front and back covers of the *New York Daily. Wow, they must have had quite a game last night.* The back cover of the paper, which led into the sports section of the paper, had a huge black-and-white photo of Marcus getting dunked on by Marc Sanford, the Miami Raptors' seven-foot-four star center, a box with the game's score 82–67, and the headline "In Your Face! It's Lights Out for Marcus King!"

Ouch . . . Well, that wouldn't make Marcus or Kareem too happy. Turning the paper over, I wondered if the loss was so bad that the reporters had continued coverage on the front of the paper.

But there, staring back out at me, was a black-and-white photo of my husband and his mistress.

Below the picture was a bright red headline that screamed, "Sex Scandal! Marcus and Laila Land Reality Show!"

Damon suddenly bounded into the room and climbed up onto the stool next to me.

"Mommy, where's my paper?" Damon asked as he sifted through the pile of papers on the counter, searching for pictures of his father. Nicole walked over to the island with Damon's waffles, set the plate in front of him, and poured some syrup on top.

"Thank you, Miss Nicole," he said. While Damon was momentarily distracted by the plate of warm waffles, I quickly folded the paper in half and put it behind my back.

"Uh, your paper didn't come today, sweetie," I said as I turned to Nicole. "Can you get Damon ready and then walk him to school?"

"Of course, Mrs. King. No problem."

"Thank you, Nicole." I kissed Damon on the forehead as he happily munched on his waffles, his long legs swinging in the chair.

With a story about Marcus and Laila's affair in a "credible" paper and not just buzzing around random online blogs, everyone would be after the story now. That meant the paparazzi would be stalking our front door for the "money shot" of the poor pathetic wife who's just found out her husband is having an affair. I knew without even looking out the window or calling down to the building doorman that hordes of reporters and photographers would be outside, waiting to catch me. I knew I couldn't risk walking Damon to school as usual.

"If there's no paper, can I watch *SportsCenter*?" Damon asked with his mouth full. As Nicole started to reach for the TV remote control on the counter, I grabbed it. She looked at me quizzically for a moment and then turned to the sink to begin washing the waffle maker.

"Uh, sorry, baby. No *SportsCenter* today. I'll turn on Nickelodeon for you." I punched the number to the kids channel into the remote. I couldn't take the chance that the *SportsCenter* anchors would cover the games Marcus was playing on and off the court. The sounds of children's giggles from the TV filled the kitchen, and fortunately Damon was immediately engrossed and forgot about his dad's game.

I turned to leave before Damon could ask me again about the newspaper and before Nicole could see the tears welling up in my eyes. I walked back to my bedroom, clutching the newspaper to my chest.

Reaching the bedroom at the end of the long hallway, I closed the door behind me and walked over to the bed. Dropping to my knees and sobbing, I unfurled the newspaper and spread it out on the gray silk duvet on the king-size sleigh bed in which Marcus and I had slept and made love throughout our eight-year marriage. The bacon churned inside my stomach as I wiped my tears with the velour cuff of my jacket and began to scan the *New York Daily* cover story about Marcus and Laila.

Unnamed sources from Glam Network, who spoke exclusively to New York Daily *on condition of anonymity, say that video vixen Laila James has just signed a seven-figure reality show deal with the popular network. "Miki [Woods], our head of reality programming, is salivating over this new show and can't wait to launch it in the summer," said one employee.*

Another source said the rising starlet's offer price jumped from six figures to seven after Woods saw X-rated text messages from New York Gladiators star Marcus King as well as racy photos of the couple in bed. "Once Miki saw those photos, she worked around the clock to get this deal signed."

James has been spotted by reporters in recent weeks, entering and exiting luxury hotels in cities where the star power forward Marcus King happens to be playing. Coincidence? We think not.

When reached for comment, James's agent, Steven Edwards, would only say, "Ms. James is a very busy woman, and she often has meetings all over the country to manage her affairs." Poor choice of words or a double entendre?

New York Daily reached out to King's longtime manager and cousin, Kareem Davis, for comment on whether the New York Gladiator would be appearing on the new Glam Network reality show. His response: "Marcus King is focused on one thing and one thing only: bringing the city of New York a championship."

After last night's bruising 80–67 loss to the third-place Miami Raptors, the Gladiators' front office and their fans likely want to see their $50 million power forward focused on the court and not on becoming a reality TV star.

I sank onto the carpeted floor and curled into a ball while crying, my body hot and sweaty, and realized why my husband had been so desperate to reach me this morning.

—

I stared at my red eyes in the mirror over the bathroom vanity and turned on the faucet to splash cold water on my face. My reflection was pathetic. Dry, puffy face. Dark circles. Frown lines on my forehead. My hair a tangled mess.

What happened to the woman I used to be?

How did I get here?

No answers came from the reflection that stared back at me. I hated myself for being in this situation. And just when I thought things couldn't get any worse with Marcus having an affair, now there was a potential reality show. Now Marcus might truly be wide open over this Laila chick, but I couldn't imagine that his sexed-out mind was so gone that he'd let his whore do a reality show off his back. That would kill his career.

More importantly, I couldn't imagine Kareem allowing his star and one-and-only client to destroy his career and Kareem's sole paycheck in the process. But maybe it wasn't just an overactive libido guiding Marcus now. Could he actually be in love with this little tramp? What happened to the Road Code?

The thought of my husband being in love with this woman was more than I could bear. I wouldn't let her have my husband or destroy my family. I was going to keep my appointment with Erin to look at houses in New Jersey, which would get me out of the city and away from the paparazzi.

I splashed some more cold water on my face, hoping to take down the puffiness. Reaching for the wide-toothed comb in the side drawer of the vanity, I took down my bun and raked the tool roughly through my tangled locks. The comb scraped along my tender scalp and pulled forcefully at the tangled strands, but I didn't care. The pain felt good. At least I could feel something. Then I reached for the brush to sweep my hair up into a neater bun and secured it with three bobby pins. A jar of Clarins moisturizer rested on the shelf under the mirror. I dipped my fingers into the cool cream and then rubbed it into my skin. Smoothing down the top of my jogging suit jacket, I decided this was the best I could do with my appearance for today and went back into my walk-in closet to grab my Gucci handbag. I put on dark-tinted

Chanel sunglasses to hide my red eyes. All I needed was for a photographer to get a shot of me with red, puffy eyes for their follow-up story. Not today.

I heard the thumping of Damon's feet running down the hallway to my bedroom. He burst into the room, calling my name.

"Mommy!" he called out in a singsong voice as I walked into the room.

"Yes, baby," I sniffed, trying to sound normal and hoping my beloved son wouldn't notice my puffy face and red eyes. I saw that he had his bright yellow backpack and jacket on, ready to go to school.

"I wanted to say bye, Mommy," Damon said as he threw himself into my arms. I hugged him tightly before he could squirm out of my embrace, eager to head off to school.

"I love you, Damon. Have a great day." I clung to him a little longer.

"See you later," he said. He then ran out the door to Nicole so that they could walk to school. The reporters would be disappointed to see Nicole taking Damon to school today and would continue to lie in wait for me, but I wasn't going to fall into their trap. Luckily, the papers had been pretty good at leaving our son alone.

I grabbed my cell phone off the nightstand. There were more missed calls from Nia. I guess Marcus had decided to stop trying to reach me. I quickly pushed the buttons to call our driver, Alex, whom I had told last night to be waiting for me at eight.

The phone rang. I thought I heard a muffled click on the line, and then Alex answered.

"Yes, Mrs. K.," Alex said when he answered my call.

"Hi, Alex. Are there reporters outside?" I asked, although I already knew the answer. I also knew that Alex always had a fresh copy of *New York Daily* with him that he read cover to cover, so no doubt he was aware of why the reporters were stalking the building. But in the few months Alex had worked for us, he had proven himself to be discreet and loyal, so he'd never tip off reporters no matter how hard they tried to cajole or even bribe him for information.

"Yes, ma'am. There are quite a few buzzards out today."

"OK. There's been a change in plans. Nicole is going to walk Damon to school, and in about thirty minutes I'm going to drive myself to New Jersey."

"Are you sure, Mrs. King? I can pull the car into the garage, and the reporters won't even see you get in." I appreciated the concern in his voice, but I couldn't risk following his suggestion.

"Unfortunately, Alex, even if you pick me up in the garage, there will be at least a couple of reporters with cars and TV news trucks that would follow us, and I don't want them to know where I'm going. So what I need for you to do is create a diversion."

"A diversion?" he asked as I hurriedly began to gather my things and drop them into an oversize Louis Vuitton tote. I stuffed my feet into some UGG boots I found in the back of my closet.

"Yes, Alex, in thirty minutes I want you to turn on the car engine and get out and open the passenger side door and stand there. The reporters will think you are waiting for me to come out, so they will be focused on the door of the building and won't see me pull out of the garage behind them."

"OK, Mrs. King. Is there anything else you need me to do?"

"If you see any of them getting antsy or looking toward the garage, pretend you have a call from me and let them hear you talking."

"Got it, Mrs. King."

"Thank you, Alex."

This plan had to work. I couldn't face the reporters today.

—

I headed to the elevator to go down to the garage. When the elevator doors opened, I noticed that Hector, the garage attendant, wasn't at his post to pull around the car. He must be on one of his extended bathroom breaks. He was a sweet old man but was always complaining about his weak bladder. The restroom for employees was at the rear of the building, so I figured it could be a while before he returned.

I ducked into his tiny office and glanced at the four security monitors, one of which showed the front of the building. There were ten to fifteen reporters and photographers with notepads, cameras, and tape recorders ready to capture the story of the day. They paced back and forth in front of the building like caged lions waiting for feeding time at the zoo. *Hate to disappoint you guys, but there will be no meal today.*

At exactly the thirty-minute mark Alex got out of the car just as I had instructed. He buttoned the jacket of his black suit, adjusted his dark glasses, and then walked around to the passenger side of the black Mercedes sedan to open the rear door. Reporters rushed to jockey for position in front of the revolving glass doors, making a pathway lined on both sides to the car so that they could be the first to get the photograph and comment from the scorned wife.

I didn't have much time. If I waited too long, I'd miss my window of opportunity because at any moment the reporters could get antsy and start to think something was up. As luck would have it, Hector, who in addition to battling incontinence was also forgetful, had left open the door to the metal box on the wall that housed all the car keys. I pushed my sunglasses up into my hair, squinted, and hurriedly tried to locate the keys to our new Jaguar XJS convertible, a gift from the Gladiators' owners when Marcus signed his new contract. I grabbed the keys off the second row from the bottom and noted the space: A4. I hastily jotted down a note for Hector to let him know I took my car and stuck it on the hook for the missing keys so that when he returned, he wouldn't think someone had stolen the car. No need to give the old man a heart attack.

Our car was at the end of the row, which was dimly lit. I made my way down the row, my steps silent in the soft boots on the concrete floor. I was just about to push the button on the key chain to unlock the door to the car when I noticed a man bent over the windshield in the shadows of the driver's side of the car.

"Hey, Hector," I said as I came closer, assuming he was doing his daily windshield washing. Startled, the man turned quickly toward me. I could see immediately that it wasn't Hector. The man, tall and heavyset with a muscular build, was dressed in dark clothing and had a black knit cap pulled down low over his forehead. His eyes were dark and hard, and there was a shadow of stubble that covered the lower half of his long face. As he began to make his way toward me, I noted that there was a large white envelope in his hand and he was wearing gloves.

I screamed, dropped my bag, and ran back toward the elevators, but the man lumbered quickly across the concrete floor.

"Come back here!" he growled as he caught up with me and tackled me to the ground.

I hit the concrete hard, knocking the air out of me. Before I could catch my breath, he grabbed my shoulder and rolled me onto my back, got on his knees, and straddled me tightly, pressing his thighs into my rib cage. His face was twisted into an angry mask. My screams echoed throughout the garage, and he leaned down to muffle them with one of his large gloved hands. He pressed his weight into me as I gasped for air. I kicked my legs and tried to claw at his face. I struggled against him with all my strength, fighting and bucking beneath him as his other hand roughly moved along the side of my breasts. His hands moved up to encircle my neck. He pressed his weight down into my pelvis to pin me down to the cold garage floor. I couldn't move.

As I stared at the roof of the garage, my eyes wide with fear and tears streaming out of the sides of my eyes, I felt his ragged hot breath along my neck. I closed my eyes tightly as he began to squeeze. I knew I was about to die in the garage.

Suddenly there was a voice shouting in the distance. There were footsteps running. And then just as abruptly as the man was on top of me, he jumped off and was gone. I rolled over onto my side, clutching my ribs, coughing and choking, and then there was blessed darkness.

CHAPTER 9

Nia

The cab driver slammed on the brakes at the corner of Park Avenue and Seventy-Fifth Street. In reflex mode, my arm swung out to push MJ back into his seat as his lightweight behind started to hurtle face-first toward the plastic partition that separated us from our driver.

"OK, Jesus, take the wheel for real," MJ said as he reached for his sunglasses, which had fallen into his lap. "Girl, you saved my life; well, maybe not my life but certainly my gorgeous face."

Muttering under my breath, I picked up my black Bottega Veneta tote that had tumbled onto the littered floor of the taxi and resisted the urge to tell our driver, Reakwon, whose name I read off the grainy black-and-white photo next to his New York City taxi license, that the brakes in his dirty-ass cab would likely work just as well if the brother lightly pushed down on them as he approached the destination instead of waiting until the last minute and trying to kill us both. My jaw tight, I swiped my American Express corporate card through the credit card reader, skipped the tip, and MJ and I jumped out of the mustard death mobile.

Deuces, Reakwon.

I tossed the heavy tote with braided shoulder straps onto my shoulder and pulled up the black cashmere cowl-neck scarf that was underneath my black Burberry trench coat around my neck and ears against the chilly fall air.

MJ and I began to make our way through the throngs of Upper East Side nannies pushing ultraprivileged toddlers in thousand-dollar strollers, heavily made-up socialites heading off to disease-du-jour benefit lunches at the Waldorf, and businessmen talking loudly into cell phones. I scanned the gold placards on the walls of the brownstones, looking desperately for the one that matched the address on the crumpled paper in my hands that I had written down twenty minutes ago when I got a call from a man named Alex. He wouldn't tell me anything over the phone beyond that he worked for Marcus and Vanessa, and that she needed to see me right away. Alarmed when he gave me the name of Prometheus Medical Associates, I asked if she was OK, but all he would say was that Vanessa wanted to see me.

After seeing the stories about Laila and Marcus in the paper, I had been trying to call Vanessa all morning. I wanted to see how she was doing as well as discuss the pressure DeAnna was putting on me to run a story on Laila's new reality show. I immediately told MJ to cancel the run-through I was about to have with our accessories editor, Sharan Ali, even though she was already wheeling racks of designer clothing down the hallway to my office. We were going to select items for a story on new fall trends. When MJ saw my hands shaking as I threw items into my bag, he insisted on tagging along, and I was thankful since I didn't know what I was going to find.

"Here it is," said MJ as he glanced back down at the paper in my hand and back up at the gold-plated placard on the outside of a five-story brownstone in the middle of the tony block.

MJ pushed the small black button on the intercom next to the door and gave our names to the curt, disembodied voice that answered. A security camera tucked into the corner of the wall turned toward us, a red light flashed twice, and then the voice told us to take the elevator up to the fourth floor before it buzzed us into the building.

The doors of the elevator opened into a small, elegant waiting room decorated in rich chocolate brown, cream, and red accents that looked more like a page ripped out of *Elle Décor* than any doctor's office in which I had ever been. There was no receptionist. A man in a dark suit put down the copy of *Time* magazine he had been reading, got up from a leather club chair, and walked over to us.

"Ms. Nia?" he asked. I could see that he had a coiled plastic headset snaking out of the collar of his shirt and into his ear.

"Uh, yes," I said, looking at him quizzically. MJ and I exchanged glances. "Are you Alex?"

"Yes, ma'am. I am. Just a moment." Alex raised his wrist to his mouth and spoke into a small microphone attached to the cuff of his suit jacket.

"Ms. Nia is here." When he received a response, he turned to MJ.

"Ms. Nia is the only one I'm authorized to send back, so you will need to wait out here with me," Alex said. I undid the belt of my jacket, took off my coat and scarf, and gave them to MJ to hold as he took a seat in one of the overstuffed wingback leather chairs and began to sulk behind his sunglasses over being left out.

"Right this way, Ms. Nia." Alex led me over to a heavy oak-paneled door that suddenly opened.

"Hi, Nia. I'm Desiree, Marcus's publicist," said a petite young woman who extended one hand to shake while she held a ringing iPhone and a BlackBerry in her other. She was dressed in a winter-white wool wrap dress that hugged her curves with black Jimmy Choo boots. Her long jet-black weave hung down her back, and heavy bangs skimmed the tops of long lashes that framed dark brown eyes. I never understood why sisters who wanted to get a weave didn't at least try to fool folks into thinking it was theirs by getting a look and length even halfway believable. Maybe she should spend less time at the salon and more time keeping her client out of the papers.

"Hello, Desiree," I said, shaking her outstretched hand. "Can you please tell me what's going on? Is Vanessa OK?"

"I'm so sorry for all the secrecy. Please, let me take you to Mrs. King." Desiree silenced the ringing iPhone and BlackBerry and led me past four closed office doors on either side of the hallway. At the end of the long hallway, Desiree knocked sharply twice on a closed door before turning the knob and holding the door open for me to enter. She did not enter the room; I heard her close the door behind me.

The room was large and looked like a luxury hotel suite except for the standard-issue hospital bed dressed with crisp white linens and a bank of blinking monitors set up in the center of the room. Heavy white curtains hung from tall windows that appeared to be tinted so that the patients could see out and enjoy the view of the Manhattan skyline without anyone on the outside being able to see in.

A nurse dressed in light pink scrubs stood by the bed. She took a plastic bag out of her pocket filled with clear fluid and hung it on a chrome IV stand, attached it to a tube, and then turned to gently insert a tiny needle into Vanessa's arm. Vanessa winced, but she didn't open her eyes.

I walked over to the bed, and when I picked up Vanessa's hand, she blinked a few times as she tried to focus on my face. A tear slid out of the corner of her eye. Underneath her eye was swollen and puffy, and her bottom lip was cut. I clutched the rail to steady myself when I saw the dark bruising on my friend's neck. I had covered enough crime scenes at the beginning of my career to know the signs of strangulation.

I began to lean down to my friend, but before either one of us could speak, I noticed some movement out of the corner of my eye and turned.

"Kareem?" I said tightly as I tilted my head upon recognizing Marcus's longtime agent. Vanessa clenched my hand when she heard me say his name.

"Hi, Nia," Kareem said as he stood up. He, too, had an iPhone and a BlackBerry in his hands along with a beat-up white envelope. Tall at six foot five and with a muscular build, he now wore custom-made $5,000 Italian suits instead of the Nike sweat suits and shorts he and Marcus used to wear when they were teammates at UCLA. Closer than most brothers, the two had grown up together in LA. Kareem's mother left the family when he was little, and his father was in and out of jail, so he spent most of his time living with his aging grandmother, in and out of juvie for minor offenses, and at Marcus's home with his aunt and cousin. The cops, who knew he had a promising future as a basketball player, tried to cut Kareem some slack, hoping the two cousins would end up in the pros together. Despite his lengthy juvenile record, he was accepted to UCLA with Marcus, and they went off to college, determined that they both would make it to the pros.

The first two years they were unstoppable, and *ESPN* magazine billed the two sophomores as the dynamic duo in a cover story predicting that Marcus and Kareem could go to numbers one and two in the draft. There was also a brief scandal that erupted their junior year involving Kareem and allegations about gambling, which were never proven. And just as Marcus and Kareem were leading their school to an NCAA championship, Kareem was struck by a hit-and-run driver on a rainy night. Kareem's left leg was shattered and, a year of painful rehab later, so were his dreams for a professional basketball career.

Equally as devastated by the accident but determined to continue to press on for himself and his friend, Marcus led UCLA to a championship and dedicated the victory to his friend who watched the game from his hospital bed. After winning the championship, Marcus felt like he had nothing left to prove on the college level and despite the pleas from his parents to finish the last few months of his senior year and get his degree—he would have been the first in their family to graduate from college—Marcus announced he was entering the NBA draft. And then Marcus fulfilled a promise to his friend by making a move that left many of the top agents and managers who had hoped to sign the young phenom shaking their heads. He announced on the night of the NBA draft that his cousin and former teammate, Kareem Davis, would be both his agent and manager.

And so Kareem came along for the ride. And when he wasn't handling business negotiations, he was inserting himself in press appearances and magazine and TV interviews, trying to get as much of his own shine as possible. His personal life was messy, and he traded off Marcus's name to bed a bevy of rotating groupies, young starlets, and R&B singers. And I was sure some of these chicks even thought Kareem was Marcus because they resembled each other so much. But once a hustler, always a hustler. Every so often there would be some incident at a nightclub or event that would hit the blogs and be all the chatter until Desiree stepped in to make it all go away. The last incident had been one for the foolywang record books when a sex tape featuring Kareem and a Hollywood actress was leaked to TMZ. The footage was so shadowy, many people initially assumed it was Marcus in the grainy video.

Over the years Kareem had managed to do a fairly decent job steering his friend's career, landing lucrative endorsement deals with sneaker companies, sports drinks, and athletic apparel, but Vanessa said there were always other agents and managers swarming around Marcus, just waiting for an opportunity to swoop in and grab him. She had tried to push Marcus to at least take some meetings with potential new representation, but Marcus wouldn't hear of it, and her suggestions only served to make Kareem her permanent enemy. Marcus and Kareem had a contract, but Vanessa hoped their contract was just the right lawyer away from being able to be broken.

Vanessa knew there was no separating the cousins, so she tried to stay out of the professional matters. But as the problems with groupies and Marcus's infidelity began to cause problems in their marriage, Vanessa couldn't help but wonder if Kareem wasn't secretly hoping their marriage would dissolve. She had told me that he knew she was pushing Marcus to drop him, so a divorce would certainly benefit him in the long run. But in the short term, she had to believe that a nasty divorce wouldn't be good for his client's image and therefore wouldn't be good for business. And, if nothing else, Kareem's sneaky behind was all about the business.

I always got a bad vibe from him. Even now, suited and booted within an inch of his life, as MJ would say, he still reminded me of one of those slick brothers on the block back in Chicago always looking for that next hustle. Kareem's insistence that the threatening e-mails Vanessa and Marcus had been receiving be kept secret didn't seem to indicate he had their family's best interest at heart.

Kareem, who was dressed in a well-tailored midnight-blue wool suit, crisp white shirt, and Hermès silk tie that he had loosened around his neck, took my extended hand and leaned in to give me a kiss on the cheek in greeting. His chestnut skin gleamed from what I imagined were regular facials, and his teeth were like two rows of gleaming white Chiclets, from cosmetic bleaching no doubt. We didn't see each other often, but since I was Damon's godmother and he was his godfather, we did interact on family occasions. And he sniffed around occasionally trying to get a little taste, but I let him know to pump the brakes since he had been so slimy and backhanded with my girl.

"What the hell happened, Kareem?" I hissed through gritted teeth as my eyes narrowed. I snatched my hand away.

"Look, let's go outside and talk. The nurse just gave Vanessa something so she can sleep." I turned back to the bed and saw that Vanessa was dozing off. I leaned over the railing of the bed and kissed her on the cheek, then followed Kareem down the hall and into a small office.

"Let me try this again, Kareem. What the fuck happened to Vanessa? And where the hell is her husband?" I said as soon as he closed the door behind him.

"Nia, I know you're upset . . . ," he started. Kareem took a seat behind the desk as if he were holding office hours. He waved at one of the chairs in front of the desk to indicate I should take a seat, but I placed my fingertips on the desk and leaned toward him.

"You're damn right I'm upset. My best friend is lying in a hospital bed, but not in a hospital. Where are we? What is this place? What the hell is going on?"

"Calm down, Nia. We all need cool heads right now. I'll explain everything. First off, we're at a private care medical service that we have a contract with. It's run by Dr. Aron Harrison who treats celebrities, politicians, and high-net-worth individuals that need not only the best medical care but also discretion."

"What happened to Vanessa, Kareem?" I was rapidly losing my patience with Marcus's cousin.

"Vanessa was attacked in the parking garage of their building this morning," Kareem said. "The attendant in the garage was away from his post, so no one was down there. When she went to get her car, some guy jumped out and grabbed her."

"Oh my God," I said as I sank down into the chair. "Is she OK . . . ?" I was afraid to ask the one question to which I didn't want the answer.

"Dr. Harrison says that she's going to be fine. She wasn't raped if that's what you're wondering."

"Thank God," I said, relief momentarily washing over me, but then I remembered the marks on her neck and face. "But she looks pretty banged up, Kareem."

"I know. Dr. Harrison ran a full battery of tests. She's got some bruised ribs and some cuts and scrapes but nothing that won't heal over time. But, of course, the attack was quite traumatic, so the doctor gave her something to relax. She's going to be fine."

I closed my eyes and let my head fall back on the top of the chair. I couldn't even imagine how terrified she must have been down there in the garage alone. And then an even scarier thought suddenly crossed my mind.

"Wait a minute, where's Damon? Was he with her?"

"No. Fortunately the nanny had taken him to school. Vanessa had an appointment to see some homes in New Jersey and was planning to drive out there."

"Where's Marcus?" I asked through clenched teeth. He couldn't still be shacked up with his gold-digging mistress with his wife lying in a hospital bed. Even that, I prayed, would be too low for Marcus.

"I booked a jet to pick him up in Detroit," Kareem said as he looked down at the platinum Rolex watch on his wrist. "He should be landing within the hour at Teterboro Airport and will be coming straight here."

"Who found Vanessa in the garage?" I asked.

"The garage attendant. When her attacker saw the attendant, he ran off."

"Do we know if Vanessa got a good look at the guy so the police have a description to go on?"

"The police were here earlier and took her statement. She was pretty shaken up, so it was difficult for her to get everything out. Perhaps she'll remember more later."

"So why is she here instead of a hospital?"

"We want to keep this as low profile as possible and out of the papers. And believe me, she's getting much better care here at the Ritz-Carlton of medical facilities. Dr. Harrison and his team are the absolute best."

"I don't know, Kareem. I think she should be in a hospital."

"Well, her husband, Marcus, wants her here. You're not her husband, Nia." Kareem said this forcefully, then looked down at his BlackBerry and scrolled through messages.

"Does her husband want her here because he's worried about his precious career? Maybe it's time he starts thinking about his wife and family and doing what's best for them instead of his damn career!" I knew people in the hall could probably hear me, but I didn't care. "I'm not going to sit up here and pretend that everything is silky smooth, like we all didn't see the paper today with the story about Marcus and Laila. It's a little late for him to play the concerned spouse."

"Look, I'm not trying to fight with you. I know we're all upset and concerned about Vanessa. But, honestly, this is the best facility, and if Marcus decides he wants to make that decision when he arrives, we'll move her, but until then I can't do anything." Kareem sat back in the chair and folded his hands, waiting for me to respond.

The door to the office opened, and Desiree stuck her head into the room.

"Excuse me, Kareem, but it's time for that two o'clock call about the *Esquire* magazine profile. Do you want to take it in here or the other office where we were working earlier?"

"Let's take it in the other office," Kareem said as he stood up, still absentmindedly checking his messages on his BlackBerry. "Feel free to stay in here, Nia, or wait in Vanessa's room. She'll probably be sleeping for another hour or so." He quickly walked out of the room with Desiree leading the way before I could respond.

I dropped my head into my hands for a moment, overwhelmed with concern for my best friend and how things were being handled. When I looked up, I noticed that Kareem left the battered white envelope he had in his hands in Nia's room on the desk. Curious, I looked back at the door to make sure it was closed and heard Desiree and Kareem's voices fade in the hallway, so I assumed that they stepped into the other office. I pulled the envelope over to my side of the desk. There was no address on the front, and it had been opened already. I pulled a sheet of paper from the envelope, and my heart began to beat faster as I clutched the chilling message.

You Will Die for Your Sins!

Was the man who attacked Vanessa the one who wrote the note?

CHAPTER 10

Vanessa

As I struggled to open my eyes, the throbbing in my head started to escalate. But at least the aching soreness that had radiated through most of my body had given in to the pain medication Dr. Harrison had given me last night. I could see the early-morning sunlight starting to peek through the sheer curtains. The only sound in the room was the soft whirring of the medical monitors and Marcus's deep rhythmic breathing.

He was seated in a chair next to the bed, his head resting on the tangled sheets and his hands holding mine. I wanted to pull my hand away, but Marcus held on to it so tightly that I didn't have the strength to do that. With my ribs bruised but fortunately not broken, I knew better than to try to sit up in the bed. Plus, I didn't want to wake him and hear more of his pathetic apologies and promises to change.

Just like the old Sunshine Anderson song goes, I'd heard it all before.

I told Marcus when he arrived that I wanted a divorce, but in those Lifetime TV movies, wasn't a near-death experience supposed to draw the estranged couple back together? I had almost been murdered in our parking garage trying to get away from reporters staked out in front of our home because of his affair with Laila James. That tramp bitch had almost gotten me killed.

She wasn't getting my family, too.

Marcus didn't know it yet, but I wasn't going anywhere, and neither was he.

CHAPTER 11

Nia

This photo shoot was a disaster.

We had been on the set for five hours already, and our photographer, Renaldo Blaze, had yet to shoot a single image of neo-soul singer Janelle Greene and her newborn twin girl and boy, Sunshine and Moon. Normally Renaldo was a pretty mellow dude since *DivaDish* kept him and his multi-culti skinny-jean-clad team of photo and lighting assistants working on the regular, but with nothing but the sounds of raised voices and crying babies coming from behind the closed door of Janelle's dressing room, even he was getting antsy.

And I needed to leave in thirty minutes to meet Terrence who wanted to download on the report he'd gotten back from his contacts at Quantico as well as his conversation with the detectives investigating the attack on Vanessa last month.

I thought we were making progress an hour ago when Janelle summoned the hair stylist and makeup artist that she had demanded be flown in first class from Detroit because she wouldn't dare work with anyone else, but there had been no indication she was anywhere near being ready.

Usually when shooting with kids, you know you're going to be popping Advil all day or throwing back tequila all night, but this was shaping up to be one for the record books. No amount of headache medicine or alcohol was going to help. Typically I would let my entertainment editor, Che Williams, handle this because she had a way of soothing even the most temperamental of celebs and coaxing the juiciest stories out of them, but because Janelle had a reputation for being emotional (industry code for just plain crazy), Che had asked me to come to today's shoot because she thought she might need reinforcements. There's a saying in the entertainment industry: never work with children or animals. After today I wanted to add "postpartum neo-soul singers desperate for a comeback" to that list as well.

I should have known it was going to be the photo shoot from hell when Janelle's PR team called me on my cell last night to discuss her ridiculous fourteen-page rider and tried to charge us for shooting Janelle and her twin babies. I informed them that not only were we not *People* magazine, but their client, while certainly talented in her own right, wasn't international superstar Angelina Jolie, so there would be no seven-figure check forthcoming for the images of Janelle and her children. But I was happy to discuss any special dietary requests, exotic flowers, and the Diptyque scented candles she had to have for her dressing room. Her publicist, Marc Q, was a fairly decent guy as far as soul-sucking publicists went. He wasn't like some of them: pathological liars who filled their clients' empty little heads with delusional thoughts of grandeur and who, thinking they were stars equal to their clients, demanded first-class travel and multiroom hotel suites for themselves. Marc told me sheepishly that he understood the requests were a shade unreasonable, but since this was what his client wanted, he had to ask.

I knew Janelle had a new album to promote, and since she had recently separated from her baby daddy, a bullet-ridden rapper named Jerome "Tech Nine" Michaels, the diva needed all the promotional help she could get. And the million of daily readers of *DivaDish* were her target audience. But we needed to tread lightly because as temperamental and crazy as Janelle might be, she could certainly take herself and her juicy breakup and comeback story over to *Vibe* or *Ebony*. This was why after four hours of shooting absolutely nothing, I hadn't shut the set down and hit her management team with a bill for the studio rental, photographer fee, lighting equipment, and catering. But something had to give because we'd be hitting overtime, and I didn't need DeAnna on my ass yet again about going over budget.

I found Che pacing back and forth in front of Janelle's closed dressing room door, nervously biting her already short nails.

"I need to talk to Marc. Can you get him for me? We're not getting anywhere, and we're about to hit overtime, which will instantly double the cost of this shoot."

"Uh, sure . . . ," Che said as she peered at me over the top of her trendy black glasses. She walked to the other side of the set and tentatively knocked on the closed door. She hadn't conducted her interview with Janelle yet, so she was loath to upset the singer until she got her exclusive. I knew there was a possibility that Janelle could shut everything down in an emotional fit if pushed, but we really didn't have a choice.

The door opened enough for Che to ask for Marc, who squeezed his thin frame out of the partially cracked door and waddled over in the superskinny black jeans secured on his nonexistent behind by a thick black leather belt with a trail of black leather studs. I never understood why grown-ass men felt the need to dress like they were in high school, and I wondered if he realized he wouldn't have to waddle if he'd just pull his damn pants up. He was going to have major hip problems in the future. Marc's fitted stonewash button-down, fresh and crisp earlier in the day, now looked rumpled, the sleeves pushed up above his bony elbows. The stress visible on his baby face made me think he probably wanted to hang himself with the slim black leather tie around his neck.

"Look, Marc," I started when the frustrated publicist plopped down on the sofa next to me, "you and I both want the same thing—a great story that gets people talking about your artist and more importantly buying her new music. And I want a great story that gets people clicking on my site. And right now neither of us has what we want."

"I know, Nia," Marc whined with exasperation in his tired voice. "I'm trying to get her to get ready to shoot, but she keeps taking calls from Jerome who's trying to talk her out of doing the story and threatening to take the babies away. He's also going in on her on Twitter as we speak."

Lord, I hate social media sometimes. Drama now breaks in real time.

MJ had been monitoring the situation on his laptop next to me, so I knew an ugly Twitter battle was brewing and that the secrecy of our shoot and our exclusive could get out. I leaned over to MJ and asked him to call Janelle's manager, a surprisingly rational white guy named Chris Matteo, to see if he could get his client to log off Twitter. I was sure he didn't want this battle any more than we did, especially since his client's baby daddy was already in hot water with authorities over a video that had surfaced last week on WorldstarHipHop of Jerome and his boys getting blow jobs from groupies in a hotel suite after a concert.

"First of all, there's no judge on the entire planet that would give a gang-affiliated, two-time-convicted drug dealer turned misogynistic rapper custody of those babies. Second of all, Janelle needs to do what's best for her damn career so she can take care of those babies. And she has to get on this set in the next fifteen minutes or we're shutting it down. I need to speak with her right now."

I really couldn't afford to shut this shoot down. I needed this story just as much as Janelle did, but I hoped my Billy badass bluff would work, because I knew no one on her squad was going to be able to get her to do anything. The problem with celebrity entourages is that no one is willing to tell the star no. No one is willing to get kicked off the gravy train by telling the star what he or she needs to hear instead of what he or she wants to hear.

"OK, but are you sure you want to talk to her?" Marc asked as we stood up to head back over to the dressing room. I slipped back on the Guiseppe Zanotti suede open-toe booties I had kicked off as the afternoon had worn on. Smoothing down the front of my black leather leggings, I put on a camel-colored oversize Donna Karan asymmetrical wrap sweater over my thin black tissue-paper T-shirt and pushed up the sleeves. It was time to do battle.

"Just clear the dressing room so Janelle and I can talk in private." I tried to sound confident as we walked, but I wasn't sure what was going to happen once we were alone. I hated celebrities. Why couldn't all stars be nice and professional like Gabrielle Union or Beyoncé?

"Don't worry, Marc," MJ said. "She's got this."

Marc went into the dressing room. Within a few minutes, the door opened, and Janelle's personal assistant/homegirl, Aisha; her best friend, Darla; her sisters, Monique and Lisa; and the Detroit hairstylist and makeup artist all filed out behind him. As Marc passed me, he squeezed my arm and shook his head.

When I walked into the room and closed the door behind me, I was pleasantly surprised to see that Janelle's hair and makeup had already been done and she was dressed in white. She was just five feet tall, and it was hard to believe that all of today's drama was emanating from that tiny body. Janelle was a dark brown beauty with large cat eyes, sharp cheekbones, full juicy lips, and a thick glossy mane of natural curly hair worn like a halo around her head. She had burst onto the music scene about five years ago with her hypnotic, husky voice that sang a string of soulful female empowerment anthems that earned her Grammy awards and a legion of young fans. But the last two years had been rough. A poorly received role in a Tyler Perry film, her volatile on-again-off-again relationship with Jerome, and her last album, for which she dropped the hit-producing team that had launched her career for some of Jerome's producers, had alienated a large part of her fan base who posted scathing comments online, saying they no longer knew who she was or for what her music stood. Marc had managed to talk sense into Janelle's head and get her to make amends with her original producing team for the release of this new album, which was starting to get a lot of buzz, but getting back with Tech would not help the comeback story.

I was happy to see the babies were sleeping peacefully in a playpen in a corner of the room despite the afternoon's ruckus. I also noticed that some of the shoes and bangles that we had pulled for the shoot were sticking out of a large bag in the corner. Dammit, I hated when celebs and their entourage took things from the shoot. Most of the time it wasn't even the celebs themselves who were trying to make off with a pair of hot new shoes or a handbag that hadn't yet hit stores but most likely one of their crew of hangers-on-type folk thinking they could cop some free clothing, shoes, or jewelry, not realizing or caring that the stylist who pulled the merchandise would have to pay the designer for the missing wares. If you had the misfortune of having to confront them about missing merchandise, they always said something like "I thought you had pulled all these things for (insert celeb name here) to take home" or "Designers always let me keep their things from the shoot," or my personal favorite, "We didn't take anything, and you can't prove it."

Janelle was seated in a director's chair with her back to the counter where a dizzying array of makeup, styling tools, and hair products was spread out.

"We need to have a come-to-Jesus, Janelle," I said, cutting to the chase although I knew I couldn't go balls to the wall just yet. I had to start with rule number one of celebrity relations—the requisite ego stroke—because most celebs were completely insecure and needed constant validation that they were still the most special thing in the world.

"You are an incredibly talented artist with millions of fans who are dying to hear your new music. They love you and can't wait to go out and start buying your album and seeing you in concert."

"Really? How do you know?" Janelle said. The ice-grill look on her face started to give way to something I would imagine no one ever got to see: vulnerability.

"Look, Janelle, ever since we started teasing this story online and promoting that it was coming, people have been posting that they can't wait for your new music. That they need your new music." I didn't tell Janelle that I told Che to turn on the comment-moderation tool for any story mentioning Janelle so that we could filter out the negative comments. I was sure some would consider that cheating, but I called it rule number two of celebrity relations: make sure those in your audience are perceived as being in the star's corner so that they come to you when they want to talk.

"I don't know. Jerome really doesn't want me to do this interview, and he's threatening to take away my kids." A tear slipped down her cheek as she reached for a tissue.

"I understand, J. But do you know what's important right now?"

"What?" she said, sniffing as she wiped her running nose.

Damn, don't mess up that makeup, I think to myself.

"What's most important, and the only thing you should be focused on, is sleeping peacefully over in that corner. Those babies, Sunshine and Moon, should be your sole focus. You have to do what's best for them. And what's best for them is for their mother to get her career back on track, not just so she can make money to take care of them, but so that their mother is happy and doing what she was born to do."

"But what if he takes them away from me?" she whined as she started to cry harder. "He's tweeting that he's going to take them away from me."

At that moment her iPhone buzzed on the counter, and she turned to grab it before I could take it away. I could tell from her expression that Jerome was calling again. If she got on that call, this shoot was dead.

"Janelle, honey, give me the phone," I said with my hand outstretched as I started to walk closer to her. "Don't answer the call. It's time for Janelle Greene to start talking care of herself and her children. No judge in the world is going to give him custody, and you know that. Give me the phone." I suddenly felt like a hostage negotiator, which I guess I kind of was since she was holding my shoot and my exclusive interview hostage. ·

It was time for rule number three of celebrity relations: show them that you identify with their work in your own life, and then quote their work from their movies, TV shows, or songs back to them.

"Last year I must have worn out your hit song 'Strong Woman' when I dumped my own man after finding out he was cheating on me and I got fired from my job all on the same day."

"Damn, sis, you broke up with your man and got fired on the same day?" she asked. She still hadn't answered the call although the phone kept ringing.

"Yes, and it was the most painful period in my life, but what got me through were your words: 'You can't beat me down. You can't take my pride. You can't make me fear. Because I'm a strong woman. Strong woman. Strong woman.'"

As I sang the last line of the song that I certainly had downloaded on my iPod but hadn't listened to more than twice, Janelle joined in, her husky voice becoming stronger with each word. She looked down at the phone screen with Tech's long dreadlocks hanging over his mean mug staring back at her, and she punched "Ignore" on the phone. She turned back to the mirror and stared at herself.

"I can do this. I am a strong woman."

"Yes, you are, Janelle. Yes, you are. And the world needs to hear your music and your story. You're going to help so many sisters with your powerful voice."

I wasn't going to take any chances that she'd get another call from crazy man, so I slipped her phone in the pocket of my sweater and took her hand to help her down from the director's chair.

"Let's go make some pretty pictures, girl," I said as we headed out the door. The room erupted in cheers and applause when we came out of the dressing room. The hair and makeup team started touching Janelle up. When MJ came over to me to give me my bag so that I could leave, I slipped him Janelle's phone and whispered in his ear that she shouldn't get this back until after the shoot and the interview.

Glancing down at my watch, I could see I needed to get a move on to meet Terrence. If Janelle hadn't wasted most of the day in her dressing room meltdown, I would have been able to preview some of the images, but I had to leave.

"Hey, Renaldo, make sure you e-mail me some images as you're shooting. I want to see how things are coming along." As I grabbed my Louis Vuitton tote stuffed with work from the office, I saw Janelle's assistant, Aisha, carrying Sunshine and Moon out of the dressing room onto the set, which reminded me of one last thing.

"MJ, make sure you tell Sharan to get all the merch from this shoot. Someone in the entourage thinks they are going on a shopping spree on our dime."

———

When I made my way downstairs from the studio, I saw Terrence leaning against a beat-up gray Lincoln sedan.

"New ride?" I asked. Dressed in dark jeans and a beige cashmere V-neck sweater and leather jacket, even standing against that beat-up car he still looked good. "This doesn't seem like the type of chariot your supermodel fiancée would ride in."

"Very funny," he said, making his way around to the passenger side door to let me in. "I checked it out from a buddy at my old precinct so we can go check on some things."

"Oooh, are we going on a stakeout?" I said as I laughed and rubbed my hands together. The comment about the fiancée had just slipped out before I could stop myself.

I caught another whiff of his new cologne. The smell was nice enough, but I preferred the natural clean soap scent he used to have when we were together. Well that doesn't matter anymore, I told myself. There's a new woman calling the shots in that department. Terrence walked around to the other side of the car and got in as I dropped my heavy bag on the floor. I dug around and pulled out the white envelope.

"It's not quite a stakeout, but you'll see, Detective," Terrence said as he started the car and pulled into the downtown traffic to head south down Broadway.

"Did you talk to Vanessa today? She's home, right?" Terrence asked.

"Yes, she's home, but I haven't talked to her since she left the doctor's office. She and Marcus are holed up in their apartment. I think they're trying to keep a low profile with the story about the attack coupled with the affair. I'm sure Kareem and his publicist are working overtime with the Gladiators to calm their concerns. This is not a good way to start off this new relationship. They don't seem like the type of organization that thinks that all press is good press."

"Definitely not. The Gladiators like to keep it clean and the focus on the team's performance on the court. But given that Marcus's wife was assaulted, they may be cutting him some slack as long as there are no new stories about Laila James and he doesn't appear in that reality show."

Within a few short blocks I started seeing signs for the Brooklyn Bridge.

"Where are we going?" I asked.

"Brooklyn."

"Why Brooklyn?"

"You'll see when we get there. Have patience." He chuckled, knowing that wasn't and had never been one of my strong suits. I reached over and began to fiddle with the radio dial in the old car.

"Hey, don't you know you don't ever touch a black man's radio?" he said in his best Chris Tucker impression as he swatted my hand way from the dashboard.

"Whatever, man," I said, laughing. "I was just trying to turn on 1010 WINS for some news after being trapped in a crazy episode of VH1's *Love and Hip-Hop* for the past five hours."

"Well that had to be fun."

"Oh, you have no idea the laughs we had. How was your day?" We were having a nice, normal after-work conversation, exchanging benign pleasantries just like any normal couple. But we were not a couple. I wondered if this felt weird to him, too.

"Good day. Very good day. Take out my iPad from my briefcase. I want you to look at a video." I picked up his black leather briefcase and put it on my lap. I could tell it was expensive; the leather was shiny and supple, and the platinum hardware gleamed. He'd never buy something like this for himself, so I knew she must have bought it. I opened up the iPad to the home screen.

"Where's the video?"

"It's in my e-mail. Look for the message from Ray Rogers with 'King Surveillance Video' in the subject line." I scanned his in-box, noticing there were quite a few unopened messages from his fiancée. When I located the e-mail from Ray, I opened the message. I pushed the button, and a grainy black-and-white video began to play, showing a steady stream of cars and cabs going by and people walking hurriedly down a street in Manhattan.

"What am I watching?" I asked, balancing the iPad on my lap.

"Keep watching," Terrence said as we crossed over the bridge into Brooklyn.

Suddenly out of the left side of the screen a large man dressed in all black came running down the street into the frame. He jumped into a car that was parked on the opposite side of the street and sped away. Then I realized what I was watching. This was the man who attacked Vanessa.

"Where did you get this?" I asked excitedly as I pushed the button to replay the video and held the iPad closer to see if I could make out the details of the man's face.

"My buddy, Detective Ray Rogers, is working the case out of the first precinct. He sent the file over. The video is from one of the city's thousands of crime watch cameras that happened to be located on the corner of Vanessa's street. Based on the time stamp on the video and Vanessa's description of her attacker, we believe this is our guy."

"Wow, this is amazing. Were you able to enhance the video to get a better look at the guy? Were there any other cameras in the area that may have provided a different angle so we could cross-reference and see his face?" I asked anxiously.

"What? Do you think this is my first case?" Terrence chuckled at my eagerness. "Of course we checked for other cameras in the area, and luckily Vanessa's building also had a camera outside that captured the license plate on the car."

"So you ran the plate, and what did you find?" I said as I twisted around to look at him.

"Yes, we ran the plate, and what we found was a name and address of one Carlo Esposito. We ran his sheet, and the twenty-three-year-old Mr. Esposito of Crown Heights, Brooklyn, has been a very busy man. He's got gang ties to the Diablo Negro crew—a cocaine, racketeering, guns, gambling, and sex-trafficking outfit with operations in Mexico, California, Arizona, Texas, and they've been pushing aggressively into New York over the last two years."

"And what is Carlo's specialty in this crew?" My body tensed. Was Vanessa targeted to be in a sex-trafficking ring?

"He's a pretty low-level enforcer type from what we can tell, but he was on the come up. Diablo Negro is one of the most vicious gangs we've ever seen, and young Carlo was trying to make a name for himself."

"But what's a guy like Carlo and a gang like Diablo Negro want with Vanessa? And is Carlo the one that's been leaving the messages?"

"Well, that's where things get even more interesting," Terrence said as he headed into the Crown Heights area of Brooklyn.

"What do you mean?"

"Carlo probably isn't even related to the threatening notes. He doesn't fit the profile worked up by my guy at Quantico. We'll look for prints on the envelope, but my best guess at this point is that he was waiting for Vanessa by her car and picked up the envelope off the windshield, just being nosy, when she came up on him. When he chased her, he still had the envelope, but he wasn't the one that left it. The stalker is someone else entirely different."

"So what you're saying is, Vanessa and Marcus are being stalked by someone, but this Carlo person attacked her for some completely unrelated reason? Was it a random attack, or was she targeted?"

"Yes, there are two people out there who have taken a very dangerous interest in Vanessa and Marcus. Carlo didn't attack Vanessa randomly— these guys don't work that way. They don't freelance. He was definitely acting on someone's order."

A chill ran down my spine as I shut down the iPad and slipped it back into Terrence's briefcase. Dealing with a crazy stalker fan was one thing, and sometimes par for the course in the high-profile world of professional sports, but why would a Mexican drug gang be after Vanessa? That piece of new information didn't make any sense.

"The police are arresting him as we speak, so hopefully we'll have some more information soon."

The car began to slow down as we approached the Quad, a nondescript four-unit brick housing project. A fleet of police cars and an ambulance were out front. A crowd of residents from the towers stood around, watching and gossiping. This wasn't looking good. I immediately wondered if the ambulance had anything to do with Carlo.

Suddenly the crowd parted as two paramedics burst through the doors of the building, wheeling a stretcher. I could see there was a large body underneath the white sheet. Terrence told me to wait by the car. He walked over to the group of police officers holding back the onlookers and then shook hands with one of the officers he seemed to know. He then ducked under the tape holding back the crowd and walked over to the stretcher. He lifted up the sheet and looked at the body. He then looked over at me and nodded his head in my direction.

Carlo was dead.

———

As we made our way back into Manhattan, I sent MJ a text and asked him to pull everything he could find on Carlo Esposito and Diablo

Negro. I needed to learn as much as I could about all of these players because since Carlo's throat had been cut, Terrence was only going to tell me so much.

We were both deep in our own thoughts as we made our way to my apartment in Chelsea when Terrence's phone rang. I looked over at the screen as he pushed "Talk" and saw that it was Vivica.

"Hey, baby," he said into the phone. My stomach clenched at the sound of him calling another woman "baby" although I knew I had no right to be upset.

"Busy day. I just left a crime scene in Brooklyn, and I've got a couple of other things to wrap up tonight, so I don't think I'm going to make dinner." I could tell she wasn't happy about that news.

"I'm sorry, Vivica," he said, lowering his voice as if he thought I couldn't hear him seated next to me. I could hear that her voice was elevated, but I couldn't make out the exact words. "Look, I'll call you later, and we can discuss it further. Do what you have to do."

"Ouch," I said. "Everything OK?"

"Yes, everything is fine," he said as his knuckles gripped the steering wheel.

"You can just let me out here, and I can grab a cab the rest of the way if you need to be somewhere."

"It's fine, Nia. Just leave it alone."

"OK, my bad . . ." We rode the rest of the way in silence. When the car pulled up in front of my apartment building, I began to gather my things to get out.

"Uh, you'll let me know about that Quantico report, right?" I said, turning to look at him.

"Oh shit. I forgot we were supposed to discuss that today. Do you want me to come up and we can go over it quickly?"

"Uh, sure. Come on up."

Why was I suddenly nervous? Terrence and I were just going to look at a file, discuss the contents, and then he was going to leave. No big deal.

I unlocked the door to my apartment and walked in, flipping on the light switches.

"Nice place," he said as he surveyed the space.

The one-bedroom loft wasn't large at only six hundred square feet, but the floor-to-ceiling windows in the sunken living room looked out to a terrace garden with a deck. The twinkling lights of the city as my backdrop had attracted me to the pricey apartment, which I decorated in a soothing palette of taupe and chocolate furniture with pops of citrus accents in the pillows. Some of my favorite elements were the bleach-blond wood floors, modern silver wall sconces, and mini crystal chandeliers. The galley kitchen, which I never used since I was in the city of endless takeout and delivery options, held my overflowing shoe and accessories collection in the cabinets. I was thankful I had resisted the urge to use the stainless steel refrigerator for more closet overflow. I grabbed a bottle of pinot, two wineglasses from the only cabinet where I stocked actual stemware, and walked back into the living room. Terrence had taken a seat on the low-slung black linen sofa and spread the contents of his briefcase out on the glass coffee table.

I placed the wineglasses on the table and took a seat next to him.

"Thanks," he said as he took a sip of the wine. "Very nice."

"Thanks. So what do we have here?" I grabbed the manila folder with the Quantico seal on the front and perused the profile they had worked up on Vanessa's stalker, but it was hard to focus with Terrence seated so close to me. I could feel the heat from his thighs as his leg pressed against mine when he leaned in to point something out.

"See, this indicates the stalker leaving the notes isn't Carlo. My guy has worked up motives and other identifiers to try to understand his, or her, behavior. For this person, the target—that would be Vanessa and Marcus—is personal. This is someone who feels a familiarity and more importantly feels like he or she is owed something. That's not the MO of Carlo and the Diablo Negro gang who are much more direct in how they conduct their business. What they do is never personal and is always about increasing their bottom line."

"But Vanessa told me she thought he was going to rape her. That seems personal."

"I'm not sure. I doubt he was sent to rape Vanessa. And he may have ended up dead because he failed at his task. But we'll learn more about that when we have his text messages translated."

"Text messages?"

"One of the officers securing the crime scene found his cell phone stuffed under the cushion of the chair he was sitting in when his throat was cut from behind. Going back through his exchanges, we saw a message with a photo of Vanessa attached."

"Oh my God, Terrence."

"We're running down the number. Hopefully it's not a disposable phone, but these guys in Diablo Negro aren't stupid. I doubt they'd take a chance communicating with a relatively low-level player like Carlo on one of their regular phones."

I took a large gulp of wine from my glass. The cool liquid did nothing to calm my nerves. I felt like Vanessa was in even more danger.

"Look, relax, Nia," Terrence said, taking my wineglass and setting it on the table. "I know you're worried about your girl, but the NYPD is all over this, and we're going to keep a patrol car on her building around the clock. And I'm sure Kareem is stepping up the private security as well. We're going to catch this guy."

I felt the sting of hot tears prickling in my eyes, and I blinked to keep them from falling. Terrence picked up the wine bottle and poured me another glass, which I accepted. I took another deep swallow to calm my fears for Vanessa and to hopefully tamp down the quickening of my pulse from being so close to Terrence again.

Suddenly he pulled me into his arms. I rested my head on his chest and against my better judgment inhaled deeply. I could feel his heart beat through the soft material of his V-neck sweater, and before I could stop myself, I placed my hand over it. It felt familiar to be in his arms again. I felt like there was something still between us. I was wondering if he felt it, too, and then I felt his lips.

He kissed the top of my head softly and stroked my short hair. I looked up at him, and then our lips connected.

Our mouths opened easily to each other, our tongues dancing like old friends reunited. His mouth was warm and wet, tasting of melted chocolate and a hint of fresh mint. Delicious and hypnotic.

I shouldn't be doing this. What we had was over. He's engaged.

But none of that seemed to matter as the rising heat of passion began to spread through both of our bodies and our limbs became entangled. His lips rained down kisses along my neck as I leaned into him, hungry for more.

He laid my body down on the sofa, and his long hard body was on top of mine. He kissed me again deeply on the mouth, his large hands moving slowly up and down the sides of my body before slipping underneath my thin T-shirt. His lips soon found my hard nipples straining up against the thin fabric of my shirt, and he pulled at them gently, torturing me. His hot breath moved over the tops of them, teasing me through the fabric. I arched up against him, my body betraying me by begging him for more. I didn't want him to stop. But as I felt the growing hardness in his pants and the silky wetness in my own panties, I knew we had to stop now or there would be no turning back.

"We shouldn't," I said huskily as I attempted to push him away, but he responded by pulling me closer.

"Nia," he groaned in my ear, his voice thick with desire. He wanted me just as much as I wanted him. I forgot the way he said my name and how that always made me tingle all over.

"No, seriously, Terrence. We have to stop." This was getting out of hand. As much as I didn't want to, I forced myself to push him away and to stand up. The room was hot, and I felt like I was suffocating. I took off the thick sweater to try to cool myself off and threw it on the chair. Terrence stood up and gathered his things as I took the wineglasses and bottle back into the kitchen. Outside of his view, I set down the glasses and bottle and leaned against the fridge.

Dammit, what had we started? I raked my fingers through my hair and tried to calm myself down. I reasoned that we hadn't actually done anything, so there was nothing to worry about, but then he hit me with a question that felt like a punch in the stomach.

"Where did we go wrong, Nia?" His dark eyes searched mine for answers and caused me to look down as I picked at invisible lint on my black T-shirt.

"Look, Terrence, what we had was a long time ago, and I don't think we should get into rehashing all of that. We both wanted and needed different things back then. And we just couldn't give it to each other."

The truth was the breakup had been hard for both of us, but we didn't have a choice. After Terrence was shot, I told him I was offered a new job in LA and that I hoped he'd come with me. Seeing him unconscious in that hospital bed was the worst night of my life. I prayed that he'd pull through and God answered. But when I begged him to leave the force and move to LA with me, he said he couldn't do it. And I said I couldn't watch him risk his life every day and wait for another phone call like the one I had received, not knowing if he was alive or dead. I couldn't live like that for him, and he said he couldn't give up on his dream for me.

"I'm sorry, Nia," Terrence said as he closed his briefcase and put on his jacket. "This won't happen again."

I was sorry, too. I was sorry we had stopped. But I couldn't say that to him now. He was engaged.

"It was my fault, too. I'm sorry. You're right, it won't happen again. I've never been the other woman, and I'm not about to start now."

As hard as it was for me to say, I knew it was the right thing to do. Terrence belonged to someone else now.

CHAPTER 12

Laila

The Glam Network camera crew trailed me as I pretended to shop at Suga' n' Spice, a trendy lingerie and sex toy store. We'd been running all over the city, shooting snippets of content so that they could cobble together clips for a ten-minute show reel they were producing to start teasing the show's premiere. And each stop required wardrobe, jewelry, a handbag change, and a new hairstyle so that all the clips looked like things were happening to me on different days. For this scene, I'd had the hairstylist put my hair up in a ponytail, and the stylist pulled some gold-threaded Miss Sixty jeans and a flowy black Narciso Rodriguez off-the-shoulder silk blouse with a keyhole design to show off my cleavage and six-inch crystal-studded Christian Louboutin Daffodil platform heels. The jeans were going to be murder to get off in the dressing room, but they appeared as if they had been painted on my body and made my ass look unbelievable on camera, so it was well worth the sacrifice.

Since the news broke that Glam Network was shooting my reality show, *Whatever Laila Wants*, the press and blogs had been going crazy, so the premiere date had been pushed up to capitalize on all the excitement and to coincide with the NBA All-Star weekend. The producer assigned to my show, Tanya Peoples, had set up this afternoon's scene as an outing for me to purchase some new goodies for an upcoming rendezvous. As I walked through the shop that was decorated like a

French boudoir, I discussed my desires with the skinny blond salesgirl, Stacey, who was eager to be on camera.

"Welcome to Suga' n' Spice. What can I help you with today?" Stacey drawled as she pretended to greet me for the first time. It was the third time we had shot this setup because this dumb salesgirl couldn't even get those two simple lines right.

"I'm looking for something sexy in red to surprise my boyfriend," I said as I sipped the champagne Stacey had poured for me upon my arrival. Unlike Stacey, I could remember my lines perfectly.

"What sort of style do you prefer?" Stacey asked as she led me over to a wall of expensive red corsets, teddies, and bra and panty sets.

"Well, we haven't seen each other in a while. He's been on the road, so I want to really blow his mind. What would you recommend?" The Glam Network legal team was nervous about my actually using Marcus's name in the show, so Miki told me to push as close to the line as possible without actually opening the network up to a lawsuit.

"Oh, that sounds fun," Stacey purred. "What kind of business is your boyfriend in?"

"Let's just say he's in professional sports and likes to go one-on-one with me."

We both laughed as I winked at Stacey and took another sip of champagne. Stacey pulled down some of the items and spread them out on top of a table so that we could select the best ones to try on. I selected three: a bra and crotchless panty set; a leather and lace corset; and a sheer teddy, and headed for the dressing room in the back of the store.

"And, cut," I heard Tanya yell to the cameraman, who had practically been running to the dressing room, hoping he was going to film me changing into this lovely lingerie. Sorry, Charlie. You'll just have to jerk off to your imagination later.

"OK, Laila, for this next scene we need you to try on the lingerie and come out to look at yourself in the mirror to see if you like the looks," Tanya said to me. "You'll ask Stacey for her opinion. And don't worry about any of the peek-a-boo parts on the lingerie; we'll blur those out on TV. Miki also suggested that you pull some things for tomorrow's photo shoot for your Times Square billboard promoting the show."

"Gotcha, Tanya," I said over my shoulder as I walked back into the dressing room. Once inside and well out of earshot of the camera, I set my champagne flute down on the small white table in the corner of the dressing room and then reached into my black quilted Dior bag for my cell phone. I hadn't been able to reach Marcus for nearly two days. Most of my text messages, e-mails, and calls went unanswered. All I had received was a short text saying he'd get back to me soon. This was not like Marcus.

Of course I had read about his wife's attack on Bossip, and it had been running on what seemed like a nonstop loop all over the TV news, but that was no reason to ignore my calls. When the news broke about the attack on Vanessa, Miki called right away, concerned that this would impact the story line in the show about my relationship with Marcus. I assured her that Marcus was fine. It wasn't like his wife was dead or anything.

But if everything was fine, why wasn't he returning my calls? Had something changed like Miki feared?

There was only one thing left to do. I had fought, clawed, and fucked my way to this point, and nothing was going to get in my way.

"Everything OK in there?" Stacey said, interrupting my thoughts with her perky voice.

"Yes, Stacey. I'll be out in a minute. Why don't you go grab me some more champagne?" I needed to send her away from the door so that I could make the call.

I turned off the microphone pack strapped to my waist, removed the strips of black tape securing the tiny microphone to the inside of my blouse, and set them both on the table next to my handbag. No way was I making the rookie mistake of letting the Glam Network sound engineer listen in on my conversation. I picked up my cell phone and dialed a number. The phone rang a few times and then went to voice mail.

Dammit, I can't reach him, either. I don't hang up the phone; it's time to leave a message.

"Kareem, this is Laila," I hissed in a low voice as I unbuttoned the tight Miss Sixty jeans to unpeel them from my body so that I could slip on the lingerie for this next scene. "You better return my call tonight. I'm not playing with you. We have a plan to follow. So don't even think about trying to fuck me over or you'll be very sorry."

I disconnected the call and then tossed the phone back into my handbag. I was sure Kareem would call me back soon. After all, he and I both knew he didn't have a choice.

CHAPTER 13

Vanessa

The tension in the apartment was so thick, we could forget needing a knife to cut it—Marcus and I needed a chain saw.

We had retreated to separate wings of the apartment. I had allowed him to come home last month since I didn't want to be alone in the apartment. We only came together to interact with Damon when he demanded we watch TV together or eat dinner. We were civil in his presence, but I'm sure the frosty chill in the air made Nicole want to turn up the thermostat in the apartment.

This morning, to escape the self-imposed prison our apartment had become, I walked down to the little mani-pedi spot around the corner after dropping Damon off at school. I was happy to see the reporters were gone so that I didn't have to worry about any prying telephoto lenses. I dipped into the small, empty salon. An attendant introduced herself as Ling and asked me to pick my nail color from the wall's cabinet. Scanning the bottles of OPI polishes, I quickly located my favorite, Lincoln Park After Dark, for both my hands and feet. Ling led me over to an elevated leather pedicure chair and turned on the massage button and heater. I dipped my feet into the warm scented water and let the jets massage my toes. I closed my eyes, my shoulders dropped, and I began to relax as I reflected on the last few days and formulated a plan.

When Marcus and I got back to our apartment that first night after I was released from Dr. Harrison's care, we retreated to separate corners of the penthouse. The next day when Marcus, who had slept in one of the guest rooms, brought a breakfast tray into our bedroom, I glanced over at the clock on the nightstand and saw that Nicole would have just dropped Damon off at school.

One look at him, my ribs throbbing from the attack, and it was war. I threw the crystal clock from the nightstand at his head. As Marcus ducked, he dropped the contents of the tray on the floor, spilling eggs, bacon, orange juice, and coffee. The clock crashed against the wall, shattering and spreading glass across the carpet.

"You have to give me some answers!" I screamed.

"I'm so sorry, V. You know I love you," he said as he walked over to the bed to hold me. Marcus seemed unsure of what to do, but he kept apologizing in his sorry-ass way, shaking his head as if even he didn't know how we had gotten here. His words were tired clichés with no meaning at this point. I pushed him away.

"What about the vows we took? What about the promises we had made to each other when we got married and you went pro? You swore to me that nothing, not a single thing, would ever come between us. Not your career, not Kareem, and not those nasty-ass groupies you can't seem to keep your hands off. Look at our life! It's a joke!"

"Vanessa, I can fix this," he pleaded. "I know you're right. I've lost sight of what matters, but I don't want to lose you and I won't lose my son." He paced in front of the bed.

"Ha! Yes, your son. The one who's counting on us to raise him together and looking to you to show him how to be a man. Is this how you show him how to be a man, by cheating on his mother with whores?"

"Look, you don't understand what life was like for me. Traveling around from city to city with everyone wanting something from you. It's hard, Vanessa. I'm just a man, and yes, I've been weak. But none of that matters now. Haven't I proved my love by giving you everything you could possibly want? The homes, the cars, the shopping sprees, the private jets, the jewelry. I work hard to provide all those things for you, so maybe this is the life of a professional athlete's wife, the price of admission."

"Everything I've ever wanted?" I screamed at him as I slapped his face hard. "I've given you everything you've ever wanted. A life. A home. A son. What about that? And as for me, the only thing I ever wanted was you, and I'd trade it all in just for that one thing. Now can you say the same?"

The weight of my words caused Marcus to fall back on the chaise lounge at the foot of our bed and drop his head into his hands. I wanted to hate him, but something inside still made me want to go to him. I steeled myself to stay where I was.

I gasped for air between sobs. Marcus came over to pick me up, but I pushed him away, screaming for him to leave our room and leave me alone. That was three days ago, and we hadn't spoken since.

My body was still sore, and I covered the bruising around my neck with turtlenecks when I was around Damon. I wasn't able to hide the swelling on my face, so we told our son that I got hit during a kickboxing class. Damon, a lover and not a fighter at age four, suggested I not go back if they were going to kick his mommy in the face. My bruised ribs were also starting to heal to the point where I barely winced when getting in and out of bed or standing from a seated position. But the physical part of healing was easy.

It was the emotional and psychological parts that were killing me. The nights were the worst. I was afraid to fall asleep and relive the attack in the parking garage. Dr. Harrison had prescribed sleeping pills, but they only made the night terrors worse because the pills were so strong, I had difficulty waking myself up out of the deep slumber and was trapped all over again with that man. I could see his ugly, twisted face and feel his hot breath on my neck. The weight of his heavy body on top of mine made me gasp for air. And unlike in real life, in the dream there was no Alex to save me, and the attack played out in an endless loop.

Most nights I slept with the lights on so that when I woke up from the nightmare, I could instantly see where I was, safe in my own bed. I also kept an extra pair of cotton pajamas on the bed next to me to change into after awaking from the nightmare because I'd be drenched in sweat as if I'd really been fighting off the man in the garage all over again.

When the detectives working on the case came by the apartment and told us that the man who attacked me was dead, I felt a tremendous sense of relief, but that didn't make the nightmares go away. They told me he was a low-level member of the Diablo Negro drug gang and that he had likely had his throat cut by a member of his own crew. Before I could ask any more questions, Marcus interrupted and said I needed my rest. He and Kareem would discuss the rest of the matter with the detectives in the library. Even though the monster haunting me in my dreams was dead, I still had a lot of questions. I couldn't help but wonder why this man had targeted me. Was my attack just a random act of violence in the big city, or had he specifically been looking for me?

The news of my attack hit the media, and the coverage was nonstop. The only good news that came out of it was that Laila was being portrayed by the media as the home-wrecking whore that she was and Marcus as the callous cheating husband. He didn't dare go out and get caught being seen with Laila. The press would have crucified him. And as for the Gladiators organization, they were very concerned. Owned by an ultraconservative hedge-fund group, the team's partners were loath to see their $150 million investment trashed in the press along with their hopes of bringing a championship to New York, so I knew without even asking that the heat had been put on Kareem to fix this nasty little matter. I could tell he was feeling the pressure from all the meetings he was having at the apartment with Marcus. Normally they talked business out in the open, but now the door was closed and the tones were hushed at times and elevated at others. Sometimes Desiree would join the strategy sessions.

With All-Star weekend approaching in just two short weeks, it was DEFCON 4 for the brand. Naturally, Marcus had been selected again to play in the All-Star game, but I'm sure he wished he hadn't been, because this year's game was being held in Phoenix, so all the stories trying to link the dead cheerleader to Marcus would likely resurface in addition to this latest news. I had also heard from Nia that Laila would be in town hosting a star-studded premiere party for her reality show. I had to attend the weekend because we were scheduled to host our annual Marcus and Vanessa King Foundation dinner to raise money for Saint Mary's Children's Hospital in Inglewood.

And just when I was sure things couldn't get any worse or any more complicated, Dr. Harrison called to tell me that I was eight weeks pregnant. I couldn't believe it. Marcus and I had been in such a deep freeze in our relationship for so long that I wondered how that was actually possible. But then I remembered that there was a night, about two months ago, before all the drama broke, when hair be damned, I slipped into the shower with Marcus after he'd come home from practicing with the team. Desperate for some physical contact and affection from a husband who was becoming increasingly distant, I slipped into the large stone shower and wrapped my arms around him, pressing my lips along his back. I took a bar of soap and began to lather his broad chest, working my way down as I pressed my full breasts into his back. Grabbing him in my soapy wet hands, I began to stroke him to arousal. He moaned with pleasure, and the hot water from the showerhead sprayed down over both of us. The steam enveloped us as I pushed him down onto the large stone seat in the corner of the shower and straddled him. Sliding down onto him, I arched my breasts into his mouth and squeezed his shoulders as he licked the water from my breasts and squeezed my hips, pulling me into him deeper. We exploded together and then went limp against the cool shower wall. After we both dried off, I suggested we get dressed and go out to enjoy a nice dinner at the new Italian restaurant that had opened around the corner from our building. Marcus hurriedly slipped into some fresh clothes and said he had to get to a meeting with Kareem about another new potential endorsement. He was out the door before I could even object or ask if we could meet later.

He didn't return home until nearly three in the morning.

After finding out from Dr. Harrison that I was pregnant, I scheduled an appointment with my regular ob-gyn, Dr. Carter, who congratulated me in confirming that I was about eight weeks along and prescribed some prenatal vitamins. As with my first pregnancy, I was having little morning sickness and I wasn't gaining weight yet, so it was easy to hide my condition. Since Marcus and I slept at opposite ends of the apartment, it wasn't like he would notice that anything was different. But things were different.

As Ling finished up my pedicure, I wiggled my glossy toes.

"Beautiful," I said to her as I slipped my freshly polished toes into the paper slippers and then climbed down from the chair to head over to the manicure station for my nails. I noticed a teaser from *Extra!* playing on the flat-screen TV mounted on the wall. The sound was off, but I could understand everything I needed to as the screen cut to a clip of the show's host, Mario Lopez, standing at the Grove, the outdoor shopping center in West Hollywood where they shot the show. The calm relaxation I had felt earlier evaporated when I saw Laila, dressed in a skintight strapless dress with her long brown hair cascading in curled waves down her back, talking to an animated Mario. Clearly that was the night's big story.

"Relax," the technician said, patting my hands that had balled into fists at the sight of the woman trying to break up my marriage. "Relax now for a good manicure."

She was right: I needed to relax. Not just for a good manicure, but so that I could be in control. And seeing Laila being interviewed on *Extra!* had given me the idea for what I was going to do next.

This bitch thought she was going to take my man, but she had another thing coming.

I was having another baby.

This was going to change everything, whether Marcus and Laila liked it or not.

CHAPTER 14

Nia

As I watched Vanessa make her way through the maze of diners to our table for lunch at DB Bistro, a trendy Midtown eatery, I could tell that something was different. And it wasn't just the oversize Chanel sunglasses she was wearing on an overcast morning that made me suspicious. Despite going through what anyone would consider two months from hell, she looked great. Dare I say she even glowed? I wasn't sure she would still have that glow, though, once I told her what Terrence and I had dug up.

"Girl, what is going on with you?" I said, laughing as she leaned in for a hug.

"What do you mean?" she said coyly as she laughed and took off her heavy gray shearling coat and tossed it, along with several Henri Bendel shopping bags, into the seat next to us. She looked great in a simple black turtleneck and black wool slacks.

"Don't play with me, girl. What's got you glowing today? Shoot, the last time I saw you with that glow, you were pregnant with Damon . . ." My voice trailed off. "Oh shit . . . *Are you pregnant?*" I said as I reached for my glass of water and took a large gulp. This was not good news.

"Yes, as a matter of fact, I am," Vanessa said with a Cheshire cat smile curved on her glossy brown lips.

"How? Why? When?" I couldn't get the questions out fast enough.

"Well, I think you're certainly old enough to know how it happened, or do you need a refresher course since you ain't had none in a while?" she said, chuckling.

"Whatever, heffa. Don't even try to play stupid with me. You know what the hell I mean. And for your information, I may not have had some in a while, but I had a near miss that you're going to want to hear about later."

"Oh, juicy. Do tell, girlfriend." She squeezed a lemon into her water glass and then began to peruse the menu. "I'm starving. What's good here?"

"Don't try to change the subject. You ain't slick. For real, what's going on?" I pushed down the menu and leaned in, staring her dead in the eye.

"OK, OK . . . Look, yes, I'm pregnant," she said as she grabbed a warm roll from the bread basket in the center of the table. "It happened a few months ago. We were in the shower and one thing led to another and now I'm pregnant. There you go, the whole story. And, no, Marcus doesn't know." Vanessa patted her still-flat stomach proudly and continued to scan the restaurant menu.

"What do you mean Marcus doesn't know? How have you not told your husband?"

"I'm just waiting for the right moment."

"Hmm . . . I don't know what your plan is, girl, but you need to stop playing games." While I knew I should be happy for my friend, the state of her marriage and the fact that there was a dangerous person out there targeting her family didn't make me think that this was the ideal time for Vanessa to be having another baby.

The waiter appeared to share the day's specials and take our orders, which provided a break in the conversation so that I could gather my thoughts. I wasn't sure if I should be happy for my best friend or sad. Any fool could see that if she was thinking that this pregnancy was going to save her train wreck of a marriage, then sister girl was sadly mistaken. I wanted to tell her that this wasn't some after-school special. This was real life, and real life doesn't end like some Lifetime movie where the long-suffering wife fights for her man and gets him in the end.

"You do realize this is completely insane? You were just attacked in your garage, you still have some crazy stalker out there, and your husband is sleeping with a wannabe reality star. Explain to me how this is the perfect time to have another baby."

"Nia, I'm fighting for my marriage and my family right now, and that's all that matters. The guy that attacked me is dead, and the police told Marcus and Kareem that it was an unfortunate random act of violence. There's nothing more to it. And as for the stalker, we haven't had a new note in over two months. Perhaps that psycho has moved on to someone else and that nightmare is over."

Her voice sounded like she desperately wanted to believe everything that she said. Because of her condition, I didn't have the heart to bring up the note that Kareem had in his possession at Dr. Harrison's office or what Terrence and I learned.

"So that brings me to my other reason for wanting to get together for lunch today." Vanessa buttered another roll from the bread basket. I had forgotten how this girl could throw down some food when pregnant.

"You mean it wasn't just for my sparkling personality?" I said mockingly. "I'm afraid to ask." I pushed my own plate away and braced myself for another nuclear bombshell.

"I want you to break the news about the pregnancy on the *DivaDish* site. I'm giving you the exclusive." She looked very pleased with herself as she dug into the grilled salmon the waiter had placed in front of her.

"Vanessa, are you sure you want to do this? As much as you know I'm all about an exclusive, and I would love to be the first to post this story, for God's sake, you haven't even told Marcus—hello, your husband—that you're pregnant." Suddenly I had lost my appetite for the rosemary roasted chicken breast and fingerling potatoes that my mouth had been watering for just a few seconds earlier.

"Nia, I'm positive," she said between bites of her fish. "This is what I want to do. And if you don't want the story, I'm sure *Ebony* or *Us Weekly* would." She had that look in her eyes that meant she had made up her mind and there was nothing I could do to change it. She was right: either I could run the story, get the credit for breaking the news, and get the spike in traffic or I could let it go to one of my competitors and get my ass handed to me by DeAnna who would no doubt be busting down my door when she found out we lost this exclusive.

"V., look, this is crazy. Why don't you take some time to think about this some more? You don't have to decide now. What's the rush?"

"Not to play the total bitch card or anything, but Nia, we've been best friends forever, and not for nothing did I basically get you this job at *DivaDish*, and if you can't do this one thing . . ." Vanessa's voice trailed off. I couldn't believe she was throwing introducing me to DeAnna back in my face, but if that was how she wanted to play, I'd treat her just like any other celebrity who had come to us with a big juicy exclusive.

"OK, Vanessa. If this is what you really want, we'll run it. But if we're going to do it, let's do it all the way. I want to crash your story into the magazine as the cover. We're going to need a photo shoot and an in-depth interview that discusses the pregnancy, the attack, Laila, and the state of your marriage. That's what people want to know. Are you really willing to go there?"

"I was hoping you would say that, Nia. I'm totally ready to give you and your team whatever you need."

"You do realize this issue will drop on the Friday of All-Star weekend?" I looked at her with an eyebrow raised, letting her know she wasn't fooling anybody and that she was playing with fire.

"Yes, of course I know. That's the perfect time." Vanessa nodded as she turned and dove back into the rest of her lunch with a self-satisfied smile.

"You are killing me right now, you know that?" I said, picking at my now-cold roasted chicken.

"Whatever, girl. You know you love me. Now let's get back to your almost getting some or whatever you were alluding to earlier. What happened? Did you get a new vibrator or something?"

"Ha, ha, very funny. No, I didn't get a new vibrator."

"Then what happened? You know you haven't had any since that jerk-off king Eric back in LA, so I'm sure you had to vacuum that thing out before getting down to the nasty," she said, chuckling.

"Last week, Terrence was at my apartment and well, I said some things and then he said some things . . . And next thing I knew we were kissing." I felt the warm blush creeping up my face as I tried to bury my face in my plate.

"Shut up, girl. And you ain't even call me! You know you are so wrong for that. What happened? You know I need all the details. And why'd you say you almost got some? I know you ain't trying to save nothing. After all, he's already had it, girl."

"Damn, V. Why you gotta be so harsh?" I said, laughing. "We started kissing and he was rubbing all over my body and, girl, you know it was feeling a little too good and then I had to tell him to stop."

"Stop? You told that fine-ass man, the love of your life, to stop?"

"Yes, Vanessa. I told him to stop. Hello, he's engaged. Remember? And to that supermodel Vivica no less."

"Whatever. You know that man isn't going to marry her. He's probably still in love with your crazy ass. You should have hit that for real."

"Hit that? Are you serious right now? Didn't I just say that man is engaged? Given what you've been going through, I figured you would be on her side. I can't do that to her. Like I told him, I've never been the other woman, and I'm not about to start now."

"I hear you and all about being the other woman, but check it, you and Terrence got some unfinished business and something deeper than what he has with Ms. Thing. And while I certainly don't advocate cheating, I do think when two people are meant to be, there's nothing that can stand in the way."

"OK, are you talking about me and Terrence right now or you and Marcus?"

"Might as well be both as far as I'm concerned. You can act like that ship has sailed if you want, but I see how your eyes light up when you talk about him like you think nobody is going to notice. I've never, in the twelve years I've known you, seen you so deep in love. And certainly not with the computer nerd in LA who used all your expensive-ass Crème de la Mer to polish his knob. *Ick . . .*"

"Well, whatever. There's nothing I can do about it now. He's engaged, and I'm not letting it go any further. What we had is officially black history. Over and out."

"Whatever you say, girl. Whatever you say."

—

When I got back to the *DivaDish* offices, MJ grabbed me at the door.

"I'm glad you're back," he whispered as we walked down the hall to my office. "DeAnna's in your office, and girlfriend is on the warpath today."

"What's got her panties twisted today?" I said as I handed MJ my trench coat and handbag.

"I don't know, but when I told her you were on your way back from lunch and that I was happy to send you right over when you returned, she just plopped her butt right down in your chair and said she'd wait."

"Shit, I'm not in the mood for her drama today." I smoothed my hair into place and took the MAC Lipglass from MJ's outstretched hand to quickly dab on my lips before entering my office.

There was DeAnna seated in my chair, scrolling through messages on her BlackBerry. I was at least glad to see she wasn't on my computer. I was sure MJ had remotely shut it down to keep it away from her prying eyes. Hopefully she hadn't snooped around my desk and seen the folder with the extensive research that MJ had compiled on Diablo

Negro. I breathed a small sigh of relief when I saw that the folder was still on the side of my computer keyboard where I had left it.

"Good afternoon, DeAnna," I said. "To what do I owe the pleasure of having you come over to my side of the floor?"

DeAnna looked up from her PDA and tapped her glossy red nails on my desk before she spoke.

"Well, I wanted to speak to you about an important new partnership that's sure to triple the traffic on your website. Is that something you could be interested in?" She raised one of her razor-thin eyebrows at me to punctuate her rhetorical question.

"That sounds exciting, DeAnna. Do tell." I remained standing because I refused to take a seat at one of the chairs in front of my own desk.

"Well, it's just come down from corporate that today we are announcing that PrimeTime Media is acquiring the Glam Network. As you know, their stable of reality TV and very desirable audience of young influentials eighteen to thirty-four years old are highly coveted and will make a great addition to our company. And our CEO wants to make sure that all the divisions of the company are incorporating Glam Network content and talent into our sites and magazines."

I swallowed hard and braced myself for the Mack truck now coming for me.

"And as part of our first initiative, *DivaDish* is going to be the exclusive event, web, and magazine partner to their hottest property, the new reality show *What Laila Wants*."

"Uh, partner?" How was I going to partner with the tramp that was breaking up my best friend's marriage?

"Yes, partner, Nia," DeAnna said, sighing at what she clearly viewed as my obtuseness.

"You and I are going to have a meeting with Miki Woods, the VP of reality programming, this afternoon at three o'clock to discuss plans for our sponsorship and coverage of Laila's premiere party at All-Star weekend in Phoenix next week. Please be prepared to discuss other ideas about how we can integrate Laila and the show into the magazine and on the site."

All I could manage was to nod my head affirmatively as my mind reeled with this new turn of events.

"Look, Nia, this isn't going to be a problem, is it?" DeAnna asked. "As I've discussed with you before, you can't let your friendships and misplaced loyalties get in the way of business. I hope I can count on you to get this done. If not, let me know, and I'll find someone who will."

With that final statement, DeAnna stood up and strode out of my office. MJ scurried in after she left and closed the door. I sat down in my chair and put my head in my hands.

"What's going on?" MJ asked. "What did she want now?"

As I ran down the details of the acquisition of Glam Network and the orders to integrate their content and talent into our properties, MJ's eyes became wide.

"You mean we have to work with that skank-ass tramp, Laila?" he said, shaking his head. "Girl, for once I wish our office was like an episode of *Mad Men* and I could get you a stiff one from the office drink cart, 'cause you need it."

"You ain't never lied, MJ. How am I going to explain to Vanessa that I now have to not only work with Laila, but I also have to sponsor her premiere party?"

"Look, she'll understand. It's business, right? It's completely out of your control. What could you possibly be expected to do about it?"

"I haven't even told you the other piece. Brace yourself," I said as I ran down Vanessa's own breaking news about her pregnancy and her request that we be the ones to break the story.

"OK, seriously. Damn a drink cart, we need to get to the nearest bar. Do not pass go and do not collect two hundred dollars. It's like we're in an episode of *One Life to Live* up in this piece."

"I know, it's crazy, right? What the hell am I going to do?"

"I don't even know, but it does, however, look like we're going to All-Star. What am I going to wear with all those handsome ball players checking me out?" MJ kicked his legs out in the chair and pointed his toes like a Vegas showgirl.

"Don't nobody at the All-Star weekend want your crazy ass," I said, sucking my teeth.

"Watch," MJ said, running his index finger down his skinny little legs. "You just wait and see. When those boys get a look at all of this? Irresistible."

"I so can't even stand you right about now," I said, shaking my head and turning to my computer while cringing at the thought of my overflowing e-mail in-box. I took the file with the Diablo Negro information and dropped it into my Louis Vuitton tote under my desk so that I wouldn't forget to take it home tonight to read.

"You know you love me. OK, back to work. I'm going to go grab Che, so you can tell her to get cracking on her big exclusive interview with Mrs. King, and I'll alert the photo editor to start coming up with concepts for the accompanying photo shoot," MJ said as he switched out of my office with thoughts of All-Star dancing in his head.

CHAPTER 15

Laila

The Los Angeles sunshine felt so good and was certainly a welcome change from cold New York in February. I'm glad Miki Woods suggested meeting in West Hollywood at the Ivy for lunch today so that we could sit outside on the patio and I could ditch the heavy layers for a cute strapless Michael Kors safari-style dress, fuchsia snakeskin ankle-wrap Manolo Blahnik sandals, and my new Gucci sunglasses. I knew I always had to be ready when the paparazzi started clicking. I'd have to make sure to stroll down Melrose and dip in and out of a few boutiques so that the photographers could get some full-length shots as well. This dress was too cute to waste on just being shot seated at a table. Plus, that wouldn't get me any more free clothes from Michael Kors if the PR rep didn't see their designs photographed on me in magazines and online.

Another bonus of today's lunch: a sister could work on her tan and get a little glow back in her brown skin while Miki discussed the launch plans for the show as well as the photo shoot for our joint *Black Enterprise* cover for a story on the big business of reality TV. This was a big week of nonstop meetings, interviews, and photo shoots leading up to the *Whatever Laila Wants* world premiere party at the Desert Palms Club in Phoenix at the end of the week. And even though a lot of the ball players were scheduled to host their own annual event that Friday night, the Glam Network events team said they were already turning people away from the party. Sounds like a good problem to have.

But a bad problem to have was that it had been two weeks since I heard from my baby, Marcus. And Kareem was suddenly a ghost as well. I understood that Marcus was holed up with that crazy wife of his, but he could at least shoot me a text message or respond to the sexy photo I sent to him from the Suga' n' Spice dressing room. I mean, damn.

Just then my thoughts were interrupted by the buzzing of an incoming text. I grabbed my iPhone from the top of the table where I had set it earlier, hoping that it was Marcus finally returning one of my many messages. I looked down at the phone. Damn, it was only Kareem.

-Just landed in LA . . . What time can U meet?
I typed back quickly: *Meet at L'Ermitage hotel, my room 1042 @ 7:00.*
-Perfect, I'm staying down the street at Four Seasons.
-Whatever, don't be late.

I tossed the phone into my new Marc Jacobs clutch I had scooped up at Neiman Marcus yesterday. Then I saw Miki pull up to the valet stand in front of the restaurant in a sleek white BMW roadster with the top down and Jay Z blasting. I got to admit, I liked her style. This cocoa-brown sister with natural curly hair that framed her face must have been at least five foot ten without heels. Wearing one of her signature Gucci suits and crisp white blouses, Miki was a powerful Hollywood player that I was happy to have on my team. She was also a serious ballbuster who, at just twenty-nine, had bulldozed her way into the reality TV space with a roster of hit after hit must-see shows. She had changed the landscape of reality TV and the Glam Network fortunes, so my agent, Steven, wasn't happy that I wanted to take today's meeting solo. He only agreed not to crash the lunch when I promised him that I wouldn't verbally agree to anything we hadn't already approved and that I, of course, wouldn't sign any papers he hadn't reviewed in advance. I told him it would all be fine and that I'd call to fill him in right after we finished.

"Hello, love," Miki said after the hostess walked her over to my table in the center of the brick patio. She had first stopped to greet Nia Long who was lunching with Gabrielle Union, and *Jet* magazine editor in chief Mitzi Miller lunching with Steve and Marjorie Harvey. I made a mental note to confirm that they were all included on the list for the launch party.

"Hi, Miki. Smooches," I said as she leaned down to kiss me on the cheek. She then set her orange Hermès portfolio and large black crocodile Birkin bag on one of the empty chairs at our table and then took off her tapered black blazer and hung it along the back of her chair.

"Whenever I have a chance to come out to Los Angeles, I always salivate for one of their delicious Cobb salads," she said as she dismissed the hovering hostess who tried to hand her a menu with a wave of one of her French-manicured hands.

"That sounds delish, Miki," I said, following her lead and handing the hostess my menu as well. Our waiter, a dead ringer for Ashton Kutcher's younger brother if I ever saw one, came over to fill our water glasses and take our drink orders.

"So, how is my newest reality star doing?" Miki asked as she smiled brightly and squeezed a fresh slice of lemon into her glass.

"I'm good, Miki. Just eager for my show to premiere. I've been tweeting and posting comments on Facebook, writing on my Tumblr, and posting photos."

"Our marketing team is so excited that you're so into social media. I think last I heard, you had over six hundred and fifty thousand followers on Twitter!"

"I broke a million last night when I posted some of the outtakes from the lingerie shopping trip. Don't worry, it wasn't too much to give away the episode, but I posted two shots and asked my fans which outfit I should wear to surprise my boyfriend. And the *Extra!* TV segment with Mario Lopez last night to tease the show helped also."

"That's great. Keep tweeting, posting to Facebook and Tumblr, Pinterest, and any other of the key social media sites. We want to continue to build the grassroots buzz for the show's launch. I want your new show to be the biggest debut our network has ever had."

"You know I'm ready to get my hustle on, Miki. Don't you worry." The waiter returned with our Cobb salads and set them in front of us.

"I'm a hustler, too, Laila. I didn't get to be VP of Reality TV at Glam Network at twenty-five without taking some risks and being able to know a star and a hot concept when I see one," she said confidently in between bites of her salad.

"And that's why I'm so thrilled to be on your team. We're going to make history because I came to win. Everybody ain't about this life. But I am, and nothing is going to stand in my way."

"I'm glad to hear that, because I have some more news for you. As you may or may not have heard, Glam Network was just acquired by PrimeTime Media Group."

Oh shit. They were taken over. Was this chick about to tell me she was leaving? I braced myself to call little Ashton back over with a stiff drink as she continued. I knew I couldn't do this show without her. I reached for my iced tea and took a long draw from the straw to calm my stomach.

"So with Glam Network being acquired by one of the largest media companies in the world, we now have many more platforms and internal partnerships that we can exploit for the launch of your show. Before I jumped on the company jet to leave New York last night, I had a meeting with DeAnna George, the president of publishing at PrimeTime Media and the editor in chief of *DivaDish*, Nia Bullock, to discuss how we can work together. She's cool. I'm sure you'll really like working with her."

"That's great, Miki. I like the sound of that and look forward to meeting her." I exhaled and took a small bite of my salad. I didn't want to risk one of the lurking paparazzi snapping an unflattering photo of me shoveling food in my mouth or chewing with big chipmunk cheeks for *Us Weekly*'s "Stars, They're Just Like Us section." No way.

"No, this is huge," Miki said as her face lit up and she became more animated. "Your show is not only going to have the full support of all the relevant magazines and websites, but *DivaDish*, along with Moët, is going to sponsor your All-Star party and stream it live on their site. Our PR team was also pushing for a magazine cover, but apparently Nia says she has some big exclusive already booked for the next issue. Not sure what could be bigger than the debut of your show, but whatever."

"I know that's right," I said as I pushed my bangs out of my eyes. "What could possibly be bigger than the launch of *Whatever Laila Wants*? It would have been great to have that cover at the All-Star launch party."

"Don't even worry about it," Miki said as she shook her head and pointed her fork at me. "Seriously, this partnership, the social media stuff you're doing, the dozen other TV interviews our PR team has set up, and the *Black Enterprise* cover, will guarantee tune-in for your show and definitely be the biggest launch we've ever had."

"Wow, Miki, I don't even know what to say. And you know I'm never speechless." Finally, things were really coming together for me.

"But I need to keep it one hundred with you, too, Laila," Miki said, her gaze turning steely. "You must deliver on Marcus King. Everyone's tuning in because they think they are going to be voyeurs into your secret relationship and your glamorous lifestyle. Your fans and viewers expect to get a window into a rarefied world that they don't have access to, and frankly they want to be judge, jury, and possibly even executioner for this scandalous relationship. You have to prepare yourself for the hate that's going to come your way. Marcus's wife, Vanessa King, while not highly visible, is well liked especially because she's the mother of his child. We tested you both in focus groups. You are going to feel the heat. But that always makes for great TV, and with as much shit as people want to talk about you, they are going to keep tuning in week after week and make you a very rich woman."

Now it was my turn to give this chick the real steely gaze.

"Let me keep it one hundred with you, too, Miki. You don't know half the things I've had to do to get here, and there's no way I'm ever going back. I don't mean to sound like Oprah in *The Color Purple*, but all my life I've had to fight. I've had haters since the day I was born, and I'll have them until the day I die. I'm about getting this money and getting my man. And there's nothing that's going to stop me, no matter what the little focus group said."

"Nice. I like your gangster. And that's exactly why I named the show *Whatever Laila Wants*. I'll ride with you until the end as long as you deliver everything we discussed. This show can be a game changer for both of us, Laila."

"Whatever you need, Miki. I got you."

"Cool. Legal is still reviewing the text messages, the tape-recorded conversations, and photos Steven sent over to make sure we have all the legal documentation we need to incorporate them into the show as needed."

"Sounds good to me," I said as I smiled and tilted my head so that the paparazzi could get a good shot of me.

—

Brixton Marshall was the celebrity stylist that Glam Network had hired to pull dresses, shoes, and accessories for tomorrow's *Black Enterprise* photo shoot with Miki, as well as for all the All-Star events, including my big launch party at the end of the week. He had just completed his run-through with me, and as I closed the door of my hotel suite behind him and his team, I was relieved to be done with my eighth appointment of the day.

I walked past the two racks of designer dresses in sequins, feathers, leather, and silk in every imaginable color that Brixton had wheeled into the room just hours earlier. I had given him two requirements for all clothing: tight and tiny. Very simple. Luckily, he had brought his seamstress with him, as most of the dresses were too long for my tastes. I wasn't some old lady, and my sexy-ass thighs that made men from coast to coast salivate were made to be seen and photographed, so we were definitely not selecting any dresses that would cover them up. I hit the Pilates studio at least three times a week, and they were ready for their close-ups.

Admittedly it had been fun playing dress up as I slipped in and out of fabulous party dresses from Dolce & Gabbana, Stella McCartney, Marchesa, and Hervé Léger for the first hour and a half, but I was worn out. I would have loved to take a nap before dinner at Crustacean in Beverly Hills with Shelly Jennings, the reporter from *Black Enterprise.*

It was only Wednesday, but I was already exhausted. I was up at the crack of dawn yawning with the hair and makeup team by seven and in the chauffeured Lincoln Navigator by eight to head to the first appointments. All day there were interviews, appearances, and branding meetings. I felt like my smile was plastered on my face. But a hustler never sleeps. Just ask Kim Kardashian.

I changed into some denim cutoff shorts and a white tank top, and put my long hair up into a ponytail to get comfortable for a few hours. Walking over to the coffee table in the living room, I pulled a bottle of red wine out of the huge gift basket stuffed with fruits, cheese, crackers, and cookies that *Black Enterprise* had sent to my suite. I poured myself a glass and went out onto the balcony to enjoy the view. As I leaned my hip up against the railing and took a sip of wine, I could see a red Lamborghini pull up to the valet stand. I wondered if it was Chris Rock or Charlie Sheen, both of whom I had scoped out in the dimly lit lobby earlier as they were taking meetings. As I leaned over the rail to get a closer look at who was getting out of the car, I made a mental note to invite him to the party as well. The driver, a very tall black man dressed in jeans and a white-and-black-striped button-down shirt, got out of the car and took off his sunglasses. It was Kareem. Good, at least his ass was on time.

Now, I'm never the type of chick to get shook. Ever. But given that I hadn't spoken with Marcus in two weeks and Miki's comments about delivering him for the show, this meeting tonight with Kareem was even more important. We had to get things ironed out tonight. I don't know what kind of game he thought he was playing, but I wasn't about to be the one that got burned. We both had too much skin in the game to walk away now.

—

"Come on in," I said, opening the door to my suite a few minutes later. Kareem smiled, but I wanted to smack the grin right off his face. He followed me down the hallway into the living room area of the suite, and I was sure he was enjoying the view of my denim shorts barely skimming the bottom of my golden brown cheeks.

Without speaking or asking, he poured himself a drink from the bottle of wine that I had just opened. As Marcus's cousin and agent, Kareem Davis certainly made the most out of his role, riding on Marcus's coattails and pretending to be the loyal, hardworking agent all these years. It had served him well.

I held out my empty wineglass to him so that he could pour me a refill as well. Kareem licked his full lips as his hooded gaze traveled up my smooth bare legs, took in the frayed denim strings from my shorts skimming across the tops of my toned thighs, and went up to my juicy breasts straining against the tight fabric of my thin tank top. I knew he could tell I wasn't wearing a bra and that excited him. Whatever. He knew it went without saying that he could look at this all he wanted, but there ain't nothing on this menu for him tonight. This brown sugar kitty kat belongs to his boy now.

Before I sat down, I walked over to close the French doors leading into the bedroom. No need to give him any ideas. That definitely wasn't jumping off tonight.

"Have a seat, Kareem," I said, motioning to the beige sofa as I walked over to sit opposite him in one of the brown arm chairs, my long toned legs dangling over the side.

"So you wanted this meeting, Laila. What's so urgent? What's on your mind?" Kareem asked as he looked down at his oversize chrome Rolex watch with the diamond face and then downed the contents of the wineglass in one gulp. Classless as always.

"You know what's on my mind. Marcus. Why hasn't he been returning my messages or made plans to get together?" I snapped.

"Well, in case you haven't read in every newspaper in the country or every website, his wife—you do remember that he has a wife, right? Well, Mrs. King was attacked, so you'll have to excuse Marcus if he can't attend to your every little need right now."

"Don't get cute, Kareem. We both know that Marcus is in love with me and wants a divorce. Just like we planned. And while I'll certainly admit it isn't the optimal time to leave his wife right at this moment, once he cuts the strings, the world will accept his decision. Vanessa King will fade into the background where she belongs. He's too big of a star for the world to turn its back on him."

"Oh really," Kareem drawled, his voice dripping with sarcasm.

"Marcus's personal life is his own. Marcus can do what he wants, and you know it's in both of our best interests for him to leave her."

"What I know is that you need to calm the hell down and fall back for a minute. Let the rumors of your affair and Vanessa's attack die down in the press. And we certainly don't need it coming up this week at All-Star."

I hated when he said her name, and that's probably why he said it, just to mess with me. Forget Vanessa King. One way or another, she was going to be out of the picture. I reached for the bottle of wine and poured myself another glass.

"In case you've forgotten, I have my show's premiere party this weekend, and I need Marcus to make an appearance. My fans and my sponsors, *DivaDish* and Moët, are expecting a big splash." Making our debut as a couple on the red carpet would make the paparazzi go wild and cement our relationship in the eyes of the public. Sure it would be a little messy, but we could ride it out. As long as we had each other, nothing else mattered.

"Wait a minute," Kareem said, leaning forward with a raised eyebrow. "Did you just say that *DivaDish* is sponsoring your premiere party?"

"Yes, I did," I huffed. "Along with Moët. Why? Is there a problem?"

Kareem collapsed back against the sofa cushions and looked up at the ceiling.

"You're just so messy, and you don't even know it. You really are a dumb bird. The editor in chief of *DivaDish*, Nia Bullock, is Vanessa King's best friend!"

While that certainly wasn't news I was aware of or expecting to hear, I was sure that Miki had that relationship under control.

"Look, Glam Network VP Miki Woods is running this thing from start to finish, so there's no way Nia is going to cross her and lose her damn job. Miki is not going to let Nia mess with her money or her ratings."

"Are you crazy?" Kareem asked as he laughed derisively and then took another sip of his wine. "No, seriously, are you out of your mind? You must be bat-shit crazy if you think Marcus is coming to your little premiere party. For God's sake, you psycho, he and his wife, Vanessa, are hosting their annual Midnight Charity Gala after the All-Star game. There's absolutely no way he can go to your party Friday night and then show up with his wife on his arm the next night in front of media from around the world, the Gladiators' front office, and our corporate sponsors. That would be career suicide and would make the LeBron James ESPN announcement debacle look like a hiccup. You have to be patient."

"Patient? I've been more than patient with this bullshit. But All-Star weekend is my official coming-out party, and I need my man on my red carpet. This is not a game."

As Kareem became more frustrated and animated, I kept my voice low and calm. He had much more to lose than I did.

"Kareem, darling, a deal was made," I said as I shrugged my shoulders. "A very serious and lucrative deal on several fronts, I might add, and I certainly don't need to tell you that if things don't work out, the consequences could be quite dire."

"We're going to play this my way," Kareem snapped. "Don't get ahead of yourself, Laila. I control Marcus. I'm the reason he's not contacting you right now, and until I say it's all clear, he won't." He poured himself another glass of wine, finishing off the bottle.

"And don't think I won't call Glam Network and get your little show shut down," he said, regaining his composure and smirking at me. "All I have to do is threaten to sue on Marcus's behalf, and your reality TV career is over."

I chuckled. Kareem had made the terrible mistake of threatening to mess with my money—*and* my man. He thought he was in control, but thanks to my boy Darryl, he was about to learn I held the cards. The tide had turned, and this punk didn't even know it.

"Well, it would certainly be a shame if my friends and I were to let Marcus find out the truth behind the car accident so many years ago," I said as I cocked my chin at Kareem, letting him know two could play at that game but only one could win. "I bet he'd be looking at you in an entirely different way if he knew what really happened that night, now wouldn't he?"

Checkmate, *bitch*.

Suddenly Kareem sprang up from the couch like a panther, and before I knew it, he had grabbed my arm and jerked me up from the chair. He pulled me roughly up against his body, my toes dangling over the carpet. His eyes were dark with anger as his face came down close to mine, his hot breath flashing in my face as he spoke with a low, dangerous tone I'd never heard before.

"Let me make myself clear, you trick-ass bitch. You better watch your mouth and watch your step. Your pussy ain't good enough to get you out of the mess you're headed toward. Trust me, I know." He laughed crudely and shoved me back down into the chair.

He leaned in over me, his large powerful arms on either side of the chair blocking my escape.

"Although I wouldn't mind tasting it one more time."

He leaned in, laughing with lust in his eyes as he began to snake his lips and slithery wet tongue along my neck while moaning. When one of his arms reached to cup my breasts, I forced myself not to recoil and pretended I was enjoying his rough touch as I leaned into his hand.

"Oh yes, baby," I moaned as I opened my legs and planted my feet flat against the floor.

"You know you want big daddy to put that long stroke on you. Ain't that right, girl?" Kareem said when he saw me part my thighs. "Say you want it, Laila." Kareem's breath quickened, and when he let go of the chair with his other arm to push down the thin straps on my tank top and his mouth began to move hungrily down to my erect nipples, I knew I had him right where I wanted him.

I grabbed his thickening manhood with both my hands and squeezed and twisted as hard as I could, just like my self-defense coordinator had shown in the class I took three years ago. I couldn't believe I remembered what to do. And it had worked! Kareem howled and jerked back hard, landing on his back on the carpeted floor with a loud thud. The people in the room below must have thought it was an earthquake. Kareem cupped his bruised manhood while he rolled around on the floor.

"You fucking bitch . . . ," he groaned. I pushed strands of hair back off my face that had worked their way loose from my ponytail during our struggle and then got up from my chair, pulled the straps of my tank top back up, and stood over him.

"Silly rabbit, haven't you ever heard no means no, muthafucka?" I said as I stepped over his body and took pleasure in the image of him writhing in pain. "Excuse me, but I need to get ready for my next meeting. Let yourself out."

Kareem struggled to catch his breath and leaned on the coffee table to try to get back up onto his feet.

"Oh, and don't forget to tell my man that I look forward to seeing him at my party Friday night. I miss him," I said as I smirked at Kareem who was now standing but still holding himself and wincing in the living room.

I then turned and opened the doors leading into the bedroom and locked them securely behind me. While I doubted Kareem would be stupid enough to try me again, I'd rather be safe than sorry. Walking into the spacious marble and glass bathroom to turn on the shower, I began to peel off my clothes and drop them onto the floor as the steam from the shower filled the glass stall.

Clearly, tonight's events had confirmed that once Marcus and I were married, I'd quickly need to figure out a way to get him to make some changes. Kareem had stepped out of line tonight; he obviously didn't know how to play his position. He'd played off Marcus's loyalty and sympathy for too long. And once Marcus knew the truth, even he would agree it was time for an upgrade.

CHAPTER 16

Nia

I was on fire for his touch.

Terrence's large hands snaked along my aching body, teasing me. I arched up off my couch to meet his hungry lips with mine as we picked up where we had left off. We couldn't stay away from each other. When he had shown up unannounced, I knew there was no use fighting what was between us.

His warm velvety tongue slipped between my swollen lips, stroking and probing. I wrapped my arms around him and began to rake my nails down his broad muscled back to the waistband of his jeans. He pushed his pelvis into mine, slowly winding his hips into me deeply.

"You taste so good," he whispered huskily in my ear as his tongue traced the outline of my ear and then flicked lightly at my earlobes. I arched my neck to give him more access. His hands reached down to the waistband of my jeans, and he pulled out my blouse and then began to unbutton it slowly. My full breasts, aching for his electric touch, strained against the pink demi-cut bra. He looked down and unclipped the delicate pearl enclosure in the front and moaned.

"You're so beautiful, Nia," he said as his dark head dipped down to encircle one of my puckered cocoa-brown nipples with his mouth. His hot breath followed by his wet mouth drove me crazy. I grabbed at his head and moved his juicy lips over to my other quivering mound. He lovingly licked at my other nipple and bit at it, causing me to moan deeply.

"Oh, is that what you want?" he asked, teasing me with his nibbles back and forth between my breasts.

"Yes," I said breathlessly. His hungry mouth moved back to my lips.

"Are you sure you want this?" he asked. He looked into my eyes, daring me to say no as one of his hands slipped down between my legs.

All I could do was moan in affirmation as I felt my body respond to his touch, warm wetness creeping into my silk panties.

"Nia. Nia. Nia . . ." I heard the deep voice ringing in my ears, and suddenly someone was knocking on the door.

I opened my eyes to answer and was startled to see MJ seated next to me, knocking on the hair dryer pushed down low over my head.

"Uh, boo, what in the Northwest hell were you dreaming about?" he asked, laughing as he cut off the hot dryer I had fallen asleep under on the top floor of Walter's Salon and Spa. I sheepishly looked around the popular Upper East Side pampering palace and was relieved to see that the two other women seated under dryers in the little alcove were too engrossed in their iPads and hadn't heard me over the sound of their own dryers. The rest of the salon was buzzing with the whir of blow-dryers and the chatter of clients gossiping while getting their hair relaxed, braided, colored, blown out, or a new weave sewn by some of the best stylists in the city. Old-school R&B was piped into the loftlike space that had exposed brick walls and bleach-blond wood floors. I looked down at the delicate gold Piaget watch on my wrist and saw I had been asleep for about twenty-five minutes.

"That must have been some dream, honey. Damn, drool and everything. Wipe your mouth." MJ handed me a tissue.

I wiped at the corners of my mouth and shook my head at him.

"What are you even doing here?" I ducked out from under the dryer and pushed the round metal hood over to the side. Reaching up to undo some of the black wrapping papers stretched around my head, I ran my fingers around the front and back of my head, praying that my hair was finally dry.

"I came to give you your phone, which you left at the office when you ran out for your hair appointment," MJ said as he handed me my white iPhone. "You're welcome, diva."

"Thanks, MJ," I said, playfully punching his arm. "Did I miss any important calls?" I said as I began to scroll through the messages.

"Terrence has been blowing up your phone like every fifteen minutes if that's what you're asking," MJ said as he crossed his legs and flicked a speck of invisible dust off the black pants he had paired with a striped Comme des Garçons T-shirt and Levi's black fitted denim jacket.

"Really?" I saw on the phone's screen that I had indeed missed five calls from Terrence but that he hadn't left a message. I punched in his number to call him back, but got his voice mail and told him to hit me back.

"Yes, really," MJ said as he smirked at me. "So what's up with you guys?" I gathered my navy patent leather Dior handbag and headed over to Walter's chair. MJ trailed me and continued to talk and type on his BlackBerry.

"All dry?" Walter asked as I slipped into his black leather chair. He ran his fingers through my short black cut and then turned to plug in the flat iron and two curling irons he would need to do my hair.

"Yes, I think we're done." Hoping to cut MJ off from pursuing his line of questioning in mixed company, I gave MJ the evil eye, like the one my mother used to give me in church when she would look down from her perch in the choir and see me cutting up in the pews. No luck.

"Good. We know we've got to get this hair right so you can fly out to Phoenix tomorrow for All-Star," Walter said as he sprayed a cloud of sheen spray on my head.

"I know that's right," MJ said, leaning up against the wall. "She can't be hanging out with me, looking busted."

"Chile, please," I said, taking my hand from under the cape and flicking it in his direction. "You already know I'm going to be looking better than you. Ain't that right, Walter?"

Walter just laughed, knowing he didn't want any part of this discussion.

"Whatever, I'm sure you'll do your best. So back to my question. What's up with you and Terrence?"

"What do you mean?" I asked.

"Don't play innocent with me. I know ya better than anyone besides maybe your momma. You got that goofy look on your face when I told you he was blowing up your phone."

"I wasn't making any face."

"Yeah, right. Like I said, I know you."

"You know we're working on this *thing* together," I said, emphasizing the word *thing* so that he wouldn't use any names in this salon with all these busybodies.

"Well, I think you're just as interested in Terrence as you are with figuring out this *thing*," MJ said with equal emphasis.

"What we had is over. He's engaged after all."

"He may be engaged, but he ain't married. Remember that scene in the movie *Brown Sugar* when Queen Latifah and Sanaa Lathan were sitting at the wedding, watching Taye Diggs about to marry Nicole Ari Parker, and Queen was poking Sanaa and telling her to do something and said, 'She's about to marry your man'?"

"Uh, yeah," I said, unsure where this little black cinema flashback was going.

"Well, *this* queen is trying to tell you to do something before someone else marries your man!"

"I can't even deal with you right now. I need to concentrate on holding my head straight so Walter can hook up my hair." Just then my phone rang. As I took it out from underneath the nylon cape, MJ leaned in to see who it was.

"Ha!" he said, laughing as I flipped him the bird and then answered Terrence's call.

"Hey," I said, trying to talk low so that MJ couldn't overhear our conversation.

"Hi, where have you been? I've been trying to reach you all day." Terrence's deep voice sent a warm feeling down my back.

"I'm at the hair salon, and I left my phone at the office, but MJ just brought it to me."

"Oh, well look. Where are you? I'll come pick you up. I've tracked down Carlo's mom in Harlem. Maybe she can give us some clues as to why her son was murdered."

I gave him the address to the salon and then ended the call.

"Coming to pick you up, huh?" MJ said, nodding at me with a knowing look in his eye.

"Yes, it's just about that thing we're working on together."

"Uh-huh. It's about that thing, all right. That thing. That thing. That thiiiinnngggg." MJ's version of Lauryn Hill's old hit song trailed off.

I made a mental note to find a new assistant.

—

Terrence and I headed up the West Side Highway to Harlem in another unmarked police car. He'd clearly taken what was available as the trash-strewn car was less than immaculate. Discarded fast-food bags littered the floor along with gum wrappers and old newspapers. And the bundle of Christmas tree air fresheners tied to the rearview mirror didn't help mask the car's odor of sweat and stale cigarettes.

"Thanks for sparing no expense on the ride," I remarked as I tried the button on the door handle to lower the window for some fresh air. Of course it was broken.

"What are you talking about?" Terrence said, laughing as he hit the dashboard with the palm of his hand. "This is one of New York's finest undercover vehicles. Do you know how many bad guys I took down in a car just like this back in the day?"

"Maybe it should stay back in the day." I chuckled, crinkling my nose at him.

"Best thing I could grab on short notice," he said. "As you can see, a brother was in court today."

I hadn't wanted to mention it, but he did look really good today in a dark gray wool suit, navy-blue pinstriped shirt, and midnight-blue silk tie knotted at his neck. He looked just as fine as he had in my dream at the hair salon, but I didn't dare tell him that, either.

"I forgot to tell you I'm heading to All-Star weekend tomorrow, too," Terrence said, changing the subject as he loosened his tie and tossed it onto the seat between us.

"Oh, really. Why?" I said, hoping my nonchalant tone hid my sudden excitement at this surprising news.

"Vivica is modeling in some annual National Basketball Wives Association charity luncheon on Saturday afternoon, and they gave her a couple of tickets to all the events, so I thought I'd tag along. I've never been to an All-Star game."

"Me neither," I said brightly, trying to mask my disappointment that his fiancée would be attending. What else did I expect? Did I think he was going to go to be with me? "So, hey, when are you and Vivica getting married?"

"August fourteen, at the Ritz-Carlton on Grand Cayman."

"Oh, that will be nice. Grand Cayman is beautiful."

"You've been there?"

"Oh, yeah, my ex-boyfriend Eric and I went there once for vacation." The lie slipped out before I could even stop myself.

"Cool. Vivica picked the place. You know, my mom was tripping at first 'cause she wanted to have it uptown and watch her baby get married at Abyssinian."

"Yes, I know Brenda Joyce wasn't too happy to hear about no Cayman Islands," I said, laughing at the thought of Ms. Brenda hearing the news.

"She got over it, though, and she's got a plane ticket and everything, so it should be pretty nice."

An awkward silence filled the car. It felt weird to be talking about his wedding when we were about to make love in my apartment just a week ago.

"So, hey uh, while I'm out there, I also want to follow up on that dead-Phoenix-dancer case," Terrence said. I was thankful he changed the subject back to something with which we were both more comfortable.

"Why?" I asked, turning in my seat to look at him as he steered the car along Amsterdam Avenue.

"I don't know. But I'm wondering if that isn't somehow connected to everything else we're looking into. I don't think it's a coincidence that the Kings started receiving those threatening e-mails and text messages after that cheerleader was found murdered."

"Maybe you're right," I said. I didn't tell him that I was working on my own cheerleader leads. I had contacted my ex, Eric, and asked him for a favor. We hadn't spoken since our breakup last year, so I hadn't been sure what to expect when I called. Eric was happy to hear from me, and we managed to even shoot the shit amicably for a few minutes before I got to the point of my call. I sent him all the text messages and e-mails Vanessa had received and asked if he and some of his hacker buddies could figure out where the threats were coming from. Luckily, I didn't have to mention anything about the hundreds of dollars in wasted face cream he'd jacked off into to get him to do me this solid. He said he was happy to do it and would get back to me within forty-eight hours.

Soon we were parked in front of one of the many tall, nondescript brick buildings on 143rd Street. We both climbed out of the car and made our way toward a group of black and Latino teens posted up in front of the building even though it was two o'clock on a school day. I wasn't sure whether it was because they knew a police car when they saw it or because Terrence, who had grown up in these same streets just a few blocks south, gave them all the universally recognized brother-man head nod and casually said, "What's up?" but the sea of hoodies, oversize jeans, white T-shirts, and Tims parted easily as we made our way into the building. We stepped into the graffitied hallway of the building's dimly lit lobby and pushed the button for the elevator. The smell of garbage and urine assaulted our nostrils and made the car I had just been complaining about seem like a lavender-scented oasis in comparison.

"Yo, the elevator's out, B," a young man tossed in our direction as he walked out from behind a metal door in the corner of the lobby leading to the stairs. He bounded out the door to meet his crew hanging in front of the building.

"Thanks, my man," Terrence said as we headed over to the stairs to begin to climb the nine flights to Maria Esposito's apartment. *She better be home*, I thought as I started up the first flight of stairs, glad I'd worn jeans and flat Prada riding boots today. Terrence followed behind me.

"You all right?" He chuckled as we reached the fourth floor and my pace began to slow. "Do I hear you wheezing up there?"

"I'm fine. You just better worry about you. You got a cushy desk job now in the DA's office, so I'm sure you're not as fit as you were when you were out jacking fools on patrol."

"Don't worry about me. I'm all good. I stays in the gym. I'm just enjoying the view," he said as I turned to look at him eyeing the back of my snug jeans.

"Keep your eyes on the stairs," I said as I swung back around, pulling down the tail of my fuchsia blouse and black Dolce & Gabbana blazer over my butt even though I switched my hips a little harder as we rounded the seventh floor.

When we reached Maria's floor, we headed down a long, dimly lit hallway. We made our way down the cracked tiled floor along a sea of banged-up brown metal doors spaced out on either side of the hallway. The smell of urine and stale reefer clung in the air, and raised voices arguing in Spanish, babies crying, and dogs barking could be heard behind different doors as we passed.

"You always take me to the nicest places," I cracked as we approached Maria's apartment at the end of the hallway. Terrence knocked on the door marked #8J. We could hear the sound of a Spanish-language television program playing loudly from behind the door.

"I think you're going to have to knock harder," I suggested.

Terrence knocked a bit more forcefully. Suddenly the television volume was lowered, and we could hear a parrot squawking in the background.

"Aaaaawk! Aaaawk! Doorbell! Doorbell!" screamed the parrot.

"*Dios mío,* I coming. I coming," a woman's voice yelled from behind the door. "Shut up, you stupido bird!"

"Who is it?" yelled the woman, who was likely straining to see through the battered peephole in the middle of her door.

"Hello, ma'am. My name is Terrence Graham. I'm with the Manhattan district attorney's office. I'm here to ask you some questions about your son, Carlo."

The woman didn't respond, although we could hear her breathing, so we knew she was still standing there.

"Ma'am, can we talk to you for a minute?" Terrence repeated. "It's about your son."

Suddenly one of the apartment doors in the middle of the hallway opened. Terrence and I turned around to see a heavyset Latino man with a jagged knife scar down the side of his left cheek and a colorful sleeve of violent-looking tattoos snaking up one of his arms step into the hallway and look in our direction. I felt Terrence's body tense up beside me, and the man stared us down for what seemed like forever. Then, just as quickly as he appeared, the man slipped on a black leather jacket over his wifebeater and then headed quickly down the stairs. I exhaled, not realizing I had been holding my breath. Terrence turned back to the door and knocked again.

"Ma'am, can we come in just for a moment?"

"I ain't talkin' to no cops!" she yelled through the door in a ragged voice I assumed was destroyed by years of smoking. Terrence lowered his tone, recognizing her concern was that she didn't want her neighbors to think she was talking to the police about anything.

"Ma'am, please, I'm not a cop. I'm with the DA's office, and I just want to talk to you for a few minutes about your son."

We heard the sound of three locks being undone and then a chain being removed. The door opened to reveal a short, chunky Hispanic woman with gray hair twisted in a severe bun at the nape of her heavily lined neck. Her eyes were dark black pools of anger, and folds of skin hung down underneath her eyes. Her lips were pulled tight in a thin pink line over her coffee- and cigarette-stained teeth. She had on a pink terry cloth housecoat over a thick cotton nightgown. Reading glasses hung on a silver chain around her neck. Her heavy, veiny legs led to feet stuffed into run-down fluffy gray slippers.

"What do you want?" she snapped with a deep heavily accented voice.

"Ma'am, I'm Terrence Graham from the district attorney's office, and my partner, Nia, and I would like to ask you a few questions about your son if you don't mind."

She opened the door a bit wider to let us into her apartment. Terrence handed Mrs. Esposito his card, and then we followed her down the narrow hallway, which was lined on both sides with piles of newspapers, magazines, clothes, and plastic containers. To say this lady was a candidate-in-the-making for the TV show *Hoarders* was an understatement. The parrot resumed its squawking when we came around the corner.

"Aaaaawk! Aaaawk! Cop! Cop!" the large green-and-yellow bird screeched from its perch in a rusted cage in the corner of the cluttered room by the window.

The only signs of family in the cluttered apartment were two large framed pictures hanging alongside each other on one of the dingy cinder-block walls. The first was a framed school picture of a boy who looked to be around eight years old smiling brightly and wearing a navy-blue private school sweater with an emblem on the breast and a white shirt. The second was a black-and-white wedding photo. The bride, who looked like a much younger and prettier version of Mrs. Esposito in a long white taffeta dress, was standing next to a tall, handsome groom in a black tuxedo.

The main room of the apartment looked like the entire contents of the home had been dumped there. Mountains of books, clothes, cans of food, plastic grocery bags, shoes, and more newspapers and magazines lay all around the room. The dusty coffee table was laden with a collection of at least forty tall Santería candles. The sofa was hidden by four overflowing laundry baskets full of clothes and children's old toys, as if someone had started on the Herculean task of trying to organize Mount Trashmore but had given up. A thirty-six-inch flat-screen TV hung over the sagging, dingy couch.

Luckily, there was no place to sit. Unsure if my latest tetanus shot was up to date, I was more than happy to stand.

"Aaaaawk! Aaaawk! Cop! Cop!" the bird screeched again.

Mrs. Esposito dropped down in the patched brown corduroy Barcalounger and pulled the black lever wrapped in duct tape to raise the cushion for her legs. I swore I saw a ball of dust come up out of the chair as if she were the Charlie Brown character Pig-Pen. She took a cigarette out of the pocket of her frayed housecoat and then reached down to dig around in her bra for some matches.

"See, even the stupid bird thinks you're a cop," she said, taking a deep drag on the cigarette and looking me up and down as she blew smoke in my direction. I tried not to shift nervously under her hardened gaze. "You got five minutes. Whatchu want to know about my son, Carlo?"

"Ma'am, when was the last time you saw your son before he was murdered last month?" Terrence asked.

"I haven't seen my son in nearly a year," she said, her eyes looking at the silent images moving across the screen of the large, old wooden floor-model TV in front of her chair. I wondered why she was watching that instead of the flat screen mounted on the wall, but I didn't ask, thinking that Mrs. Esposito barely wanted to talk to Terrence, let alone his "partner."

"Why is that, Mrs. Esposito?" Terrence asked.

"Because I told him I never wanted to see him again," she said feistily as she took another deep drag of the cigarette and then tapped it on the edge of the overflowing glass ashtray on the metal TV tray next to her chair.

"And why is that?"

"'Cause 'bout two years ago he start runnin' wit that gang. I said, 'Carlo, me and Papi didn't raise you to be no thug.' But he don' listen. He disgrace his father's memory. God rest his soul." She looked over at the wedding picture posted on the wall and made the sign of the cross.

"My husband, Hector, he was a good man. He work hard for thirty-seven years for the New York City Transit Authority as a bus driver before he died five years ago. He worked his fingers to the bone to provide for me and Carlo. But Carlo don't wanna work real job. He want fast money, flashy cars, *putas!*"

"If you don't mind me asking, Mrs. Esposito, where did you get the flat-screen TV?" I asked, finally working up the courage to speak up and follow a hunch.

"Who you, welfare worker? What you care where I get my TV?" she sneered.

"Well, I was just wondering as that's a really nice expensive TV, yet you're choosing to watch your telenovela *Diario de Mi Familia* on this older TV," I said, gesturing to the model resting on the worn carpet.

"Ah, whatchu you know about *Mi Familia?*" she said, lying back in her chair and looking at me skeptically.

"*Muy poco,*" I said, holding up my index finger and thumb and smiling at her to try to break the ice. "I know sweet little Rosario better watch her back and her man Ricardo with that blond hussy Carmacita." For once I was thankful to have taken in some of MJ's ramblings while he was talking to his boy toy du jour, Ricardo, who had just landed a small part on *Mi Familia*.

"I know, *Mami*! Right, I knew that Carmacita was no good!" she said, beginning to get animated. We exchanged a few more thoughts on the popular Spanish-language drama, and then I came back around to the TV.

"But why don't you watch the show on that beautiful flat screen, Señora? Then you can see all the drama in HD," I said.

"I'll never watch that TV," she said as her shoulders slumped and her eyes began to look far off.

"Why, Mrs. Esposito?" I asked, even though I already knew the answer.

"Carlo. He bought that TV with his drug money," she said, spitting out the words. "He mount it on the wall when he know I be out at Mass. I come home and he say, 'Surprise, *Mami*! Look what I done for you.' I tell him get out; I don't want none of his drug money. That was the last time I see him."

"Mrs. Esposito, did your son ever tell you who he was working for?" Terrence asked.

"No," she said, sniffing, and her voice went down to a hoarse whisper. "I don't ask and he don't say."

"Mrs. Esposito, have you ever heard of Diablo Negro?" Terrence pressed. At the mention of the notorious drug cartel, Mrs. Esposito's shoulders tensed as the parrot began to squawk excitedly from its cage again.

"Aaaaawk! Aaaawk! Diablo! Diablo!" The parrot hopped around the cage, repeating itself loudly.

Mrs. Esposito lowered the footrest on her chair and then stood up.

"Look what you've done now! I'll never get that damn bird to shut up now. I think it's time for you to go." She began shooing us back down the cluttered hallway toward the door as the bird continued to screech.

"Aaaaawk! Aaaawk! Diablo! Diablo!" As the bird screamed, Mrs. Esposito became more and more insistent that we leave despite Terrence's pleas for just a couple more questions.

"People will hear that loco bird all over the building," she hissed. "You have to leave now."

"Mrs. Esposito, according to the images I reviewed from the crime scene, your son had a parrot in his apartment. Please, was there anything your son ever said to you about Diablo Negro?"

"Are you crazy? You're going to get me killed talking about those people," she hissed as she opened her door, stuck her head out, and looked around. Once she felt the coast was clear for us to leave, she opened it wider and stood aside for us to depart.

"Now get out and don't ever come back! I don't talk to no cops!" she yelled loudly into the hallway, putting on a show for her neighbors. As I walked by her to follow Terrence out of the apartment, she whispered something in my ear.

"I find this at the bottom of the parrot's cage," Mrs. Esposito said as she furtively pressed something in my hand and then slammed the door behind us.

I looked down in my hand and saw a small key with an orange MTA tag on it. I nudged Terrence who looked down at the key and then took it and slipped it into his pocket.

As Terrence and I walked back down the hallway toward the stairs, I saw that the door for the apartment where the large tattooed man in the leather jacket had exited was slightly cracked. I could tell Terrence noticed it, too, because he suddenly took my arm at the elbow as if to hurry us along to the stairs. As we began to descend the stairs, we both heard a second door slam shut.

We made it quickly down to the lobby and back out the front door of the building to the car. As we stood in front of the car doors, we looked up toward the eighth floor of the building. The man with the leather jacket was standing in the window, his massive arms folded across his broad chest, as he stared down at us, making sure that we left.

—

Once we turned onto the West Side Highway heading back into Midtown Manhattan, Terrence took the key from his pocket and handed it to me.

"What's the tag say?" he asked. The short key, which looked like it was for some kind of old train station locker, had writing stamped into the plastic orange casing that covered the top of the key.

"Uh, it looks like Port Authority, Section one-four-six, Box fifteen," I said, squinting at the worn letters. "I think that's what it says."

"That's strange, because ever since 9/11, none of the New York City transportation stations have storage lockers for fear of terrorists planting bombs. So it can't be for one of those lockers, because why would Carlo have this key stashed in the bottom of his parrot's cage?"

"I don't know, but he must not have wanted anyone to find it," I said, turning the key over in my hand to inspect it.

"Well, he hid it in the place that no one looked because his apartment had been ransacked pretty thoroughly by whoever killed him." Terrence thought some more and then reached into the breast pocket of his suit jacket for his phone, punched in a number, and put the call on speaker.

"Yo, Peter. It's Terrence. What's up, man?" he said as he turned left onto Forty-Second Street and headed east.

"Well, well, well. If it ain't Mr. Big-Time District Attorney Terrence Graham." A deep voice with a thick New York accent filled the car.

"Aw, man. You know how I do. How's your beautiful wife, Annemarie, doing?"

"Pregnant. Again. Twins," the voice said, snorting.

"What? Pregnant again. How many is that for you guys? Like five?"

"Six, brother. You know we're good Irish Catholics, so . . ."

"I'll say. Saint Peter must be loving you guys. Congratulations, man. You still the Port Authority division?"

"Hell, yeah. Why, what's up?"

"I'm curious. You guys got any lockers still in your station for citizens?"

"Nah, you know Giuliani got rid of those things after 9/11. If you can't carry all your stuff, you're shit out of luck at the Port."

"What about lockers for bus drivers and other employees?"

"Yeah, of course, the employees have their lockers, but even those are likely coming out soon."

"Pete, I've got a key that says Section one-four-six, Box fifteen. That one of your keys?"

"Hold on a minute," he said. We heard typing on a keyboard in the background for a few seconds, and then he was back on the line. "Yeah, that's one of ours. Uh, it looks like it's in the older area of the terminal on the southwest corner. It's the one the bus drivers use. Computer says it's assigned to Hector Esposito."

"Thanks, Pete. Anything else?"

"Wait a minute. Yeah uh-huh. Here it goes. It says Esposito's retired, and the box hasn't been reassigned."

"That's perfect, Pete. Hey, when are you going to let me buy you a drink to celebrate those twins?"

"My number hasn't changed, and neither has my drink. You know where to find me, Mr. Big-Time DA."

"All right, I'll catch you at McHenry's next Thursday. First round's on me."

"Second round's on you, too," he said. "Catch you next week, Chief. Hey, make sure you bring that supermodel fiancée that me and the guys see you with in all the papers. We need something beautiful to look at if your ugly mug is going to be there."

"Very funny, O'Doyle. See you next week." Terrence ended the call and seemed put off by me hearing the end of the conversation.

"Great, so we know that the key is for an actual locker," I said, trying to sound cheerful and not reveal any of the ache that had suddenly gripped my stomach. Terrence pulled the car to a stop and parked in one of the emergency unloading zones in front of the Port Authority. Having police plates had its privileges.

We headed into the cavernous Port Authority building. It was nearing rush hour, so the place was crawling with people in a hurry to catch a bus or train. As we moved deeper into the bowels of the station, the crowd thickened, and Terrence and I were separated as people weaved in between us. Terrence grabbed my hand and pulled me along. His large hand enveloped mine, and I held on tightly as he parted the crowd and followed a sign marked "Employee Lockers." When he tried to push open the door, he found it was locked. Luckily, just that second a man came out. Before the door could swing shut again, Terrence stuck his foot in it. We were in.

The old locker room must have been a relic from when the station was first built. It was dank and dark with a hard stone floor and exposed pipes running overhead. Fortunately, no one else was in there. We made our way over to the section marked 146 and began to scan the rows of metal lockers, looking for number 15.

"Got it. Here it is," Terrence said as he sat down on the end of a long wooden bench and faced a box marked number 15.

I handed him the key. He slipped it in the lock and turned. The metal-vented door swung open on its hinge.

"Let's see what Carlo's been stashing in his old man's locker that he didn't want anyone to find at his apartment." I peered over his shoulder into the locker. Terrence, not wanting to destroy any fingerprints, used a penlight to show the contents. There were four stacks of cash deep in the back, a couple of watches, some old family photos, a wallet, and two passports with different identities. Using a pen, Terrence flipped open the wallet to find a fake driver's license with Carlo's face and the name of Carlo Ramirez. When he tilted the wallet up for closer inspection, an airplane boarding pass slipped onto the ground. I took a tissue from the pocket of my blazer and used it to pick up the ticket.

"Look," I said, gasping as I read the destination on the boarding pass. It was for a flight to Phoenix.

"Well, what do you suppose Carlo was doing in Phoenix?" Terrence asked.

"I don't know. But something tells me if we cross-reference the date on this boarding pass to the day of the murder of the Phoenix cheerleader, there's going to be some overlap," I said excitedly. I set my handbag down on the bench next to Marcus and then dug around to find my notebook. Flipping the pages, I located the key date. Kalinda was found shot in the head June 16; and the medical examiner said she died June 7.

"That's within forty-eight hours of our new friend, Carlo Ramirez, landing in Phoenix," said Terrence.

"So what's a killer in the Diablo Negro cartel doing taking a trip to Phoenix?"

"Looks like it's a good thing we're going to Phoenix, so we can figure that out," Terrence said as he dropped the boarding pass back into the locker and shut the door and then put the key back in his pocket. Both of us were deep in thought as we made our way back through the even denser crowd to the front of the Port Authority. Terrence tried to take my hand again so that we could stay together, but I slipped just out of reach.

Finally we reached the front entrance and stepped out into the cool evening air. I turned to Terrence, eager to get home to see if Eric and his hacker friends had dug up anything from the e-mails. Maybe they were tied to what we discovered today as well.

"Thanks for today. I think I'll jump in a cab and head home," I said.

"I can take you home. It's not a problem. That way we can talk this out some more," he said, looking at me quizzically.

"No, really it's OK. I'll see you in Phoenix." I flagged down a taxi and jumped in before he could object further. I sank into the backseat of the car, which unfortunately smelled no better than the car Terrence had been driving, and let my mind wonder about what Carlo had been doing in Phoenix and why it was best that Terrence not take me home because I knew I wouldn't be strong enough to turn him away a second time.

CHAPTER 17

Vanessa

The private plane touched down smoothly on the tarmac in Phoenix. Damon clapped his hands excitedly.

"Mr. and Mrs. King, welcome to Phoenix," the flight attendant said into the intercom. "The local time is nine thirty a.m., and the temperature is a gorgeous eighty-six degrees and sunny."

"Daddy, we're home!" Damon shouted, bouncing on his father's lap as the plane continued to taxi slowly on the runway of the private airstrip. Damon didn't yet consider New York home, so ever since we told him we were going to Phoenix, he'd been saying we were going home.

"Well, you're halfway right, little man," Marcus said, hugging Damon tightly and leaning over to look out the window with his son. "We're back in your hometown, but we live in New York now."

"We're home, Daddy!" Damon squealed again.

"Whatever you say, buddy," Marcus said, laughing.

"Are we going to our house, Daddy?"

"No, Son. Remember I told you we sold our house in Phoenix, and we're going to stay in a hotel this time?"

"OK, Daddy."

I loved the sight of the two of them together and the sound of their laughter, and that was why everything had to go according to plan this weekend because no two-bit trick was going to break up my family.

I was glad to be on the ground as well. I had been running back and forth to the bathroom, fighting nausea so many times during the flight, I was sure Marcus would begin to suspect something was up. I'd never had morning sickness with Damon, but this time was clearly different. Luckily, Marcus had slept most of the way with his large Beats earphones glued to his ears while he rested up for the nonstop weekend of events. If anyone suspected anything, it was Nicole, who passed me some saltine crackers after my fourth time rushing to the bathroom. I knew she wouldn't say anything, so I wasn't concerned.

When the plane came to a stop, I looked out the window and saw two black Lincoln Navigators parked at the end of a black carpet. Kareem and Desiree were standing next to one while they both talked on their cell phones.

"You're not coming to the hotel with us, Marcus?" I asked, turning back to look at my husband.

"No, babe. I have to go meet with Kareem and take pictures with the East team. I'll catch up with you guys for a late lunch back at the hotel around one o'clock." He turned and set Damon on the floor, and began to gather his earphones and magazines to toss into his Louis Vuitton tote.

"Why don't you take Damon with you?" I said, knowing as soon as I said it that Damon would beg to go until his father let him.

Five, four, three, two . . .

"Daddy, please. Can I go with you? Please, Daddy!" Damon said, his eyes wide with the prospect of going with his dad and seeing his uncle Kareem. He hopped up and down on one leg excitedly.

"You guys will have fun together, and I can focus on going over the final plans and review the auction items for our Midnight Gala tomorrow," I said to Marcus.

Of course I had an ulterior motive. If Damon was with Marcus, he'd have to take Nicole, too, and that meant he couldn't get into any trouble with all the hoes trolling around everywhere. Although there was only one ho I was really focused on this weekend. Plus, that would give me enough time to have the important meeting I was planning.

Marcus tried to look at me with pleading eyes, but I ducked my head, pretending not to see him as I gathered my things to toss in my Bottega Veneta tote.

"Have fun with Daddy and Uncle Kareem, sweetie," I said as I kissed my little man on the cheek and then grabbed my bag and Gucci train case. I made my way to the front of the plane where the door had just opened.

Damon skipped down the aisle, holding his father's hand, and Nicole followed them out of the plane, carrying her purse and Damon's bag filled with toys and snacks.

As we all made our way off the plane, we could see luggage handlers taking out our suitcases from the luggage compartment. They piled the eight pieces of trunks, suitcases, and garment bags onto a trolley cart and rolled them over to the parked SUVs to begin loading everything into the back.

"Uncle Kareem!" Damon squirmed out of his dad's arms and ran over to his favorite uncle. Kareem dropped down on one knee and scooped up his godson.

"What's up, D? How was your flight?" Kareem asked as he slipped his phone back in his pocket.

"Good, Uncle Kareem. Guess what?" Damon said, looking up at his uncle and taking his face between his two little chubby hands.

"What?"

"I'm coming with you and Daddy today! Daddy said I could."

"He did? Well, if Daddy says you can, then that's all good with me." I had watched Kareem's face closely to see if he looked frustrated with this unexpected piece of news, but he took it in stride.

"All right, baby. We'll see you back at the hotel later." Marcus leaned down to kiss me on the cheek, but I quickly turned my head so that he got my lips instead.

"OK, baby. Don't be gone long. I have something important I need to talk to you about." I looked deep into my husband's eyes and kissed him back. After I pulled away, I looked over at Kareem.

"Take care of my men," I tossed over my shoulder as the driver helped me into my waiting car.

"Don't I always, Vanessa?" he said with one of his fake smiles. I slammed the door closed. I smiled as I leaned back into the seat, knowing that I would have the pleasure of wiping that smile off his smug face for good this weekend.

As the truck began to leave the airport to head to the Four Seasons hotel, I pulled my cell phone out of my bag and shot off a text message confirming the time and location of my afternoon meeting.

Your days are numbered, Kareem Davis, and you don't even know it yet.

—

There was a knock on the door of the hotel suite right on cue. *Damn, that girl is never late,* I thought as I walked across the marble foyer to open the door.

"What's up?" I said, hugging Nia. She had called a few minutes ago, asking if she could come see me because she had some good news and some bad news to share. I'd never heard her sound that cryptic before, and she said she couldn't tell me over the phone, so I told her to come on over.

"Hey, girl. How are you feeling?"

"Good. Come in the bedroom. I'm trying to figure out which gown I'm wearing to the gala tomorrow night."

"I only have thirty minutes. I'm meeting Terrence across town in an hour," she said. That worked perfectly for me since my meeting was due to start in forty-five minutes, and I couldn't afford to be late.

"Terrence? What's Terrence doing in Phoenix?" I said as I held a red sequined one-shoulder gown up against my body and looked at my reflection in the mirror.

"You ought to know. His fiancée is modeling in your damn fashion show," she said, flopping down on the king-size bed.

"What on earth are you talking about, crazy? There's no fashion show at our Midnight Gala."

"No, not the gala. Vivica's modeling at the Basketball Wives charity fashion show bullshit."

"Oh, that's right," I said, snapping my fingers. "I remember now. Girl, I barely even go to that thing. I pop in and make an appearance and pop right back out. My first couple of years in the league I was all up in there joining committees, hosting events. Shoot, now? I'm focused on me and mine. I don't have time for the petty gossip and nonsense, which is all that thing really is, anyway."

"Whatever the fuck ever. The fact of the matter is he's here because of her."

"Look, that's your own damn fault," I said, turning back toward the mirror to hold a short strapless black lace dress with a train up against my body.

"What's that supposed to mean?" she snapped.

Sighing, I turned around and came over to sit with Nia on the bed.

"What it means, dear sister, is that I know both of y'all are still in love with each other, and you need to just go ahead and tell him how you feel. Don't be scurrrrred, girl."

"I can't do that. He's engaged," Nia whined.

"Look, until he's married, all bets are off."

"Is that how you felt when you and Marcus got engaged and all those tricks were throwing their panties at your man, showing up naked in his hotel shower? You do remember that one, right?"

"Chile, I had forgotten about that one. He called me from the road, half-scared to death, telling me about the naked woman who had snuck into his hotel room and was hiding in his shower."

"And I had to talk you out of jumping on a plane to get to wherever the hell he was playing and tracking that bitch down. Remember?"

"Yes, Lord, I sure do. Wow." I got lost in my thoughts for a moment, looking at how far we'd come. We went from him being scared of the crazed groupies he found in his shower to me having to accept the

Road Code to where we were today. My stomach jumped as I thought about what I had to tell him tonight.

"Hey, on the phone yesterday, you said you had some good news and some bad news for me. What's up?"

"OK, which do you want first?" she said, sighing deeply.

"Damn, girl. What is it? Give me the bad first so you can leave on a high note."

"OK, here we go. I hate to even mention this heffa's name, especially since you and Marcus are in such a good place right now." I felt my body tensing up as she went on to explain how her company had acquired the network that was producing Laila James's reality show, that all the publications were required to support the show, and *DivaDish* was going to be the sponsor for her premiere party tonight.

"I really tried to get out of it, Vanessa. I swear I did," Nia said as she searched my eyes pleadingly.

"Let me mull that one over a bit while you give me the good news," I said, thinking it better be great fucking news to get over the stinking betrayal I felt.

She reached into her bag and pulled out a magazine and placed it in my hands.

"This is the good news. This is your magazine cover that I'm going to reveal at Laila's party tonight."

I usually don't like any pictures of myself, but I had to admit Nia's team had done a wonderful job. She had selected the shot of me wearing a bright pink off-the-shoulder Oscar de la Renta dress. My neck was laced with piles of gorgeous silver necklaces, and my hair was blown out sleek and straight and swept to the side. The makeup was flawless. I looked confident, happy, knowing.

And while the photo was gorgeous, the cover line stole the show: "Marcus and Vanessa King on rebuilding their marriage and welcoming a new baby."

There was also a quote: "'We couldn't be happier,'" I read aloud.

"So what do you think?" Nia asked, leaning over my shoulder to look at the cover. "Please tell me you love it."

"It's really beautiful, Nia. Thank you so much." I hugged my friend. I knew she had no choice in the party, but she was more than making up for it by debuting my cover tonight. It was perfect. She had no idea what this meant to me and what it meant to our family.

"Wait until you read the story. I think Che did a great job, although I was sorry to hear that Marcus was never able to sit down for an actual interview with her due to his crazy game-and-practice schedule. But the quotes he e-mailed were great."

I slid off the bed and began to put the three gowns back on their hangers, fussing with the rack so that Nia couldn't see the disappointment on my face.

"So how was your flight? Did your stomach bother you?" Nia asked as she slipped the magazine back into her bag.

"I'm good. Next week I'll officially clear my first trimester, and all the morning sickness will be gone," I said, laughing. "I'll be so glad when I can stop all this sneaking around." As soon as I said the words, I wanted to pull them back in.

"'Sneaking around'?" Nia asked, walking over to stand in front of me. "What do you mean 'sneaking around'? Oh my God, you still haven't told Marcus, have you?"

"No," I admitted. "I'm going to do it tonight."

"What do you mean you haven't told him? What about all those quotes that Marcus e-mailed to my editor about how happy he was about the baby?"

I stiffened my shoulders and stared back at her with a hard glint in my eye.

"Look, I'm going to tell him tonight, and all those things I said in the magazine are going to be true."

"Going to be true? Are you nuts? That's not how it works, Vanessa!"

"Look, don't try to get all high and mighty with me right now. Look at how you sold your best friend down the river by working with a woman who is trying to destroy my family," I yelled back at her.

"You know I didn't have a choice, Vanessa!"

"We always have choices, Nia. And I've made mine. The magazine will make its debut tonight at Laila's party, and I'll tell my husband that he's going to be a father again. End of story. Even I couldn't have dreamed that the magazine would be debuting the cover at that whore's little party," I said, clapping my hands. I knew I must have sounded and looked crazy, but I didn't care. It was time for payback and for Laila to learn what it felt like to be humiliated.

"You know I'm your girl forever and always, but you better have my back when the ish hits the fan with DeAnna for dropping this bomb at the party we're sponsoring. You do realize I could get fired for this?" she asked me.

"Look, Nia, you wanted a big story, and I gave you one. So now let's just sit back and watch the fireworks."

—

When Nia left, she wasn't totally happy with me, but she'd get over it. I was confident that my plan would prove fruitful for the both of us.

The next knock at the door was also exactly on time. And after my last meeting, I was looking forward to this one, which was hopefully going to bring me more good news.

"Mrs. King," said the tall gentleman in an expensive black suit, crisp white shirt, and yellow Hermès tie as I opened the door. His dark hair and piercing blue eyes complemented his tan features, reminding me of Tom Cruise.

"Mr. Knight, please come in," I said as I shook his outstretched hand.

"Thank you, Mrs. King. It's such a pleasure to finally meet you in person."

"The pleasure is all mine. We've certainly been texting and e-mailing for quite some time. Please call me Vanessa." I led him into our suite, and we walked past the formal dining room and into the sunken living room.

"And please call me John," he said as he unbuttoned his suit jacket and took a seat on the long gray sofa.

"I'd offer you a drink, John, but frankly we don't have much time. My husband will be here in about thirty minutes, and he'd go ballistic if he saw you here, so let's get down to business, shall we?" I asked as I took a seat next to him on the sofa.

"That sounds good to me," John said, smiling as he reached into his briefcase.

"Good," I said with a smile of my own. "So, John, tell me how your firm, Knight Sports Management, plans to take my husband Marcus King's career to the next level and how you're going to get him out of his contract with that thieving son of a bitch, Kareem Davis."

—

I closed the door behind John and ran into the bedroom, giddy with excitement. The Knight Sports Management proposal had exceeded my wildest expectations. While we hadn't had time to go through the entire proposal, John hit the high points, outlining a top-tier strategy about how to make Marcus an international star.

But the most illuminating part of the meeting had to be the research Knight's team had done reconstructing Marcus's earnings over the past year and matching that up with the forensic accountant's audit I had begun when we first got to New York. I always suspected that Kareem was skimming money, but I had no way of proving it. Now, thanks to Knight, I had all the proof I needed and then some.

He also shared one cautionary note: with all the recent drama Marcus and I had been going through, John heard that the Gladiators' owners were getting nervous. They were concerned that Marcus could get involved with a career-ending scandal and, even worse, that winning basketball games didn't seem to be his priority. John assured me that he understood that all athletes go through rough patches, but one of the things that his firm specialized in was crisis management and making unwanted people and problems go away.

The buzzing of my phone on the nightstand interrupted my reverie. I rolled over to pick it up and read the incoming text message.

What I read made me drop the phone and scream. This couldn't be happening again.

Welcome back to Phoenix, bitch! Are you ready to die?

CHAPTER 18

Nia

As the elevator doors opened into the crowded lobby of the Ritz-Carlton hotel, I reconsidered if it was a good idea to come downstairs to meet MJ. My intention was to order a very large alcoholic beverage and download to MJ my disastrous confrontation with Vanessa, but the sea of bodies cut off a direct path to the bar. The lobby was packed with clusters of B-list celebrities and their entourages, basketball players in warm-up suits and sunglasses, and women dressed in what can only charitably be described as damn near nothing. Cameras were snapping, video cameras shooting, and phone and room numbers were exchanged. I felt like I had stumbled into hedonism.

This wasn't a professional sports weekend; this was Freaknik for grown-ups. All these people weren't staying at the hotel, but the earnest hotel staff conferring behind the check-in desk felt powerless to stop everyone who had turned their elegant lobby into a makeshift nightclub. But then the scent of reefer wafted in the air, and I knew the party in the lobby would be over soon. Any moment hotel security, backed up by Phoenix police, would sweep in and order anyone without a hotel key to leave.

"Excuse me," I said as I twisted my body sideways to squeeze between masses of oiled and scented bodies. It was slowgoing. At about the halfway point, I tried to jump up to see over the heads of the people in front of me to make sure I was even headed in the right direction. A woman, wearing a short orange silk halter dress that looked like she fell into a paper shredder on the way to the hotel, snapped at me angrily when I accidently came down on her diamond-encrusted big toe stuffed in an open-toe crystal sandal.

"Watch it, *bitch!*" she said, popping her gum as she whipped around, slapping me in the face with a mass of Indian-hair extensions in a confection of curls that looked straight off the Miss America pageant.

I smiled and apologized to the young woman, hoping to diffuse a potential episode of *When Sisters Attack*, but her girls didn't want to let it go.

"Nuh uh, girrrrrl. I know she didn't just step on your fresh diamond pedi," said one of her friends who was clad in a fuchsia copy of the shredded dress worn by the offended party.

"Is you crazy? You know how much I paid for this pedicure?" the woman with the helmet of hair said as she reached down to rub her foot dramatically. A chorus of "I know that's right" rained down on my head.

"I'm so sorry," I said, craning my neck to see if I could make a quick escape, but my path was blocked by the crowd of men talking loudly about all the women they intended to sleep with this weekend.

"I know you ain't trying to just run off like you ain't just step on my damn foot," the woman started again, stepping closer to me. Did she really want to fight in the middle of the Ritz-Carlton? I couldn't imagine being a grown woman and fighting over stepping on someone's toe, but I also knew enough from growing up on the streets of the Chi that this young woman felt like I had disrespected her in front of her friends, and she wasn't going to stand for that. I hadn't fought anybody since I was sixteen and had to throw down with a girl from another block after she accused me of trying to talk to her boyfriend at a skating party. I was nice with my hands, thanks to my uncle Frank, and back in the day we could have gone back and forth barking at each other until one of us jumped, but those days were far behind . . . for me at least.

Suddenly MJ appeared by my side. He was not exactly giving me a fighting chance at 140 pounds, but it least there would be a witness to my side of the story when we were all inevitably arrested.

"Hi, Nia, everything OK?" MJ asked, lifting his stunner shades. "Hi, ladies. Love the dresses. Fierce!"

"Thanks, boo boo, but your friend here just fucked up my fifty-dollar pedicure, and I ain't havin' it," the woman said.

"Oh, that's Nia. She's always so clumsy," MJ said, putting his skinny arm around my shoulders as I gave him the side eye.

"What's your name, honey?" MJ said to the woman who was still huffing and puffing as he reached into his nylon Prada cross-body bag and pulled out a white envelope.

"Remy Cherelle," she said with her hand on her hip and a sculpted eyebrow raised.

"Well, Remy Cherelle, please, you and your gorgeous friends must accept our invitation to join us for the premiere party for Laila James's new reality show, *What Laila Wants*, at the Inferno tonight." He handed each of the four young women a ticket to the party.

"Eww, Serena, girl. We goin' to Laila's party!" squealed Remy Cherelle as she looked at her ticket and then high-fived her twin in the fuchsia dress.

"That's hot, girl!" Serena said.

"Ballin'!" the girls screamed in unison. Jim Jones would be so proud.

"I told y'all we were going to be ballin' this weekend," said Remy, taking credit for getting her crew tickets to one of the hottest parties in town. "And you broke bitches ain't even want to chip in gas money for the trip from Houston!"

"You right, girl. You right," another of Remy's crew said with a nod. She had decided to break ranks on the fashion front and wear white leather jeans that looked like they had been painted on her curvaceous body, a black leather halter top, and a black rhinestone-studded cowboy hat.

"I hope y'all got some more fabulous dresses, because this party is going to be off the chain, Ms. Remy," MJ said, smiling as he tucked the envelope with the rest of his comp tickets back in his bag. He's always very adept at diffusing tense situations.

"You know we do, boo. What's your name?" Remy asked MJ, her new bestie.

"I'm MJ, and this is Nia Bullock, the editor in chief of *DivaDish*," MJ replied as he picked up my arm to extend it to Remy.

"Nice to meet you," Remy said, shaking both of our hands.

"Nice to meet you, too, Remy," I managed to squeeze out. "I look forward to seeing you guys tonight."

"We wouldn't miss it," Serena chimed in excitedly. "Laila is a pimp for real. She got that Marcus King on lock, and I can't wait to watch her show." Before I can say anything else to put my foot back in my mouth, MJ tells the 2 Live Crew extras "toodles" before leading me through the crowd to the bar.

"Thanks, MJ," I yelled over the crowd. "You know I didn't want to have to show that chick how we get down in Chicago."

"Yeah, right," MJ snorted. "That's all I need, to have to be bailing your crazy behind out of a Phoenix jail during All-Star weekend. DeAnna would *looove* that!"

"No doubt."

We finally made our way to the entrance of the Club Bar. The thin blond hostess asked to see my room key, explaining that they were trying to keep the bar space free for hotel guests and their parties. Good, at least it would be quiet in there.

As I dug around in my Gucci tote for the key, the hostess asked, "How many people are in your party, Ms. Bullock?"

"Two," I responded, holding up the key.

"OK, just a moment, please. I'll go get a table set up for you."

"Thank you," I replied. I put the key back in my handbag and heard a man's voice call my name.

"Nia! Hey, Nia, over here."

I looked to see where the voice was coming from, and that's when I saw Eric squeezing through the crowd and making his way over to MJ and me.

"Eric?" I said as he reached down to hug me. "What are you doing here?"

MJ slipped his shades down on his nose and looked over the tops of the frames at my ex-boyfriend.

"Well, one of my boys works for Nike, and he had an extra ticket to the game, so he invited me to come down. Plus, I knew you were going to be here, and I got that information you were looking for." Eric patted the breast pocket of the tan linen sports coat he was wearing over a chambray shirt that was tucked into dark blue jeans. I hadn't seen him since the day he moved out. I had even blocked him on Facebook so that I wouldn't have to see his updates and photos on the feeds of mutual friends. He looked like he had lost a few pounds. His face was clean-shaven, hair freshly cut.

"You look good, Nia," Eric said, swallowing hard.

"Uh, thanks. It was nice of you to bring it over to me in person, but you could have just called," I said, shifting in my Valentino suede heels. Suddenly I was glad I had changed after leaving Vanessa's room into a black-and-white off-the-shoulder Derek Lam blouse and skinny black jeans.

The hostess then returned, and MJ said we'd now need a table for three, clearly getting the vibe that Eric wasn't leaving anytime soon.

"No problem," the hostess said brightly as she turned and headed back into the Club Bar to now secure seating for three.

"You cut your hair. I like it," Eric said as he reached out to touch my hair.

"Thanks," I said. He and MJ shook hands cordially, although I knew Eric was still on MJ's shit list.

Before MJ could inject himself into the awkwardness of this moment, I heard another man's voice calling my name.

"Nia! Hey, there you are," Terrence said as he made his way through the hotel crowd. Wearing dark black jeans, a crisp white shirt, and a steel gray sports coat with dark navy-blue threads that matched the pocket square, he also looked really good.

"Aww, shit, now," MJ whispered under his breath. "This is getting good." The hostess returned to the stand, ready to lead us to the table for three, when MJ leaned over and told her we'd now need a table for four. She nodded and headed back into the bar to find another table.

"Hi, Terrence," I said as he bent down to kiss me on the cheek.

"What's up, MJ, right?" Terrence said as he gave MJ some dap. "Nice to finally meet you. I've heard a lot about you."

"Oh, likewise. I've heard a lot about you, too."

I could tell from the sound of MJ's voice that he was enjoying this just a little too much.

"What are you doing here, Terrence?" Didn't I just say the exact same thing to Eric?

"I've been calling you, but you didn't pick up, so I came over to your hotel to see if I could catch you. I just received some more information on Carlo's activities while he was in Phoenix."

"Oh, I see," I said. I hadn't noticed any missed calls on my phone.

I looked back at Eric who was looking at me quizzically. Clearly an introduction was in order. But how was I supposed to introduce my ex to my ex? I had to bite the bullet.

"Uh, Terrence, this is my uh, friend Eric from LA. He's tracked down that information we were looking for on the ISP address. And, Eric, this is Terrence, my friend from New York who works in the DA's office. His fiancée is modeling in the National Basketball Wives Association fashion show tomorrow afternoon, so that's why he's here." I knew this was an awkward way to introduce them to each other, but I honestly had no idea what to say.

As Terrence and Eric shook hands, I could see each sizing up the other. I had told Eric about my relationship with Terrence when we started living together during one of those new-couple conversations where you count down your most significant relationships. As for Terrence, he had a mind like a steel trap, so I knew he remembered that I said I had been dating someone seriously in LA named Eric before I took the job at *DivaDish*. I hadn't told him why we broke up. Too embarrassing.

"Nice to meet you, man," Terrence said.

"Nice to meet you, too," Eric said.

Fortunately, the hostess returned, and she seemed happy to see that my party hadn't yet expanded again. She led us through the dark mahogany bar to a circular dark wood table in a corner of the room and left us with cocktail menus. Terrence was seated on my left and Eric on my right. I could see MJ trying to keep it together as he took a seat across from me. Suddenly the room felt very warm.

An awkward silence settled around the table as we all studied the cocktail menu as if our lives depended on it.

"Well, Nia, I think we should have their signature drink, the Purple Diva," MJ said, breaking the silence. "But this Chanel No. 6 could be fun, too."

"Mmm, Purple Diva sounds fun," I said, dying to drink anything at this point. "What's in it?"

"Vodka, blueberries, lemon, and basil," MJ said, reading the ingredients.

"Perfect," I said as the waiter reappeared to take our orders. I asked for two Purple Divas for MJ and myself.

"I'll have a scotch, neat," Terrence said, handing the waiter his menu.

"And I'll have a beer. Do you have Blue Moon?" Eric asked when it was his turn to order.

"Absolutely, sir."

Not wanting the strained silence to return to the table and eager to shut down this meeting as quickly as possible, I dove in. "So, Eric, you said you got the information on the real ISP address for the computer that's been sending Vanessa and Marcus the threatening e-mails and text messages."

The waiter returned with our drinks, and I tried to not swallow my entire cocktail in one gulp.

"Uh, yeah," Eric said as he pulled a piece of paper out of the breast pocket of his jacket. "The person sending these messages clearly had no intention of ever being found. They were good."

"But not as good as you and your friends, right?" I asked.

"Of course not," Eric said. "No one's better than me."

Why did I have the feeling he wasn't just talking about computing?

"So what did you guys find out?" Terrence asked, taking a sip of his scotch.

"Well, the address the e-mails were coming from and the phone numbers used for the text messages were fake."

"But we knew that already. My guys down at Quantico dug that up weeks ago," Terrence said dismissively.

"Yes, but that's where mere mortals stop and where I take over. Where your guys ended is exactly where the person sending those messages wanted you to end. Most government agencies, and certainly local government agencies, don't have the technology, or frankly the talent, to be able to go deeper and break through these networks."

"So how deep did you go?" Terrence shot back.

Was this really happening?

I took another large swallow of the cool purple liquid.

"Oh, I went all the way, brother. Trust me," Eric said with a hint of cocky bravado in his voice I'd never heard before. MJ kicked me under the table, clearly enjoying their exchange.

"So look. Here's what they did. They used software that basically makes it impossible for their computer's IP address to be tracked and then connected it to a VPN, virtual private network, where they basically rented a remote computer to route all of their Internet traffic through Sweden."

"Wow, that's quite elaborate," I said, signaling the waiter for another cocktail. "Like you said, this person clearly didn't want to be found."

"Yes, but I did find them." Eric took a swallow of his beer, drawing out the suspense. He smoothed out the paper on the table and read the name and address of the person who had been sending Vanessa and Marcus death threats.

"Well, that can't be possible?" I said as the waiter set down my second Purple Diva in front of me on the table.

"Why do you say that?" asked Eric.

"Because she's dead," Terrence said, setting his empty glass down on the table.

"Kalinda Walters was killed, shot in the head," I said, fishing out one of the blueberries from my drink and popping it into my mouth. "So unless God has Wi-Fi . . . ?"

"I'm one hundred percent certain that this is the originating IP address, so if you're serious about catching the person stalking your friend, then if I were you, I'd pay this location a visit," Eric said confidently as he pushed the piece of paper across the table to me.

—

MJ headed up to his room to go over the final details for tonight's party while Terrence, Eric, and I walked out into the blazing-hot Phoenix afternoon. The front of the hotel looked like the showroom of a luxury-car dealership where several Mercedes, Lamborghinis, BMW roadsters, Porsches, and Maybachs were lined up. Valets desperately tried to manage the flow of cars while keeping a smile on their faces.

"It looks like the address is about twenty minutes away," Terrence said, fiddling with the GPS on his iPhone. "We can take my car."

As Terrence walked over to the crowded valet stand, Eric pulled me over into the shade under a large canopy.

"Thank you for tracking down this information," I said. "I know it was a lot of work, and I know you didn't have to do that for me."

"No, it was my pleasure," Eric said, still holding on to my arm. "You know I'd do anything for you, Nia."

"I know," I said, looking down at the limestone ground.

"So, do you think I can see you again before you head back to New York?"

"Um . . . I don't know, Eric. I mean my schedule is pretty crazy this weekend with the party and everything."

"I know you're busy, but I'd really like to have a chance to talk to you." I looked up into his dark brown eyes as he smiled down at me. "Come on, Nia. Meet me for a drink."

"We just had a drink," I said playfully as I saw Terrence begin to make his way back over to us. "OK, look, I'll call you later, and we'll work something out."

"Thanks, Nia," he said as he leaned down to kiss me on the cheek. "I look forward to it."

"All set," Terrence said as he cleared his throat and motioned to the black Lexus waiting at the curb.

"Thanks again, Eric," I said. "I'll call you later."

"Yeah, thanks, Eric," Terrence said, extending his hand. "We really appreciate all your, uh, work."

"No problem," Eric said, staring Terrence dead in the eye and shaking his hand. "Glad I could help."

Why did I feel like they were still sizing each other up?

"Be careful, Nia," Eric called after me as the valet helped me slide into the front seat of the waiting car.

"Don't worry, Eric," Terrence tossed over his shoulder as he walked around to the driver's side of the car. "She's with me."

—

Terrence steered the Lexus smoothly along the Phoenix streets while I adjusted the air-conditioning vents to direct the cool air onto my legs. It had to be a hundred degrees outside, and having drinks with both my exes wasn't helping.

It had been weird to see Eric again. He looked good and had clearly gotten his life together. I was happy for him but wasn't sure why he thought we needed to see each other again. Since he had gone through all the considerable trouble of tracking down the information for this stalker, however, I at least owed him another drink. But he needed to understand that I was trying to focus on moving forward, and he was a painful memory from the past. So why did it feel like the same thinking applied to Terrence as well? At least Terrence was engaged, so he was off-limits.

"So what made you reach out to your ex?" Terrence asked. "I mean Eric, not me."

"Very funny," I said. "Look, how many computer hackers do you know? If you know the best, you reach out to him. We weren't really getting anywhere with your contacts."

"Is that the only reason?" he asked, looking at me through his dark sunglasses.

"Of course that's the only reason," I snapped. "But even if it wasn't, what business would that be of yours?"

"OK, OK . . . Damn, I was just asking. You're right, it's none of my business."

"Exactly. Anyway, where's your fiancée?"

"Not that it's any of your business, but we arrived this afternoon, and I dropped her off to rehearse for the fashion show before I headed over to your hotel."

"Oh, she needs to practice walking?" I couldn't stop myself from the snide remark.

"I don't know what they do at these things," he said, laughing. "I just know she'll be there for the next four hours and then we're going to dinner."

So I guess that meant he wasn't going to come to my party tonight. Not like I had formally invited him, but I had secretly hoped that he'd want to come. Of course then that would mean that he'd be with her, and I certainly didn't want the supermodel on the red carpet of my party. That's the last thing I wanted to see.

"Well, then we've got two hours to figure out why threatening e-mails are coming from a dead woman's computer," I said.

"According to the Phoenix police files, Kalinda Walters lived with a roommate, a Sean Beckman. A computer science major at the University of Arizona."

"Sounds like we may have our guy," I said, looking at the window.

Terrence stopped the car in front of the Gardens, a large stucco apartment complex forty-five minutes from our hotel. A few palm trees lined the street. A little boy sped down the block on his bicycle while another boy trailed him on his scooter. We walked into the brick courtyard of the complex past several rows of metal mailboxes and a swimming pool full of young co-eds splashing around in the cool blue water. Just being out of the car for five minutes left me dying to join them as a trail of sweat made its way down my back.

We got to building C and walked up two flights of stairs to unit 2D. When Terrence knocked on the door, a small dog could be heard barking behind the door.

"Yeah, who is it?" a man's voice said.

"Sean Beckman? My name is Terrence Graham, and I need to talk to you about Kalinda Walters."

The door opened to reveal a thin man in his early twenties with pale freckled skin and a shock of curly red hair. He was wearing a large white T-shirt with a University of Arizona logo on the front, socks, and flip-flops. And even though he was wearing baggy basketball shorts, I doubted he'd ever played the game a day in his life.

"Are you from the police department?" he asked, looking at us skeptically.

"Not exactly, Sean," Terrence said. "I'm from the New York district attorney's office, and I'd like to ask you a few questions about the e-mails coming from this apartment to Marcus and Vanessa King."

Sean immediately tried to slam the door, but Terrence jammed his foot in the doorway.

"Look, Sean. We won't take up too much of your time. We just want to ask you a few questions. You can let us in now to talk, or we can come back with a few officers from the Phoenix police department and have an entirely different type of conversation."

"I don't have to let you in," he insisted as he pressed his thin body up against the door, still trying in vain to push it closed.

"No, you're right, you don't have to let us in," I said, leaning in so that Sean could see my face. "But I also don't think you want us to continue this conversation in front of your apartment so all your neighbors can hear about you sending threatening e-mails from a dead woman's computer."

Reluctantly Sean opened the door and let us enter the apartment. We walked by the small kitchen with a cracked linoleum floor and sink full of dirty dishes. Just off the entryway was a tiny living room sparsely decorated with a cheap but serviceable black IKEA sofa, two matching chairs, and a black wooden coffee table littered with half-empty coffee mugs, dirty paper plates, and a MacBook Air. A large University of Arizona pennant hung over the couch. The black TV stand across the room held a large television, a few textbooks, a PlayStation console, and two framed pictures of Kalinda. In one, she was fresh-faced and smiling, standing next to Sean in a graduation cap and gown and holding the dog that greeted us. In the other, she wore tight gold spandex shorts and a matching black-and-gold halter top, the dance uniform of the Phoenix Lasers.

The barking little dog, a small white and gray poodle, hopped around our feet excitedly.

"Down, Chee Chee. Stop it," Sean said as he scooped up the little dog. He walked to the back of the apartment and put the small ball of fur into one of the bedrooms and shut the door behind him.

Joining us back in the living room, Sean invited us to have a seat on the sofa and shifted nervously on his feet.

"Cute dog," I said, motioning to the photo of the three of them on the TV stand.

"Thanks. I got Chee Chee for Kalinda as a graduation present. She loved that dog. But you're not here to talk about Kalinda, right?" Sean asked as he took a seat in one of the well-worn chairs. It was obvious from the way he said her name that he had more than a roommate interest in the slain dancer.

"What are you talking about, Sean?" Terrence asked. "We want to talk about the letters."

"The letters!" Sean shouted as he fought to keep back the angry tears welling up in his eyes. "I can't believe you guys are here harassing me, and Marcus King's the one that murdered Kalinda."

"Look, calm down, Sean," I said, trying to start over. "We just want to find out what happened. Let's start from the beginning. Why were you sending the e-mails, and why were you using Kalinda's computer?"

"Why should I tell you two anything? The cops don't believe me, and you guys won't, either."

"Sean, we're just looking to clear up some things, so the more cooperative you are now, the easier it will be down the line," Terrence said.

"I told the cops everything I knew already, and they didn't believe me. They believed that lying son of a bitch King."

"What exactly did you tell the police, Sean?" I asked.

"Tell us everything and start from the beginning," Terrence said.

I could see that Sean was really getting worked up and was probably going to shut down on us any minute.

"Who are you, anyway?" Sean asked, suddenly turning to me. "Are you with the district attorney's office, too?"

"No, my name is Nia Bullock, Sean. And I'm a reporter."

"Are you writing a story on Kalinda?" he said with a tinge of hope in his voice.

"Not exactly, Sean. But I can tell you cared about your friend Kalinda a great deal. How long were you all friends?"

"We moved in together her senior year to save on rent. She was a great friend and such a nice person. She was just as beautiful on the inside as she was on the outside."

"It sounds like you guys were good friends. Did things between you and Kalinda ever go further than that?" I asked. Maybe the roommate got jealous of the relationship with Marcus and killed her in a jealous rage.

"Are you kidding?" Sean snorted. "As you can see, we're kind of the poster couple for Beauty and the Geek. Kalinda and I were just friends. Would I have liked for it to have been more? Sure. But I knew that was never going to happen, so I settled for having her as a friend. I didn't have many of those around campus since I spent most of my time in the computer lab."

"So why didn't Kalinda move out after she graduated last year and landed a job dancing with the Phoenix Lasers?" Terrence asked.

"Those dancers don't make shit. I made more at my summer internship at Google last summer than Kalinda made in her first year. She thought it was going to be all glamorous dancing and being on TV, but it was a lot of hard work, and she had to deal with a lot of rules she didn't like."

"What kind of rules?" I asked.

"The dancers weren't allowed to date the players, and if someone found out that they were, the dancer would immediately be fired. Kalinda complained about that rule because she said the players were always coming onto her and some of the other girls. She said some of them were kind of cute, but she didn't want to lose her job."

"Did she like her job?" I asked.

"Yeah, she did. She loved to dance and liked the attention she got."

"Did Kalinda get a lot of attention?" Terrence asked. "Did that bother you, Sean?" I could tell he was picking up on my thought that maybe this kid had been jealous and afraid Kalinda was going to leave him.

"Look, I know what you're thinking. The police thought the same thing in the beginning, but I'm not some crazy jealous stalker dude who killed my roommate because I was in love with her. Did I care about Kalinda? Yes. But I'd never hurt her."

"So what do you think happened to Kalinda?" I asked.

"About two months before Kalinda died, she started seeing some new guy. She was real secretive about it, which was unusual for her because she was always pretty open about who she was seeing. I met other guys when they came to the apartment, or I'd hear her talking on the phone with them or she and her friends would talk about them when they'd come over. But this new guy? Nothing. Whenever I asked her why she was being so secretive, she'd say she couldn't tell me. Her Facebook status, which usually said 'In a relationship' when she was seeing someone, was changed to 'It's complicated.' Then one day I was taking out the trash and saw her getting into a black Porsche Panamera with dark tinted windows and flashy rims, and I assumed she was seeing some rich married guy who didn't want his wife to find out."

"You didn't see the driver or anything else?" Terrence asked.

"Nope, like I said, the windows were tinted. I did see the license plate, though, and I remember it because I have a photographic memory."

"Did you ever see the car again?"

"No, not that car. But another time I saw her getting into a Mercedes with tinted windows, and I memorized that plate as well."

"Anything else in your mind that made this relationship stand out from the rest?" Terrence asked.

"Well, the gifts."

"What gifts?" Terrence and I asked in unison.

"You saw how Kalinda looked. I mean, it wasn't unusual for guys to buy her stuff, but this was on a whole other level. She started coming home with expensive jewelry, fur coats, and shit."

"Why didn't the police try to track down those purchases?"

"Well, you see, that's the thing," Sean said leaning forward. "Two days after Kalinda's body was found, someone broke into our apartment and stole all that stuff."

"Did they take anything else?" I asked.

"No, the only things missing were from Kalinda's room. They didn't take any of my computer equipment, the TV, PlayStation, or anything."

"What did the police say?" Terrence asked.

"Yeah, and how are you tying this all to Marcus King? You said she knew there was a policy against dating players, and that she didn't want to lose her job."

"Well, the day Kalinda went missing, it was Friday, and she said she was going away for the weekend with the mystery guy. She thought things were getting pretty serious. She didn't know where they were going. She said he just told her to pack for warm weather and meet him at the airport that afternoon. So when Monday came around and no Kalinda, I'm thinking maybe they decided to stay a little longer. Then Tuesday came and one of the other dancers called me and said Kalinda didn't show up for practice. So then I started to worry, and I called the police."

"And Wednesday the body was found," Terrence said, completing the story.

"Yeah, Wednesday the police came to the apartment and said they needed me to come down to the medical examiner's office and ID a body," Sean said, his voice choking up with emotion. "I couldn't believe what that monster had done to her body. How could someone do that to another person?"

"I'm very sorry, Sean. I know it had to be hard for you to see your friend like that," I said.

"Yeah, but what came next was much worse. The cops asked me a lot of questions, and at first it seemed like they were trying to finger me for the murder, but I got crossed off the list once they confirmed that I was at the annual Hackers United convention in Las Vegas that weekend and there were several witnesses who saw me there. I told them they needed to find this guy she was dating. I recalled the license plate numbers I had seen, broke into the DMV mainframe, and found the cars' registered owner."

"Who was it?" I asked, holding my breath.

"The great Marcus King," Sean said. "I gave the cops the information, and they said they'd look into it, but then they came back a few days later, claiming Marcus had an airtight alibi."

"What was it?" Terrence said.

"He was playing the Dallas Panthers at an away game that night," Terrence said, flipping through his copy of the police file.

"But what about the break-in to your apartment and the stuff you said was stolen?" I asked.

"They didn't believe my story about all the gifts King had bought her. If that stuff hadn't been stolen, they could have gone back to the stores and found out who made the purchases. I didn't have any proof beyond some photos she had taken of herself in the mink jacket and a necklace that she had posted on Facebook."

"Anything else unusual about the break-in?" I asked.

"No, nothing really. This is a pretty safe neighborhood."

"Are you sure?" Terrence pushed. "No strange faces in the neighborhood around the time Kalinda disappeared?"

"Well, not to profile or anything, but a couple of days before the break-in, I thought I kept seeing the same large Hispanic dude in front of the building waiting in his car. I think it was a black Nissan, but I didn't see the plate."

"Did you tell the police?" I asked as I rummaged in my bag to locate a photo of Carlo. Terrence had confirmed that Carlo had rented a black Nissan Maxima from Hertz when he landed in Phoenix two days before Kalinda was killed.

"Of course I did, but those lazy assholes brushed it off. Not that I could blame them. It's Phoenix after all, so the description of 'Hispanic guy in a car' doesn't really take you too far."

"Is this the man you saw watching you from the car?" I asked as I placed the black-and-white photo of Carlo in front of Sean.

"Uh, yeah, I think so. I mean, he had sunglasses on, but I'm pretty sure that's him," Sean said as he looked closely at the photo. "Who is this guy?"

"Don't worry about that right now," Terrence said as he took the photo from Sean and gave it back to me. "Look, the only thing we can tell you at this point for sure is that Marcus King did not murder Kalinda and you need to stop harassing them."

"Did that man you just showed me kill Kalinda? Maybe he was working for King," Sean exclaimed, unwilling to let go of his theory about his friend's murder.

"Leave that to us to figure out, Sean," Terrence said. "But trust me when I say you should leave Marcus and Vanessa King alone."

"Well, I'm not sorry for what I did. That bastard deserves to fry for what he did to Kalinda," Sean said as his face began to turn red and he raked his bony fingers through his curly hair in frustration.

"Sean, listen to me," I said. "The police are right. Marcus King did not murder your friend. Trust me."

"OK, then what do you want from me? Am I in trouble?" Sean whined. "Are the Kings pressing charges?"

"Look, if you promise not to send any more threatening e-mails or text messages, then we'll talk to the Kings," I said.

"So why did you start sending those messages?" Terrence asked.

"After the fucking cops refused to follow up anymore, because it was my word against King's, I leaked some information to some of the local papers, hoping they'd investigate, but aside from a few gossipy stories about King possibly sleeping with Kalinda, nobody picked up the trail until you guys showed up today."

"So you started sending those messages to Marcus and Vanessa because you thought he'd gotten away with murder," I said. "We know how you sent the text messages and e-mails, but how'd you get the notes delivered to their homes?"

"There are underground hacker networks full of people who will deliver stuff for the right fee," Sean snorted. "Look, Kalinda said they were getting serious, and she wanted to marry him. But this King guy was already married, and there's no way he was ever going to leave his wife and kid for some dancer. Even I know that."

"So you think Marcus King killed Kalinda when she saw that King wasn't going to leave his wife?" Terrence said with a raised eyebrow.

"Kalinda was used to getting what she wanted. She definitely wasn't used to guys telling her no. I think maybe Kalinda threatened to tell his wife or something, and he flipped out. And then he put her body out in the desert, hoping no one would find it."

"Sean, we appreciate all your help. Like I said, Marcus King didn't kill your friend. Stop sending the messages before you get into some trouble that you can't hack your way out of."

"Feel free to reach out if you think of anything else that might be helpful," Terrence said, handing Sean his card.

"Are you around the rest of the weekend in case we have more questions?" I asked, turning the knob to open the door.

"Yeah, I'm around all weekend. I'm working on my senior project," Sean said as he placed the card in the pocket of his baggy shorts.

"Good, we'll be in touch if we have any further questions," Terrence said as he stepped out of the cramped apartment and into the sunshine with me and slipped on his sunglasses.

"Please find out who killed Kalinda," Sean said as he leaned against the doorjamb, squinting in the sunlight as he looked down at the pool full of people having fun in the cool water. "Whoever did this deserves to pay for what they did to my friend."

CHAPTER 19

Laila

Fresh from the shower, I stood in front of the mirrored closet in my W hotel suite and admired the view. Then I stretched out on my stomach on the bed, naked except for my Prada python platform sandals and a diamond-studded belly chain. I thought about all the wonderful things that were going to happen tonight and the insurance policy I was creating as I took a deep drag on the joint Darryl had given me earlier to relax. My fingers skipped along the tops of my breasts and moved slowly down toward the moisture between my thighs. Wet. Ready.

I heard the knock on the door and called out to my handsome visitor to come in. I had left the door ajar so that I would be lounging, ready and waiting. I kneeled in the bed, my hands on my knees.

Marcus strode purposefully into the bedroom. I hadn't seen him in weeks, and my whole body ached for him to be inside me. He was dressed in a black Tom Ford suit, black shirt, and black tie with huge diamond cuff links at the sleeves. His perfectly smooth chocolate skin glistened. His hair was freshly lined and his facial hair neatly trimmed. His eyes were deep dark pools framed by long silky lashes, and his lips were full and juicy and eager for my kiss. Unable to wait any longer, I began to crawl toward him on the bed, my hair falling into my eyes. I knew how he loved seeing me beg for it.

"Hello, baby," I drawled huskily, my voice deep with desire. "I've missed you."

"Laila, we need to talk," Marcus said as he picked up the robe that lay across the settee at the end of the bed and tossed it at me. "Put on some clothes. I don't have much time."

He walked back into the living room. Confused, I climbed down off the bed and wrapped the silk robe around my body, then followed him into the main area of my suite. I came up behind him and wrapped my arms around his waist; letting the robe fall open, I pressed my body against his. I was sure he could feel my heat through his clothes. My hand began to slide down the front of his slacks, reaching for the long, hard chocolate treat I couldn't wait to slide into my mouth. He pulled away from me and then turned around to face me. He looked like he was steeling himself to say something.

"Marcus, baby, what's wrong? Aren't you happy to see me?" I smiled as I opened the robe and let it fall to the floor in a silky red puddle.

"Look, I came here to tell you that it's over," he said in a tone I had never heard before. He ran his hand across the top of his head. "Things have gotten out of control. I have to focus on my career and my marriage. I can't afford any more distractions."

"Distractions?" I said, putting my hand on my hip, the diamond belly chain cutting into my skin. "Is that all I am to you? A distraction?"

"Look, baby. This is the way the game goes. We had fun, but now I've got to go back to real life. I've got to get focused back on what matters and take care of business."

I couldn't believe what I was hearing. Maybe Darryl gave me some fucked-up shit and the weed was making me hear things. I stepped forward again and dropped down on my knees in front of him, my hands desperately clawing at the silver YSL belt buckle on his slacks.

"Laila, get up," he said, pulling me up from the floor by my elbows and leading me over to the sofa to sit down. He didn't sit down next to me.

"I don't know how else to say this. We're done. It's over. Now, look, Kareem is going to contact you in a few days and take care of you. We had fun while it lasted and there's no need for you to walk away empty-handed." And with that last little insult, he kissed me on the top of my head and headed out the door.

When the door to the suite closed, Darryl burst out of the mirrored closet in the bedroom and came out into the living room with his video camera dangling from his hand.

"What the hell just happened, Laila?" he asked, looking back and forth between me and the door. "I didn't catch anything on tape. What happened to the wild, crazy sex tape I was going to record and leak to the press in case we needed it?"

I slumped down on the floor next to my robe and said three words I had never said in my entire life: "He dumped me." Tears began to fall as my body was racked with huge sobs. Where the hell did I go wrong? What happened, and how did Kareem double-cross me?

"Look, stop crying," Darryl said as he put his camera on the table and helped me stand. He grabbed the robe from the floor and wrapped it around my naked body. He led me back into the bedroom, and I sat on the bed.

"I'm going to take care of this. We're going to get this money. Trust me." Darryl took his cell phone out of the back pocket of his baggy jeans and placed a call. When the person on the other line picked up, Darryl began to speak to them rapidly in Spanish.

"Pull yourself together, Laila. It's time to move to plan B," Darryl said as he slid the phone back into his pocket and sat beside me on the bed, stroking my hair.

"Plan B?" I asked, looking up at him, mascara mixing with my tears and running down my cheeks.

"Yep, you know real gangstas always have a plan B. And your boy D just called in the cavalry."

CHAPTER 20

Vanessa

Two large bodyguards shielded Marcus as he strode out of the front entrance of the W hotel, holding back the crowd of screaming fans and groupies clamoring for his autograph and attention. He unbuttoned his suit jacket and slipped into the back of the waiting SUV next to me. One of the bodyguards took the driver's seat after closing the door behind Marcus while the other folded his large frame into the front passenger seat.

"It's done," my husband said as he took my hand and brought it to his lips.

"Good," I said quietly as I smoothed down the front of my strapless red sequined Versace gown, trying to hold myself back from asking for the details of his final meeting with Laila James. Had she cried? Had she begged him to stay? Had she screamed?

I looked out the window as the chauffeured SUV turned out of the crowded hotel parking lot and glided smoothly down the dark Phoenix city streets on the way to our next engagement. I could tell that Marcus was dreading this one as well, but at least this time I would be right by his side as he delivered the unfortunate news.

I felt my phone vibrating in my Alexander McQueen snakeskin box clutch. When I took it out, I saw a text message from Nia and smiled.

We found ur stalker. He won't b bothering U anymore. TTYL.

I exhaled deeply as I put the phone back into my clutch. Even after our fight this afternoon, I trusted Nia with my life. She wouldn't play with something this serious, so I knew if she said this person wouldn't be bothering us anymore, then my family and I were safe. I looked over at my husband and thought about telling him, but he looked deep in thought about how life was about to change forever. I'll tell him later on tonight.

"Hey," I said to Marcus as I squeezed his hand and searched his eyes. "Baby, don't worry. You're doing the right thing. You have no other choice."

"I know, but do we have to do this tonight?"

"Yes, sweetheart," I said gently but firmly. "We do. It's time."

"I know, baby. I just never imagined we'd end up here after everything we've been through together."

"I know, honey," I said, stroking his hand lightly with my glossy silver nails. "I didn't, either." That last part was a lie, but he didn't need to know that.

I opened my Christian Dior compact to freshen my makeup. Felecia, my makeup artist, had done a wonderful job. My dark brown skin glowed, the golden bronzer highlighted my cheeks, and the silver and gold smoky eye shadow and long silk eye lash extensions really made my eyes pop. I applied another coat of glossy red Versace lipstick and then smoothed down the sides of my hair. The stylist had flat-ironed my thick black hair into supersleek straight waves with a jagged part down the middle. And he had sworn on his life that it would stand up to the desert heat. I didn't want to look crazy on the red carpet when we got to Kevin Hart's comedy jam later on that night.

The SUV made a left turn into the parking lot of the Nikko Tower. Designed by the Orito Group out of Japan to great acclaim, it was a stunning sixty-floor construct of twisted burnished metal and glass, and it was one of Phoenix's newest and most exclusive office buildings. We stepped out into the evening's dry heat, and the bodyguards escorted us into the glass lobby's cool interior. A lone security guard stood watch at a large marble desk facing a bank of computer monitors in the center of the modern lobby. The only sound was that of a janitor cleaning the already sparkling floors with an automatic polisher. Out of the bank of thirty elevators a bespectacled man in a dark navy-blue pinstriped suit and red tie made his way over to us.

"Mr. and Mrs. King, welcome," the man said, and his voice had the faintest hint of a British accent. "I'm James Van Helsen. And I've been asked to bring you both up to the executive boardroom on the seventieth floor."

"Thank you, James," I said. As I looped my arm through Marcus's, I could feel his body tense over what he knew he needed to do. I hoped he wasn't getting cold feet.

"Now, will your security team be joining us, or will they be waiting for you in the lobby?" James asked the both of us.

Before Marcus could speak, I jumped in.

"They'll be joining us for the first meeting but not the second," I said firmly.

"Very good, Mrs. King. We're happy to have them join the first meeting, but I'm afraid I must ask an indelicate question. Are these gentlemen armed?"

"Yes, of course," I said.

"Unfortunately, as a matter of protocol, no weapons are allowed on the seventieth floor. So I'm afraid I must ask that they leave their weapons down here." James motioned for the security guard to come over to us and addressed our bodyguards. "If you don't mind, could you place your weapons in this security box? You can claim them straight away when you come back down to the lobby. Clarence won't let anything happen, I can assure you of that.

"If you'll just follow me this way."

I signaled to Bruce and Tyson, who I knew could kill anyone with their bare hands in seconds to protect this family, to hand over their weapons. They opened their suit jackets and removed nine-millimeter guns from their holsters and placed them in the metal box. James closed the box, locked it, and gave the key to Bruce.

"Thank you so much for your understanding. Now if you will all follow me, please."

James began to lead us over to the bank of elevators, and my Rick Owens ankle-wrap stilettos clicked along the marble floor. James inserted a key in the panel on the wall, and the doors to a private elevator opened. There were only two buttons on the panel on the inside of this elevator, one for the lobby and one for the seventieth floor. James once again inserted the key and then pushed the button for the top floor. The elevator silently glided up to the top floor of the building, and then the doors opened into a large reception area framed all around by a bank of floor-to-ceiling windows that looked out onto the twinkling Phoenix skyline and the desert mountains. A receptionist with a severe black bob, wearing a black dress with a mandarin collar, sat behind a large walnut reception desk, typing on a computer. She barely looked up at us as James escorted us past her desk as if it were normal to see a meeting conducted at this hour on a Friday night.

We walked down a long carpeted hallway, its walls decorated with works of art I had only previously seen in art books or museums. I must have counted at least two Picassos and a Renoir by the time we made it to the end of the hallway and stood in front of two walnut doors with brushed metal handles shaped like rams' ears.

"Are you ready, Mr. and Mrs. King?" James asked, turning to us as he stopped in front of the doors.

I looked at my husband because, even though I had gotten us to this point, he was the one who had to make the final call.

"Yes," he said firmly as he inhaled deeply. I clasped his hand tightly and gave it a reassuring squeeze.

"Very well," James said as he pushed open the doors. The executive boardroom was one of the largest rooms I had ever seen. The same bank of floor-to-ceiling windows showed off the skyline in here as well. We made our way into the room as James escorted us down to the end of the long glass table that sliced down the center of the room. A stenographer, a blond woman also in a black dress with a mandarin collar, was seated on the opposite side of the table, fingers poised above the keys and ready to begin. Two men in dark suits got up from their chairs as we approached, and James introduced them.

"Mrs. and Mrs. King, please meet Cedric Jameson and Cristoff Warner, the two senior partners who will be overseeing this evening's transaction." We shook hands with the two men, who both looked to be in their early fifties, and then we took our seats next to them at the table. James instructed Bruce and Tyson to stand by the door.

With that, James left the room and returned a few minutes later with a familiar face through a side door at the same end of the room.

"What the hell is going on, Marcus?" Kareem thundered as he walked into the boardroom and saw his best friend, his wife, and their lawyers. James instructed him to take a seat across the table from us and then sat down in the empty chair next to me.

The stenographer began to type.

CHAPTER 21

Nia

The photographers screamed out names to get the line of reality
TV stars, R&B singers, and rappers to stop along the red carpet
so that they could get their shot. But as soon as the woman of the hour
hit the carpet for her premiere party, only one name was heard.

Her firm golden-brown body was encased in a flesh-toned strapless
minidress laced with chunks of crystal in strategic places. One shiny
cluster hugged each of her full breasts, another fanned across her bikini
line, and then a line snaked down the back of the dress over the crack
of her ample bottom. Her long light brown hair with golden highlights
was piled down the center of her head in a cascading Mohawk of curls.
Her fire-engine-red lips curved into a seductive smile as she placed her
gold-studded talons on her hips and blew kisses to the photographers.

"Laila! Laila! Laila!"

Glam Network's newest star had turned the pack of photographers
into a frenzied pool of sharks all trying to get the perfect shot of the
one-of-a-kind dress that with one false move would present a priceless
image. MJ and I watched Laila pirouette on her sky-high Christian
Louboutin crocodile and sequined platform pumps on the red carpet
while she waved to the screaming fans lined up five rows deep behind
the police barricades in front of Inferno.

Luckily, the *DivaDish* video team had prime placement in order
to live stream the party on our website. So far, Tanya, the reality show's
executive producer, had told me we had about seventy-five thousand

people logged on, and she expected that number to grow throughout the night as they kept posting updates and photos.

MJ and I made our way through the tight security line into the already packed nightclub. DJ Kid Capri, who we had flown in from New York, was lighting up the turntables and waved at us from the DJ booth.

"Looks like a packed house," I said, trying to make myself heard over the noise.

"Yeah, good turnout," said MJ, whose black suit was accessorized with oversize chrome zippers along the lapels.

"Great party for our last hurrah," I said as I hung on MJ's shoulders. I had told him that once I revealed this cover, I was probably going to get fired. So for the second time in a year, we'd both be out of a job over something I did. MJ took it all in stride as usual and said we should enjoy the night because there was no telling what might happen.

"Now why aren't you on the red carpet taking pictures with the person you're hosting this party for, Miss Thing?" MJ said, moving his little skinny hips to the beat of Beyoncé's "Drunk in Love."

"You know why," I huffed. "It's bad enough I have to host this damn party for the woman sleeping with my best friend's man, but I don't have to take any damn pictures with her, too!" Besides, even though I was looking good in the short Junya Watanabe floral lace shift dress and Manolo Blahnik black patent leather booties MJ had picked out for me, I wasn't trying to stand next to someone basically wearing a body stocking.

"I think someone may disagree with that," MJ said in his singsong voice as I turned around to face someone tapping me on the shoulder.

"Why aren't you taking pictures with Laila?" DeAnna snapped. She was dressed in a fitted red suit with skinny pants and sans blouse, her large breasts visible between the curved lapels of the suit. Her long black hair was slicked back in a severe chignon at the nape of her neck.

"I was coming in to check on how things were going," I yelled as DJ Nice started the opening chords of Jay Z's "99 Problems" and the club erupted.

"What?" she screamed back at me, straining to hear what I was saying as people rushed by, jostling her to get to the dance floor at the center of the two-story club. I decided to use this to my advantage, so I moved my lips, saying nothing, and made a few hand gestures like I had to go find someone, and then turned and left her standing there. Hopefully she would get crushed in the stampede.

As MJ and I made our way deeper into the club and headed upstairs to the VIP section, I saw Miki Woods in a black suit, lounging on one of the white sofas and chatting with comedian Kevin Hart. I knew I needed to talk to her now before the cover was revealed and Laila, our new corporate brand thanks to the merger, was humiliated, but I wasn't sure what to say. Once it came out, the only thing left to say would be, "Nice working with you." I flashed my all-access pass at the security guard stationed at the VIP entrance, and he removed the rope to let me in. From the tray of one of the waiters I accepted a La-lini, tonight's signature champagne cocktail compliments of tonight's other sponsor, Moët, and made my way over to Miki.

"Hi, Nia," Miki squealed when she saw me, jumping up from the couch. She introduced MJ and me to Kevin, who gave us some passes for his midnight comedy showcase and told us he expected to see us there.

"All right, all right, all right!" I said, making an embarrassing attempt to impersonate Kevin's dad from his famous act. He and MJ just looked at me like I was stupid as hell. I took another large sip of my drink. MJ shook his head and walked Kevin out of VIP, hopefully explaining to him that I'd suffered a brain injury as a child.

"How's it going, Miki?" I said, sitting down next to her on the sofa and taking a sip of my champagne cocktail.

"I'm good. Great party, Nia. Congratulations." Miki held up her own glass for a toast. We clinked glasses.

"Thanks, Miki," I said.

"Now that Glam Network is a part of PrimeTime Media, there are big plans in the works. The key word is expansion. We're going to need people with bold ideas, fresh perspectives, and the ability to execute. I hear good things about you, and from what I've seen, you got this partnership up and running quickly for the launch of Laila's show, so I'd say you are one of those people. Would you agree?"

I was taken aback by her question. While I knew I was good at what I did, I didn't expect she'd be thinking so highly of me in a few minutes when the new cover with Vanessa's story and fake interview with Marcus were revealed.

"I like to think I have some good ideas," I said, not wanting to put myself out there too far, seeing as DeAnna would probably be firing me by the end of the night.

"Don't play yourself short, Nia. As a woman of color in the business world, you can't afford to do that. You've got to learn how to promote your value. Look, I know good talent when I see it, and I look forward to expanding this partnership and getting things moving in exciting new directions."

She was right. Whoever got anywhere by not stepping up and showing people what she could do? No one. And even though I was quite sure I would end the night unemployed, I spent the next twenty minutes talking to Miki about all the ideas that I had shared with DeAnna over the last six months that she'd either ignored or shoved in a drawer never to see the light of day. She seemed especially interested in my ideas about creating local content with the *DivaDish* brand in ten key markets.

"Where would you start?" Miki asked. It had been so long since anyone had showed a genuine interest in my ideas, I almost thought she was being sarcastic.

"I'd like to start in DC and capture that entire Maryland, Virginia, DC market, and then explore Atlanta, Detroit, Houston, Chicago,

Charlotte, St. Louis as key markets, and then conduct some research to identify the next four targets."

"That's a great idea. And do you think you could handle all those editions along with your current responsibilities?"

"Absolutely, I have a great team. They are nimble, hardworking, and passionate about the brand."

Just as I finished talking about my team, DeAnna squeezed through the VIP crowd and made her way over to us. I could tell by the way she looked at me that she wasn't happy to see me talking to Miki. She also expected me to get up and make room for her next to Miki.

"Hi, DeAnna," Miki said. "I was just complimenting Nia on this great party and discussing some of her exciting plans for the *DivaDish* brand. Sounds like you've got a real winner here."

Damn, now why'd she have to go and tell DeAnna all that? Even though she had dismissed or ignored most of my ideas, I knew DeAnna was extremely territorial and wouldn't like hearing that I was discussing anything about the *Diva* brand with Miki. As I began to get up from the sofa to make room for Miki, MJ walked over with a microphone and Laila.

"It's time for the cover reveal," he said, handing me the microphone. He might as well have said, "It's time to walk the plank." "They want you and Laila over by the railing overlooking the dance floor, and Tanya will project the cover image on the wall above the DJ booth and then roll the clip of Laila's show."

MJ led Laila and me over to the railing and gave me the microphone. Laila's makeup artist rushed over to powder her nose and freshen her lipstick. Her hairstylist quickly fluffed up her curls. I looked down and saw Tanya Peoples getting her crew into position on the stage.

MJ spoke into his headset to cue DJ Nice to cut the music and introduce me, and then MJ gave me the cue to start speaking.

"Ladies and gentlemen, on behalf of *DivaDish*, Moët, and Glam Network, it is my pleasure to welcome you to the world premiere party for Laila James's hot new reality show, *Whatever Laila Wants*!" The room erupted in cheers, whistles, and thunderous applause. Just as I was about to reveal the cover, Laila grabbed the microphone from my hand and stepped in front of me.

"How's everyone doing tonight?" Laila purred into the microphone as she blew kisses down to the cheering fans below. "Welcome to my party for my new show, *Whatever Laila Wants* . . . I'd like to thank Glam Network for launching my show and Moët for sponsoring this fabulous party. Can we get a hand for Moët and Glam Network, everybody?"

I couldn't believe she was snubbing me and the *DivaDish* brand at the party we were hosting for her.

"And now, for the moment you've all been waiting for. It's the world premiere of my clip from my new show, *Whatever Laila Wants* . . . Hit it!" Since Tanya had been instructed to show the cover first and then the video, it took her a few seconds to pull up the show clip.

"I said, roll the clip!" Laila said forcefully with a hard smile on her face. "Let's give these people a sneak peek at what they really came to see!"

The clip for *Whatever Laila Wants* began to play, showing various scenes of Laila in New York City and Los Angeles. There were clips of Laila shopping, dipping in and out of luxury boutiques, trying on lingerie, in business meetings, out at nightclubs surrounded by groups of men, and, of course, the requisite celebrity cameos. But the part of the clip that caused my stomach to drop was the way the producer had interspersed allusions to her relationship with Marcus. There was Laila rolling around in a hotel suite wearing a number 17 New York Gladiators jersey and panties reading the *New York Daily* story about her and Marcus getting caught leaving the hotel, footage of her at Gladiator games, cheering on the sidelines, and cutaways that made it look like Marcus was waving to her. This was much worse than I could have even imagined. I looked over at MJ and motioned for him to close his mouth, which was hanging open in shock. Laila looked back at me and sneered before turning to address her fans again.

"So what do y'all think?" Laila roared, pumping her fist in the air, which caused her skimpy dress to rise, nearly displacing the strategically placed crystals of her gown. "Did your girl Laila put it down or what?"

The crowd in the club started cheering in response.

"Laila! Laila! Laila! Laila!"

"Are y'all ready for the drama?" she asked, holding out the microphone for the crowd's response.

"Are you ready for the sexy?"

"Are you ready for my new show!"

I needed to get out of there and get some air, but I knew I had to do my job first. I snatched back the microphone as Laila adjusted her dress.

"One more round of applause for Laila James, ladies and gentlemen!" The crowd cheered again and then quieted down as I motioned for silence. "As Laila mentioned, this is her night, and it's a special one as she prepares to launch her exciting new reality show. Well, we all know nothing makes for a better reality show than a little drama, so with that I present the new cover of *DivaDish* magazine and our exclusive interview with Vanessa King!"

Tanya punched the button on her computer, and the cover of Vanessa King announcing her pregnancy was revealed. There was a loud audible gasp from the crowd as everyone took in the beautiful image of Vanessa cradling her stomach and read the cover line about her and Marcus working things out. The crowd erupted in applause and cheers that were even louder than before. Suddenly they began chanting again.

"Vanessa! Vanessa! Vanessa! Vanessa!"

"What the fuck is this?" screamed Laila, not realizing the microphone I was holding was still hot and that the cameras from the live stream were trained right on her. Her face was twisted into an ugly mask, her mouth in a menacing scowl.

"You bitch! I knew you were out to get me. I know you're friends with Vanessa! You did this on purpose!"

"Like you said, get ready for the drama, right?" I quipped, leaning in and whispering in her ear as I dropped the microphone at her feet.

I began to make my way back through the crowd of speechless Moët and Glam Network executives to DeAnna and Miki who were both on their feet by the couch. No time like the present to get fired. DeAnna's face was twisted in a similar angry mask, blood rushing up her neck to her cheeks. Miki was typing furiously on her BlackBerry as she and her assistant walked past me out of the VIP area without saying a word. I couldn't believe what I had just done, but I didn't really have a choice.

"Are you crazy?" DeAnna screeched as she grabbed my arm and pulled me into a corner behind a tall plastic palm tree. "What the hell was that stunt you just pulled?"

"It wasn't a stunt, DeAnna," I said as I jerked my arm away from her. "We had a great exclusive, and I ran with it. Any editor would have done the same thing."

"I warned you that your loyalties to Vanessa were going to get you in trouble!"

"This wasn't about any loyalty to Vanessa. Like I said, I did what any editor would have done in my position."

"Oh, really . . . You think so? What about our corporate partnership with Glam Network, Nia? Did you think of that?"

"I did what you asked me to do, DeAnna. I threw Laila a party, and I got our brand unbelievable buzz. People are going to be tweeting and posting comments about this party and Laila's upcoming show for weeks. And traffic and sales are going to be through the roof!" I was desperately trying to spin some sort of tale to make it seem like tonight's events were to our advantage, but she wasn't buying it.

"Did you see how fast Miki Woods hightailed it out of here tonight after you pulled this little surprise? She's probably hopping on a plane right now back to New York to put your head on a platter!" I knew she was right, but I didn't want to admit it and show DeAnna my fear.

"I was just doing my job," I asserted, tired of being bullied by this woman. In the world of reality TV, all drama is good drama. But I didn't expect DeAnna to understand that.

"What job?" DeAnna sneered as she raked her cold hard black eyes up and down my body.

CHAPTER 22

Vanessa

The stenographer typed quietly and efficiently across the table as Kareem faced the evidence in front of him. There was no way out, and the bastard knew it. A satisfied smile curved across my lips.

James and the two partners had done an excellent job of laying out Kareem's complex web of financial deception that had begun the night Marcus announced that his cousin would become his manager and agent.

When Marcus signed the management documents that Kareem had hastily drawn up within a week of his announcement, what Marcus hadn't realized was the stack of documents also included a power of attorney.

James, in his clipped British accent, began to walk everyone through what had happened next. Over the years, he said, Kareem had surreptitiously built layer upon layer of shell companies, created fake employees and fraudulent expenses, and billed all of his own personal expenses, including the mortgages for his three homes, clothing, groceries and all of his cars, to bilk nearly $120 million from Marcus, approximately half of his earnings over the past eight years.

Seeing the devastated look on Kareem's face as he was presented with document after document that the firm's forensic accounting team had created chronicling every single dollar he had stolen from

Marcus over the past eight years made their $100,000 retainer and $2,500 hourly fee well worth it in my opinion.

Nearing the close of the meeting, Cedric really earned his money when he began to lay out Kareem's relationship with Laila. He presented a folder to each of us, complete with photographs of the former couple, cell phone records, and e-mail exchanges outlining their plans to leak sightings, text messages, and photos to the media. Their ultimate plan, said James, pausing for dramatic effect, was to get me out of the picture and Laila installed as the new Mrs. King for both of their financial benefit.

While Marcus had thought he was prepared for walking into this evening, I think seeing it all laid out in front of him in black and white with page after page of stolen money and copies of text messages and e-mails unearthed by private investigators was harder than he thought. After being shocked into silence for most of the meeting, he suddenly spoke up.

"How could you do this to me?" Marcus said, his voice choked up in a hoarse whisper. "You were my brother." He couldn't even look across the table at Kareem. I took his hand under the table.

Kareem, his broad shoulders deflated and head hung low, pushed through the pile of papers as if searching for something that would wipe away all of the damning evidence.

"Answer me, dammit!" Marcus said, pounding his fist on the table. "You fucking answer me!"

Kareem refused to meet Marcus's gaze, so I motioned to Cristoff, the second senior partner, to continue.

Cristoff nodded and cleared his throat before he began his part of the evening's presentation. He slid a gray legal-size folder containing a packet of documents across the conference room table to Kareem.

"Mr. Davis, we've taken steps to unravel your agreement with Mr. King, and as such you will sign this agreement that will dissolve your management agreement and power of attorney with Mr. King effective immediately. As such, the mortgages on your three homes, all contents therein, tags and titles for your six cars, have all been ceased and are in the process of being liquidated. All the credit cards in the name of Marcus King Holdings have also been canceled. Against our recommendation, the Kings have decided that you walk away today, keeping whatever you currently have on deposit at your bank."

Cristoff pushed a few buttons on his iPad to pull up Kareem's account and then, looking over the top of his reading glasses, said, "For the recording of this meeting, the stenographer is to note that Mr. Davis's bank balance as of this moment, held in a Merrill Lynch CMA account, is $235,987.34. Consider that a very generous severance package, Mr. Davis, especially since it goes against our recommendation, that Mr. King is declining to press charges and send you to jail for a very long time."

Kareem exploded out of his chair, knocking it back on the floor. "You can't do this to me!" he yelled as he pounded on the table with both his hands. "Marcus, I made you the star you are. You wouldn't be where you are today if it weren't for me."

"Are you kidding me, man?" Marcus snapped through gritted teeth. He pushed his chair back from the table and stood up. As he leaned forward across the table, his eyes bulging and face tense with rage, his body was coiled and ready to pounce. "You stole money from me, from my family, when I would have given you anything!"

"You don't know what I've done for you," Kareem retorted, desperately shaking his head.

"What you've done for me? Let me see what you've done for me." Marcus counted down the irreversible offenses on his fingers. "You've stolen half my money. You've tried to break up my marriage. You've betrayed your godson.

"I loved you like my own brother. Made you the godfather to my son. I've had you in my home. I've asked you to protect my wife, and all this time it was just about the money with you. All about the money. You were never my brother."

"Don't try to blame your sneaking around on me, partner. No sir," Kareem said. "You liked fucking all those freaks and had me running around making airplane reservations, hooking up hotels and shit. Don't act like you were just an innocent bystander. Yeah, everything was all good while I was hooking up your little rendezvous with Laila, but now you want to act all high and mighty like you weren't down for the game."

It hurt me to hear about all the other women, although I had suspected that Kareem had been facilitating Marcus's hookups with groupies all this years.

"Yes, you're right, Kareem. I've done my dirt, I've disrespected my wife and my vows, and I have to try my damnedest to make amends for that with her and with God. And you're going to have to do your damnedest to make things right with God yourself, but don't ever come looking for me to forgive your punk ass."

"Punk? Who you calling a punk! You don't even know half the things I've done for you!" Suddenly Kareem crossed over to Marcus in three quick strides and grabbed his cousin's lapels, pulling him close into his face.

"You don't know what I've done for you!" he screamed desperately, his eyes wild with fear and anger. As Marcus fought to free himself, Tyson and Bruce bounded across the room and wrestled Kareem off Marcus.

"Get off me! Let me go!" Kareem tried to twist out of the tight hold of the two bodyguards, but with one on each side of him, they easily pulled the two men apart.

"You don't even know what you're doing! You can't cut me off! I know this isn't you, man. I know it's Vanessa's idea. We family, man! She's always tried to come between us!" Kareem was desperate now, begging for his life.

"No one brought this on but you, Kareem! We're finished. I kept my promise. I said we'd make it to the NBA together, and we did. Now it's over. You betrayed me in the worst way possible."

Suddenly Kareem turned his anger on me as I came up beside my husband. "Fuck you, Vanessa," he sneered, straining against the bodyguards holding him in the chair. "You bitch. I'll get you for this! I swear I will!"

Suddenly Marcus wrestled his way out of the bodyguard's grasp and lunged forward to punch Kareem hard across the face as he sat in the chair. "Don't you ever say my wife's name again!"

Tyson stepped forward to block Marcus from taking another shot. Kareem turned his head to the side and spit some blood onto the carpet and rubbed his aching jaw. Marcus took one last look at Kareem, then came back over to me and grabbed my hand to leave. As I quickly grabbed my purse, I took one last look at Kareem, and my lips curved into a satisfied smile.

As we made our way out of the conference room, Marcus tossed over his shoulder to Tyson and Bruce, "Make sure that muthafucka doesn't leave this room until he signs those documents."

—

Before James escorted Marcus and me to our third and final meeting of the evening, I asked him to give us a moment of privacy in the hallway. He gladly obliged and slipped into an office down the hall.

"Are you OK, baby?" I took Marcus's hands in mine and looked into his eyes, which were filled with pain. "I know that was hard for you." I would have given anything for him not to have to go through that pain of betrayal, but it had been necessary. He needed to know the truth. And now we could forge a new future free from Kareem and free from Laila.

"I just can't believe K. would do that to me," he said, a tear slipping out of his eye. I reached up and brushed it away and hugged my husband close.

"Baby, I know he was like your brother, but this world is vicious, and he got greedy and turned on us. But at least now you know."

"But look at what I almost let him do to us," he said, his lips in my ear. "I almost let all the bullshit kill our marriage. I almost lost everything that mattered."

"I won't pretend you haven't hurt me. But it's for better or worse with us. I knew from the beginning that this wasn't going to be easy, but I knew it would always be worth it. You can always trust me, baby. You know that I'll always have your back. I'll always hold you down. I love you, Marcus. Always have, always will."

"I don't deserve you, Vanessa. I really don't."

"Yes, you do, Marcus. We deserve each other, and we're going to be together forever because that's how we do. Today is the first day of the rest of our lives, baby. It can be that way if we want it to."

"Oh God, Vanessa. Can't we do this next meeting later? I just want to go back to the hotel and be with you." His warm breath tickled my ear as his embrace tightened. I hugged him and then stepped back to look into his eyes.

"I would love nothing better than to go back to the hotel, but we've got to take this last meeting because you need to make some more money to take care of your growing family," I said as I placed his hand on my stomach.

"You're pregnant?" he said, his eyes suddenly wide with delight and surprise.

"Yes, baby. We're pregnant." I smiled. Marcus picked me up and hugged me hard, swinging me around in the dimly lit hallway just as James returned to retrieve us for the meeting.

He walked us down to a large glass conference room. There were about ten young men and women seated around the large glass table, and they all stood up and started clapping when we walked in.

"Marcus King, it's a pleasure to finally meet you," John Knight said as he made his way over to us from the head of the room. "Mrs. King, so lovely to see you also. I trust our lawyer and team of forensic accountants were helpful with your last meeting and that you're ready to move forward with Knight Sports Management."

"Absolutely," Marcus said, extending his hand to John while keeping his other arm firmly around my waist.

CHAPTER 23

Nia

The shot clock counted down the seconds as the All-Star team from the East set up a nice three-point opportunity. Marcus dribbled down low and pushed past Easton Miles, the six-foot-ten guard for the West, pump-faked, and then floated the ball into the basket.

"That's my baby," Vanessa said, jumping up from her courtside seat to clap for her husband as he ran down the court and winked at her.

"Would you sit your happy ass down and act like you been somewhere before," I said, clowning her as I jerked on the coattail of the peplum-style mustard yellow Prada blazer she wore with black stretch denim jeans tucked into Jimmy Choo boots. I pulled her down onto the cushioned chair next to me.

"Whatever, hater," she said, taking a sip of her lemonade. "You know you're excited to be sitting here with me cheering for the East."

"I hate to break it to you, boo, but I'm cheering for the West tonight," I said as I pumped my fist in the air, yelling for Easton to pick up the pace as he faced off against Marcus again.

"Not in my seats you ain't," Vanessa said, looking at me in mock horror with her hair cocked to the side. "You better get right or get to steppin'."

"Dang, is that how you'd treat your girl after all these years?" I asked, feigning shock. "I mean, I tracked down your stalker and humiliated that tramp, and that's all the thanks I get?" I dipped a large chip into my nacho sauce, trying not to spill another gob of melted cheese on my Balmain ruffled motorcycle jacket.

"Aww, you know you my girl," Vanessa said reaching over to hug me from the side and jostling my nachos in the process.

"Watch it, girl. Don't be messing up my outfit getting cheese every-where," I said.

"No for real, girl," Vanessa said as she kept her eyes on the court as the clock crept toward the halftime show featuring Usher and Justin Bieber. "You really looked out for me and my family, and I'll never forget that. I'm sorry DeAnna got so upset with you."

"I know, V. I'll just have to face the music when I get back to New York on Monday. I'm sure DeAnna won't be able to wait until the end of the week to give me my walking papers."

"I don't know, girl. Something tells me things are going to work out," she said as she squeezed my arm and reached for another chip.

"Well, you must be the only one," I said.

"I can't believe you said the stalker was some crazy computer nerd who thought Marcus killed that cheerleader," Vanessa said, changing the subject.

I didn't tell her that I wasn't quite convinced that Marcus hadn't had something to do with her, but I'd need some more information for that. And I really didn't want to get into that part of the story, given how happy she and Marcus were right now. I hadn't seen them this happy in years. She was glowing, and he was looking at her and smiling in a way I hadn't seen in a long time.

I was so excited when she called me early this morning to tell me all about last night's events. I was just as shocked as she was to learn of Kareem's embezzlement but glad to know that he was out of their lives. When I told her about how I handled the cover release with Laila, she had screamed into the phone and said she would have given anything to be a fly on the wall to see that heffa's face cracked on the floor. She said she knew something big must have happened, because as soon as they left their meeting with Knight Sports Management, both her phone and Marcus's started blowing up with congratulatory text messages, calls, and e-mails. I told her I was glad she had told her husband before the news broke all over Twitter and Facebook.

When I asked her why the news wasn't out that Marcus had signed with a new manager, she said that they'd all agreed to get through All-Star and wait until they got back to New York next week and could meet with the team owners. Everyone had been sworn to secrecy. Even Kareem had been forced to sign a confidentiality agreement. That seemed smart. No need to let Kareem's news overshadow the good news about a new baby.

"So that guy was so fixated on Marcus, what did he mean by 'I know what you did'?" Vanessa asked as she leaned over to dip into my nachos.

"He thought that Marcus had killed Kalinda because she had threatened to tell you about the relationship." I paused, waiting to see what she would say.

"Well, Marcus and I had the true come-to-Jesus conversation late last night, and he confessed all his dirt. And you know don't no brother ever confess all the dirt unless he's caught red-handed, and he swore he never slept with that dancer. You may call me stupid and naïve, but at that point there was no need for Marcus to lie to me, so I believe him."

Strangely I was beginning to believe him also.

"OK, but there's one thing I can't figure out."

"What's that?" she said, waving to friends on the other side of the court.

"The roommate said that twice he caught the guy she was seeing picking her up, and he noted the license plate. After the police found her body in the desert, he searched the DMV database and found that the car was registered to Marcus."

"What kind of cars were they?" Vanessa said, stiffening in her seat.

"One was a Porsche sedan and the other a Mercedes," I answered reluctantly for fear I was going to give her an answer she didn't want to hear.

"That's interesting because we don't own any Porsche sedans, but someone I know does," Vanessa said, crossing her arms across her chest and looking at me intently. Suddenly I realized who she was talking about.

"Kareem? He has a Porsche? But why would his car be registered in Marcus's name?"

"Remember I told how the forensic accountants uncovered that he was running all his expenses, mortgages, credit cards, everything, through Marcus's name and our holding company?"

"Yes, I remember."

"Well, we also found out that all the titles and registrations for the cars were in Marcus's name as well. That's why the plate check came up with his name."

So Kareem had been the one dating Kalinda and didn't want anyone to know. But had he been the one to kill the young girl and dump her carved-up body in the desert, or had he hired Carlo to do it?

"The roommate said that the police told him that Marcus had an alibi that weekend the girl was murdered because he was playing in a game in Dallas. Do you happen to know if Kareem was at that game as well?" If he was at the game, that would certainly rule him out, but that didn't mean he couldn't have contracted Carlo to kill Kalinda.

"One thing I can say about Kareem is that fool never missed a game. Away or home, his ass was always there watching his boy play."

"But then why was she killed? Kareem isn't married, so the cheerleader wasn't a threat to him."

"I don't know, girl, but looking at the report the accountants and lawyers pieced together, girlfriend must have been having a good time on my husband's dime. There were bills for jewelry, furs, shoes, spa visits, and trips to the Caribbean and Mexico."

"Wait a minute," I said, grabbing her arm. "Did you say there were receipts for trips to Mexico?"

"Yeah, um, there were a couple of trips to Mexico if I remember correctly."

"Do you remember what part of Mexico?"

"Why, you and Terrence planning a getaway?" she teased.

"No, we're not. But do you remember what part?"

"I can't remember the cities, but they had weird names I had never heard of. Didn't sound like any of the major tourist spots, but maybe he'd found some new superexclusive getaway."

Just as the buzzer sounded for halftime, I quickly gathered my handbag and pushed the rest of the nacho container and my beverage back under my chair.

"I have to go, Vanessa. I'll catch you later at your Midnight Gala."

"But I thought we were going to watch Usher?" she said, looking perplexed as I pulled out my cell phone and dialed Terrence. "Where are you going?"

"I have to go check on something. I'll catch you later." As I walked along the court toward the exit, I held the phone up to my ear.

"Come on, Terrence. Pick up the phone . . . ," I muttered to myself as I wove in and out of the thickening crowd. He said Vivica had gotten tickets to the game, so I knew he had to be here somewhere.

When his voice mail picked up after several rings, I had no choice but to leave a message. This couldn't wait.

"Terrence, Vanessa just told me that Kareem owned the cars that Sean saw. He was the one dating Kalinda. I'm headed back over to Sean's to confirm something on Kalinda's Facebook account. I may have found our link to Diablo. Call me back."

I headed out of the crowded arena to grab a taxi.

—

When the driver pulled up in front of Sean's apartment complex twenty minutes later, I told him there was an extra twenty-five dollars in it if he waited for me. I didn't think it would take long to check Kalinda's Facebook account, and if my hunch was right, I would be one step closer to figuring out why Diablo was involved with the murder of a dancer and why they tried to kill Vanessa.

I walked through the courtyard, which had been full of sunshine and laughter yesterday afternoon when Terrence and I were last here, but now, at nine thirty at night, it was dark and quiet. The only sounds were the muted voices of residents talking from their open windows and my heels on the cobblestone pavement. I made my way back to Sean's building and climbed the two flights of stairs. I walked down the length of the breezeway to Sean's apartment and knocked on the door. I thought I heard footsteps behind the door, but then several seconds passed and no one answered. I knocked again and received no response. Not even the little dog was barking.

"Sean," I called out through the slightly cracked window that looked into the kitchen. "It's Nia Bullock. I need to ask you another question." I tried to peek through the blinds but couldn't see anything. Yesterday they had been wide open, but tonight they were closed tight. I knocked on the door again.

Sean had said he'd be around all weekend working on his senior project, so why wasn't he answering the door? He could have stepped out to get a pizza or something, although judging from the number of food delivery menus I saw stacked on the kitchen counter, there was no reason for him to ever leave the apartment.

Maybe he had his headphones on and couldn't hear me knocking. I reached for the doorknob and turned it. I'd never been one to break and enter, but I really needed to see Kalinda's Facebook account. I pushed open the door and stepped into the small entryway. The only light in the apartment came from the glow of the PlayStation console on the TV stand and Sean's open laptop on the table. He had to be here. I closed the door behind me just in case the dog ran out of one of the bedrooms. I didn't want her to get loose.

"Sean," I called again, not wanting to scare him in his own apartment. No answer. I took a deep breath and began to walk farther into the apartment. As I made my way past the TV stand toward the bedrooms at the back of the apartment, I noticed that Kalinda's laptop was no longer on the shelf of the coffee table.

I could see a light from under the door of one of the bedrooms.

"Sean," I said again, louder this time. I knocked on the bedroom door but got no response. Like a scene from a horror movie, I felt the hairs on the back of my neck stand up as I turned the knob to walk into the bedroom.

"Oh my God," I screamed. My hand flew up to my mouth as I felt my stomach lurch. There was Sean lying on the bed, his arms down by his side, one of his pale hairy legs hanging off the edge of the unmade bed. His face was bruised and bloody, and the side of his head looked like it had been bashed in with a blunt instrument. His tongue hung out of his mouth to the side, his eyes bulging open in sheer terror.

As I took in the gruesome scene, I saw a ball of fur caked in blood by Sean's foot. Chee Chee was dead, too. I turned suddenly to run out of the apartment, breathing hard as I banged my leg into the coffee table. That's when I realized I wasn't alone. A large shadow jumped out of the corner by the couch and suddenly a man wearing a black nylon face mask was on top of me. I hit the ground and felt his gloved hands slip around my throat as I tried to buck and twist from under his heavy weight. As we struggled, I heard the sound of running footsteps in the distance and someone calling my name.

"Nia!"

I knew I had to try to scream. I managed to free one of my arms and pushed the flat side of my palm up as hard as I could into his chin. I connected. The man groaned, and when he grabbed his face in pain, I could see tattooed skin on the side of his neck. I screamed as loud as I could and fought back against the man whose face I couldn't see. Then I heard the footsteps getting closer, and the man jumped up and ran out of the apartment.

I rolled over on my side, choking and gasping for air. Terrence burst into the apartment and rushed over to me on the floor.

"Nia! Nia! Talk to me, baby. Are you OK?" He pulled me up off the floor and onto his lap.

I clung to his jacket, hot tears streaming down my face as I tried to catch my breath.

"Oh my God, Nia . . . ," he whispered in my ear as he stroked my hair. "If that man had killed you, I don't know what I would have done. Could you see who it was?"

I tried to choke out the words.

"What did you say, Nia?" Terrence said as he leaned down to hear my hoarse whisper.

"Diablo," I said, reaching up to touch the side of Terrence's neck. "Tattoo."

The man who had attacked me, and had killed Sean, had a black tattoo of a devil on his neck, the sign of Diablo Negro.

CHAPTER 24

Laila

Thank God for invisible tape, I thought, as the stylist placed the clear strips along my breasts so that the red-crystal-encrusted Zac Posen bustier would stay up. The matching satin micro miniskirt had a plume of netting down the back like a peacock's train, which skimmed the back of my neon blue Jimmy Choo ankle-wrap sandals. As I pirouetted in front of the mirror, I noticed that my makeup artist had been successful in reducing the puffiness and splotchy redness on my face from my tears.

After being humiliated at my own party by Nia Bullock, I had come back to my room in tears. No one had ever gotten the best of me like that. I hadn't even been able to connect with Miki, so I could only imagine what her reaction was to the magazine cover. Would she cancel my show? Would everything I had worked so hard for be lost?

My attempts to reach Kareem had also gone unanswered, so Darryl said it was time for us to take matters into our own hands. He reached out to DJ Williams, the league's new bad boy who had a reputation for fighting both on and off the court, making it rain hundred-dollar bills in the strip club he owned in his native Atlanta and being suspended for spitting on a fan who had booed him during a game. Darryl had done business with him in the past, and he asked DJ if he wanted to go to a party with me. Of course, DJ had jumped at the chance and told Darryl he was down for whatever. I agreed with Darryl that DJ would be the perfect escort for this evening's grand finale.

"Looking good, girl," Darryl said as he leaned against the doorway to the bathroom while I looked into the mirror and fluffed up my long curls.

"And you know this, man," I said, turning to pop my lip gloss into my black Chanel clutch. "Let's do this."

As we made our way into the living room, Tanya Peoples and the rest of the Glam Network camera crew began to assemble to head out with us. I guessed that if Miki was intent on canceling my show due to yesterday's events, she would have told the camera crew to stop filming. Since they were there, it was my duty to give them some footage they would never forget.

———

DJ's paws were all over me. I scooted away as far as I could in the stretch Lincoln Navigator limousine, inching closer to the door. Darryl, who sat across from me, was sandwiched between four of DJ's boys and the Glam Network cameraman and was typing away on his iPhone, so he didn't see me signaling for help. With the cabin of the truck smelling like reefer and the Hennessy flowing, DJ was clearly in the mood to get acquainted. And seeing as how he was a professional athlete making serious paper, he didn't have much experience these days with being turned down. As far as he was concerned, everyone was available to him.

"What's good, Ma?" DJ asked, breath hot in my ear as he put his beefy arm around me and tried to pull me closer to his rock-hard six-foot-ten frame. He was young with only two years in the league, but the TMZ poster boy was determined to make a name for himself. Luckily, tonight he had forgone his eponymous denim line and put on an actual black suit like a grown-ass man. A web of interlocking tattoos of crosses, vines, and guns snaked down his neck into the collar of his red shirt and across his broad light-brown chest. Unfortunately, it was too late for me to change when I saw that we were color coordinated, looking like we were going to some ghetto-ass prom. DJ's massive thigh pressed into mine as his hand grazed the edge of my short red skirt. He wore dark sunglasses, but I could tell that his eyes were undressing what he thought was his girl for the night. I didn't want to have to check this fool for real because I needed him tonight, but he was definitely not getting any of this kitty kat tonight or ever.

"Now, DJ," I purred in an ear that had a five-carat stud attached to the lobe and then stroked his bald head, "relax, baby. We've got all night." I made sure to smile for the camera filming us as we rode to the party, and I carefully tugged at the short hemline of my skirt to pull it down.

"I know, but for real, girl, you got a brother trippin' looking all delicious. Let's skip this party shit and go back to my hotel." He licked his lips and looked at me over the tops of his glasses.

"Save something for later," I said, pressing a bloodred nail on his full lips. I had to pull it back quickly when I saw him open his mouth so that his tongue could lick me. "This is a very special evening, baby. And I think you're really going to enjoy yourself. I guarantee."

"All I need to enjoy myself is your fine ass naked in my bed, for real," DJ said, his lips nibbling along my neck as he tried to slip a hand between my thighs. "For real, let's go. I want you for real."

"I know you do, baby," I said, crossing my legs to block the probing fingers that wanted to get to the honeypot and give his boys a freaky little show. "But I have a surprise for you that will make you want me even more. Trust me." I stared into his eyes, pressed my breast into his chest, and licked my lips to tease him as the Navigator came to a stop in front of the Biltmore Estate. A quick glance at my watch showed it was just past midnight.

Showtime.

I climbed carefully out of the truck so as not to give DJ's boys a flash of the goodies and stood next to DJ whose large hand slid down my back and rested on my ass. I knew it would be pointless to move it at this point, but the camera was filming.

"Yo, where we at?" DJ asked, giving my cheek a squeeze, while the production assistant put on his microphone pack. When Darryl had told DJ that the network would be filming our little date, he had been more than up for getting some screen time, because in his mind any press was good press.

"Just a party we were invited to," I lied as another production assistant slipped the cold microphone pack down the back of my bustier and then clipped the small black mic on the front of one of the crystals. I reached back to fluff up the plume netting on the back of my skirt. DJ looked back to enjoy the view as well.

"All right now, you know I can't wait to get up under that skirt tonight," he said, adjusting the front of his pants. "You got me ready to take off right now."

"I know you can't," I said, trying not to laugh at him. Poor baby, he actually thought he was getting some of this tonight.

Tanya led us, along with DJ's requisite entourage, into the building's lobby.

The building, which had once been a luxury hotel, had been recently reopened as an event space. Tonight the grand marble and glass foyer was festooned with a purple and green Mardi Gras theme. With the evening's event in full swing, we could make out the sounds of music and laughter coming from behind the closed ballroom doors. The check-in table was empty. A couple, dressed in black or white as the invitation had requested, had on brightly decorated masks and headed back into the ballroom. As the door opened, we could hear John Legend playing the piano and singing.

A large banner hung from the ceiling announcing tonight's event. The cameraman zoomed in on the logo as DJ read the words.

"'Welcome to the Marcus and Vanessa King Midnight Mardi Gras Gala. A fund-raiser for Saint Mary's Children's Hospital.'"

I managed to refrain from telling DJ "Good job" for reading so well as I saw two Biltmore security guards in black pants and white shirts heading over to us. Darryl cut them off, and with his back to the view of the cameras, took a large stack of cash from his pocket. Peeling off a couple of hundreds, he pressed a few folded bills into both of their hands. Suddenly, the guards realized they were due for a break.

"Yo, son, this is Marcus's joint?" DJ asked me.

"Yes," I said in a clipped tone but trying to smile. "Is that a problem?"

"It ain't no problem for me. For real, though. But it might be a problem for King," DJ snorted as he gave his boys some dap. DJ was an ideal escort for this evening because he and Marcus got into it on the court two weeks ago when DJ got ejected from the game for a flagrant foul on Marcus. The league had suspended him for three games, which included playing in the All-Star game. Ever since, he'd been barking at Marcus on Twitter, but Marcus, of course, hadn't responded. Marcus was the king of the league and didn't have to address this kid. Ordinarily I wouldn't have addressed this kid, either, but I knew seeing me with DJ would get under Marcus's skin. It probably wouldn't help relations between the two players that Marcus had won the All-Star MVP title for the second year in a row.

I slipped on my silver crystal-studded mask. When the producer tried to hand DJ a black one, he pushed it away.

"I ain't wearing that bullshit. Let that muthafucka see my pretty face."

Whatever, I thought. *You're cute and all, but no one will be looking at you anyway.*

John Legend was wrapping up his set when we walked into the darkened ballroom and those in the audience were on their feet clapping. Huge masks, flowers, and beads decorated the large space, and the hundred tables were laced with Mardi Gras beads and flowers. As we walked down the center aisle of the room, I could feel the hot stares of people as they saw me in my bright red dress in clear violation of the evening's dress code. There were murmurs and gasps as people began to recognize me. I could see out of the corner of my eye that some of the event's organizers were scurrying around in the corner, trying to figure out what to do.

An efficient-looking woman in a black suit and glasses rushed up to us, waving her clipboard in my face.

"I'm sorry, but you all have to leave," she said, trying to block our path. The band on the stage played as John Legend made his way offstage while the audience continued to applaud. I pointed at my ear and pretended I couldn't hear her over the music and the crowd, and I pushed past her with one camera in front of us and one behind us. The producer scurried ahead and began to scout around for two seats at the front of the room as if we were being escorted to our assigned seats. Brilliant.

I could see that DJ had his eyes fixed on a table at the front of the room. The hosts for the evenings had their backs to the room as they applauded John Legend's performance, so they didn't see us making our way down the aisle. Marcus wore a black custom-fit tuxedo with a black shirt and bow tie, and Vanessa, the lady of the evening until I arrived, of course, had on a long strapless red sequined gown with her black hair blown out sleek and straight with a center part. Marcus put an arm around his wife's waist and drew her close to him as he leaned down and kissed the top of her head, and I nearly stumbled on the carpet as my stomach tightened at the sight.

That was my man. And that should be our baby we were celebrating. She had ruined everything we had. He didn't love her. I knew he didn't love her. He couldn't. He loved me and we were supposed to be together. If it weren't for that baby, he wouldn't even be trying to reconcile with his wife. I knew that, and she knew that, too. It would be a PR disaster for Marcus to leave his pregnant wife for me, but I had to let him know that I'd wait for him. No matter how long it took.

More guests in the room began to turn and look at us as the applause died down and the sound of shocked chatter filled the room. As Marcus and Vanessa turned to take their seats, the frazzled woman in the black suit scurried over to their table and whispered something in Vanessa's ear. That was when she looked up and saw me. I saw her eyes narrow through her black velvet and diamond-studded mask.

Bring it on, bitch.

DJ's boys were laughing loudly as they walked behind us. There were only two seats at the table the producer identified, so they would have to stand. As we got closer to the table, Marcus and Vanessa rushed over, both of their expressions tight with controlled rage. DJ palmed my ass and pulled me closer as he removed his shades and tucked them into the breast pocket of his jacket.

"What the hell are you doing here?" Marcus hissed. The Glam Network cameras jockeyed for position as they encircled us. DJ's boys filled in the gaps between the camera and sound techs, locking the four of us inside the tense circle just a few feet away from each other. Each of us, I imagined, wanted to rip the other apart. As I sized up Vanessa through my mask, my gaze unconsciously raked down her body to her stomach. Reflexively she put her left hand with her wedding ring over the small roundness barely visible in the sequined dress. But I saw the bump in her dress, and she knew it. I looked back up at her eyes, which were flashing with anger and something else—triumph.

"Ease up, man. We just wanted to congratulate you on your MVP," DJ said sarcastically.

"Really?" Marcus said, looking DJ up and down. "Maybe next year you'll get to play and you'll have a shot. But in the meantime, I asked what the hell are you doing here?"

"Hello, Marcus," I said, drawing my lover's name out like a silken caress and refusing to acknowledge Vanessa. "So good to see you again. Thanks for the invitation."

"Laila, you have to leave. I don't want you here," Marcus said. His words cut into my heart, but I knew they were just for Vanessa's benefit. What else could he say?

"I'm sure you don't mean that, Marcus," I said. I wanted to reach out and touch him and let him know that I forgave him for what he said yesterday. I knew he just said those things because of Vanessa being pregnant. He really didn't want to be with her; he wanted to be with me. I fingered the large pear-shaped diamond pendant hanging around my neck that Marcus had given me for my birthday. I knew he remembered the necklace.

"You must leave now," Vanessa said through pinched lips, refusing to be ignored at her own event by her husband's former mistress. Her hands were now clutched in the folds of the heavy sequined fabric of her long dress. Her friend Nia, dressed in a one-shoulder black gown, appeared at her side and whispered in her ear, trying to pull her away.

"Really, Vanessa?" I said haughtily. "And who's going to make us leave?"

I couldn't stand to look at her or Nia. I hated them both. I couldn't stand the thought that Vanessa was carrying Marcus's child. That should be our baby. I ignored her, flipping my hair back over my shoulder, and then I turned to DJ.

Vanessa and Nia turned to look for the event's organizer who stood outside the circle, whispering desperately into a walkie-talkie to call up security. Fortunately, Darryl had taken care of that by giving the two guards in the lobby enough to share with the other Biltmore rent-a-cops. What I didn't see was Marcus's private security detail that Darryl wouldn't have been able to convince to take an extended break. Maybe they were in the back, assisting with security for John Legend.

"Don't be mad at me, baby. We just wanted to support your event," I said, stroking DJ's arm and turning my attention back to Marcus. I saw Vanessa's body tense when I called her husband "baby" right in front of her. But she needed to learn even if it was the hard way. Marcus was my baby. Not hers. They were the past, and I was going to be his future, baby or no baby.

If I could just get him to look at me. His steely gaze was locked on DJ just like when they were on the court. But I needed Marcus to look into my eyes so that he could see that I still loved him. I still wanted him just as much as he wanted me. He had to look at me and see that I could wait. I could wait for Vanessa to have the baby, and then we could go back to the way things were. I needed to break through the arctic chill I saw in his eyes. He refused to look at me with Vanessa standing right next to him.

But like crazy-ass Glenn Close said in *Fatal Attraction*, I wasn't going to be ignored.

"DJ, didn't you say you wanted to make a donation to Marcus's little charity?" I said. I was hoping this young boy was bright enough to pick up on my cue. He hesitated for just a moment, looked at me quizzically, and then snapped his fingers twice at one of his boys who immediately produced a large ball of cash and handed it to him.

"Yeah, Laila, baby," DJ said, his lips curled into a sardonic twist as he unfolded the thick ball of cash his boy handed to him. "You're right, I wanted to give something for the kids." And with that, just like he and his boys liked to do in the strip club, DJ began to flick the bills in a rolling motion into the air, making it rain hundred-dollar bills down on Marcus and Vanessa. DJ's boys erupted into howls of deep laughter.

"Yo, son, you gon' make him dance for that shit," one of DJ's boys quipped as he doubled over and guffawed loudly.

"Nah, man, but maybe his little wifey wants to shake that ass for some of daddy's cash," DJ said as he looked Vanessa up and down, daring Marcus to do something. The rain of money continued to fall arrogantly down onto the couple as if in slow motion.

Suddenly Marcus snapped and lunged at DJ, throwing a punch that landed right on his nose. Blood gushed out of his nose, and the ballroom erupted in screams and shouts as the sounds of chairs being overturned and glass breaking filled the air. DJ wiped the blood from his face, spit onto the ballroom floor, and then drew back and punched Marcus. Then the two men were locked with their arms swinging, trying to land blows. The Glam Network camera crew was jostled back, and they tried to regain their footing to continue shooting. As DJ's boys prepared to jump in, some of Marcus's teammates jumped up from their tables and rushed over to help.

Nia and the party organizer tried to extricate Vanessa from the growing swarm of people as she screamed for Marcus to stop fighting. A wall of black-suited bodies bumped into me, knocking me onto the carpeted floor of the ballroom. As I quickly got up on my knees to avoid being trampled by the growing crowd of fighting men, I saw Nia trying to lead a tearful, screaming Vanessa away from the crowd.

"Marcus! Marcus!" Vanessa's arms flailed in the air to grab her husband from the escalating brawl. The sound of her voice screeched in my ears like nails on a chalkboard. This was all her fault as far as I was concerned. Before Nia could get her friend away from the crowd and safely on the other side of the room, I lunged and grabbed onto the end of Vanessa's dress and jerked as hard as I could on the end of the gown. Vanessa flew backward onto the floor, losing her grip on Nia's hand. I backed out of the crowd and knelt under the skirt of the table. I lifted the linen fabric and could see that Vanessa was down on the ground. Her sequined form was soon swallowed up by the fighting men stampeding to get at one another. They couldn't see or hear the woman screaming on the floor between their legs. The tangle of legs and shoes swarmed around her as she curled her body into a tight ball, trying to shield her stomach.

"*Vanessa! Vanessa!*"

Nia jumped up and down as she screamed for Vanessa. I could see the sheer panic and fear in her eyes as she tried to break into the crowd of bodies to reach her friend.

As the mass of fighting bodies shifted deeper into the ballroom, I began to crawl out from under the table. Just as I stood up, someone stepped on the plume of netting on the back of my skirt, ripping it off. Suddenly I felt a pair of strong arms lifting me up and back onto my feet. I pushed my tangle of hair off my face and turned around, hoping to see Marcus. But it was Darryl.

The swarm of fighting bodies had grown to over twenty people. The Mardi Gras decorations crashed to the floor as streams of screaming guests tried to make their way out of the ballroom, tripping and falling over one another. As I steadied myself on my feet, I could see over the top of Darryl's head that Marcus's private security guards, Tyson and Bruce, were quickly bounding across the tops of the tables to get to their boss. As they reached the edge of the crowd, they dove into the middle of the fray. Bruce head-butted his way through two fights and then smashed his elbow into the throat of one of DJ's boys as he made his way to Marcus who was still wrestling with DJ. Tyson threw four quick punches, blowing back a couple of the fighters so that he could get down to the ground and the ball of red sequins on the floor. He came up holding Vanessa's limp body in his arms. Putting his head down, he rammed his way back out of the crowd, moving quickly out to the entrance where I could hear the wail of police sirens and paramedics.

"We gotta get out of here," Darryl yelled as he quickly turned and pushed through the crowd of onlookers, leading me away from the fight as the cameras continued to roll.

CHAPTER 25

Nia

The taxi pulled up in front of the Ritz-Carlton. The valet opened the door and tipped his hat as I paid the driver and exited into the crisp predawn morning. I carried my shoes in one hand and tried to hold close what used to be a modest split up the front of my black J. Mendel silk dress; it was now ripped open to the tops of my thighs as I dragged myself into the lobby of the hotel. The tile floor felt cool to my bare tired feet. Dark sunglasses shielded my bloodshot eyes and runny mascara.

I knew I must have looked crazy to the hotel staff, scurrying around the lobby in the early-morning hours, but since it was All-Star weekend, I'm sure they had seen worse. As I made my way to the elevators, I passed a man wearing dark jeans and a white linen shirt who was sleeping in a chair next to a potted palm tree.

"Terrence?" I said quizzically, wondering what he was doing sleeping in the lobby of my hotel. The sound of my voice stirred him from his sleep, and he jumped up from the chair.

"Oh my God, Nia, where have you been?" he barked with concern in his eyes as he grabbed my bruised shoulders and took in my torn dress. I recoiled in pain, and as I reached up to rub my aching shoulder, my dress flew open.

"Terrence, what do you want?" I said. I was bone tired and not in the mood for any more drama. I closed the opening of my dress and pushed the button for the elevator.

"Where have you been? I've been waiting for you for hours." He followed me onto the waiting elevator. "I heard about the brawl on the news, but when I went over there, I couldn't find you. No one could tell me where you were. I've been trying to reach you for hours. When you insisted on going to the party after leaving Sean's apartment, I knew it wasn't a good idea!"

"Terrence, can't we do this another time? I'm exhausted." I pushed the button for the twenty-eighth floor and the elevator doors closed. I hadn't wanted to go to the gala, either, but I had promised Vanessa I would be there.

"No, this can't wait, Nia. I was worried sick about you! What happened?" His warm hand reached out to caress my sore shoulder, but I jerked away from his touch again. After what I had seen tonight at the hospital, I just wasn't in the mood for any more drama. And complicated relationships cause nothing but drama.

"In case you don't remember the last time I saw you, you were getting attacked in Sean's apartment by someone tied to one of the most vicious drug cartels in the country. How do I know he didn't come back for you at the party?"

"Look, Terrence, no one tried to kill me at the party," I said dismissively, walking off the elevator when the doors opened for my floor. "Shouldn't you be with your fiancée anyway? What are you even doing here at my hotel? Shouldn't you be with her?"

"Maybe I don't want to be with her." His response stopped me in my tracks as I started to make my way down the hallway.

"Really?" I snorted, sick of the game we had been playing for months. "Go home to your fiancée, Terrence. Leave me alone." I turned away as a single tear slid down my face behind my sunglasses. My nerves were brittle, and my emotions raw. The last thing I wanted was for him to see me crying. After what I had just witnessed at the hospital, I couldn't handle another emotional confrontation.

In front of my door, I reached into my clutch and pulled out my room key, causing my cell phone to tumble onto the floor. Before I could stop him, Terrence bent down to pick up the buzzing phone. I knew before I saw it that it was another incoming text from Eric. He had been texting me all night, checking in with me after hearing about the fight on the news.

I'm glad ur OK. Get some sleep. Call U later.

Terrence handed me the phone. I could tell he saw the message.

"Glad to see someone knows that you're OK," he snapped sarcastically.

"Whatever, Terrence," I said with a sigh. "Who I text and who I talk to isn't any of your business." I shoved the phone back in my bag and opened the door to my room. I turned to say good night and to close the door, but he followed me into the room.

"Well, come on in," I said. It was my turn to be sarcastic. I followed him into the living room area of my small one-room suite and tossed my shoes and bag on the chair. I really wanted to take off the tight dress, which I felt like I'd been wearing for three days.

"What do you want, Terrence?" I asked again as I walked over to the large windows and opened the curtains. The view overlooked the hotel courtyard, which was full of desert flowers. There was a lone swimmer in the lap pool. The sun continued to rise in the early-morning sky.

"I want to know that you're OK. I need to know that you're OK."

"I'm fine, Terrence," I said, my voice sounding high and shrill in my own ears. The evening's events whirled around in my head. I couldn't stop the tears this time. Terrence led me over to the sofa as I sobbed, and he cradled me in his arms. I rested my head against his chest and cried from the depths of my soul for my best friend and the baby she had lost.

When I caught my breath, I told Terrence what happened—Laila, DJ, the camera crew, the fight. I shuddered as I recalled seeing Vanessa trampled by the fighting crowd and not being able to reach her. Tyson had gotten Vanessa out to the paramedics while Bruce had freed Marcus from the brawl and got him to the ambulance. I jumped in a cab and followed them to the hospital, but it was too late. There was nothing the doctors could do. I stood in the hallway of the hospital room and heard Vanessa scream when the doctor told her the news. I saw Marcus hold on to his broken wife as they both cried and mourned the loss of the baby they had already come to love.

"It was my fault Vanessa lost the baby," I mumbled. "If I hadn't let go of her hand . . ."

"No, it wasn't," Terrence said, lifting my chin and looking into my eyes. "Look at me, Nia. It wasn't your fault. There's nothing you could have done." He held me as I cried, rocking me in his arms.

I felt the heat from his body. His hand came up and stroked my hair.

"Don't do that, Terrence," I said huskily. I couldn't think when he touched me. Despite my tiredness, I could feel the electricity between us.

"Why not, Nia?" He continued to stroke my arms. I could feel his warm breath in my hair as he sighed deeply.

"Because you have a fiancée. Did you forget about her?"

"I can't forget about you, Nia. As much as I want to, I can't. And I told Vivica that tonight after we got into a huge fight when I told her I had to leave to find out if you were all right."

"Look, no one asked you to check on me. You don't need to check up on me," I choked out as I tried to pull away from him. "Now go back to your fiancée. I'm sure you can patch things up."

"I don't want to patch things up. I want you. I always wanted you." Then Terrence's lips were on mine, kissing me softly yet insistently. His mouth was sweet, warm, and wet. Heat raced through my veins. My fingers danced across the front of his shirt, making a path toward his taut stomach. Reaching under the shirt, I felt his smooth hot skin as he moaned into my mouth. My fingers lingered around his belt buckle, and I could feel him starting to surge to life.

Suddenly he pulled away from me.

"We shouldn't be doing this, Nia. You're tired. You're emotional. I don't want you to do something you'll regret in the morning."

"It's already morning, Terrence. No more regrets," I said as I rained kisses along his neck. There would be no turning back this time.

"Nia . . . ," he groaned into my ear as his lips and teeth nibbled at my earlobe. His hands cupped my breasts through the silken fabric of my gown. His thumb played across my hardening nipple, teasing me with spikes of pleasure and causing me to arch forward into his hands, craving his mouth on my body. He slid the single shoulder strap of the gown off my shoulder and unzipped the dress.

Emboldened, I pushed away and stood up in front of him. Staring into eyes full of hunger and passion, I shimmied the dress down around my hips and let the fabric fall into a pool of silk around my feet. Standing in front of him with a hand on my hip, I let him take in the view of my black lace demi-cut strapless bra and wisp of a matching thong. Turning around, I bent over in front of him to pick up my dress.

"You're not playing fair," he said huskily, reaching out to caress my bare full cheek.

"I know." I took his hand and led him into the bedroom. The curtains were closed, so the room was still dim. I pushed him down onto the crisp white duvet. His dark skin gleamed against the stark white bedding. I stood between his legs, muscled thighs that strained against his jeans, unbuttoned his linen shirt, and pushed it off his broad muscled shoulders. His chest was tight and hard. He was so damn sexy.

"You know I love you, Nia," he said, cupping my face and pulling my mouth down to his. He nibbled at my lips and then plunged his slippery tongue into my waiting mouth. He pulled his mouth away from mine.

"Nia, I love you," he said again, looking deep into my eyes as his hand stroked the side of my face. I let my guard down, relaxing into his embrace, and released the words I'd never thought I'd ever say to him again. There was no need to hold back ever again.

"I love you, too, Terrence," I whispered as a single tear fell onto his chest. "But so much has happened . . .

"When I saw you after you got shot lying in that hospital bed, I knew I couldn't stand the thought of going through that again. Not knowing if you were going to live or die, so I begged you to come to LA with me, hoping that would keep you safe." The memory of seeing him lying in that hospital bed, hooked up to machines and going in and out of surgery, caused me to shiver. It had been the scariest forty-eight hours of my life. The decision to leave had been so hard, but I knew I had to pursue my dreams and couldn't bear watching him go out into those dangerous streets night after night, not knowing if he was going to come back to me.

"Baby, I'm sorry you had to go through that. But I'm OK. Nothing is ever going to happen to me. None of that matters. We're both in New York now, and nothing is going to keep us apart."

"But what about Vivica?" I said, afraid of his answer.

"Like I said, when I told her last night that I had to find you, she knew before I was even willing to admit to myself that I was still in love with you. At first I tried to deny it, but it was true."

I couldn't believe what I was hearing. Was it possible that we had found our way back to each other after all of these years?

"We can figure this out. I know we can, Nia. We both love each other, and that's the only thing that matters."

His lips were suddenly on my mouth again as he flipped me over onto the bed, and I felt his delicious weight on top of my body. I raked my nails along his muscled back and opened my legs to wrap around his waist, pulling him into me even more deeply. I reached in between us to undo his belt buckle and open his pants. I held him, feeling him grow and surge in my hand, and heard him moan with pleasure at my touch.

As I massaged him, the warm wetness of his tongue licked hungrily along my neck. I moaned in disappointment as he slipped out of my hand. My back arched as he made his way down to my breasts, which were straining against the cups of my bra for his touch. I was so hungry for him, and he sensed my impatience.

"Relax, baby," he said with a deep moan as he pushed me gently back down into the soft, cool folds of the bed. "We've got all day. And I want to taste and enjoy every inch of you." My body tingled with anticipation as I felt warm silkiness between my thighs.

While one hand skimmed along the edges of the delicate lace bra, his other wandered slowly down the curves of my body along my hips and thighs and then back up along my arm. His hand caressed the side of my face as his thumb stroked my lower lip. I sighed deeply and opened my mouth and sucked lightly on it, giving him a promise of the warm wetness that was to come.

My body was on fire, but I knew he was intent on taking his time as our bodies got reacquainted. I could feel the pulsating weight between his legs pressing urgently into the middle of my thigh as he slid down my body. My hands caressed the short dark hairs on his head.

His tongue lapped warm wet circles along my bra as he teased me with his mouth. I grabbed his shoulders until he finally opened the delicate diamond clasp. Just as my breasts spilled out of the cups, he traced his tongue across my erect nipples, which had been craving his touch. His lips sucked and pulled gently on one as his fingers tugged and pinched lightly at the other. It was exquisite torture.

Suddenly he kissed me again, more urgently this time as his hips thrust into mine. The silkiness between my legs turned into a throbbing ache as I felt him straining against his jeans to get to me.

"Maybe the wait's not going to be as long as you think," I said softly, joking as I pressed my warm wetness into him. He laughed throatily as he slid down my body, his mouth stopping again to rain strokes of his tongue along my breasts to my smooth stomach. I tried to control the quiver I felt in my legs as his hot breath moved along my belly button to the waistband of my thong.

"Are you shaking?" he asked as he looked up at me and laughed. His kisses were torture as his lips moved along the silk band around my hips and then his dark head moved lower between my legs. I inhaled sharply as he began to stroke me through the panties with his tongue. My body arched to meet him, my legs shaking. His teasing rhythm with both his tongue and fingers through the material became more insistent as I felt waves of ecstasy build. I moaned and squeezed his body, urging him to increase the pace as tiny quakes of pleasure rocketed through my body. He finally pushed aside the delicate material and plunged his tongue deep inside me. I felt like I was floating above the bed as my breathing quickened, and I moaned his name over and over again.

"I love it when you respond to me like that," he said as he stepped out of his jeans and black fitted boxers, looking quite pleased with himself. Taking in the sight of his rippled naked body, I stretched my body as a smile danced across my lips.

"And I love it when you make me feel like that," I said huskily as I wiggled out of the thong. I wagged my finger for him to join me. As he slipped onto the bed, I straddled his pelvis, pushing my silky folds up against his hardness. I leaned down to kiss him and asked if he had a condom. He rolled over to the side of the bed and reached down to his jeans for a foil-wrapped square. A few seconds later he was back underneath me.

As I enveloped him inside my tight warmth, I looked up at the ceiling and then closed my eyes as I enjoyed the delicious ride.

"Damn, Nia . . . ," he moaned huskily. We were both lost in the thrusts of pleasure and reconnection as our bodies became one. He pushed up against me and sat up in the bed so that we were eye to eye as I braced my knees against the mattress and placed my arms around his back and slid slowly up and down.

"Oh God. Nia." Suddenly he put his arm around my waist and flipped me onto my back. I wrapped my legs around his hips, pulling him into me as my arms wrapped around his back. As my tongue traced along his collarbone, I tasted the salt of perspiration as his pace increased. He pushed me down deeper into the bed as we looked into each other's eyes. Our breathing quickened as we started to climb the summit, feeling the first teases of our orgasms.

"Nia . . . Nia . . . Nia," Terrence moaned in my ear as I clenched his back and felt the tingles of pleasure rising. He thrust into me harder as he caressed my cheek and felt my muscles tighten around him as both of our bodies contracted in warm, delicious waves of aftershocks.

Exhausted, we both collapsed. Unable to move as our bodies struggled to regulate our breathing, Terrence gathered me in his arms and rolled over on his back. I rested my head against his chest and threw my leg across his thighs, trying to get closer to him.

"That was amazing," Terrence said when he caught his breath. He stroked my hair and kissed the top of my head.

"I would have to agree," I said as I nestled into the crook of his arm.

As I listened to his beating heart—his breathing slowed into a rhythmic pace, his chest rising up and down slowly—I fought to keep my own eyes open. It felt good to be in his arms again. Safe. Protected. Loved.

For this moment nothing else mattered.

—

I stretched against Terrence's warm naked body and yawned. The curtains were still closed in the bedroom, so I couldn't tell what time it was. With Terrence's heavy arm across my waist, I sat up as best I could and looked over at the clock on the nightstand. It was almost noon. We'd been asleep for about four hours, and my flight was at two thirty.

I looked down at Terrence who was beginning to stir from his sleep, his long thick eyelashes starting to open. His arm tightened around my waist as he felt me trying to sit up. I kissed his strong jawline and stroked the smooth deep brown skin along his cheek, then made my way to his full, juicy lips, which were now curved into a smile.

"Wake up," I said softly in his ear. "It's almost time to check out."

He smiled sleepily, baring his perfect white teeth, and stretched his long toned body.

"Check out? You mean you're kicking me out?"

"Yep, time to go back to New York. We have a case to solve, remember? Diablo Negro ring a bell?"

"All you can think about is Diablo Negro after all I did for you last night . . . I mean this morning?" he said teasingly as he glanced over at the clock on the nightstand.

"What you did for me?" I said, laughing as I punched his shoulder playfully.

"Yes, hello, two orgasms? Does that ring a bell?" he said as he rolled over on top of me.

"Hmm . . . ," I said, placing my finger on my cheek. "I don't think I remember that at all. Are you sure?"

"Well, I guess I'm just going to have to refresh your memory." Terrence kissed me deeply as I felt him swelling again under the sheets.

"Mmm . . . As tempting as that may be, we have to check out of here, and I've got a flight to catch back to New York. Don't you have a flight to catch, too?" He was moving his hips in small circular motions as his lips grazed my neck, so I could tell he wasn't listening to a word I said. And I knew as the heat began to spread in my own body that if he didn't get off me soon, we'd never make our flights.

The sudden ringing of the phone interrupted the moment. I pushed up against him to roll over and answer it. As I tried to focus on the person talking on the phone, Terrence began to massage my back.

I put the phone against my chest.

"What are you doing?" I hissed, trying to sound serious, but with his lips snaking a trail along my shoulders, it was difficult to concentrate.

"Go ahead, talk on the phone," he said mischievously. He knew I couldn't concentrate.

I put the phone back up to my ear, intent on rushing off whoever this was.

"Uh . . . hello," I said, hoping I didn't sound breathless. "Stop it."

"Stop what, Nia? It's me, Eric. Are you OK?" Shit, why did it have to be Eric on the phone now? Terrence's breath was hot in my ear as he nibbled along my lobe, quickening his pace and then slowing down, driving me crazy.

"Uh . . . yeah, I'm fine," I said, closing my eyes, delirious as I pushed back into Terrence's thrusts. "Look, um, can I call you back? I'm in the middle of something."

"Yeah, she's in the middle of something," Terrence said in a husky whisper as his hand snaked around my body and squeezed my breast. I tried to shush him by putting my finger to my lips.

"I'm downstairs and wanted to come up to talk," Eric said.

"No!" I said, trying to squelch the moan I felt rising in the back of my throat. "Um, I'm going to have to call you back later . . ."

"But I'm right downstairs," Eric said insistently. "I just need to see you before you leave this afternoon."

"Now's not a good time, Eric," I said, his name slipping out in frustration. At the sound of my ex's name, Terrence reached around to take the phone from me.

"Yeah, now's not a good time, Eric," Terrence said tersely into the phone before placing it back down on the cradle. Before it could ring again, Terrence hit the "Do Not Disturb" button on the phone's base.

"Now, where were we?" he said as the waves of heat climbed between our thighs. I guessed we'd both be taking later flights home.

CHAPTER 26

Vanessa

The doctor was speaking, but I couldn't hear anything he said. I looked out the hospital window at the gleaming Phoenix skyline and wondered how the sun could be shining so brightly on the worst day of our lives.

Marcus, still dressed in his black tuxedo with the shirt open and the bow tie stuffed in his pocket, stood stone-faced by my bedside as the doctor continued to speak. His knuckles were bruised and his lip was cut. The emergency room doctors had stitched up a deep gash above his right eye, but otherwise he was uninjured.

"Mr. and Mrs. King, while I know the thought of having more children right now probably seems premature, I want to let you know that you will be able to get pregnant again," Dr. Barrett said in an efficient tone as he flipped through my medical chart and made a few notations with his pen. My mind had shut down last night after he told us about the miscarriage. The last clear thought I remember was the sound of someone screaming "No!" over and over again, and then there was sleep. The nurse must have given me something to knock me out. I rested fitfully and kept imagining myself falling back down on the floor over and over again with a menacing tangle of feet stomping around me as I curled into a ball, trying to protect my baby and screaming for Marcus to help me.

"Dr. Barrett, when can my wife go home?" Marcus asked, his deep voice tired and heavy. "We're traveling by private plane, so there's a bedroom where she can lie down. We could also take a nurse with her if necessary."

"Well, I don't see any reason why she can't leave tomorrow morning. Traveling privately certainly helps. I'd just like to keep her here for one more night of observation. And, of course, she should see her own doctor when she gets back home to New York." The doctor placed the chart back in the stand at the end of the bed and then left the room.

I felt Marcus's hand reach for mine as he sat down in the metal chair next to the bed, but I pulled my hand away.

"Vanessa, please," Marcus choked out. "Baby, I'm so sorry." He tried to reach for my hand again. I didn't have the strength to pull away a second time.

"Look at me, Vanessa, please," he pleaded from the side of the bed. But I couldn't. I didn't want to see his face. It was his fault we had lost the baby.

Suddenly the door to my room swung open, and I felt Marcus tense up. Earlier some aggressive paparazzi had been spotted by hospital personnel on the floor, so I knew Marcus had stationed Tyson and Bruce outside the door. I thought it had to be the doctor or the nurses coming to poke and prod me again or deliver one of those awful meals that always went untouched.

"Mommy! Daddy!" Damon's little voice echoed around the room as he came bounding across the floor followed by Nicole. Before he could jump up on the hospital bed, Marcus caught him and, scooping up our son in his arms, planted a kiss on his cheek.

"Hey, little man," Marcus said hoarsely, trying to clear his throat and change his expression to not look so worried. "How are you?"

"Good, Daddy." Damon kissed his father on the cheek and then squirmed in his father's arms, trying to get down onto the bed to get to me. I reached out for him. I needed to hold my child.

"Be careful with your mom, D. She's not feeling well." Marcus carefully placed our son on the side of my bed. Damon wrapped his chubby brown arms around me and laid his head on my chest. I wrapped my arms around my son, inhaling his fresh scent of soap and lotion. I stroked his curls and hugged him tightly against my body as tears slipped out of my eyes before I could stop them. I was glad Damon couldn't see my face. I turned away from the window and saw Nicole quietly slip out of the room.

"What's wrong with you, Mommy?" Damon asked as he sat up on the bed, his legs dangling over the side. He looked at me quizzically with the same large brown eyes as his father and reached out one of his small fingers to wipe my tears. "Don't cry, Mommy. It's OK. Where do you hurt? Do you want me to kiss it and make it better?"

I smiled and wished his sweet little kiss could make it all better. Marcus took a tissue out of his pocket, turned away from us, and walked over to the window. I was thankful we hadn't yet told Damon that I was pregnant. We had been planning to tell him at a special family dinner when we returned home.

"Mommy is fine, baby," I said, rubbing the top of his head. "Don't you worry. I had a little accident at a party, and the doctors want to check me out. We're all going to go home together tomorrow. Don't you worry about anything."

"Good, I'm ready to go home," Damon said, hopping down off the bed.

"You are?" Marcus asked, turning away from the window and stuffing the tissue into his pocket. "Why are you so eager to get home?"

"Because, Daddy, I want to see my friends at school," Damon said as he flew around the room with his arms outstretched, pretending to be an airplane.

"You'll be home tomorrow, and you can go back to school the day after that," I said, trying to prop myself up on the pillows. Marcus handed me the remote control to adjust the bed. I took it without looking at him.

"OK, Mommy," Damon said. Nicole came back in the room with a bottle of chocolate milk from the vending machine for Damon and asked if she should take him back to the hotel. Marcus picked up Damon and leaned him over the bed to kiss me good-bye.

"I'll see you tomorrow, Damon," I said as I kissed his cheek and squeezed his arms. Marcus walked them out of the room, and I heard him explain to Nicole that we would be leaving tomorrow and to get our things packed.

He returned to my bedside and sat down in the chair, once again reaching for my hand. I inhaled deeply and felt the tears coming down again. I couldn't stop them as ragged aching sobs ripped through my body. I tried to pull my hand away from his, but he wouldn't let me, holding my hand tightly and laying his head down on top of it. I could feel the moisture of his own tears on my hand. My other hand reached over to pound the top of his head as hoarse screams escaped my lips.

"I hate you, Marcus! I hate you!" I punched his shoulders as we both cried over the loss of our child. The pain was deep and cavernous, and I wondered if we would ever heal.

"Please, Vanessa," he said, looking up at me with tears streaming down his face. His brown eyes beseeched me to hear him out. "Listen to me."

I couldn't look at his face. The face that had lied to me so many times. The face that had cheated on me. The face that had gotten us to this point. I closed my eyes and collapsed back against the pillows. I couldn't believe that less than twenty-four hours ago we had been so happy, making a fresh start, excising both Kareem and Laila from our lives.

"Vanessa, I know you're devastated right now, and I am, too. We lost our child, Vanessa. That was my baby, too. And I'll never forgive myself for putting you in that situation. I know if I'd never slept with Laila, none of this would have happened. But, Vanessa, I can't lose you, too. Not now."

I shook my head against the pillow, my free hand lying across my stomach. Nothing he said mattered. Nothing he said could change what had happened. Nothing would bring back our baby.

"You have no idea how I feel, Marcus," I said, spitting out the words. "I've taken your bullshit for too long. You let this life twist you up, and it got you thinking the rules didn't apply to you. You were above it all. You could do whatever you wanted and sleep with whomever you wanted. How do you think that made me feel? This life? You wanted this life, Marcus. Not me. All I ever wanted was you!"

"Vanessa, I know I've put you through hell. I know you've given everything to our marriage and that I took it for granted, but we were back on the right path. You showed me that. You showed me the right way."

"Yes, Marcus." A bitter edge he hadn't heard before crept into my voice. "You're right, I gave you everything. I fought for us when you were too selfish to fight for us. I fought for us when you were out fucking that whore and your best friend was stealing all your money!"

Marcus exhaled deeply as if my words were like physical blows punching him in the gut. I stared up at the hospital ceiling through my tears, praying to God that he would just leave.

"Vanessa, I'm begging you, baby. Don't do this to us. Don't leave me. Don't leave our family. I'm so broken, Vanessa. I'm sorry."

"You're sorry? Now you're sorry?" I said, my voice rising and shrill. I couldn't stop myself from saying the thing that was really at the crux of my pain. "I'll tell you why your ass is sorry, Marcus! You're sorry because you didn't protect me last night, Marcus. And you didn't protect your child!"

Marcus's large shoulders shook at the pain of my words, and he clenched his fists into tight balls.

"You didn't protect your child, Marcus! You were too busy fighting and protecting your ego while I was getting trampled on!" The memory of being trapped on the ground, clawing and trying to find a way out and then just wrapping myself in a tight ball, sent a chill down my spine. I shook my head to push away the memory.

"Is that what you think?" he said, looking at me, pain etched on his face so deep that it looked like his face would be frozen that way forever. "Is that what you think? That last night was about my ego? Last night I was trying to protect you. I had no idea it was going to turn into that brawl. You're right. I should have gotten you out of there, but I was so focused on DJ . . ." He trailed off as I cut in.

"Yes, you were focused on DJ because he was with your whore!" I spat out at him.

"What?" he said, looking up at me incredulously. "You think I attacked DJ because of Laila? No, Vanessa. Listen to me. That had nothing, absolutely nothing, to do with Laila. I meant what I said to you before: it was over between us. I punched DJ because of what he said about you and how he tried to disrespect us at our event. Vanessa, that was all about you, not Laila. I need you to know that."

I closed my eyes against the wave of fresh tears. He took my clenched fist and pried my fingers open, lacing his fingers tightly through mine.

"Vanessa, I know you're hurt. I am, too. I know you don't believe me, but I'm telling you the truth, and I'll live the rest of my days blaming myself for not protecting our child. Baby, I'm begging you. We lost our baby, but I can't lose you and Damon, too."

The raw pain in his voice sliced into me. I saw his own hurt and anger at himself radiating in his eyes as he pleaded with me and pulled me into his arms. We were carrying the same wound.

CHAPTER 27

Laila

I checked my iPhone yet again for a message. Nothing. Zippo. Zilch. No call or returned message from Miki Woods or anyone at Glam Network since I had returned to New York a few weeks ago. At first I thought maybe radio silence was a good thing because she hadn't reached out to say they were canceling the show after the party debacle. And even I had to admit that things had gotten out of control at Marcus and Vanessa's gala, but I was sure the cameras had caught a lot of good footage that they could edit into a great episode.

The league's commissioner had come down hard on DJ with so many witnesses swearing to the fact that he and his boys had started the brawl. The gritty cell phone footage that popped up all over YouTube and the gossip blogs also didn't help his case. Marcus, the league's golden boy and the one whose team had a shot at the play-offs for the first time in a decade, was let off with a slap on the wrist.

There had, of course, been no word from Marcus this week. With his wife rushed to the hospital, I knew he couldn't reach out, but I was sure all wasn't lost. Now that Vanessa had lost the baby, he no longer had to stay with her and he could be with me. I just needed to get to him. I knew if we could just be in the same room, I could convince him that we were meant to be together and then I could get the reality show back on track. But I couldn't reach him. The number I had for him had been disconnected, so I had no way to talk with him directly. Since Kareem was fired, I hadn't wanted to reach out to him, thinking he couldn't do anything for me, but he just might be the only one who could hook this up.

Scrolling through my contacts, I pulled up his number.

"Hello," he answered gruffly into the phone after the fourth ring. I knew I was going to have to use some honey to get his help.

"Hi, Kareem," I purred into the phone. "I missed you at the party in Vegas. Where were you?" I hadn't seen Kareem that night at the party and was surprised that he hadn't jumped into the fight to protect his best friend and his star client. Of course, Darryl had told me rumors were swirling that Kareem had been cut, so I knew he needed me just as much as I needed him.

"Uh . . . I was there, but I was in the back. Yeah, in the back handling some details. Why, what have you heard?" His voice sounded suspicious as if something was wrong.

"Nothing, baby. Chill. I need to see you," I said.

"You do?" he said, snorting into the phone and then laughing. "And why is that? Marcus not returning your calls after the shit you pulled in Phoenix?"

"That wasn't me. That was crazy DJ. Whatever. I need to see you. When can we hook up?"

"Oh, so you want to see big daddy now, huh?" I heard him swallow something and clear his throat. "You know all you got to do is say the word and I'm there."

"Let's cut the shit, Kareem," I hissed into the phone. "You know we both have to get this deal back on track. And neither one of us has a lot of time to make that happen."

"I'll be out of town the next two days, but I'll call you to set up a meeting when I get back," he said before hanging up.

I put the phone back on my nightstand and reclined against the pillows. Kareem was desperate right now, and desperate men were dangerous. I dialed Darryl to fill him in on my conversation.

"Sounds like you might need something with you when you meet with Kareem," Darryl said, the sounds of the city in the background.

"What did you have in mind?" I said.

"Let me know when he calls you to arrange the meeting. I'll contact our friends and get you a gun that can't be traced just in case he causes trouble. That wouldn't be good for business."

CHAPTER 28

Nia

The walk to DeAnna's office was long. I imagined this was what it would have been like for prisoners walking to the guillotine. I hadn't seen DeAnna since we'd gotten back from Phoenix. I had heard she'd been behind closed doors much of the last two weeks, and I assumed she was busy working with HR and the legal department to get her ducks in a row to break my contract and follow through on her promise to fire me. And since I knew she was going to fire me anyway, I decided there was no need for me to have the website or magazine cover any of the stories about the brawl at the gala and Vanessa's miscarriage. I was not going to add to my friend's misery.

The rumors were circulating heavily that Glam Network was going to cancel Laila's show due to the fight she caused at Marcus and Vanessa's party and the subsequent backlash in the press and on social media. And once word got out that Vanessa had lost the baby, Laila was officially the most hated black woman in America. But in my experience, I knew that some media execs would think that was another reason to tune in to her reality show, to see the woman you love to hate.

When MJ poked his head into my office during a cover meeting to tell me DeAnna's office had called, I was glad I had told him a week ago to pack up our essentials. I knew the call would be coming, so there was no need to suffer the added humiliation, yet again, of security standing over us as we cleaned out our desks before being escorted out of the building.

As I approached DeAnna's corner of the floor, I smoothed down the front of my black Prada dress with the A-line skirt and adjusted the hot pink Michael Kors belt that matched my pumps. Clearly it was fitting that I was wearing black today. I saw DeAnna's regular assistant wasn't at her desk guarding her door as usual. A petite woman with short natural hair typed away on a keyboard. DeAnna must have brought in a temp for the day.

"Hi, I'm Nia Bullock. I'm here to see DeAnna," I said. The young woman looked up and smiled brightly.

"Hi, Ms. Bullock. I'm Terry. She's expecting you." Terry walked around her desk and led me to DeAnna's office and then opened the door. But when I walked in, it was Miki Woods I saw sitting behind DeAnna's desk. *Shit*, I thought to myself, *DeAnna took this all the way up to corporate, and now because I fucked over Glam Network, this chick is the one to fire me.*

"Hi, Nia. Come on in." Miki smiled and walked from behind the desk to sit in one of the leather chairs. I took a seat opposite Miki and looked around for DeAnna, sure that crazy bitch was about to pop out from behind the sofa or out of the closet at any moment to gloat over getting me fired.

"I'm sure you're wondering why I called you here," Miki started, taking a sip from the cup of coffee that Terry handed to her. "I really enjoyed our conversation in Phoenix, and I wanted to follow up."

Now I'm really confused. First, no DeAnna and now Miki's talking about following up on our conversation. I didn't say anything and waited for her to continue.

"I liked your expansion plans for the *Diva* brand. You've got good instincts, and your business is solid."

"OK, but what about the party?" I asked, looking at her with an eyebrow raised as I crossed my legs.

"Ah, yes, the party. Well, your live stream of the event was the highest-rated stream we've had. So your instincts were spot-on."

"But what about Laila and the show and the cover story on Vanessa?"

"What are you talking about? That was great! Breaking the story at her party was huge. You know what gets people talking and tuning in. It didn't matter to me that people hated Laila and rooted for Vanessa. That's great TV!"

"So you're moving ahead with Laila's show?" I asked, still unsure of what was going on and when DeAnna was going to pop out of the closet.

"No, of course not. Thanks to you." Miki smiled as she took another sip of her coffee. If the show was canceled, why was she smiling? "I can't thank you enough for having Vanessa call me."

"Vanessa called you?" Why would Vanessa have called Miki?

"Yes, of course. And when she said that you had suggested she pitch me on the idea of switching horses, I thought it was brilliant!"

"Switching horses?" I said, repeating her words. I was thoroughly confused. Now there were horses in the show?

"This is exactly what I'm talking about, Nia. You have a sharp mind and see how things can be bigger than they already are. And telling Vanessa to call me and getting her to agree that she and Marcus would do a reality show made the idea of killing Laila's show a no-brainer."

Suddenly everything made sense. In an effort to save my job and get back at Laila, no doubt, Vanessa had called Miki and told her that I had convinced her to do her own reality show with Marcus. She hadn't mentioned anything to me about this the last time I saw her. The only thing she seemed focused on was rebuilding her marriage with Marcus through thrice-weekly counseling sessions. But clearly, she was also focused on getting revenge against Laila and making sure she didn't make a dime off being tied to her husband.

"So you're going to do a reality show with Marcus and Vanessa?"

"Yes, all thanks to you." Miki jumped up from her chair and began to walk around DeAnna's office, talking about how big the show was going to be and how she was so excited to be working with them.

"OK, but where's DeAnna?" I asked, still needing one piece of today's puzzle clarified.

"Well, unfortunately DeAnna didn't share my enthusiasm for your career, and when she tried to get you fired, I had to step in. DeAnna is no longer with the company. And now the digital division reports to me."

"So you're my new boss?" This was officially the weirdest meeting I'd ever had.

"Yep, and we've got big plans. I want you to get started on drafting your expansion plan. I want to see a full budget and revenue plan worked up by next week, and I agree that we should start immediately. Are you ready to move to DC?"

The rest of the meeting passed in a blur as Miki prattled on excitedly about the plans for *Diva's* expansion and Marcus and Vanessa's new show. I nodded my head in the right places and jotted down what I hoped were relevant notes as my head spun.

When I got back to my office, I told MJ what happened.

"Hallelu-jer!" he said in his best Madea voice as he slapped me a high five. "Now I don't have to sell this body on the street to pay my rent, honey."

"Well, that's good, because you wouldn't have gotten much," I shot back as I walked into my office and closed my door so that I could call Terrence. How could I tell him about moving to DC when we had just gotten back together?

"Hey, baby. I was just thinking about you," he said, picking up on the third ring. "I called you a few minutes ago, but MJ said you were in with DeAnna. Is everything OK? Did you get fired like you thought?"

"Uh . . . well, I didn't get fired. In fact, I think I just got promoted."

"That's great, Nia! We'll have to celebrate over dinner tonight. I also have some news about Diablo."

"What is it?" My ears perked up as I pushed aside thoughts of DC.

"Well, I followed up on Kalinda's Facebook account and used the location services feature to see where some of the pictures were taken that she posted right around the time that Kareem took those trips to Mexico."

"And what did you find?"

"Well, if he was with Kalinda, then he was in Tijuana and Zitácuaro, two of the main locations for Diablo Negro outposts. And you're really going to love me for this one: we ran all of Carlo's passports that we found in that locker at Port Authority, and it turns out he had been to those same cities at least four times in the last year."

"So you think Kareem is somehow tied to Diablo? Why would he be mixed up with those guys? Drugs?"

"I don't think it's drugs. I had one of my buddies put in some calls to UCLA where Marcus and Kareem played basketball in college and pull their college files. Marcus was clean as a whistle. But the NCAA had investigated Kareem for possibly shaving points during his junior year."

"What do you mean 'shaving points'?"

"Shaving points is when a player manages the score of a game by making fewer shots or throwing a game."

"What does that have to do with Diablo?"

"The NCAA was never able to prove anything, but typically when you're talking about point shaving, the player is tied to a bookie or loan shark, and Diablo, in addition to many other operations, is also heavy into sports gambling."

"So how does Diablo end up trying to kill Vanessa, and why'd they kill Kareem's girlfriend Kalinda and then Sean?"

"I haven't figured out that piece yet. All I know is that we can tie Kareem to the same cities in Mexico where Diablo has a stronghold, and at one time he could have been throwing games for the Diablo crew."

"But what about when he got in that car accident?"

"Well, that's also an interesting point. The night of the accident, Kareem and Marcus had a sweet last-minute victory against Duke to go to the championship. In fact, Kareem sank the winning shot. I wonder if Diablo told Kareem to throw the game and when he didn't, they ended his career."

"OK," I said, warming up to Terrence's theory. "That would make sense, because I remember after the accident Vanessa telling me how devastated Marcus was that they never caught the driver because Kareem was never able to give any identifying details about the car. Maybe he knew who ran him over all along."

"Very good. Now you see where I'm headed."

"OK, but if Diablo did end his career, why would Kareem still be working with them? He doesn't have anything to offer now. He can't throw any more games for them or anything. He doesn't even play anymore."

"No, but up until a month ago he had something even more valuable."

"He had Marcus King," I said as I fell back into my chair with the realization. "But wait a minute—Marcus would never throw any games. And he's playing better than ever. The Gladiators are headed to the play-offs next week."

"Remember how you said Vanessa's lawyers found out through the forensic accountant that Kareem was stealing about half of Marcus's money? Well, once you're into Diablo Negro, you can't get out. I think Kareem was paying Diablo all these years out of Marcus's earnings."

As I wrapped my mind around all that Terrence was theorizing, my mind zeroed in on something that Vanessa had said to me two weeks ago after the news broke that Marcus had taken on a new agent.

"Wow, that would make sense because Vanessa said that when the accountants identified all his assets, all he had was a little over two hundred thousand dollars in the bank. They couldn't find any trace of the tens of millions of dollars he'd taken from Marcus and Vanessa's accounts."

"Exactly," Terrence said. "The money had to have gone somewhere, and I'd bet anything it's gone to Diablo all these years."

"OK, but none of that explains why Diablo killed Kalinda and Sean and attacked Vanessa."

"Look, we'll talk some more about it over dinner. What time can you be ready?"

I glanced at the calendar on my computer screen and saw that MJ had rescheduled the interrupted cover meeting for later in the afternoon. I also had two other meetings with the fashion and beauty teams to review the summer trends that they wanted to shoot for the magazine. I wouldn't be able to get out of here for a while, but fortunately Terrence's day sounded just as busy.

"I have to be in court in thirty minutes, and then I have to wrap a few things. I'll come get you around five o'clock, and then we can go out and celebrate your promotion."

"Perfect. See you then." I hung up the phone with my mind whirling over the Diablo connection to Kareem and the fact that I hadn't told Terrence that my new boss had just asked me to move to Washington, DC.

CHAPTER 29

Vanessa

After I put Damon down for his afternoon nap, I headed into the master bathroom to run a hot bath. My aching muscles, still sore from yoga that morning, called out for a warm soak. As I started to fill the large Jacuzzi in the center of the master bathroom, I sprinkled in some lavender bath salts and then dimmed the lights. I pushed some buttons on the iPod dock, and the sounds of Jill Scott filled the room.

I was beyond tired. It had been a long day already and an even longer week. Going to counseling with Marcus three times a week was intense and draining. But unlike in the past when I had begged him to go and he had just sat on the couch saying whatever he thought I wanted to hear, this time he was the one who had found Dr. Gordon, a gentle and well-respected marriage counselor in Midtown. And this time he was fully engaged, searching for answers for his behavior and holding himself accountable. The sessions delved into the challenges in our marriage and the loss of our baby since that was something with which we were both still dealing. Marcus had also requested some solo sessions with Dr. Gordon, which was encouraging. I knew he needed to work through his issues of Kareem's betrayal.

One of the other things we discussed was the new reality show deal with Glam Network. Marcus had been surprised that I had expressed an interest in doing something so public, especially with the network that had been promoting Laila's show. I explained to him that by doing the show, we could effectively kill Laila's show and all the talk about their relationship. At first, Dr. Gordon didn't think it was a good idea for us to be entering into such an arrangement, but when I explained to her that I really wanted to use this show as a platform to build awareness for our family foundation and show people how hard we were working on our relationship, she agreed that it could be good for us. Of course, I hadn't mentioned that I also wanted to show the world that Laila hadn't gotten the best of me, but no need to tell the therapist that little nugget.

Dropping my jeans and T-shirt on the floor, I stepped out of my bra and panties. I groaned in appreciation as I slipped into the warm bath and leaned back on the terry cloth pillow attached to the back of the tub.

Shit, I thought as I sat up in the tub, I forgot to put my hair up. Too late now. The steam was already doing its magic. I settled back against the pillow and closed my eyes.

"All I need now is a glass of wine." I chuckled to myself.

"Are you sure that's all you need?" Marcus's deep voice startled me. Dressed in black jeans, a camel sports coat, and a black turtleneck, he looked so good.

"Oh, hi. I didn't hear you come in." I swirled the water around in the tub, suddenly feeling vulnerable and wishing I'd put in some bubble bath so that I'd at least have the bubbles to hide under.

"Mind if I join you?" he asked. Dr. Gordon had been encouraging us to explore some intimate moments with each other, but anything we had done since returning from Phoenix a month ago had fallen flat and felt tense. After everything we had been through, we felt awkward with each other. But I knew we had to break through this barrier if we were really going to have a shot at saving our marriage.

"There's more than enough room," I said, sweeping my fingers across the water. The tub could probably hold four people. As he began to take off his clothes, I pretended to look away. He took off his jacket and tossed it onto the chair next to my vanity. He lifted the cashmere turtleneck over his head, and I watched in the mirror how the muscles in his arms and chest rippled. Before I could blink, his pants and underwear had dropped to the floor. I closed my eyes and leaned back against the pillow. The water was about to get a lot hotter.

As I felt him lower himself into the other end of the tub, the water rose to cover the tops of my breasts. Even though the tub was large, it wasn't long enough for his legs to stretch out, so he bent them at the knees, placing a foot on either side of my thighs.

"The water feels good," Marcus said as he moaned and leaned his head back against the other end of the tub. "But you know what would feel even better?"

"What?"

"If you would come over here and let me hold you," he said in a husky whisper that had a hint of vulnerability. I hesitated for a moment but then turned around and slid across the tub into his arms and between his legs. My back relaxed against his muscled chest as his arms wrapped around me.

We both reclined in the water, listening to the music, our eyes closed. Marcus's arms stroked my arms lazily in the water as he planted soft kisses on the top of my head.

"Thank you, Vanessa," Marcus said.

"For what?" I asked, relaxing deeper into his embrace, seduced by the smell of the lavender, Jill's voice, and the warm water.

"For this. For us. For everything." His hands suddenly lifted me up and turned me around to face him. He pulled my mouth down to his as his other arm encircled my waist, keeping our bodies pressed together in the warm water. My tongue hungrily danced around his as I tasted crisp peppermint and a hint of coffee in his warm wet mouth.

I could feel him swelling beneath me as he pressed my body into his and began to kiss me again. One of his hands tangled in my hair as he held my mouth firmly on his. He kissed me deeply as if he wanted to taste every corner. I kissed him back just as passionately and ground my hips into his.

Suddenly, a voice we both loved could be heard outside the door.

"Mommy, are you in there? I'm hungry." Marcus and I both laughed at the sound of our son's voice interrupting our lovemaking.

"We'll continue this later," I said as I took one last nibble on Marcus's lower lip before stepping out of the tub and wrapping my wet body in the large peach bath sheet hanging on the wall.

"I'm going to hold you to that," Marcus said with a frustrated chuckle as he sank deeper into the water.

"You better," I tossed over my shoulder as I turned the knob to let our son into the bathroom.

CHAPTER 30

Laila

The small chrome gun felt light in my hands as I raised it and aimed the muzzle at the man seated in my living room.

"What are you doing, Laila?" Darryl exclaimed, waving his hands in the air. "Are you crazy? You don't point a loaded gun unless you plan to use it."

"Maybe I am planning to use it," I retorted as I lowered the weapon and turned the gun over, inspecting it closely. Darryl walked over to me and took the gun away, ejecting the magazine.

"I'll put that back in when you're ready to leave," he said sarcastically as he sat back down in the chair.

"What are you so scared of? You know I'd never hurt you." I walked over to Darryl and, sitting on his lap, hugged him.

"Yeah, but there are lots of people who have gotten their heads blown off because someone was playing around. I don't play with guns. Now, what time are you meeting Kareem?"

"He told me to meet him at six o'clock," I said as I hopped off his lap and went over to the bar to mix myself a drink.

"You sure you don't want me to come with you?" Darryl asked.

"I'll be fine. Besides, we can't hide you in the closet again if he's already there. I'll have your little friend with me. You can put the gun over there with my purse and my trench coat."

I was hoping I wouldn't have to use the gun tonight but was prepared if I did. I had been glad to finally hear from him. We had a lot to talk about, and from the tone in his messages, it seemed like he wanted to pick up where we had left off. He was going to have to agree to do things my way or suffer the unfortunate consequences. That had been the order that had come down. But I was hoping there was still a way for me to get what I wanted, and I was determined that Kareem was going to help me.

CHAPTER 31

Vanessa

As the three of us left the small Italian restaurant, we saw that a large crowd had gathered outside. Fans cheered for Marcus and snapped photos with their cell phones and clamored for autographs. Going out for an early dinner before Marcus headed to practice had been a last-minute decision, so we hadn't brought Tyson and Bruce. After signing a few autographs for fans counting on Marcus to take the Gladiators to the championship, he ducked into the waiting SUV and slid in next to Damon and me. Alex pulled slowly away from the curb of cheering fans.

Damon chatted excitedly with his dad on the way home as the car made its way back downtown.

"Can I wait up for you tonight, Daddy?" Damon asked, hoping his father would let him skip his strict seven thirty bedtime to play some more video games. Marcus and I looked at each other and smiled over our son's head, both thinking about the promise we had made to each other to pick up where we left off in the bathroom earlier this afternoon.

"Not tonight, little man," Marcus said. "You've got a big day at school tomorrow, so you've got to go to sleep."

"Can't I just stay up this one time, please?" he begged, looking up at his father. I knew it was my turn to be bad cop, and I was more than happy to do so since I had plans for his father later on. I told him that his father had said no and that he could stay up late another night or I would even take him to practice one night. He seemed to like that idea and settled back into his seat for the rest of the short ride home.

Once we were home, Marcus changed his clothes quickly so that he could head out the door for the special late-night practice. It was unusual for the team to practice in the evenings, but with the championship within reach, Marcus said the coach wanted them to run some new plays and sharpen their defense.

"Promise you'll wait up for me," Marcus said as he leaned over and kissed me while I stood in the kitchen making Damon's lunch for school.

"Promise me you won't sap all your energy on the court tonight and that you'll have enough for me later," I said, popping one of the strawberries into his mouth that I was cutting up to put in a sandwich bag.

"You know I will," he said as he smiled. The door closed behind him. I finished preparing Damon's lunch and then walked to his bedroom to ask Nicole to get him ready for his bath.

"You can leave as soon as you're done, Nicole," I said, eager to have the apartment to myself so that I could set the mood for Marcus's return.

A few minutes later the intercom buzzed, announcing that we had a visitor. The doorman said Alex, our driver, needed to drop something off. I told him to send him up and opened the door to await his arrival.

"Hi, Mrs. King," Alex said as he came off the elevator and approached the door. "Sorry, to disturb you, but I think Mr. King left his phone in the car when I dropped him off at practice, so I wanted to leave it here in case he needed it tonight."

"Yep, that's his phone. Thank you, Alex," I said, taking the BlackBerry from him and closing the door behind him. As I walked down the hallway, the phone vibrated with an incoming text. Before I could stop myself, I looked down at the phone to see who the message was from. As the initials LJ popped up on the screen, I felt my legs give out, and I crumpled onto the floor in the hallway. Laila James.

Suddenly I felt sick to my stomach. My face flushed hot with blinding rage, and my hands were shaking as I tried to push the buttons to pull up the message.

See you soon, baby. Wet and ready . . .

As I pulled up the screen to show their entire exchange, I banged my head against the wall. How could I have been so stupid? How could I have believed him? I could see it had all been a lie as I read their entire exchange, which had started while we were all together at dinner:

> LJ: *Me so horny. See U soon?*
> Marcus: *Yes. Can't wait. Trying to get away.*
> LJ: *Where?*
> Marcus: *Four Seasons. Our suite. 6:00. Be ready for me.*
> LJ: *Always ready for U. Luv U! Been tooooo long.*
> Marcus: *Too long for me 2. I luv U 2. I'm ready now!!!!!*
> LJ: *What did U tell V?*
> Marcus: *At practice . . .*
> LJ: *She believed that????*
> Marcus: *She believes whatever I tell her. Don't worry about her. Worry about what I'm about to do to U!*
> LJ: *OOOOOh. Can't wait 2 CU!*
> Marcus: *Be naked!*
> LJ: *See U soon, baby. Wet and ready!!!!*

As I sat in a heap on the floor with my back up against the wall and reread the text exchange between Marcus and Laila, the red-hot fury continued to build. I felt like someone had reached inside my body and ripped my heart out of my chest. It had all been a lie. Everything he said in Phoenix about never seeing her again. Everything he said in the hospital about making it up to me. Everything he said in Dr. Gordon's office week after week about changing his life. It had all been a fucking lie.

I stumbled to my feet and threw the phone hard against the wall, watching it shatter, and then turned and ran into our bedroom. I pulled open the door to Marcus's closet, my eyes scanning the racks of neatly hung clothes, the shelves of gleaming shoes and fresh sneakers. I walked to the back of the closet and dropped down on my knees. Feeling back into the deep recesses of the closet underneath the hanging shirts, I felt the cold metal box. I pulled the safe out into the middle of the floor. My hands still shaking, I tried the combination, which was Damon's birthday. The first time it didn't work. Wiping my hands on my pants, I told myself to calm down. I slowly turned the dial and tried the combination again. The lights flashed on the display, and the door swung open. Pushing aside our passports, some insurance papers, and a stack of cash, I reached into the box for the gun.

Pulling out the nine-millimeter gun that Kareem had gotten for us in Phoenix after we started to receive the threatening e-mails, I held it in one hand and reached back into the safe for the clip. I pushed it into the bottom of the gun until I heard it click into place.

CHAPTER 32

Nia

After reviewing the mock-up of the Keri Hilson cover for the latest issue of the magazine, I turned back to my computer and pulled up Kalinda's Facebook page again. It had been hard to stay focused on work today. I looked intently at the photo of the once-vibrant cheerleader, wishing her image would start talking to me so that I could figure out why Diablo Negro had Carlo kill her.

"You still staring at the dead girl?" MJ said, strolling into my office and placing some layouts in my overflowing in-box. I filled him in on what Terrence had shared about Kareem's possible connection to Diablo Negro.

"Diablo Negro? If he's mixed up with those guys, he's in some serious shit."

"What do you mean? And how do you even know?"

"Girl, please. Those guys are bad news. I watch Lester Holt on *Dateline*. I know."

"Oh, really," I said, only half listening to my crazy assistant as I picked up the layout of next week's cover story on Rihanna and began to mark the pages up with my pen. "And what exactly did Lester Holt say about Diablo Negro?"

"I know you're not really listening, but I'm going to tell you anyway. So about a month ago, me and Ricardo were watching a story on *Dateline* about this guy—"

"So this is what you and your boyfriend do on Friday nights?" I said, cutting him off and laughing. "You guys sit up in bed watching *Dateline?*"

"Look, I know now that you and Terrence are all lovey-dovey again and he's giving it to you on the regular, but I know you aren't trying to mock me. Whatever. Just listen to my story, dang. So, anyway, they had this story on about the Diablo cartel, but what was fascinating was the family of this guy they profiled had gone into hiding because their son had gotten mixed up with Diablo over some sports betting the kid had set up at some college down south. Anyway, the boy owed them like a ton of money, and the family had scraped it together somehow to pay Diablo, but then the cartel said they had to keep paying regardless. The family didn't have any more money, so the kid took off running, and the Diablos came to the family and said they had to keep paying. When they refused, a couple of days later they found the boy's sister in the trunk of a car all carved up. The reporter said that was one of the things that made this gang so vicious was that once you were tied to them, that was it. You, your family, whoever—you were bound for life."

"Wait a minute," I said, looking up from my layout. "So if that's true, then maybe with all the talk about Marcus's possible one-hundred-fifty-million-dollar contract with the Gladiators, Kareem tried to pull away, and Diablo sent him a message by killing Kalinda."

"That sounds like their style," MJ said.

"That still doesn't explain why they would go after Vanessa. And now what happens to someone like Kareem who no longer has access to the money he was paying Diablo?" As soon as I asked the question, a cold chill ran down my spine. I didn't want to hear MJ's answer.

"Well, my guess would be that Diablo is going to find a way to get their money regardless. Those Diablo guys never back off. Kareem will have to find a way to get their money, or Marcus will."

I grabbed my phone off the desk, dialed Vanessa's cell number, and put the call on speaker while I threw my things into my handbag. After the call went straight to voice mail, I tried the house phone.

"Hello, King residence," a woman's voice answered.

"Hello, Nicole?" I asked. "This is Nia. Is Vanessa there?" *Please God let her be there.*

"No, I'm sorry. She just rushed out."

"Is Marcus there?"

"No, I think Mr. King is at practice."

"Did Vanessa say where she was going?"

"No, not really but . . ." The nanny's voice trailed off. I could tell she wanted to say something else but wasn't sure if she should.

"What is it, Nicole? What were you about to say?"

"Well, it's just that she looked really upset when she left. Like she had been crying. She asked me to stay with Damon until she returned."

"Are you sure she didn't say anything about where she was going? Please, Nicole, try to remember. It's important."

"I thought I heard her mumble something about catching somebody at the Four Seasons as she headed out the door."

I thanked Nicole and told her to tell Vanessa to call me right away if she came back to the apartment.

"What do you need me to do?" MJ asked as he got my coat from the closet and handed it to me.

"Call Terrence and tell him to meet me at the Four Seasons right now," I said as I threw my khaki trench coat on over my dress and grabbed my handbag. "I'm not exactly sure what's going on, but you don't have to be Lester Holt to figure out it's not good."

CHAPTER 33

Vanessa

Promises were made.

Tears began to stream down my cheeks behind my sunglasses. Slipping the steel-plated gun out of my pocket, I stepped out of the shadows and raised the gun level with his broad muscled back like they taught me at the gun range in Phoenix. I could barely see his dark head as he moved up and down while thrusting into her, so I knew it would be easier to hit him in the back. I was glad I couldn't see his face, because that might have stopped me.

I pulled the trigger twice.

After all, promises were made.

One bullet hit him in his shoulder and the other in his lower back. Laila screamed as his body slumped down on top of her. As she screamed and tried to push Marcus off her, I moved to get a better shot at her.

"No, please! No, please don't shoot!" Laila begged, her voice quivering as she saw me step out from the shadows.

"No, Vanessa! Please, no!" She struggled to pull the bedsheet stained with his dark red blood up around her naked body. I wanted to tell her it was much too late for modesty.

I raised the gun again and pulled the trigger. The bullet hit Laila right above her left eyebrow, and her head slammed back against the large leather quilted headboard with the force of the bullet. A single trail of blood began to stream down her face.

It was done.

As the enormity of what I had done started to creep into my consciousness, my body shook and I dropped the gun on the floor. A low guttural animal scream sounded as I fell onto the floor. It was me. I had killed my husband and his mistress.

Suddenly the bedroom doors burst open. When I whirled around to see if it was the police, I saw Tyson and Bruce walking toward me. One scooped up the gun off the floor and then began to make his way over to the bed.

"No! Don't touch him," I screamed as he went over to the side of the bed and felt Marcus's neck for a pulse. I tried to run over to the bed, but Tyson held me firmly around the waist and lifted me off the ground. As he carried me out of the room, I screamed for Marcus. When we reached the elevator, Tyson put me down on the ground, and, keeping his viselike arm around my waist, he shoved a hard piece of metal in my side and looked at me. His hard black eyes glinted with menace, and his lips were twisted in a snarl.

"Shut your fucking mouth. We're walking out of this hotel. If you make one fucking sound, I'll put a bullet in your head just like you did to Laila in there, and then I'll go to your home and do the same to Damon. Do you understand?" Hearing my son's name, a fresh stream of tears fell down my face, and my legs suddenly felt weak. I shook my head vigorously, my eyes wide with fear. Where was he going to take me?

The elevator arrived, and we rode down to the lobby in silence. As the doors opened, he shoved the gun hard into my side again and secured his arm around my waist.

"Now, walk through this lobby and out the front door like everything is just fine," Tyson snarled as we began to walk across the marble floor. No one seemed to notice us, and as we passed the front desk again, Christian's head was down, so even he didn't see me leave the building.

We stepped outside, and he walked me over to the waiting black limousine where Alex was holding the door open. When Tyson shoved me into the backseat, I fell onto the floor of the car as he climbed in next to me. Alex quickly closed the door and then walked around to the driver's side and got in. The car began to pull away from the hotel. I regained my balance and climbed back onto the seat when I heard another voice in the car.

"*Vanessa?*"

I pushed my hair out of my eyes and took off my sunglasses so that I could adjust my vision inside the car's dark interior.

Across from me at the end of the car's cabin was Marcus. His hands were bound in front of him in black plastic handcuffs. Another heavy-set man sat next to him with a gun pressed into his side.

Suddenly both men took out black hoods and, putting them over our heads, ordered us not to talk as the car continued on to its destination.

CHAPTER 34

Nia

As the cab came to a screeching halt across the street from the Four Seasons, I saw a line of police cars, two ambulances, and a couple of local news trucks parked in front. I shoved some money over the seat at the driver and got out of the cab. Dodging cars, I quickly crossed the four lanes of traffic on Fifty-Seventh Street and saw Terrence pacing in front of the hotel as cops ran in and out of the building.

"Terrence!" I yelled through tears as I made my way over to him.

"Nia, it's not pretty," he said to me as I rushed onto the crowded sidewalk in front of the hotel, thinking my best friend was dead.

Just as I turned to ask Terrence this question, a line of officers began shouting to clear the sidewalk of onlookers who had gathered on both sides of the entrance. Terrence flashed his DA badge and took me inside the lobby, which had been cleared of all the guests. The elevator doors opened, and two paramedics came out with a body covered with a white sheet.

"Oh my God. Vanessa!" My hand flew up to cover my mouth. I tried to run over to the body, but Terrence held me back.

"It's not what you think, Nia!" he said as I struggled against him. "It's not Vanessa."

As his words penetrated my thoughts, Terrence flashed his badge at the paramedics and walked over to look at the body. He lifted up the sheet. I braced myself before looking down. It was Laila with a single bullet hole in her forehead. Her face, once beautiful, was twisted into a macabre mask. Her eyes were wide open, displaying the paralyzed fear she must have felt in her last moments. Blood ran down her face and into her long streaked hair.

My mind raced. Had Vanessa killed Laila? How had she even known she was going to be at the hotel? Was she with Marcus? I didn't want to believe that he would cheat on Vanessa after all they had been through, but what else could have happened?

"Who killed Laila?" I asked as Terrence lowered the sheet back over her face and the paramedics made their way out of the hotel to the waiting medical examiner's truck.

"That's what I want to ask this guy," Terrence said, gesturing toward the elevator doors, which had just opened. The police escorted out a man on a stretcher. He was naked from the waist up with a swath of white gauze and tape across his shoulder and his rib cage. A paramedic trailed alongside, carrying an IV attached to a needle in the man's arm. His other arm was handcuffed to the stretcher.

As the stretcher made its way across the lobby, the man raised his head and our eyes met.

It was Kareem.

Dazed by his wounds, Kareem didn't speak as the police rolled him out the front door of the hotel to the waiting ambulance. As he hit the curb, news reporters, cameramen, and photographers surged forward, shouting questions and snapping pictures.

A police detective in a tired brown suit and faded yellow shirt walked back into the building and headed toward Terrence.

"Nice night for a murder, huh, Terrence?" the detective asked as he shook Terrence's hand. "What brings the DA's office out tonight?"

"A high-profile murder in one of the city's best hotels always gets on our radar. You know the mayor's going to be all over this one. What do you have so far, Detective?"

"Well, we need to do some forensics, but on the surface it looks like a lover's spat. Found the vic naked in the bed, single gunshot wound to the head. The perpetrator, also naked, was sprawled out on the floor with two wounds, one in the shoulder and one in the lower back. Found one gun at the scene."

The detective held up a dark blue NYPD evidence bag and pulled out a plastic bag with a nine-millimeter gun inside.

"Looks like they may have struggled over the gun and both got shot, but we'll see what ballistics confirms."

"No witnesses?" Terrence asked.

"We still need to take a bunch of statements from the hotel staff and some of the guests, but so far no one recalls anything unusual."

"Thanks, Detective. Keep me posted." Terrence steered me out of the lobby back out onto the street, and over to his waiting car.

"Do you think that detective was right?" I asked as he held the passenger side door open and I slipped into the front seat.

"I don't know. We'll see what the tests say, but that still doesn't explain where Vanessa is and why she came to this hotel."

"What if Diablo Negro was waiting for her here?" I closed my eyes, fearful that my friend had been abducted by the vicious cartel. Vanessa didn't deserve this. She was just getting her life and her marriage back on track. Terrence reached across the seat of the car to grab my hand.

"She's going to be OK, Nia. We're going to find her. Let's head back to the apartment and wait until she comes home."

Just then my cell phone rang. I dug frantically in my bag, hoping it was Vanessa, but when I looked at the screen, I saw it was the office calling.

"Hello?" I answered abruptly, thinking it was probably just MJ checking in to see if we'd found Vanessa.

"Hey, Nia," said MJ. "Did you find Vanessa?"

"No, not yet. Did she try to call the office?"

"No, but I have an idea about how you may be able to find her. Let me call you back." When the line went dead, I told Terrence what MJ had said.

Terrence pulled the car over when MJ called back fifteen minutes later. I put the call on speaker so that he could hear the conversation.

"OK, I called over to Miki Woods's office and spoke with one of the producers on Marcus and Vanessa's new show that I'm friendly with. And he told me that as part of our production plans, they sometimes have the crews trail the subjects to capture them without knowing they're being filmed so they act really natural. Sometimes they end up using the footage in the show or use it for focus-group testing. So the crew has been watching Vanessa and Marcus for a few days now, just catching them out running errands, nothing major or too invasive but—"

"MJ, did they have a crew on them tonight?" I asked, cutting him off.

"Yes, girl. The producer said that her team had just sent an update saying that they followed a limousine that had both Marcus and Vanessa in the back out to a warehouse in Rahway, New Jersey. They had to leave to head back to the city for another shoot."

"MJ, you're the best!" I exclaimed. "E-mail me the directions to the warehouse."

"Already done, boss lady. Let me know what you find out."

"Thanks, MJ!"

Terrence grabbed his cell phone after I hung up and put his own call on speaker as he whipped the car around in the middle of the street and headed across town to the Lincoln Tunnel.

"Lee Howard," a deep gravelly voice growled when the call connected.

"Lee, it's Terrence."

"What's up, man? Long time no hear now that you wear a suit for a living." The voice chuckled on the other end of the line.

"Very funny, Lee. Look, I've got a possible hostage situation with a high-value target at a warehouse in Rahway, New Jersey. I believe they are being held by Diablo Negro."

"Sounds like my kind of party," Lee said, his deep voice perking up with interest.

"That's exactly why I called you ex–Navy Seals guys instead of my boys in NYPD. I need a team with special–forces type experience. Who's working tonight? I need your best crash team to meet me out there stat. They're going to need to come in heavy, but we need the high-value targets alive. No mistakes."

"No problem. I've got the perfect team. They've been pulling most of the antiterrorism raids throughout the tri-state but nothing much lately, so they'll be happy to have some real fun for a change."

"Again, brother. We need the targets alive, a husband and wife. I'll share more details when you guys get there."

"No problem. We're on our way." The phone line went dead.

CHAPTER 35

Vanessa

I shivered in the cold metal chair to which I was tied. Underneath the stifling hood, I struggled to regulate my breathing and stay calm and not panic. We had to make it out of here alive, and home to Damon.

I still wasn't sure what was going on. Marcus and I had both been taken out of the car, but then we were separated. I had been relieved to see Marcus in the back of the car, but now I didn't know who I had killed with Laila. But what about the text messages I saw between him and Laila? Had someone set me up?

I could hear a group of men standing around us, their voices, speaking in Spanish, echoed around the cavernous space. From the different tones of their voices, I imagined there were about five or six men in the room with us. Suddenly I heard heavy footsteps on the concrete floor heading in my direction. The hood was pulled roughly off my head. I shook my hair out of my eyes, squinted, and adjusted my eyes to the dim lighting in the warehouse.

The large space was also an airplane hangar. Two black SUVs and a small private jet were parked at the end of the room by the huge hangar doors. Several aisles of floor-to-ceiling metal shelves lined both sides of the space and stocked old, rusted shipping containers. The voices I had heard belonged to five men stationed around the room, each holding semiautomatic weapons, their arms folded in front of them. Suddenly the door to the plane opened, and the stairs lowered. Two men walked down the stairs and made their way toward a large metal table with a briefcase on top and two chairs set up in front of me. As the two men got closer, I saw that I knew one of them.

"John?" I said, looking into the face of Marcus's new agent.

"Mrs. King, it's always a pleasure to see you," John said in the same pleasant tone he would use as if we were meeting in a conference room instead of a warehouse in the middle of nowhere. "Of course I wish it were under better circumstances." He unbuttoned the jacket of his navy-blue suit and took a seat behind the table next to the other man, whom I didn't recognize.

I took his age to be about sixty. He was tall and trim, and he wore an expensive gray suit, crisp white shirt, and a red silk tie. His salt-and-pepper hair was combed back. His face was a deep tan as if he spent a lot of time in the sun; he had dark black eyes and thin lips pressed into a tense line. He leaned over to John and said something in Spanish.

"Ah, yes, let us get started," John said as he turned to one of the men. "Can you please ask Mr. King to join us?" The man jogged over to a door leading to an office and went inside. He walked Marcus into the room flanked by Bruce. As Marcus got closer, he looked over at me and tried to reach for me, but Bruce jabbed him sharply in the ribs with the butt of his gun and motioned for him to continue to the table.

Seeing that my husband was still alive and hadn't been killed by these animals, I exhaled for a moment, but the aching pit in my stomach tightened. I had to bite my lip to keep from crying out for him, certain that would only make our situation worse.

"Welcome, Mr. King," John said as Marcus was led to the table, his hands still restrained by the plastic handcuffs in front of him.

"What the fuck is going on, John?" Marcus growled as he shook off Bruce and the other man holding him. "What are you doing with my wife? Whatever you want, you can get it from me and let her go!"

The man seated next to John leaned over again to whisper something in his ear.

"Well, it's not quite that simple, you see. Because right now your wife could be wanted for murder, so it's probably not a good idea for her to leave just yet."

"What the hell are you talking about?" Marcus barked, looking back and forth between me and John.

"Well, it seems that your wife, in a fit of jealous fury, shot and killed your former mistress this evening."

Marcus whipped his head around to look at me. I dropped my head down, unable to meet his searching gaze.

"Oh, wait, there's more. You see, it also appears that she shot Kareem as well, thinking it was you. But don't you worry, he survived his injuries."

"Vanessa, what is he talking about?" Marcus asked, desperate for my answer.

I looked up and explained that Alex had given me his phone, and I had seen some text messages saying that he and Laila were planning to meet at the hotel.

"But Vanessa, I have my phone. What are you talking about?" Marcus pleaded.

"But I saw the messages," I said.

"No, actually Mrs. King, you didn't see Marcus's phone," John said, interrupting. "What you saw was a duplicate phone that we loaded some messages onto so you would think your husband was meeting his former lover."

"You son of a bitch!" Marcus tried to lunge at John, but the two men held on to him.

"Why, John?" I screamed at him as I strained against the ropes, almost toppling over the chair.

"Leverage, of course," John said. "Now we're the only ones that know that you were in that hotel room and pulled the trigger. And right now the only fingerprints that the police are going to find on the gun that you dropped at the scene will have Kareem's prints on them, so unless we say otherwise, he'll take the wrap for the murder you committed."

"But what do you want? You're already my agent," Marcus spat out at him.

"It's not what I want that matters," John said as he turned to the man seated next to him. "At this point all that matters is what Mr. Quadron and Diablo Negro want."

Both Marcus and I stiffened at the mention of Diablo Negro. All of a sudden it felt like I had ice water running through my veins. We had both heard of the infamous drug cartel, but I couldn't fathom what they would want with us. Marcus never even used drugs in college, let alone now. My head was spinning.

Suddenly, the man, who up until now had spoken only Spanish to John, began to speak in English. His voice had a heavy Mexican accent as he started to explain why we were all here. He said Diablo Negro had first become involved with Kareem ten years ago when he and Marcus played together in college. Apparently, Kareem had in fact been involved with the cartel's gambling business and agreed to shave points off games in exchange for money. But when their team went to the play-offs and he was supposed to throw the game, Kareem didn't, and Diablo lost a lot of money. Ten million dollars to be exact. Well, after that night, some of their associates paid him a visit to explain the error of his ways, but Kareem ran out of his dorm room. When their colleagues tried to catch up with him, they struck Kareem with their car, ending his career. But while Kareem had paid for a portion of his crime, that still didn't address the problem of the lost $10 million, to which 50 percent interest was added each week.

"And when you announced that Kareem was going to be your agent, he told us he'd found a way to pay us back," said Mr. Quadron with a sliver of a smile across his cold, hard face.

"So Kareem used the money from my first contract to pay back the ten million dollars plus interest?" Marcus asked.

"Well, by then the ten million had turned into fifty million, so it just kept growing, and Kareem, seeing no other way, sold us half your contract."

"What do you mean he sold you half my contract?"

"What I mean, Mr. King, is that for every dollar you earned since you started in the NBA, from your salary as a player to endorsements and business ventures, we've received half."

My mind was reeling to hear that Kareem had gotten us in bed with these monsters and given half of Marcus's earnings over the years to these bloodsuckers.

"But he must have paid you off at some point," Marcus said. "So why was he still paying you?"

"Certainly he repaid the original loss and interest, but once he gave us fifty percent of your earnings, we couldn't imagine walking away from that kind of money. So we told him we'd like to continue our arrangement."

"Then what happened?" Marcus asked. I could tell he was afraid of the answer.

"Well, that's when you signed your one-hundred-fifty-million-dollar contract with the Gladiators, so Kareem decided he wanted out, but we paid his little girlfriend a visit that seemed to convince him that it was in his best interest to stay."

"What girlfriend?"

"The little dancer, Kalinda, I think her name was. Such a pretty girl. It was a shame to see her pretty face and body carved up that way."

I shivered in my chair, again remembering the newspaper descriptions of what had been done to that poor girl's body. Like Nia had said, the stalker who ran the license plate on the car and thought he had seen Marcus had it all wrong. The girl's murder had been a message to Kareem.

The man resumed his story and said that once Kareem was back in line, another snag in their lucrative arrangement arose when we got to

New York and rumors started circulating that I wanted to find a new agent for Marcus.

"So meeting you was no accident, John," I said, looking at the agent that had introduced himself to me at an NBA charity event in Phoenix that I hosted about a month before we moved to New York. I'd thought it was such good fortune that the Knight Sports Management Group had signed on at the last minute to be the title sponsor of our event. John had attended the event and chatted me up throughout the evening, planting the seeds of change.

"Nothing is ever an accident," John said, smiling. "And so when you got to New York and reached out to me, we knew we had a backup plan in place in case Marcus did decide to fire Kareem."

"But why would you need that? Kareem, aside from stealing my money to pay you guys, was loyal," Marcus asked, still unclear as to how we ended up here.

"Well, Kareem was getting messy. After the unfortunate demise of his girlfriend, he became reckless, and we knew we could no longer count on him to handle our business interests effectively. And that's where Laila came in."

"Laila?" Marcus hissed. "She was working for you guys, too?"

"Not as directly as Kareem, but through her friend, Darryl, with whom we had a significant cocaine business in LA, we were able to get her to work her charms on you as well. The plan was for you to leave your wife for her, and then our interests would be protected, and we wouldn't need Kareem at all."

Ever since Kareem and Laila had come into our lives, they had both caused us nothing but heartache and pain, manipulating and twisting emotions for their own gain and destroying our family in the process. They both deserved to burn in hell.

John said that to get Kareem back in line, they had sent one of their men to our home to get to me.

"You sent someone to attack my wife!" Marcus broke free from the men and lunged across the small table to grab John by his lapels.

"No, Marcus!" I screamed as Tyson pulled Marcus away from John. The other man struck him with the butt of his gun in the side of his ribs. The sight of Marcus doubled over in excruciating pain was too much for me, but when his head came up, his face was more determined than ever, his eyes flashed with hot anger, and his nostrils flared as he breathed.

My mind flashed back to the attack in the parking garage. It hadn't been random at all. Diablo had sent that man to kill me.

"To answer your question," John said while smoothing the lapels of his jacket, "Carlo was interrupted and didn't finish the job. A mistake that cost him dearly. After that, there was too much media attention, so we decided that the best way to protect our investment was a more direct approach, so I reached out to your wife again and started the process of showing you Kareem's deception so you would fire him.

"It was kind of you not to press charges against him for stealing your money, but now you'll have to decide if he goes to jail for the murder of Laila and Kalinda or if Vanessa will. We've set Kareem up to take the fall with his prints on the gun, the same gun that was used to kill Kalinda. All you have to do is continue our little arrangement of fifty percent of your income coming directly to us. Otherwise, your wife goes to jail for two murders and an attempt on Kareem's life, and we'll have to end your career in a similar manner as Kareem's."

Mr. Quadron raised his hand and motioned to one of the armed guards stationed on the other side of the room. The man removed a large rusted pipe from behind his back and lumbered over to John.

"Breaking kneecaps is such a cliché but certainly effective when you're dealing with a professional athlete, wouldn't you say?" John chortled as he opened the briefcase on the table and pulled out a sheaf of documents and a pen. "So what will it be, Mr. King? A continuation of our previous financial arrangement, or do you want your wife to go to jail and your career to be ended? The choice is yours."

CHAPTER 36

Nia

Within minutes of our arrival outside the warehouse in Rahway, Lee, a burly mean-looking guy with coal-black eyes, and six other men dressed in black fatigues tucked into black combat boots, bulletproof vests, and high-tech earpieces had arrived in a reinforced SUV that looked like it could take out a brick wall. They surveyed the exterior of the warehouse, and Lee sent one of the men he called Bishop to assess points of entry and find the best way to approach without being detected by Diablo Negro.

When Bishop returned, he laid out the setup inside. He said he counted ten armed men inside the main area of the warehouse and that there were likely at least two other men on the plane inside. My blood ran cold when he said that Vanessa was tied to a chair and that Marcus's hands were cuffed and he was being held by two men. There were also two men seated at a table. He assumed they were in charge of the situation. He showed Terrence a photo of the two men that he took with his infrared telephoto camera.

"That's Pablo Quadron, head of Diablo Negro, on the right, but I'm not sure who the other guy is with him," Terrence confirmed.

Within twenty minutes Terrence and Lee came up with a plan to have three men scale the exterior wall and go into the building through the air shaft. Three of the other men would cover the back entrance and wait for their leader's signal.

Terrence changed out of his suit jacket and tie and took a vest from Lee's outstretched hand.

"What are you doing?" I cried as I grabbed his arm and pulled him around behind his car, my eyes wide with fear because I already knew the answer. The thought of him going into that warehouse and facing Diablo Negro made me flash back to the nightmare of seeing him lying in that hospital bed fighting for his life. I couldn't go there again.

"Nia, I have to go. Lee and I will take the guy at the front, and we'll get Marcus and Vanessa. These guys are the best. Trust me. I used to work with them. Everything is going to be OK." He took his jacket and put it around my shoulders, then pulled me close to his body. He pulled my chin up so that I would look him in the eye.

"Nothing is going to happen to me, Nia. I promise." He leaned his head down and kissed me on my trembling mouth. I kissed him back hard, my arms wrapping around his waist tightly as I tried to hold him with me a little while longer.

"You better come back to me," I whispered hoarsely.

He hugged me and then walked back over to Lee and the team to review the plan one last time and load the semiautomatic that Lee tossed to him from the back of the SUV. Within seconds they all disappeared into the overgrown brush.

I wrapped Terrence's jacket tighter around my shaking body as I closed my eyes and prayed silently. I inhaled the scent of his jacket. The cologne scent was gone. It just smelled like him.

CHAPTER 37

Vanessa

John spread the legal papers out on the table, explaining that while they were sure that Marcus, unlike Kareem, was a man of his word, he would need to sign a new management agreement that would allow Knight Sports Management to take 50 percent in fees so that it looked like a legal business arrangement. John would in turn then pay Mr. Quadron the fees.

"I need to talk to my wife," Marcus said as he jerked away from the men holding him and walked over to me. He bent down on one knee and leaned into my ear, his head resting on my shoulder. My arms strained against the ropes. I wanted to hold him so badly.

"Baby, I'm so sorry I got us into this mess," he said as I rested my head against his and let my lips brush across his cheek.

"I'm the one who should be sorry. I brought John into our lives, and if I hadn't killed Laila, they wouldn't have anything to hold over you."

"The only reason I'm signing these papers is because I can't bear the thought of you going to jail. I could deal with not playing basketball again, but I can't ever deal with not having you."

I closed my eyes as a tear fell onto the side of Marcus's face.

"And I could bear the thought of going to jail, but I couldn't ever stand by and watch someone hurt you. It would kill me."

As we absorbed the enormity of what was about to happen, along with the uncertainty that even if he signed the papers, Diablo

Negro could still hurt us, we didn't want to leave each other's side. But Bruce came back over and jerked Marcus up onto his feet, then led him back over to the table.

"If I do this, you'll let us go?" Marcus asked as he held his hands out so that Bruce could remove the handcuffs and he could sign the documents, giving away half his fortune to save me.

"Of course, Mr. King. We want you to get back out on that court just as much as you do," John said, his eyes gleaming with triumph.

"And no one ever touches my wife again," he snarled, looking directly at Pablo Quadron.

"As long as our arrangement stands, you have no problems, I can assure you," Mr. Quadron said as John removed a black Montblanc pen from the breast pocket of his suit jacket and laid it on top of the contracts.

As Marcus bent down to pick up the pen, a large explosion sounded and glass shattered all around us. I ducked my head and screamed as shards of glass rained down from the top of the glass and metal-framed roof, followed by long black ropes. Three men rappelled down the ropes, and then there was smoke in the room and gunfire, but all I heard was my own screaming.

"Marcus! Marcus!" I screamed as I rocked and strained against the tight ropes holding me firmly to the chair. I could see Marcus jabbing his elbow deep into Tyson's neck through the smoke. Then he quickly turned to me and ran.

John flipped the table over and grabbed the briefcase and began to run with Mr. Quadron toward the plane. But their escape was cut off as three more men burst through the hangar doors, guns blazing.

As bullets continued to fly, Marcus made it across the room to me in five quick steps and scooped me up while I was still tied to the chair. I buried my head in his chest as he turned and ran, flanked by Terrence and another man dressed in all black who covered our escape by firing rounds from his semiautomatic weapon.

I shut my eyes tight as a last image of our son smiling flashed through my mind.

I was sure we were about to die.

CHAPTER 38

Nia

I hadn't expected to be packing up my office twice within one year. But if I had learned anything, it was to always expect the unexpected. MJ walked into my office, carrying more boxes and a tape gun.

"How did we accumulate so much stuff in just a year?" he asked as he folded the corrugated boxes into shape.

"I don't even know," I said, turning around to survey the chaotic scene of half-packed boxes around the office. There would be no refuge at home, either, since my apartment was also in a half-packed state. "But I hope we can wrap this up today because I can't stand the thought of looking at this mess any longer."

"I'm going to stay late tonight and finish it up so I can focus on getting my own shit together," he said, whipping the tape gun across to seal the top of a box full of books under the coffee table.

"Thanks, MJ. That would be great. I'm going to try to finish up as much as I can before I head out for my dinner."

The move to DC had been a difficult decision, but Miki really hadn't given me a choice. As the new head of both the TV and publishing division, she was eager to get her expansion plans moving. But while I appreciated her support for my ideas, which was certainly a welcome departure from DeAnna, I quickly found out that woman had only one speed: Go! Within two weeks of our conversation during which she announced that she was taking over our publishing unit, she asked me to present to her and the board my plans for the *DivaDish* brand. Within a week of my pitch, I officially got the green light to move forward.

I was excited about the prospect of leading the charge to develop the *Diva* brand and had decided I needed to be in DC for at least the next six to eight months to get *DCDiva* launched. I would take the shuttle back and forth to New York as necessary to continue to oversee the magazine and DivaDish.com. It was going to be a huge challenge, but finally I had the opportunity to fully run my own business without worrying about the meddling hands of someone like DeAnna or the sneakiness of someone like Kris Kensington throwing me under the bus. Office politics had never been my thing, and I looked forward to focusing on doing my job and not having to worry about my colleagues trying to stab me in the back.

The other exciting part of the expansion plans was my interest in covering another type of celebrity: politicians. In DC, the celebs were the members of the Congressional Black Caucus, DC's black power brokers, society mavens, and the web of six-figure strategists and lobbyists that really made the Beltway work. And our initial research had shown that some of these folks were even more scandalous than the coked-up, philandering, tantrum-throwing stars we had been covering, so we should have a successful launch for our magazine and website.

And thanks to Vanessa, I was heading to DC on a high note businesswise. After she and Marcus were rescued from the warehouse last month, she had given *Diva* the one and only interview about their kidnapping by Diablo Negro. The exclusive account of their harrowing experience and glossy photos of the happy family in their new home in Alpine, New Jersey, had skyrocketed our newsstand sales for our bestselling issue ever, and the web tease resulted in tripling our traffic.

And while Che had done an excellent job on the story, there was one piece of information I knew I had to get from Vanessa herself.

—

The Midtown restaurant, Jezebel, was quiet, as the dinner crowd wouldn't be arriving for at least another hour. I had requested an early reservation so that I could get back to my apartment to finish packing before my flight to DC in the morning. A slim hostess dressed in all black led me to a corner of the restaurant.

Seated in the roomy white leather banquette, Vanessa flipped through a copy of the new issue of the magazine featuring her cover story. She looked so happy. She was dressed in a bright berry-colored fitted dress with cap sleeves, with her hair cut into a sleek asymmetrical bob. Her face glowed with very little makeup—only a hint of gloss on her lips, some bronzer on her cheeks, and some mascara to frame her large brown eyes.

"Nice job, girl," she said as she pushed the long side bang off her face. I leaned down to kiss her cheek and then slid in next to her.

"Nice job yourself. That issue is flying off the stands. Are you guys happy with the story and the photos?"

"Yes, everything turned out great." She put the magazine back in her purse and gave the waiter her drink order of iced tea. I ordered a glass of merlot and perused the menu.

"So, are you all packed and ready to go?" Vanessa asked.

"Just a few things to throw in the suitcases tonight and I'll be done. MJ is packing up what we need for the office tonight and shipping that out. Hopefully it will all be set up within a few days so we can get right to work."

"That's great, girl. I'm really proud of you." Vanessa raised her glass to mine in a toast. "You've busted your ass, and now it's really paying off. Cheers!" The waiter returned to the table and took our orders.

"Thanks, V. You know, I can hardly believe it, but it's really happening. You know I love New York, but I've also always wanted to live in DC. MJ found this fabulous real estate agent who got me this cute little town house in Georgetown to sublet and is coordinating all the elements of the move. I can't wait for you to see it."

"Well, now that I've got you back on the East Coast, I'm not going to let you get away that easily, so I hope your town house has a guest room so I can come visit."

"Yes, it does, but you know I'll be in New York a couple days a week as well."

"And is it work or pleasure that will be bringing you back to New York?" Vanessa asked coyly as she took another sip of her tea and winked at me.

"Whatever. You know you better come and bring my godson to DC to see me. Although I know you can't do too much right now with your man taking his team to the championship." Marcus had come back to the court with a vengeance, lighting up the boards and rallying his teammates to step up their games as well, and it had paid off. For the first time in ten years, the New York Gladiators were playing in the championship. But facing the New Orleans Dragons would not be easy.

"Isn't it exciting? Marcus and his team are so focused right now. They are really determined to win this and bring New York a championship."

"That's great, Vanessa. I'm so happy for you both. How are things going between you guys?"

"Well, you know it was hard when we had to face all the news about Kareem, Laila, John, and Diablo. I think Marcus felt betrayed by everyone and like he had been played for a fool, and it nearly cost him everything. We've continued to see the therapist at least once a week, which has helped, and we are both committed to making our marriage not only work, but better than it ever was." As she continued to talk about how their weekly therapy sessions were bringing them closer together and their plans to try to have another baby after the season ended, I could see the pure happiness in her face. I hadn't seen my girl look like that in a long time. She and Marcus seemed like they had a real fighting chance.

"I'm really happy for you, V."

"But you know none of that would have been possible if you and Terrence hadn't found us in that warehouse. I was never so happy to see Terrence in all my life!"

"And I was never so happy to see the three of you and Marcus when you all came busting out of that warehouse. I was scared to death."

"You were scared? Try being carried out strapped to a chair, not knowing if bullets were going to cut you down at any moment." Vanessa shuddered with the memory of that wild night as she dove into her entrée. "I still have nightmares."

"I was glad you called for dinner. Now that you're a Jersey resident, what brings you into the city this evening?" The waiter cleared our entrées, and we both passed on dessert, so Vanessa asked for the check.

"I had a potential endorsement meeting for Marcus this afternoon, and after dinner I'm meeting him at the Habitat for Humanity event at Cartier where the Glam crew will be following us all night." Miki had convinced Vanessa that it would be a good idea to start taping the reality show as soon as possible as they rebuilt their lives after the kidnapping and Marcus led his team to the championship. Clearly that woman had the golden gift of the gab, because normally Vanessa was such a private person that I couldn't believe she had even agreed to allow the cameras to follow them during this intimate moment in their lives.

"How is it having the cameras following you, Kim Kardashian?"

"Whatever, heffa. It was hard at first, but honestly now it's like I forget they are even there."

"OK, but don't let me turn on the show and see your ass throwing drinks in folks' faces and pulling out weaves and ish like those other reality shows," I joked as she placed her American Express black card on top of the bill.

"Never that. Always classy."

"Yes, that you are, my dear. And I have to thank you again for approaching Miki about doing the show and telling her it was my idea. What made you do that?"

"I felt bad about deceiving you in Phoenix about the cover story on the pregnancy announcement. You put your job on the line for me, so I thought if there was a way for me to save your job, I should do it."

"And it didn't hurt that you killed Laila's show in the process, right?" I looked at her underneath my lowered lashes as she smirked while signing the credit card slip for dinner.

"Well, I never explicitly told Miki she needed to cancel Laila's show. I think she saw the merits on her own of signing our show and cutting Laila loose, especially after I told her that I'd hate to have to include her and the network in a suit against Laila for causing me to lose my baby."

"What do you mean?"

"Remember at the gala when you were trying to pull me away from the fight and suddenly I fell back into the crowd?"

"Yeah . . . I always thought someone stepped on your dress."

"I fell because something pulled me back onto the ground. At first I thought maybe someone had stepped on my dress, too, but when I replayed that image over in my mind, I remember seeing Laila skulking around on the ground and going to crawl under a table. I know that bitch pulled me down, and after I told Miki to check all of her camera footage, she seemed to see things my way."

"Wow, no wonder she was so eager to get that deal done and cut ties with Laila. A lawsuit would have been a huge black eye for the network and likely ended her career."

"Exactly. And following my plan, everybody wins."

"I ain't mad at your gangsta, girl," I said, raising my glass to her again before taking a sip. "But, speaking of Laila, there's one thing I've never been able to figure out."

"What's that?" she asked, putting her credit card back into her wallet.

"What were you doing at the Four Seasons?" I said. Just as the detective had said, Kareem's prints were the only ones found on the gun, and he told the prosecutor that it was a lover's quarrel between the two of them, but I still had my suspicions that wasn't the whole truth.

"What do you mean?"

"Don't you think it's kind of strange that Diablo's crew happened to snatch you up in front of the same hotel where someone had just killed your husband's former mistress?"

As I braced myself for my best friend's answer, Vanessa took her black Prada makeup bag out of her navy-blue Dior handbag and removed her gold compact and lip gloss, and then touched up her lips in the mirror.

"No comment," she said as she snapped the compact closed and dropped everything back in her bag, leaned over and kissed me, and then slid out of the booth and headed for the door, toward the waiting cameras.

—

Turning the key in the lock of my apartment door, I could see that thanks to the efforts of Denise and her team at the Organized Home, my apartment no longer looked like the war zone I had left this morning. All of the boxes were sealed, labeled, and stacked neatly in the hallway, ready to be shipped out in the morning. So just as she had promised, all I needed to do was focus on packing an overnight bag and my toiletries. I wonder what it would cost to have this woman run every aspect of my life.

Just as I had taken off my clothes and changed into a pair of black leggings and an old Harvard T-shirt, the doorbell rang. I padded down the hallway in my bare feet, thinking it had to be someone from Denise's team with a last-minute job since the doorman hadn't buzzed to announce a visitor. When I opened the door, a large white bag of Chinese food greeted me. I couldn't see his face behind the bag, but I recognized my deliveryman immediately.

"What are you doing here?" I asked, smiling happily as Terrence lowered the bag and leaned in to kiss me. "I thought you weren't going to be back from DC until later."

"We wrapped up early, so I jumped on the shuttle to get back and help you pack and feed you dinner. But it looks like you don't need me. Nice job." Terrence followed me down the hallway past neat rows of boxes into the living room.

"Well, it's very kind of you, but as you can see, for once I've got everything under control. And I already ate."

"Well, then you won't mind if I eat. I'm starving. Haven't eaten all day," Terrence said as he took a seat on the couch, opened the bag, and set out a couple of white takeout containers on the coffee table.

I curled up next to him on the couch and reached for a fortune cookie, but he swatted my hand away.

"No food, no fortune. It's bad luck," he said, separating the wooden chopsticks and diving into his kung pao chicken.

"Where the hell did you get that from? You don't even know what you're talking about," I said, laughing as I threw my legs across his lap and put my arms around his waist and nibbled on his ear.

"I thought you said you weren't hungry," Terrence said, moaning as my tongue traveled down his neck and my hand began to unbutton his shirt.

"I said I already ate. But I didn't say I wasn't hungry," I said, laughing softly. "But I'll let you finish so you can get your strength up."

"Oh, so it's like that. You're just going to tease a brother and then try to send him back to his food?" Terrence put his chopsticks down, flipped me onto the couch, and laid his body on top of mine. His lips were hot and wet along my neck.

"I was just trying to help you out," I said as he reached under my thin T-shirt and found my breast. I moaned and closed my eyes as I wrapped my arms around his neck. Suddenly he sat back up on the couch and returned to his food.

"Yeah, you're right. I should eat first," he smirked, shoving some rice in his mouth as he watched me pull my shirt down and struggle to sit up on the couch.

"You'll pay for that later," I said playfully, punching him on the arm. "Promise?"

"Oh, I promise. So how was the Diablo meeting in Washington?" I sat up and picked at a spicy pepper over his shoulder and popped it into my mouth.

"Good meeting. We reviewed our entire case on Diablo with the FBI team, and they are going to give us all the resources we need to build an airtight case for kidnapping, racketeering, and drug smuggling. Quadron's operation is vast and growing. They deal in marijuana and opium poppy, grown mainly in the mountains of southwest Mexico. They also control the meth traffic. Pablo Quadron is the brother of Geraldo Quadron, the head of the Diablo Negro family, and he's been responsible for their other side businesses—sports betting, sex trafficking, and their expansion into meth. The FBI and DEA have been after the major players in Diablo for years and considered them one of their biggest threats, calling them a clear and present danger to America and its citizens. Pablo Quadron alone is believed to be responsible for the deaths of thousands of people, including at least fifteen DEA agents. He's a big fish, and we got him."

"I'm proud of you, baby," I said, planting a kiss on his cheek as I breathed yet another sigh of relief that he and his team made it out of that warehouse alive. Seeing him run out of there pulling Marcus and Vanessa along had been the happiest sight of my life.

"And is Kareem talking yet? Will he testify against Diablo?"

Kareem had kept his silence and refused to answer any questions about Diablo when Terrence and the prosecutor tried to question him with his lawyer after his arrest. Even when the district attorney intimated there was the potential of a lighter sentence for helping the state build its case against the drug cartel, he still refused.

"Unfortunately, Kareem won't be saying anything to anyone anymore. He was found dead in Rikers yard this morning. He was lying on the weight bench and someone dropped a hundred-pound weight on his face and neck."

"Oh my God . . ." My hand flew up to my mouth. I knew Terrence had questioned Vanessa about why she went to the Four Seasons that night but hadn't gotten any further than I had with her at our dinner tonight. And I knew we were both thinking the same thing right now: with Kareem dead, no one could ever point the finger at Vanessa for Laila's murder. "Do they know who did it?"

"Of course no one is talking, but I've got to believe it's Diablo. But there's no way right now to tie them to Kareem's murder."

"So what happens now?"

"We'll continue to build our case and prosecute both Pablo and John." Terrence finished his meal and put the containers back into the bag and then fell back against the couch.

"And what will be your involvement?" I was pretty sure I already knew the answer.

"On the flight back, my boss, District Attorney Kimberly Williams, told me she wanted me to lead the prosecution."

"Oh my God, that's huge, Terrence! I'm so proud of you. This is going to be the case that makes your career and leads to the district attorney's office, something you've always wanted." Even as I said the words, I felt myself deflating because I knew this case would consume him for months and require all of his time and attention. Where would that leave us? It was bad enough that I was going to be living in DC for several months and traveling back and forth, but this was too much.

"Hey, what's wrong?" he said lifting my chin, which had dropped down to my chest as I played with the hem of my T-shirt.

"Nothing. I'm really happy for you. This is big." I looked around the apartment at all the boxes packed and ready to go to Washington, wondering why it seemed like we were always moving in opposite directions.

"Yes, it's big, but it's not bigger than us." He lifted my chin with his finger, and the dark brown eyes, framed by endless lashes, that I loved looking into had a seriousness that wasn't there before. "Nothing is bigger than us, and nothing is getting in the way, Nia." He dipped his head down and kissed me. His tongue searched for mine as he pushed me back down onto the couch.

I curled my arms around his neck and sighed deeply.

"I love you, Terrence," I said, willing myself to believe that we could make a long-distance relationship work during the busiest time of both of our careers.

"I love you, too, Nia. Nothing is going to come between us. Now about that promise you made earlier . . ."

CHAPTER 1

S he could hear the sounds of the party through the vent. The tinkling of laughter, deep self-important voices, champagne glasses clinking, and a jazz quartet playing softly.

It was all so civilized. Unlike what was happening to her.

The sharp blade of the man's knife moved along her trembling inner thigh as the man's ragged breathing quickened. She turned her throbbing head to the side and closed her eyes tight against the sight of him pushing her legs apart on the hard wooden desk. As tears ran down the side of her swollen face, she felt two more pairs of hands holding her body down, one at her shoulders and the other at her feet, pawing at what was left of the dress she had borrowed from Nia and ripping away the shreds of once-beautiful red velvet fabric. There was no use crying out now. Not that she could anyway; they had started by breaking her jaw.

Through her hazy consciousness, she heard the band stop playing, and with the sound of polite applause, she knew that the black-tie members of Washington's elite were now taking their seats at their $50,000 tables in the hotel's grand ballroom. It was time for this evening's program to begin to kick off the annual African American Congressional Caucus weekend.

They heard the music stop, too, so the men knew unfortunately they would not be able to savor the capture of their prey tonight. One of them was now inside her, grunting. He grabbed at her hair to pull her close to the face that she had always thought so handsome but was now twisted into an unrecognizable mask of hate as he spat guttural curses in her ear. The other two men lowered the zippers on their tuxedo pants as they growled at him to hurry up so that they could have their turn. They knew there wasn't much time left; if they weren't back in that ballroom soon, they would certainly be missed.

As she began to lose consciousness for the last time, she heard through the vent the announcement that everyone in the ballroom had been waiting for all night.

"Ladies and gentlemen, I present to you, the president of the United States." As the band began to play the thunderous tones of "Hail to the Chief," the audience rose once again to applaud.

Exhale TV

ABOUT
THE AUTHOR

Angela Burt-Murray is the cofounder of CocoaFab.com, former editor in chief of *Essence* magazine, and a self-confessed cupcake and reality TV junkie. She is the cohost of the talk show *Exhale* and coauthor of the humor book *The Angry Black Woman's Guide to Life* and the novel *The Vow*. She resides in Atlanta with her husband, Leonard; two sons, Solomon and Ellison; and a ridiculously lazy bulldog named Cosby.